Intents & Purposes

SIMON TEMPRELL was born in Chesterfield, Derbyshire, and raised in nearby Clowne. He attended the Plymouth Art & Design College before moving to London in 1982. After working as a window dresser at Harrods, he started his own interior design business in 1986, moving to Brussels in 1990 and Washington, DC in 1992.

Continuing his design business, he lives in Virginia and began writing as a hobby in 1994. His first book *The Rich Man's Table* was published by Pan Macmillan in 2000, followed by *Previous Convictions* and *Bitter & Twisted*.

Intents & Purposes is his first self-published novel.

Praise for *The Rich Man's Table:*

'An astonishingly accomplished comic novel that out-fabs *Absolutely Fabulous,* outpaces *Tales of the City* for plot, and outcamps E.F Benson's Mapp and Lucia novels for waspish social commentary ...Temprell's nerve is breathtaking'

Robb Cassy, *Bookseller*

Also by Simon Temprell

The Rich Man's Table

Previous Convictions

Bitter & Twisted

SIMON TEMPRELL

Intents

&

Purposes

www.lulu.com

First published 2008 by Lulu.com

www.lulu.com

ISBN 978-1-4357-1687-2

For Nelson

Acknowledgements

Love and thanks to my Gran whose letters inspired me to create the character of Tallulah's grandmother in this book.

Thanks also to Millie Knox and the Chantry of the Silver Veil for welcoming me in to their community

The front cover of this book is a revised version of an original design by Jake Catt. The author photo on the back cover was taken by Jiorgos Vouros.

Intents

&

Purposes

Death

I died at seven minutes past midnight, serenaded by Simon & Garfunkel as I plunged to my death.

Hello darkness, my old friend.

The Snake Pass is a scenic but treacherous stretch of road that winds across the moorland between Ladybower reservoir and Glossop. There are steep ravines to one side of this infamous stretch of road and it has a poor accident record. When I was a kid I used to stare out of my dad's car window and look down at the rusty relics of vehicles that had somehow found their way down there and it seemed unbelievable to me that people would just drive over the edge like that.

There was a serene moment of suspended animation as if dangling from a parachute and I could see every detail of my dashboard; illuminated phosphorescent green and achingly *real.* A split second before the car exploded I became disengaged – miraculously free from my seat belt – and tugged effortlessly through the roof and upwards as though attached to an invisible bungee cord; catapulted out of the flames like a spiritual phoenix.

I knew the instant that it happened that I was dead.

Out of darkness comes light; and suddenly everything made sense.

Veronica

Veronica Rustin can't afford to leave anything to chance: She has bleached her hair, changed her name and travelled over six thousand miles in five days to escape the crime she has committed. And now she has arrived at her final destination; Brown Bread Cottage on the edge of the Derbyshire Peak District.

It would probably make more sense for a fugitive like Veronica to seek refuge and anonymity in the middle of a sprawling city like London or Paris but she has developed a desperate urge to avoid human contact wherever possible. On the flight from Miami to Frankfurt she travelled first class for the privacy it afforded her; keeping her eye-shades on for the entire nine hours and refusing all offers of food and drink beyond two bottles of spring water. She took sleeping pills, plugged her ears and slept on the flat-bed with the complimentary duvet pulled up to her chin. Her sleep was mercifully dreamless and she woke feeling startled and slightly confused when the lights came on for breakfast.

She spent one night in a small privately owned hotel in Frankfurt before taking another flight to Vienna. From Vienna she took the hydrofoil down the Danube to Budapest where she spent another night in a ghastly little place with a shared bathroom and rats scrabbling in the walls before embarking on a gruelling journey across Europe by train to eventually find herself in London this morning in the middle of the rush-hour. The smell of hot fuel, baking croissants and damp English autumn greeted Veronica the second she stepped down from the train carriage on to the platform and it was like opening the lid of a trunk filled with things long forgotten.

Under less dramatic circumstances she might have been thrilled to be back in London after all these years but her only concern this morning was to get across town to St. Pancras from where she could catch a final train up to Chesterfield.

She emerged from the station to stand in line for a black cab and the mossy dampness of the morning air curled around her with lazy indifference. The sun made patterns through the mist and steamed the windows of the cab as they wove between buses and cars in a slow, agonizing crawl from one train station to another. Familiar buildings nudged Veronica's memory and infused her with a strange kind of melancholy for a time when life was uncomplicated and simple. It was like flicking through the yellowed pages of an old photograph album and recognizing the imperceptible passage of time.

First Class on British trains is surprisingly civilized and Veronica was pleasantly positioned in an almost empty carriage where she was offered complimentary tea, coffee and newspapers while the staggeringly grimy outskirts of London receded behind her to reveal the streaky amber and gold of the countryside. Cows perused the vast fields, their heads bent towards the earth and their tails swishing nonchalantly as they snorted clouds of moisture in to the morning air. Hedgerows crammed with brambles and wild flowers flashed by like sepia prints from school textbooks and inspired visions of cross-country runs and nature walks. Her childhood came tumbling back towards her in a scattering of lost memories and reminiscence.

She rented a car in Chesterfield. The short walk from the station to the car rental office was overlooked by the Crooked Spire; a twisted witch's hat of

3

unseasoned timber leaning precariously against a stubborn expanse of patchy grey sky. The sun seemed to bleed from behind the texture of the cloud-cover creating a small patch of nicotine yellow in an otherwise colourless sheet of October noon. The girl at the rental place was cheerful; her accent achingly familiar and charming to Veronica.

"I hope you don't mind," apologized the young girl with the tightly-bound pony-tail and the golden heart necklace, "we don't have the car you booked but we can offer you a free up-grade to a Toyota Avensis automatic if that's OK?"

Veronica was relieved. She had somehow imagined that she would be able to cope with a stick-shift but after five days of travelling and very little sleep the thought of attempting the navigation of the English countryside after all these years away was making her nervous. Bad enough that she would have to drive on the left and sit on the right, but to tackle a gear stick at the same time; that would have been suicide in her current state of mind.

She pulled out of the car park with caution and juddered uncertainly across several roundabouts until she was safely out of the town centre and headed out towards the tranquillity of the surrounding countryside.

From this point forward Veronica Rustin has become Nicole Harvey; a name invented by her friend Daphne who joked that Veronica's new persona should reflect her love of shopping. And so they took the name of Veronica's favourite London department store and turned it in to a credit card, a bank account and a French ID. She still has her British passport but decided that it was safer to travel through Europe as a French woman, just in case. It is impossible to know how clever the authorities can be at tracking somebody down and

4

Veronica has watched enough movies to understand the importance of false documentation.

The rental cottage was booked via the internet from Vienna. It was chosen for its location and its lack of glamour in order to fool any would-be pursuants. A woman like Veronica Rustin would be more at home in an opulently decorated boutique hotel than a place described as 'quaint' in a holiday brochure catering to 'nature-lovers, hikers and young families.'

Nicole Harvey, despite her rather sophisticated name, is a different kind of woman from Veronica Rustin and she is looking for peace and solitude in a place without bell-boys, chamber-maids or front desk clerks. Brown Bread Cottage is situated less than a mile outside Castleton; a quaint tourist spot with a humble population of about twelve hundred residents. There is a ruined castle, several underground caverns and mile upon mile of bleak, unspoilt Derbyshire moorland where Nicole can vanish for a while until she decides what to do next. She has booked the cottage for a month and the owner – a Mrs. Harris – told her that it is empty for most of the winter so she can extend the lease if needs be.

It is already starting to grow dark by the time Nicole pulls in to the lane leading to Brown Bread Cottage. She checks her watch. It is only four o' clock. She had forgotten how England is at this time of the year.

Tallulah

Back in the afternoon gloaming of Chesterfield, beneath the shadow of the twisted spire of St. Mary's & All Saints, lives a woman called Tallulah Clegg.

The name Tallulah couldn't be tagged to a more inappropriate person and it remains a mystery to this day why Patricia Clegg named her only daughter after an immoral, promiscuous, bisexual, drug addicted actress. Maybe there was more to Tallulah's mother than met the eye or maybe it was merely the fact that *Lifeboat* was one of her favourite Hitchcock films. Whatever the reason, Tallulah Clegg is the antithesis of everything Ms. Bankhead was reputed to stand for.

Here she is, scantily dressed and splattered with bright red paint. The paint isn't exactly what she was expecting. On the chart it looked rich and velvety like the inside of a jewellery box but on her wall it looks more like tinned tomato soup. She hopes it will calm down as it dries because even in this light – and it's a cloudy October afternoon – she can tell it is a highly unsuitable colour for a kitchen. It is the kind of colour they use in Chinese chip shops. It is a colour that has been splashed across Tallulah's thoughts for several months now; insistent and worrying like a throbbing tooth that will have to be removed. The colour should be called 'Phone Box' or 'London Bus' but it is called, unfathomably, 'Charisma'. Tallulah wonders who sits down every day to think up the names for all those paint colours and what kind of qualifications does someone need to get such a job?

What is the colour of cancer?

Tallulah is certain it would be something ugly like puce or the greenish-purple of a violent bruise. Like a chart in an old-fashioned butcher's shop each part of the body is designated a corresponding colour and Tallulah wonders what colour her breasts would be. Pink seems to be the obvious choice. Despite morbid thoughts about cancer and mysterious lumps Tallulah is in a positive frame of mind. Today is her day off and although it is a Wednesday she enjoys being at home when most other people are at work. It feels special to have a day off during the week and there are all manner of interesting things on the telly during the daytime.

"Maizy dotes and dozy dotes and little lamsytivey, a diddle-e-eye-de-do, wouldn't you?"

She sings loudly as she paints her kitchen walls bright red, blithely unaware that the words to her song bear little resemblance to the actual gobbledegook she is singing.

It is a song her mother used to sing as she mashed the potatoes; her rhythmic clanging accompaniment dislodging the clumps stuck to the masher. It is a song that accompanied many household chores from polishing the brass to cleaning the upstairs windows with the sash jammed down to hold her thighs in place as she sat precariously on the outside ledge.

> *Wipe it on Windolene, wipe it off Windolene,*
> *That's how to get your windows clean,*
> *Wipe it off straight away, wipe it off no delay,*
> *So easy with new Windolene!*

Tallulah's mother had a limited repertoire of songs that she reserved for household chores and the same songs have stayed with Tallulah all these years. Even as a small child Tallulah had a memory for songs and jingles. She only had to listen to a tune a few times before she had the lyrics off pat. The bus conductors used to give her rolls of unused tickets in return for a song or two and she was richly rewarded every Christmas when she would trail around the neighbourhood singing carols at people's doors.

Tallulah is the kind of woman you might stand behind at the supermarket, her meagre groceries lined up on the rubber conveyor belt as testament to her sad little life: Tins of fruit cocktail, evaporated milk, instant coffee and those miniature tins of baked beans with pork sausages. Thank goodness Tallulah doesn't like cats otherwise there'd be the obligatory tin of Whiskers to complete the pathetic picture of spinsterdom.

Tallulah's kitchen is quite spacious for such a small house but that's because these houses were built at a time when the kitchen was the hub of the household. A time when women stayed at home and cooked three full meals a day. A time when doing the laundry was a full day's work. This kitchen was never fully modernized and so there are a lot of things to pull away from the walls before Tallulah can paint behind them. She briefly considered painting *around* everything but she knew that those dirty yellow patches of oil-based gloss, spattered with grease and dead insects, would spoil the satisfaction of a job well done. She's never been one for sweeping dust under the rug and although the ancient cooker and the powder blue Formica kitchenette were both pretty hefty she managed to yank them in to the centre of the room all by herself.

> *Flash lifts dirt away – soon everything's bright*
> *You've got a sunshine house – what a lovely sight!*

Red isn't the kind of colour you'd expect someone like Tallulah to choose, it's totally out of character. She's never been particularly keen on strong colours, preferring softer, more peaceful shades but a TV design show put the idea in to her head and it's been buzzing around in there for a couple of years. The designer did a bedroom in a rich crimson colour with dark purple curtains and a four-poster bed and it looked so sumptuous and inviting that Tallulah thought she might try it herself. She must be off her rocker thinking it would work in an unmodernized 1950's kitchen but she keeps reminding herself that it's only a couple of tins of paint and if she really hates it when it's done she can paint over it again.

If only life were that easy.

She stands on the top step of her ladder to reach the highest part of the wall and the roller makes wide, shocking tracks across the dingy primrose that's been there for the past twenty-odd years. The walls at one time were papered with Chianti bottles and strings of onions and it is still there beneath the thick layers of gloss. There are patches of it visible now that the cooker has been pulled out and it startled Tallulah with its familiarity when she first caught sight. She hasn't seen that paper since she was a teenager but the coarse design and gaudy colours are as fresh to her now as they were back then. It's funny how a badly sketched wine bottle can immediately bring back the smell of the chip pan and the plump, sputtering sausages that her mum used to fry up for Saturday tea.

It's really too dark to be painting now. The fluorescent strip in the middle of the kitchen ceiling casts unfriendly shadows and Tallulah can't tell if she's missing a few spots so she climbs down from her perch and places the murderously red roller in to its gory tray of paint. The back of her hand and forearm are peppered with tiny pin-pricks of paint and she stares at the effect as though mesmerized by something more sinister. She imagines her body as a giant expanse of calm icy water where the insignificant tips of gigantic icebergs barely break the surface.

Disaster is merely waiting to happen.

Duck or Grouse

Nicole Harvey (and we must become accustomed to using her new name otherwise things will just become too confusing) sits in the front of her rental car for a moment and surveys the place that will be her home for the next few weeks. Brown Bread Cottage is the kind of flat-fronted stone-built hideaway that one might expect in this part of the world. It isn't what you would call quaint but it isn't ugly either. It has the kind of no-nonsense symmetry you might find outlined in a child's colouring-book; the blue-painted door smack in the centre with four windows and a chimney, encompassed by a moss-encrusted drystone wall that has disintegrated in two or three places. It is flint-faced and sensible with an unkempt garden that frames the slightly off-kilter profile of the cottage like a tangled beard. The cottage looks out over a wide expanse of meadow dotted with trees and dissected with more drystone walls. At this time of the day the sky is layered with strands of yellow and salmon as though composed of mineral formations compressed and buried beneath the peat-brown weight of evening. To a woman who has spent the past fifteen years living in ocean-front condominium buildings this bucolic scene is as alien as a moonscape, despite the fact that this country was once her home.

She gets out of the car and takes a deep breath. The loamy smell of earth and mushrooms, of ferns and bracken is overwhelming for a moment and there is an eerie silence broken only by the rapid scolding alarm of a blackbird in a nearby tree. There is no breeze but the air is chilled by dampness and Nicole pulls her jacket further across her chest as she retrieves her suitcase from the back of the car. She is travelling light. She brought only the barest of essentials and there is something undeniably liberating about carry-on baggage from which there is no requirement to be parted. Anyway, it offers the opportunity of going shopping when she feels up to it.

The key to the cottage is on the window ledge, behind the potted ivies. There is a stone frog perched amidst the shrubs and an enamelled sign above the low blue door that reads 'duck or grouse'. The key turns easily in the lock and Nicole pushes the door open to reveal a small low-beamed sitting room with whitewashed walls and a wide-plank floor. It smells of dried flowers and chimney smoke. Because the window is small, leaded and deep-set there is very little light inside the cottage and when Nicole turns on the wall-lights they cast a rosy glow across the uneven texture of the roughly-hewn walls and ceiling.

Everything is as one might expect; spindly, uncomfortable-looking furniture upholstered in William Morris fabric, horse-brasses, corn dollies and commemorative plates on the walls, a log-burning fireplace blackened with years of soot and a coffee table underneath which somebody has placed an ancient game of Monopoly and a battered deck of cards. Nicole hasn't been in a room like this for many years and she feels overly large and polished, like an adult encroaching on a child's Wendy house. Her head is only a few inches from the ceiling and the floorboards creak ominously as she steps forward to place her case on the sofa. It is a room for knitting and crossword puzzles and listening to the wireless on rainy afternoons.

The tiny kitchen has just enough counter space to make a sandwich but there is an oversized stone sink with a gathered curtain underneath to hide the plumbing. The view from the window is picturesque but vacant due to the fact that the fields seem to stretch in to infinity with very little to break the monotony. There is a small patch of back garden with a wooden table and two chairs, an ornamental wheelbarrow filled with dead plants and a washing-line strung between the eaves of the cottage and a crooked wooden post from which hangs a string bag of clothes-pegs. The back door is badly warped and Nicole can see daylight creeping in around the edges.

There is a dining room on the other side of the central staircase and upstairs there are two bedrooms and a bathroom. The antiquated plumbing boasts a hot water geyser above the deep enamelled bath tub (decades of tide-marks etched into the pitted surface and green streaks running down from the brass taps as though they are suffering from a severe sinus infection). The toilet has a wooden seat and the kind of elevated cistern that sits against the ceiling with a metal chain and the manufacturer's trademark embossed in to the ironwork. Nicole is relieved to see a nice thick roll of pink 2-ply and not a sheaf of torn newspaper squares held together with a piece of garden twine.

The larger of the two bedrooms has a double bed so it makes sense for Nicole to use that one, despite the fact that the smaller room has a nicer view and prettier wallpaper. She sits on the edge of the bed to test the dubious-looking mattress and, as suspected, the coiled springs creak with protest and the bed dips with a dusty sigh. The linens are clean (she sniffs them and they smell of fabric softener) and an electric radiator ticks contentedly beneath the window, taking the edge off the chill and emanating a faint burnt-paint smell. All-in-all it could be much worse, thinks Nicole as she removes her jacket and drapes it over the iron bedpost.

Beyond Repair

Tallulah goes to the kitchen sink and runs warm water across her hands and arms. With a squirt of washing-up liquid she scrubs at the freckled red paint with a small nail brush. She sings as she scrubs and her gaze scans the back yard where her washing trembles slightly in the fading light.

Now hands that do dishes can feel soft as your face with mild green Fairy Liquid.

The nights are drawing in and the clocks go back on Saturday night.

Tallulah has lived in this house all her life. Her parents rented it from the council and then Margaret Thatcher's government decided to offer it to them at a ridiculously low price and they were sensible enough to take it. Dad had just received several thousand from the NCB for losing his finger in an industrial accident and so it was all rather opportune. They mortgaged the house, installed gas central heating and changed the stair carpet. Tallulah can remember the atmosphere of affluence for those first few months after it was finished; they'd have relatives over for Sunday tea just so that they could take them upstairs to show them the landing. There used to be a lot of relatives back then. Tallulah wonders what happened to them all. They disappeared when her parents died.

Wiping herself on a tea towel she stares at the stranded cooker with its charred and blackened eye-level grill. She wonders, idly, just how many slices of toast have browned under that series of inconsistent flames. All those between-meal-times when a couple of slices of bread and a can of mushroom and bacon Toast Toppers would fill the hunger gap. The ancient cooker is leaning slightly because it is usually propped up on a couple of tiles where one of the feet fell off several years ago. One of the knobs is missing and Tallulah has to use a pair of pliers if she wants to use all four jets although she doesn't do much cooking. There's nobody to cook for and she prefers to eat things she can pop in the microwave. Oh yes, she *does* have a microwave. It was one of the first things she bought after Dad died and it was worth every penny.

Really there's no need for a kitchen this size now she's on her own; she could make do with an electric kettle, a little fridge and her microwave and she'd be set. The last thing Tallulah actually *cooked* in the oven was a shepherd's pie and that was the summer when Princess Diana died; Tallulah can remember adding the salt of her tears to the frying pan. She is scared to death of the pilot light and keeps the gas turned off at the mains so as to prevent explosions.

The telly is on in the other room. She likes to leave it switched on for company and it's nice to hear voices around the house, especially in the evenings. They have always been big on the telly in her family and even when they had company the sound was just turned down so people could make conversation without losing track of what was going on in the outside world. Back then it was the telly that bound people to the house on certain nights and Tallulah can remember how they'd all sit round the fire on a Saturday night watching Morecombe & Wise or the *Generation Game* with a huge chunky bar of Galaxy from the corner shop and a bottle of lager for Dad. No video recorders in those days. No DVD rentals. She used to love Saturday nights with the curtains pulled and the gas fire on, listening to the sound of jovial voices in the street when people turned out of the pub at eleven. Sometimes, on the run-up to

Christmas, she would be allowed a small Snowball in one of the little gold-rimmed glasses her mum kept in the cocktail cabinet and the Advocaat would leave a little yellow line on her top lip.

These days Saturday nights are mostly quiet.

They re-vamped the social club to make it in to one of those fruit-machine, pub-grub kind of places and now the nocturnal noises from the street are more sinister; breaking glass, dogs barking and the occasional echo of late night drunks weaving their way through the back streets on their way home. Nobody leaves their door unlocked any more. Most of the cars have safety devices clamped to their steering wheels and it's not safe to walk down by the rec' after dark. It's all drugs and teenagers on the dole so Tallulah always walks the long way round on her way home from work in the winter. Just the other afternoon some kids threw a pop bottle at her and called her names from across the street. It's not like it used to be when gangs of kids played Hide & Seek for hours on end.

Coming, ready or not!

The hall is dimly illuminated because the bulb's gone at the bottom of the stairs. Tallulah makes her way upstairs and tries to remember what it was like when the carpet had some pile to it. Oh those first few months were wonderful! They would run up and down in their bare feet and they thought they were royalty. Now the complicated pattern of swirling gold and red is worn away to the jute backing in several spots and it has adopted a kind of greasy sheen as though impregnated with years of cooking fat; uncleanable and beyond repair.

She can hear next-door shouting at the kids; muffled thuds and high-pitched screams reverberate through the wall as evidence of another life being conducted somewhere else. The bulb at the top of the stairs hangs in a dusty red mop-cap of a shade with bright yellow fringe and it casts long, menacing shadows across the landing like the fingers of an outstretched hand. Up here the air is cooler because Tallulah hasn't turned on the heating yet (she's been using the plug-in electric fire in the living room for the past few days.) There is also a very different smell up here from the main floor of the house. Downstairs it smells perpetually of greasy food and cigarette smoke despite the fact that Tallulah has put a Glade plug-in in almost every available socket. But upstairs there is a slightly damp odour which lingers even on the hottest of August nights. It is the smell of old wallpaper paste, warped floorboards and the stagnant air of the attic above. It is the smell of old ladies' talcum powder and long-forgotten board games.

Tallulah stands in the open doorway of the bathroom and in the mirror she looks like a sagging dimpled mattress. She had no old clothes to wear for decorating so she is wearing some bargain pieces from the annual sale at work. The bra is expensively made from dove grey silk but it is slightly too small for her and it cuts in to her breasts at the top and rides up underneath. She quickly averts her eyes from her mounds and bulges and she moves south. Her pants are peach coloured satin but the cream lace on the trim is partially shredded. The fabric is expensive but over-washed. She looks like a kinky, overstuffed scarecrow or a blow-up doll; the kind men buy in sex shops for their own private satisfaction. Chance would be a fine thing! Tallulah doesn't know what it's like to have a man inside her. She has no idea what a real-life naked man looks like. Even a vinyl blow-up sex doll has more fun than she does.

"Jimmy crack corn and I don't care, Jimmy crack corn and I don't care, Jimmy crack corn and I don't care, my master's gone away."

She hums the tune almost soundlessly under her breath as she turns to one side and sucks in her stomach. It doesn't flatten out, it merely turns in to a wobbling crater of putty coloured flesh and it depresses Tallulah to acknowledge that she is past the age of caring. She's too old now to think about going to the gym and, anyway, Lennie Johnson from number fifty-three was carried out of the gym on a stretcher a few weeks ago so what's the point in that? There was a time when she used to watch her weight and worry about gaining a few extra pounds but the days of Slimcea bread and Ayds slimming toffees are long gone and Tallulah eats more-or-less what she wants.

Show them you're a Slimcea girl
You're a slim girl in a new and exciting world!
Show them you're a Slimcea girl!

What's the use of a twenty-seven inch waist if the rest of your body is dying?

The washer on the bath tap is worn-out and water gurgles in the drain as it is swallowed away. The bathroom is austere by modern standards. It is as cold and impersonal as a morgue and the lighting is harsh. The window has a pane of patterned glass to protect the privacy of the occupant from prying eyes and on the sill she keeps her father's aftershave bottles, most of them practically empty or rusting around the metal stoppers.

Denim; for men who don't have to try too hard!

Hai Karate; be careful how you use it!

Old Spice; the mark of a man!

Sometimes Tallulah splashes a little on to the palms of her hands to bring back the smells of the past.

She will have to take a bath. Her chest is streaked with paint and she's got some in her hair as well. She opens the airing cupboard and switches on the immersion. A spider scuttles away from the light and disappears behind the tank where the lagging has disintegrated. Tallulah shivers. It won't be long before she has to start using the heating again but she's been putting it off. The bathroom has a wall-mounted electric heater with a pull-cord switch but it has been broken for years so Tallulah has to leave the bathroom door open all through the winter otherwise ice forms on the inside of the window. The central heating only stretches as far as two of the bedrooms upstairs and so the bathroom and the lumber room are like Siberia in winter. She has a fan heater but it uses too much electricity so she only plugs it in when the temperature gets really low.

Seven — we live on Economy Seven,
Cheaper electricity — heaven!

Tiny Lives

Of course Nicole has absolutely no provisions aside from a bottle of duty-free vodka and a muesli bar so she is forced to consider a run-out to find a local shop. She suspects that Castleton closes-down at five-thirty and wonders where the nearest supermarket might be. Do they have supermarkets out here in the middle of the wilds? If she had somewhere to connect to the internet she might be able to look-up the information but there isn't even a phone at Brown Bread Cottage. She will just have to drive around until she finds something. It is practically dark outside and the thought of navigating those narrow roads again fills her with dread. She is exhausted; gritty-eyed and greasy-skinned from days of travelling and sleeping in strange beds. She would like to soak in the bath and fall in to bed but she knows she will probably wake in the middle of the night feeling ravenously hungry or desperate for a cup of coffee so she fetches her jacket, grabs her bag and heads out to the car.

The evening sky is chaotic with stars; minute dust-particles of light like spilled talcum on navy-blue linen. A plane winks its way silently high overhead and Nicole wonders where it is headed. Difficult to imagine the passengers sitting up there being served drinks and salted peanuts, all of them totally oblivious to the tiny lives going on down here. Just for a moment Nicole feels totally alone and a shivery panic trembles through her chest so that she has to pause for a moment by the gate and breathe deeply. The smell of decomposing leaves and cow manure hang in the air, suffusing the evening dampness with a strange melancholy. Why does she suddenly experience a sharp mental image of infant-school coat-pegs; each one marked with a picture so that the children can find their way back to anoraks and bobble-hats at playtime? An apple, a pair of cherries, a tug-boat and a kite; Nicole had forgotten all about that until this very minute.

She drives carefully back the way she came and, as suspected, Castleton appears to be closed for the day. Only the pubs remain brightly illuminated and although it might be sensible for Nicole to go inside one of them to ask for information she isn't up to the kind of scrutiny she is certain she will receive in such an establishment. Her memory of English pubs is one of dart-boards and salt-n-vinegar crisps, of gouty men in tweed jackets and blousy women sipping gin and orange. The bars in

America are so different; especially the kind that Nicole is used to frequenting in Miami.

Miami; it seems so far away to her already and she's only been gone for five days. She wonders what Gideon is doing at this very minute. She can practically hear the foul language from here. He will be hating her as much as she hates him and he will be formulating a plan to find her and drag her back for justice. Gideon isn't the kind of man who releases a grudge lightly and he will be blind with rage; suffocating with indignant fury and hungry for retribution. The thought causes Nicole to smile as she drives through the narrow main street of the village. She will call Daphne later and find out all the news. The thought of it all unfolding four thousand miles away is almost as delicious as a soap-opera and Nicole would give anything to be a fly on the wall.

A Silent Killer

The telephone suddenly breaks the silence and Tallulah freezes for a moment, her hand still on the handle of the airing cupboard. She hates the sound of the phone, it is loud and intrusive and it's usually a wrong number of somebody trying to sell her life insurance or double glazing. It continues to ring in the hallway downstairs and still she waits. Goose pimples rise on her arms. There is an old dressing gown hooked over the back of the bathroom door, it is a slippery satin thing that somebody once gave her father as a misguided Christmas present, the kind of thing he would never use. Tallulah slips it on over her underwear and immediately feels colder than before. The phone continues to ring with an insistence that is surprising. Usually they give up after the eighth or ninth ring. She knows that as soon as she decides to go downstairs to answer it the phone will stop ringing so she doesn't rush to get it.

"I didn't think you were there," it is Tallulah's grandmother, "I let it ring because I was sure you said today was your day off. It's not as though you'd be going out anywhere on a week night."

Gladys Clegg lives alone in a little council bungalow on the other side of town and although Tallulah doesn't visit her as often as she should they usually talk on the phone a couple of times a week. The conversation is usually one-sided and all Tallulah has to do is listen.

"Hello, Gran, I was just about to run myself a bath. I've been painting the kitchen."

"Painting? Oh, that's nice, duck. I haven't got my teeth in so you'll have to excuse my slurring. That new set have been giving me gyp so I've left them out today." There is a moment of silence and Tallulah can hear her gran breathing heavily at the other end of the line.

"Are you all right, Gran? You sound a bit under-the-weather."

"Oh, duck; I don't know how to tell you this. I've been having a bit of a cry and had to pull myself together before I phoned you. It's our Robert; he was killed in a car crash on the Snake late last night."

"Oh no!" gasps Tallulah as she sinks down on to the bottom step, pulling her bare feet up under the hem of the slippery dressing gown.

"Your Auntie June just phoned me and apparently they've had the police round in the estate and everything. Isn't that awful? I've been choked since she called me, thinking about when you were all little and used to come round for ice-cream money. He was a lovely lad. I only saw him on Sunday. They came round for half an hour on their way home from their dinner. I don't see too much of him these days. It's a bit of a drive from his house and now that June and Ted live over the other side of Brimington I don't really get to see any of them as much as I'd like."

"Oh that's awful, Gran. I haven't seen Rob since Janice's wedding but he seemed so much happier since the divorce."

"Yes, well I don't know why he'd want to live out there in the Peak District but June reckons he was shattered after Julie left him for that other bloke and he just wanted to get away from everything and be on his own. I always said that Julie was a bit of a slapper and I was proved right. All fur-coat and no knickers, that one. I had her pegged the day he brought her over to meet me. You'd think they would have popped over to see me more often, wouldn't you, but I haven't seen hide nor hair of *her* since those kids from the estate were sniffing glue behind my shed and that must be over two years ago now. June and Ted are only twenty minutes away but Ted just had his piles banded so I suppose he doesn't like to sit for long. June sounded terrible, but that's only to be expected when you're on chemotherapy. They think they've caught it in time but you never know, do you? It's *insidious* is cancer; a silent killer."

Tallulah pulls the thin silk across her chest. Gran likes to use long words from the dictionary. She does a lot of reading. Tallulah needs to trim her toenails. Tallulah doesn't want to get on to the subject of cancer, thank you very much.

"So how did the accident happen, Gran?"

"They don't know, really, but he drove the car through the metal barriers and went right over the side. Car burst in to flames when it hit the bottom and our Rob was dead by the time the ambulance got to him. I couldn't believe it when our June rang this afternoon, it only seems like yesterday when you two would come round on your bikes together. Actually, when the phone rang I thought it was the council calling to complain about the old carpet I'd put out for the bin men. You know they don't take just *anything* any more; you have to ring them up if you want them to take anything more than your usual rubbish and then they take weeks before they come."

Tallulah is thinking about Robert. She can remember playing marbles with him on their driveway and making dens in the hedge. He used to have a razor-cut and Oxford Bags. She still thinks of him as a boy of thirteen with a centre parting and a mood ring.

"I'm sorry, what did you say, Gran?"

"I said I'm getting now as I don't want to move these days but I'm still mobile. If only I could just walk down to the shop and back but I'm not grumbling as there are such a lot of people with cancer and I've had a good life, duck. I'm not complaining. If only I could shift this wind, I've been rifting all day."

Tallulah is certain that all anyone talks about these days is cancer. Every time she turns on the telly there are women wearing pink ribbons and turbans talking about their 'survival' and their courage. People are dying all over the place and the statistics are in the papers to prove it. It is a word printed in dark black ink and feared by all. It is a word that even comedians find hard to make fun of.

"I'll have to find out about the funeral. I expect it'll be sometime next week. I'm not sure if I can get the time off work but I'd like to send some flowers."

"Well you wouldn't catch me going to any funerals. I've never liked funerals and at my age I can't be standing about in draughty churches. The last funeral

I went to was your granddad's and that was enough for me. The next funeral I go to, duck, I'll be in a box!"

When Tallulah puts down the phone she wonders what made her gran so hard and so indifferent to death. It must be something to do with her age and the changes she has witnessed during her lifetime. Hardness of character comes from hardship in life and Tallulah's gran has certainly not enjoyed some of the privileges that young people these days seem to demand.

Gladys Clegg has lived in the same village all her life, from cradle to (eventual) grave, and she can still remember what it was like to wear a flapper dress and work 'in service' for a few shillings a week. She has never owned her own home or even a car and things like credit cards, bank loans and mortgages are a mystery to her. Gladys comes from a generation and class where TV's were rented and a three-piece suite was only possible if you resorted to Hire Purchase. Milk was delivered daily and left on the doorstep, dripping was saved in an earthenware bowl and spread on toast that had been browned on the end of a toasting fork in front of the open fire, clothes were washed by hand and put through the mangle.

Although Tallulah doesn't have much by today's standards she can't complain when she considers the kind of life her gran has lived. This house is paid-off, she's got a Mastercard in her purse (which she has never used) and there are always chocolate biscuits in the pantry. Her job doesn't pay much but it's enough to get by on and there are a couple of thousand in her savings account in the event of an emergency. She is *rich* by comparison and, consequently, according to Gran, Tallulah is as soft as the rest of today's youth.

"The young 'uns today want everything *now*, they're not prepared to save up for anything. They get married and buy houses and they want to fill those houses with dishwashers and tumble-dryers and fitted carpets while their debts pile up like horse muck around them. Nobody actually has any *real* money any more, it's all on the never-never. Instead of loan sharks there's credit card companies and instead of bailiffs there's bankruptcy court. Bankruptcy? Ha! It's just an excuse to write off their debts, clean the slate and start all over again. This country has gone to the dogs."

And Tallulah, to a certain degree, has to agree. But what does it all mean when young men like Robert have their life snuffed out in an instant? What is the importance of a second or third mortgage if you might pop your clogs at any moment? Perhaps the young people today have got their priorities right, grabbing everything immediately instead of waiting until they're too old or too cold to appreciate it? What does Gran have to show for ninety-six years of poverty? And what did Tallulah's parents gain by putting away every spare penny they earned? They could have sold this house and rented a little flat somewhere by the sea, living very comfortably off the profit until they died. But it was important for them to leave Tallulah an inheritance and so they went without holidays and frivolous shopping sprees to provide for their daughter. And that bold black word with the capital 'C' caught up with them both before they reached sixty.

From the living room Tallulah can hear the sound of people cheering and clapping as somebody else wins the jackpot and, for the first time since she discovered the lump in her breast, she feels choked with fear.

Stone Cold

Nicole wakes with a start and for a moment she hasn't got a clue where she is. She steadies herself against the sloping mattress, the quilt pulled up beneath her nostrils and the drowsy scent of her dreams puffing up in ripples of flannelette. She senses that the room is cold even though she is buried beneath a mountain of feather and down. The curtains are drawn but the flimsy, un-lined material does little to block the gritty morning light. Birds are the only sound for a second or two until the mobile phone rings again to rouse Nicole from her temporary bewilderment.

The phone is on the bedside table next to a glass of water. The glass is cranberry-coloured; thick and clumsy with air bubbles trapped inside like recently formed ice. It stands on a crocheted doily made from coarse unbleached string.

"Ronnie? It's Daph."

"Christ! What time is it?"

"Four in the morning. Jake just went to bed so I sneaked out. I'm on the beach."

Nicole hears a gust of sea-breeze; a hollow echo in Daphne's phone. She pictures the endless stretch of dark sand and water, dotted with lifeguard stations and wooden huts advertising *ceviche* and smoothies. There is probably a cruise ship floating aimlessly out to sea; brightly illuminated and massive against the flicker of distant lightning.

"Ugh! I was in such a deep sleep. I've been sleeping for hours." Nicole picks up her watch and checks the time; it is just after nine.

"Are you in England?"

"Yeah, I got here yesterday. I'm at the cottage."

"Is everything OK?"

"Yeah, everything's fine. This place is pretty basic but it's remote and it's clean. If you could see me now you'd piss yourself; I'm wearing my socks in bed! It's, like, forty degrees over here."

Daphne chuckles at the image. Nicole imagines her friend walking slowly across the tightly packed sand; criss-crossed with tyre marks and worn thin like an old carpet where a layer of concrete is showing through. She can't count the times she has walked that same strip late at night when searching for answers to sleepless questions. She remembers one night, after a particularly violent row with Gideon, stalking off to the beach at three in the morning and spending the night perched on top of a mound of stacked sun-loungers watching the digital clock from the tower on Lincoln Road and waiting for the first streaks of morning to appear on the horizon.

"Gideon's going fucking crazy! We met him for drinks at the Delano and Jake tried to calm him down but he was wasted and we had to leave because he was making so much noise. He wants to kill you, Ronnie. I'm not joking; he really wants to kill you."

Nicole pulls on her robe and levers herself uneasily to the edge of the creaking mass of springs and eiderdown. She reaches out to touch the radiator; it is stone cold.

"Sweetie, he already did his damndest to kill me. The bastard deserves everything that's coming to him. Shouldn't he be worrying about that bitch Courtney if he's so enamoured with her? Having lived with Gideon for all these years I wouldn't be surprised if he dumps her *pronto* now that she's flawed goods."

"Honey, I'm not even sure that he *knows* about Courtney. It's not common knowledge and she's keeping it very close to her chest for obvious reasons.

She's still dancing at Club Madonna and turning tricks so I guess she's not too concerned about it. Right now Gideon's way more furious about the money you took than anything else. I don't think he knows yet *how* much you took but he's got a good idea. He's talking about bringing in the cops and hiring a private investigator."

"Well, we knew that would happen. Let's hope my convoluted trip across Europe puts them off the scent."

"He has already mentioned England, of course, and is threatening to come over there himself to look for you."

Nicole allows herself a nervous giggle. "This is a small country, Daph, but it's not *that* small. He'll never find me here, he'll probably go to London, hang around in a hotel bar for a few days, call a couple of friends and then come back home to drown his sorrows between the silicone tits of that filthy whore he's banging."

"Listen, Ronnie, I know this has been really difficult for you but you've done the right thing. Gideon doesn't give a shit about anyone but himself. Jake told me yesterday that Gideon went out on Tuesday night, got wasted and ended-up spending the night with that bleached-blonde scag from the Van Dyke. He boasted to Jake about it; told him that the bitch deserves all she gets for being so easy. When he told me that I felt so glad that you're out of it, Ronnie. He's on self-destruct."

"Under any other circumstances I'd be loving every minute of this, Daph, but now that I'm here I've got way too much time to think and I'm scared shitless. I don't know anybody over here any more and even if I did I wouldn't be able to get in touch with them. I'll probably spend a few days acclimatizing myself to this place and then I'll have to go in to Manchester to get myself sorted out."

"Not London?" suggests Daphne, her voice carried away on another gust of Miami breeze.

"No, London's too risky. There's always the possibility somebody might recognize me and even though I'm a blonde now I doubt that I'd fool anyone. It's better to stick to the provinces for the time being."

"Look, I've got to go, Ronnie; I don't want Jake suspecting anything. I'll try to call you again in the next couple of days but don't call *me*. I'm supposed to be in Orlando working a bachelor party this weekend but I think I'm going to blow it off; the stripping is really getting me down and I keep hoping that I'll hear from that director I told you about. Just take care and relax for a few days. Do those breathing exercises and take a couple of Ativan. You've done it, girl, you've really done it!"

"I love you, Daph."

"Love you too, honey. Bye."

And Nicole flips her mobile together like a powder compact and yanks back the bedroom curtains to face the day.

Removed from Reality

There are muffins for breakfast (the kind her mother used to call pikelets; rubbery, open-textured things to be drenched with melted butter) with Rose's lime marmalade and (sadly) *instant* coffee. Nicole was lucky last night as she drove out of Castleton she found a small general store that was still open so she filled a basket with all manner of peculiar food items; brand names she had forgotten about, things that are quintessentially British such as Branston pickle, chocolate digestives and Tizer. The lady in the shop was friendly but not particularly inquisitive; one of the advantages of choosing a tourist area in which to hide. Nicole had returned to the cottage with her bag of groceries and dinner consisted of Heinz beans on toast with grated cheddar, a glass of merlot and an entire chocolate orange. She watched TV for a while until she dozed off on the uncomfortable sofa and finally made it up to bed at around eight-thirty.

The weather is colder today and there is a bit of a breeze. They are carving pumpkins on the morning show and Nicole, still in her bath robe, finishes off her coffee and wonders how she will spend her first day in Derbyshire. She isn't familiar with the surrounding area but she does have a map and a guide book. The novelty of being here creates a strange kind of holiday environment, despite the fact that she feels oddly displaced and totally removed from reality. Derbyshire was never a county she visited when she lived in England; she went to Alton Towers once on a school trip but apart from that she spent most of her formative years around London.

Nicole was born in Surrey. Her father was a bus driver and her mother worked in a health clinic as a receptionist. Her childhood was uneventful – ordinary – and although she made it through to grammar school she was never much of an academic. Nicole was more interested in clothes and pop music than algebra and alum crystals. She discovered sex at an early age, despite the fact that her parents were tight-lipped on the subject and preferred to change channels rather than watch unnecessary intimacy on their TV screen.

Nicole has *never* been prudish, despite her upbringing. As a teenager she *was* naïve when it came to matters of a sexual nature. Her parents never attempted to discuss the euphemistic activities of the birds and the bees with their daughter and sex education in the 1970's was nothing more than ninety minutes in the biology lab with an animated film and 'anonymous' questions written on scraps of paper, tossed in to a bag to be read out and answered by the teacher.

'If I wank too much will my knob drop off?'

'Why are my balls hairy?'

'Can I stop myself getting pregnant if I jump up and down and squirt Dettol up my vadge after I've had sex?'

This last question was probably a bona fide cry for help from Donna Bagshot who, at the age of fourteen, was shagging just about every sixth-former who owned a motorbike. Nicole sat next to Donna every week in Music and while the rest of the class listened to *The Lark Ascending* or something experimental played on bongo drums Donna described her latest conquests in graphic detail. Nicole was fascinated and strangely titillated by Donna's lurid stories and yet she doubted she could ever do the things that Donna did. A year later Donna was knocked-up and had to leave school early to bring up the first of her three illegitimate children in a council flat with her Down's Syndrome sister.

Nicole lost her virginity when she was nineteen, to the wine waiter of a restaurant where she worked as a waitress every weekend. He was nine years older than Nicole and he was married with two kids. He flirted with her from the very first day she started but it took him almost a year before he got in her knickers. José was Spanish with a 'reputation' but Nicole believed she was in love and so she allowed him to sidle up behind her one night in the basement when she was clocking-out. They ended-up in the men's changing room with Nicole jammed up against the wall, her legs wrapped uncomfortably around José's waist while he pounded in to her with all the finesse of a Bull Mastiff. They had to do it quickly because they were afraid somebody might walk in and José pulled out at the crucial moment and made a mess of Nicole's black skirt. The whole episode was over within a couple of minutes and, huddled at the back of the number fourteen bus, Nicole cried all the way home.

The second man to have his way with Nicole was her first husband, Marc. Marc worked at the same department store as Nicole and they met at the display department Christmas party. Nicole was rather drunk on too many free vodka and tonics and Marc ravaged her in the back of his Ford Escort. They were married the following summer and Nicole moved in to Marc's three-bedroom Victorian terrace in Holloway, left the department store and started her own party planning business.

Sex with Marc was like Sunday lunch; predictable, tasty but somewhat uninspired. At first they were having sex two or three times a night and Nicole was under the misguided impression that Marc was some kind of super-stud. But it wasn't long before she discovered that her husband was unable to achieve orgasm while inside her and could only complete the act if he manipulated himself while she tugged on his scrotum.

"I've never been able to come inside a woman," admitted Marc one night after a particularly frantic attempt by Nicole to sit astride him when she thought he'd reached the point of no return with a fistful of baby lotion. "I didn't lose my virginity until I was thirty-one so masturbation was my only form of release up until then." Nicole was shocked. She had somehow assumed that Marc had been sexually active for *years* before he met her but it turned out that all of his previous relationships had been purely platonic aside from some 'heavy petting' and an episode with an electric toothbrush. Fortunately, for Nicole, Marc's previous girlfriend had finally taken matters to hand and taught him the rudiments of copulation so although he was unable to deposit his seed in the appropriate repository he could at least satisfy his sexual partners with relentless vigour.

There will always be those who find sex a fascinating topic and others who would rather watch Jane Asher make a birthday cake than see her flailing around in a TV play with her titties out (and, yes, let me assure you, the actress-cum-cake-maker *has* done both!) Each to their own. Leave the room, change the channel or close the book; nobody is going to force you to witness something you'd rather ignore.

So, Nicole discovered pornography, sex toys and casual sex and by the time she divorced Marc and moved in to her own flat she was fairly addicted to all three. At the age of twenty-seven she was earning a decent wage as a party planner and cashing-in on the soaring economy of the mid-eighties. She had clients not only in London but also in Paris, Frankfurt and Milan and her reputation as a design maverick was spreading rapidly through certain circles of society. During that time she didn't have much time for relationships and her focus was on her career. She had a couple of short-term flings but nothing worth getting excited about. And then she met Gideon; Gideon the American with the square jaw and the glamorous sports car.

Gideon Rustin was young and wealthy and smart and sexy and he was the kind of husband Nicole could wear on her arm like a Prada handbag. It didn't matter that he wasn't interested in the same things as her; it was of little concern that he bought most of his clothes at Gap and only got his hair cut four times a year. When a man is young he can get away with that kind of bohemian behaviour and when a man is *wealthy* he can do just about anything he pleases. He allowed Nicole to dress him up for special occasions so she wouldn't have to feel embarrassed by his lack of sartorial elegance at charity functions and red-carpet events but he was more at home in a baggy tee-shirt and jeans than he ever was in the designer clothes that Nicole liked to buy for him in London.

Gideon Rustin was CEO of a computer software business that he created at the astonishing age of twenty-one. Nicole met Gideon when she was contracted to plan his coming-of-age birthday party. It wasn't exactly love at first sight, in fact Gideon was a most objectionable client to work with and Nicole very nearly abandoned the project following a debacle over her choice of table centrepieces. At the time she failed to understand how an apparently jumped-up little computer nerd could possibly have an opinion on Singapore orchids and yet he surprised her with his knowledge of exotic flowers.

It didn't take long for Nicole to discover that Gideon had a strong opinion on just about everything and she learned never to underestimate his innate sense of style and sophistication. It was Gideon who helped design Nicole's wedding gown, Gideon who chose their first house and it was Gideon who had the final say on all of their interior design projects. You might think that Nicole, being a design professional herself, would take umbrage at this invasion of her expertise but she respected Gideon's decisions and sometimes wondered if maybe she was never anything more than mediocre in the field.

Everybody envied them. They had every trapping of success and Nicole was free to live out her fantasies without recrimination. She was wealthy and beautiful and something of a celebrity in the social circles that mattered to her. Then, in the early nineties, Gideon suffered some kind of mental short-circuit (probably sparked by too much coke and ecstasy) and decided that he wanted to jack-in the computer business and move to Miami to buy a chain of gyms. That was when everything started to fall apart.

False Gods

Thinking about Gideon makes Nicole uncomfortable. It is difficult to equate the man she knows now with the man he was back then. Miami changed him irrevocably. His soft, fuzzy edges and his lack of convention became swamped by the superficiality of his new image-conscious friends and within the space of a year Gideon adopted a new kind of personality and dressed it in designer clothes.

He was never a jealous person and he viewed sex and love as two entirely separate compartments of his marriage. Right from the beginning he was open with Nicole about his opinions on monogamy and although it worried Nicole somewhat (she thought he was sugar-coating his inability to commit to marriage) she agreed to try a more open arrangement in their relationship. She had her first threesome with Gideon a fortnight after they met and despite the fact that she had to lock herself in the bathroom for twenty minutes to get her mind around the sight of Gideon getting his bottom licked by a slut in a cheap under-wired bra she was able to hold herself together.

"I don't understand why you were jealous," exclaimed Gideon after the other woman had left. "It's just sex! You have to stop placing so much importance on something that is little more than a recreational activity. I have sex because it feels good but, for me, it means nothing more than a good massage or a game of squash. I've never been able to understand the way society dictates that sex is something sacred and if you ask me there would be a hell of a lot less cheats and liars in this world if everyone could just get over the puritanical crap that's been hammered in to us since birth."

Nicole wanted to tell Gideon that she thought he was over-simplifying the situation, that his opinion was not the norm and that most people are just too insecure to allow their partners to have complete sexual freedom. But she didn't know him well enough at the time and she didn't want to appear priggish so she merely stated that it would take some getting used to but that she wasn't averse to the idea. They were having great sex when it was just the two of them so she participated in a few more threesomes and gradually her inhibitions began to slip away.

She soon started to realize that by bringing in a third party they were avoiding the inevitable erosion of novelty in their sex life and there was none of the formulaic monotony that many couples have to deal with when they've been together for a while. But once they moved to Miami the dynamic changed and Gideon stopped including his wife in his sexual exploits. He started hanging out with his new friends until the early hours of the morning and Nicole had to accept the fact that he was surrounded every day by beautiful women who were more interested in his bank account than his marital status. It was around that time Nicole had her first *real* affair. His name was James and he was British. They had fifteen glorious months together before he was killed in a speedboat accident off the Florida Keys and Nicole never really recovered from the tragedy.

Nicole's enviable lifestyle continued to attract attention but it was as hollow and brittle as she felt inside. She had become the stylish woman of a certain age who refused to allow herself the indignity of growing old gracefully. She attended obligatory charity functions with Gideon for the publicity it generated and she was perceived as aloof and impenetrable by her contemporaries; those women who hadn't weathered the ravages of time quite so gracefully. They speculated spitefully on the firmness of her skin and the gymnastic grace of her figure and swallowed their envy like chunks of stale bread whenever they saw her out with Gideon, her young, handsome, *wealthy* husband.

But, like worshipping false gods, envying Nicole was a misguided pastime because, despite all the obvious trappings of wealth, beauty and success, she was a deeply troubled person and her life was falling apart. She began to find it difficult to live in a world where she regarded the majority of people as a waste of space.

Simple day-to-day activities outside the walls of her home drove her to distraction and she couldn't cope with the simple fact that she was merely another mortal on this planet of six billion. Surely five billion of those people could be exterminated and the world would be a better place? The simple *inconvenience* of co-existing with those people was enough to send anyone over the edge; the reckless drivers, the common *hoi polloi* who littered South Beach with their push-chairs and snotty-nosed kids, the rude telephone operators and officious police officers, the 'full' sign at the car park, the lack of reservations at the best restaurants, the so-called

Christians and the prudish neo-puritans who complained to the newspapers whenever they saw a pair of tits on their TV screens. The world seemed to be crammed with objectionable, irritating, worthless animals bringing absolutely nothing to the table but their own sense of importance.

And then she found out about Courtney and everything changed forever. Nicole was well aware that Gideon was screwing-around and she was quite prepared to accept that inevitable fact. She didn't even mind that he was having an affair; after all, she herself had been in love with James while continuing the public side of her marriage to appease the publicists and the facile circle of friends with whom they were forced to fraternize. Only Daphne knew the real truth behind Nicole's marriage and it was Daphne who finally brought the stupefying facts to Nicole's attention.

Leaving the dregs of her coffee in the bottom of the cup Nicole takes her things through to the kitchen sink and pauses for a moment to look out over the serenity of the Derbyshire countryside. She barely recognizes the woman she has become and yet she feels more comfortable in her skin this morning than she has felt in many years. In order to move forward she was forced to move back and now that she's here – despite all the anger and fear involved – she is certain that the shredded mess of her life will mould itself in to a new shape and she will find the strength to invent herself again.

All Shapes & Sizes

"She comes out of hospital tomorrow. She's been in since last Friday. They were coming to my bungalow for the ash from the fire to mix with their soil when she tripped over a mound in the road just below the tollbar. She sustained a fractured knee and Geoffrey went to see her Sunday and she's got a plaster from her thigh to her ankle. I don't know how Arthur will manage with it not to come off for six weeks."

Tallulah's gran called again last night. Ostensibly she called to give Tallulah more details of Robert's untimely death and plans for the funeral but she moved swiftly on to subjects of a more trivial nature.

"I thought Doris and Arthur had moved to Great Yarmouth?" mumbled Tallulah as she attempted to stretch the phone cord over to the living room door so she could continue watching the telly.

"No, duck, they moved back a few months ago but they don't go out as often now as they've got a satellite dish. Mind you, I don't blame them because there've been a few burglaries on their street. It's time something was done because everything's getting out of hand. I wish I was in the government; I'd show 'em. Bring back the birch. Bring back hanging, that's what I'd do!"

"Listen, Gran, I've got to go now but I'll call you tomorrow and come and see you this weekend sometime, OK?"

"All right, duck. It'll be lovely to see you, despite the sad circumstances, and I've just got a new second-hand cooker so you can come for your Sunday dinner if you want. It's been grand since they converted me to gas because they were only giving us six small bags of coal a

month and it wasn't like the stuff your granddad used to
get when he worked at the pit."

"OK, well I'll give you a ring tomorrow night
after I've been to see Auntie June and Uncle Ted."

And so Tallulah is here, after work on a
Thursday evening, wondering what to expect from the
bereaved parents.

Ted and June Clegg live on a new housing estate
where the brick is a deep burnished red and the windows
are mullioned.   Even the sliding patio doors are
mullioned. This is a modern day Tudor village complete
with half-timbered facades and zigzag brickwork and this
is the first time Tallulah has been to visit her aunt and
uncle in years.

Tallulah enters the estate by foot, coming from
the bus stop at the end of the road. The evening sky is
streaked with shades of autumn and although the wind
has died down it is still very chilly. Most of the leaves
have already fallen and the trees are beginning to take on
the appearance of winter. It will be Halloween in a
couple of days and then Bonfire Night. The kids round
Tallulah's way have been letting off bangers every night
for weeks and she'll be glad when it's all over.

She's been at work all day and her feet are killing
her. She really doesn't want to be here and wishes she
had been firmer when Gran dropped heavy hints that it
would be only right and proper for Tallulah to visit her
aunt and uncle after such a tragic loss. After all, Tallulah
did used to spend quite a bit of time playing over there in
the summer holidays and Robert *was* exactly the same age
as her.   It's just that Tallulah hates these kinds of
confrontations, these awkward social events where she
never quite knows what to say. Auntie June and Uncle
Ted will be devastated and probably want to be left alone
right now and Tallulah is afraid that she has nothing to

tell them that will make any difference. All the usual platitudes about death and sympathy run through her head as she makes her way to the house and she can't seem to think of anything comforting or wise to offer up in the way of condolences.

And there's something else that is bothering Tallulah as she keeps her head down and walks briskly across the street, she is terrified of seeing Auntie June and her cancer.

The lump in Tallulah's left breast sits heavily on her mind. It has been there now for many months and every morning Tallulah checks to see if it might have diminished or dissolved during the night. But it seems to be resolute in its size and density and sometimes she even imagines that it is getting bigger. She hasn't said anything to anyone. It's not easy maintaining a cheerful disposition when you're off to the toilet three times a day to fumble under your bra for reassurances that never come.

Tallulah works in a small lingerie boutique for a Frenchman they call Mr. B (because when he first arrived in England nobody could pronounce his surname properly). Mr. B makes custom undergarments for wealthy women and his speciality is traditional and rather brutal-looking corsetry for the fashion industry. They sell pieces from other French manufacturers but everything is very expensive and even with her staff discount Tallulah can't afford to wear the things she sells. If Tallulah had a spare two hundred quid she wouldn't be spending it on an uplift bra. She has worked for Mr. B since the sweet factory closed down in Chesterfield and although the work is undemanding and sometimes tedious she finds the peaceful atmosphere of the boutique a relief after twenty-five years on the production-line at Trebor. Tallulah hasn't touched a boiled sweet since her first week at the factory when she ate so many that she vomited on the bus going home.

There are two other 'girls' at Mr. B's and although they're all over thirty he still prefers to refer to them as his girls. Junie Starr is the manager and she has been with Mr. B for thirty years while Sue Covey is a trainee. There is a workshop upstairs where Mr. B employs five seamstresses and he has a small factory in Lille where they construct the more complicated under garments. Tallulah's title is Assistant Manger but with only three of them working in the shop she doesn't have much opportunity to wield her status. The only time she has any sense of authority is when Junie takes her annual holidays and then Tallulah is allowed to process orders and report directly to Mr. B. It's an easy life for minimum wages and Tallulah allows herself few luxuries.

Tits of all shapes and sizes are exposed to Tallulah on a daily basis so you would think that she'd be perfectly comfortable discussing her own when she's at work but Tallulah was brought up to ignore her private parts as one might ignore what goes on under the bonnet of a brightly polished car. Tallulah treats the discovery of the lump in her breast as she would an ominous rattle in the engine; she keeps driving and hopes it goes away on its own. She has managed to avoid all scheduled mammograms, ignoring her doctor's advice and preferring ignorance over fear. Tallulah has never had any kind of operation, no major illnesses and she is fortunate that her teeth are still going strong because she hasn't been to see the dentist since she bashed the last one in the face when she was nine years old. She has a phobia of hospitals and her worst nightmares are often based around the discovery of horrible disfigurements on her body. Sometimes she wakes in a cold sweat having just spat out her entire set of teeth or having sprouted alarming lumps and sores on her limbs. She can't even watch *Casualty* without a clutch of anxiety in the pit of her stomach.

Sackcloth & Ashes

Ted and June's house stands alone in a narrow strip of land. Similar houses flank either side, all of then immaculately groomed and impeccably landscaped. The lights are on but the curtains are drawn so Tallulah can only see shadow and light through the Sanderson cabbage roses. She wonders if Auntie June might be tucked beneath a blanket on the sofa with her head wrapped in some kind of turban or – worse yet – a wig. Will Uncle Ted be sitting in the armchair staring down at a large framed photograph of Robert while his tea goes cold on the side? Tallulah prepares herself for the worst so she is startled when she knocks at the door and hears laughter from the other side of the glass panel.

They are watching the telly. Well, the telly is on but Tallulah can't be sure they were actually watching it. Maybe the sound of the newsreaders is soothing background noise in a house where death and disease hang in the air like silently drifting cobwebs. But the gas fire is on and there are chocolate biscuits on the coffee table and Tallulah is slightly alarmed to find Auntie June doubled over with laughter. The room is over-heated and there is a strange burning smell. Uncle Ted is standing by the painting of the stampeding elephants and he has a cigarette between his fingers, hanging limply by his side as he clutches his stomach with the other hand. He is laughing too.

Tallulah isn't quite sure how to react so she just stands in the middle of the Axminster in her overcoat and bobble hat and she smiles along with them. "So, what's the joke?" she asks as she starts to unbutton her coat.

June manages to compose herself sufficiently to address her niece; she is still clutching a cushion to her stomach. "Oh, it's nothing very funny, love. We're smoking marijuana and it makes us a bit giddy". And with this June starts to splutter and she looks up hopelessly at Ted at which point they both explode in to laughter once again.

"*Marijuana?*" gasps Tallulah, looking first at Auntie June and then at Uncle Ted, "that's *illegal!*"

But this just causes her aunt and uncle to laugh even louder so Tallulah removes her hat, shoves it in to the pocket of her coat and hangs the coat over the back of a dining chair. "Where on earth did you get marijuana?"

"It was our Rob who gave us this last lot," answers Auntie June, swiping at her eyes with the sleeve of her cardigan, "he got it when I started on chemo because it stops me being sick."

"Yeah, he was a good lad," muses Uncle Ted who has suddenly turned introspective, staring down at the tips of his carpet slippers.

"We'd never tried it before," explains June, "but when I started on the therapy I was feeling sick as a dog and it was our Rob as suggested smoking a bit of marijuana. It's not illegal if it's for medical reasons, you see, and our Rob seemed to get his hands on some fairly quickly. It's *lovely!* Do you want a bit, Tal? Ted, give our Tally a puff on that thing."

"Not for me, Auntie June, I don't smoke *normal* cigarettes and I don't take drugs. Does your doctor know that you're smoking that stuff?"

"Oh yes, love, he said it was a bloody good idea! He's a grand doctor; a young bloke, probably in his thirties, wouldn't you say, Ted?   And handsome? – crikey, love - he'd give that George Clooney a run for his money, I can tell you!"

"Sit down, duck, you look like Lizzie Dripping standing over there." Uncle Ted motions towards the bottle green Dralon sofa with the tasselled fringe. "I know you probably expected us to be wearing sackcloth and ashes for our Rob but, the fact is, it's not really sunk in for us yet. We've both been trying to imagine him not being here any more but we can't seem to get a handle on it. We've had a bit of a weep, of course, but I can't say we feel bereaved. Not yet, anyway. Perhaps things'll be different at the funeral."

"Oh you don't have to explain – or apologize – to me, Uncle Ted. I'm just glad to see that you're both looking so well considering the stuff you've been going through recently. How are *you* feeling, Auntie June?"

"You know, Tally love, it's not so bad." June shifts back in her armchair and raises her ankle to rest on top of a small embroidered stool. Her complexion is a little less rosy than usual and her eyes are hollow and smudged with shadow. "The day after the chemo is usually the worst but if I smoke a few puffs of this stuff I can generally get through it without vomiting. There's no pain, you see, not from the cancer. It's the *worry* that affects you more than anything. And it's hard on your Uncle Ted, isn't it, love? I have always said it's harder for the one who *isn't* ill; the husband or the wife, like."

"I'll go and put the kettle on," announces Ted as he stubs out the butt of the badly-rolled joint in a small crystal ashtray, "Your Auntie June wanted to have a word with you anyway and I've got a couple of things to do in the shed." And he goes through in to the kitchen, pulling the glass panelled door silently behind him. As he does so the bulb in the standard lamp suddenly pops, throwing the corner of the room in to shadow.

"That's funny," comments Auntie June, turning to look at the lamp, "that's the third bulb that's gone since yesterday."

"So what's the word you wanted with me, then?" asks Tallulah, leaning forward to place her elbows firmly on her knees, "Gran didn't mention anything to me; she just said that you might like to see me. Is there something you need me to help you with, Auntie June?"

"Oh your Gran never says what she means; she's been talking in riddles all her life and she loves a bit of intrigue. It was your Gran who suggested that you might be able to use some of our Rob's stuff, that's all. Your Uncle Ted was telling her that we've got to empty out that house of his and get rid of his stuff but that we didn't know anyone we'd trust to do it. Your Gran said that she though there might be some things that you could use, like his computer and stuff, and then we got to thinking that you are really the only person we can ask to help us clear out his belongings. There's no way in hell we'd ask Julie because, as far as we're concerned, the divorce shut her out of our lives forever, thank God! She's taken enough from our Rob as it is and she's not getting another penny from this family."

Tallulah reaches out across the narrow coffee table to touch her aunt's knee; it is a simple movement but it transmits the appropriate amount of sympathy in such a situation and Tallulah is an expert at offering sympathy. "Isn't it a bit early to be thinking about these things? Perhaps we should wait until after the funeral to talk about it, eh?"

"No, love, it's important for me and your Uncle Ted to start on these things because, between us, we can't seem to concentrate on anything for more than a few minutes. We've never been to his house, you see; our Rob has always been funny like that; secretive, like. Even when he was married to Julie we'd only go over to the old house on Boxing Day and Easter Sunday. Rob liked his privacy and we think he preferred to see us here, in our own home, where we *belong*."

"Well, is there a rush to do this?" asks Tallulah, sitting back against the sofa cushions, "you don't need to sell the house straight away, do you?"

"Yes we do, love. You see the house is only worth a few thousand more now than when our Rob bought it and the next mortgage payment is due at the end of the month. Every month that passes will be another mortgage cheque from *our* bank account, whittling away the small amount of money that'll be left over after the solicitors and estate agents have had their cut. We can't afford for it to stay around for too long. There are no savings and no life insurance, you see, and because there was no will it will be up to us to sort out all his dealings."

"It'll be a bit funny, going in to Rob's house seeing as how I haven't seen much of him these past few years. I don't really *know* him any more."

"Well we don't know much more. He kept his private life to himself and we learned to stop asking him. Living out there all on his own just didn't seem natural to us but he kept telling us that it was what he wanted. Kept going on about how he wanted to live his life on his own terms. He seemed happy enough when he came over here but he didn't stay in touch with anyone else and we never met any of his new friends, if he had any."

"Perhaps we could go there together, the first time?" suggests Tallulah, hopefully.

"Oh no, love, that's the point of asking you to do it; we don't *want* to go to our Rob's place. We want to remember him how he was when he was alive and that house and all the stuff in it has got nothing to do with our son. Whatever kind of private life he was leading out there we just don't want to know about it. And it's not just that we're worried he might have some porno mags stuffed under his bed or some bones in the cellar; it's just that we don't want to see *evidence* of the life we were excluded from. He'd want all of that kept private. If he didn't want to share it with us while he was alive he wouldn't want us prying now."

Tallulah wonders just how complicated this act of charity might become. For a start she doesn't have a car and Rob's house is way out in the Peak District. Secondly it will take weeks to sort through all his stuff unless she arranges for somebody to come and empty the house in to a skip, but that would be a bit ruthless. She'd hate to think that *her* life might one day be reduced to a mound of useless rubbish.

Ted comes in to the room carrying a wicker tray of tea things. "So has she asked you about our Rob's place then?" And he places the tray on the coffee table, next to the chocolate biscuits.

Tallulah nods and offers her uncle a smile of reassurance, "Yes, we've been talking about it and, of course I'd be happy to help out."

"We'll reimburse any expenses, of course," explains Ted as he stands back from the tea tray to warm his bum against the gas fire, "transportation, cleaning bills, anything you might have to pay for out of your own pocket. We can give you the keys to our car if you like."

"I can't drive, Uncle Ted. I took some lessons when I was eighteen but I never took my test," smiles Tallulah, "we can sort out the money and stuff later on."

"Well, anything you want to take for yourself, you're welcome to it."

"Thanks."

But Tallulah is dismayed by the prospect. She wishes she were stronger in character; the kind of person who can say no when they don't want to do something. But how can she say no to Auntie June with cancer and Uncle Ted with banded piles just one day after their only son has been killed in a car accident?

She plucks the knitted cosy off the teapot and places her fingers around the warm china handle.

"Shall I be mother?" she asks, with one eyebrow raised. And Ted leans forward to put a drop of milk in to each of the three cups.

Robert

Oh yes, I was upset but it wasn't suicide that sent me over the edge of the ravine. Not *conscious* suicide, at any rate. The psychoanalysts would have us believe that everything is pre-meditated, that we are not always aware of the driving force behind our actions but believe me when I say that I had no intention of killing myself.

I'd had another pointless phone conversation with Julie – acrimonious as always – and maybe I shouldn't have gone out in the car so late at night, especially as I'd downed a couple of very generous glasses of Ursula's dandelion wine. Sometimes I would drive out to Ladybower late at night; stop the car somewhere off the beaten track and smoke a joint while looking up at the stars. I liked to imagine the submerged ruins of Ashopton village like a watery ghost town beneath the still waters of the reservoir and although I never saw the church spire (it was destroyed in the

1970's to stop people from swimming out to it) my mother used to tell me how it would protrude from the water during drought season.

I don't know why I decided to drive through the Snake Pass. It seemed like a good idea at the time and I was high so I imagined it might be something of a trip to open the car windows and drive along that wild and majestic road with my music blaring out in to the night.

The car went through the metal barrier, the air-bag inflated and for a couple of seconds I was flying in slow-motion. This is what it must feel like to jump out of a plane, I thought to myself in that moment of unspeakable calm before impact. There was no time for fear; there was just a sense of inevitability and although my life didn't flash before my eyes there *was* a sudden jolt of understanding. All my questions were answered in that split second before the car exploded and the feeling of relief was miraculous.

Simple Pleasures

It has been an unexpectedly pleasant day and Nicole can't remember when such simple pleasures satisfied her in this way. Now that she is growing accustomed to driving on the wrong side of the road she has discovered a renewed excitement in the simple navigation of country roads. In Miami the drivers are aggressive and dangerous; many of them uninsured and nonchalant about the possibility of getting in to an accident. The freeways are like race-tracks with maniacs switching lanes without indicating and driving way above the speed limits and Nicole can't remember the last time she went out for a drive for the sheer pleasure of it. In Miami she would invariably return home seething with rage at the arrogance or sheer indifference of a fellow driver and occasionally she would scare herself by reacting violently towards a particularly objectionable jerk. People running red lights, honking horns at stop signs, giving her the 'bird' when she failed to get out of their way in the fast lane; Miami is the capitol of rude, self-centred egotists.

Nicole is amazed that people in England still raise their hand in a salute when she stops to let them pass; they wave her ahead at junctions and always use their blinkers to indicate when they're turning. One gentleman actually got out of his car to point Nicole in to a tight parking space at the Chatsworth farm shop and he wasn't pan-handling or looking to get her phone number. Amazing!

She spent a very happy hour in the farm shop buying all manner of delicious delicacies; it was like a mini Harrods food hall with servers in straw boaters and pristine white aprons, baskets piled high with fresh produce and home-baked specialities. The packaging and presentation was so tempting that Nicole wildly over-spent and now has enough food to keep her going for the entire week. She was seduced by childish things like ginger beer in old-fashioned bottles, elderflower wine, leek and walnut sausages, massive scones called Fat Rascals and rhubarb preserves. It wasn't until she got back in to the car and made the calculations in her head that she realized how much she had spent.

She avoided the main towns and kept to the smaller roads, following her instinct and refusing to consult a map until it was time to head back to the cottage. She is disappointed that many of the stately homes are closed for the season but Chatsworth is still open and she spent the afternoon touring the house before indulging in an extravagantly fattening cream tea in the wonderfully comprehensive restaurant there.

Coming from a world of low-carb, low-fat, sugar-free dieting she felt positively wicked sitting down to clotted cream scones and egg mayonnaise sandwiches. And everyone was so polite! Neatly-dressed couples and retirees talked quietly at each table, nodding and smiling at each other as they returned their dirty trays to the conveyor belts. Where are the yobs and football hooligans that Nicole was so worried about before she came over here? Probably in Manchester and Leeds; cities with football clubs and council houses. She doubts that Lager Louts would be interested in herbal tea and seventeenth century tapestries.

When she got back to Castleton she parked the car and took a stroll around the village centre despite the fact that the weather suddenly became much colder. A sharp breeze scattered the last remaining leaves along the narrow pavements and Nicole took refuge in some of the tourist shops along the way to stay warm. She bought a pair of earrings set with the local Blue John stone, a large slab of chocolate fudge and a decent pair of walking shoes. The clothing wasn't worth considering because it was mainly geared towards the kind of people who find comfort in waxed canvas and Arran knits. She briefly considered a rather quirky padded jacket with a detachable hood until she realized that she was getting carried away by the novelty of Country Living. Apparently they have a branch of Harvey Nichols in Leeds and Manchester now so she will save her clothes shopping until she feels brave enough to tackle the city.

There is a funny little second-hand knick-knack shop tucked away in a picturesque corner by the bridge and the man who owns it has stuck up wry hand-written notices to amuse his customers. There was one that particularly tickled Nicole, it read: 'And for my American customers, there is no such thing as a thousand dollar treasure for fifty pence!' And over by a collection of mis-matched teacups and saucers another sign read; "I don't serve afternoon tea or little tarts.' Nicole bought a silver-plated tea-strainer for one pound fifty and a couple of Daphne du Maurier novels she hasn't read since she was at school.

For most of the day she didn't think about Gideon or the mess he has created. There were a couple of times when the reality of her situation landed with a sickening thud against the lining of her stomach but she focussed her attention on something else and the fear in her gut dissolved away to nothing more than a nagging sense of apprehension. She doesn't want to face up to the difficult challenge ahead, she just wants to bury her head in the sand for a while and bask in the simple fact that she has escaped from the vile, corrupt little world where she lived so smugly in her state of self-denial. It only takes a few days away from Miami to realize just how unhealthy and poisonous that kind of environment can be if you allow yourself to believe in it. It's hard to reconcile that just a few weeks ago Nicole was sufficiently delusional to allow Gideon his conjugal rights despite the fact that the sight of his drug-induced erection revolted her to the point of gagging. What kind of woman allows herself to be used in that way? What does it say about her self-respect? She feels now that she will never have sex again. She wants to soak in a bath of lavender and rose petals and wear crisp white cotton to bed. She would like to erase her sex, neuter herself with a row of neat little stitches and cover it over with a clean bandage.

She is forty-six years old and already her periods are less regular. Hopefully menopause will soon staunch the monthly flow of blood and render her barren. Nicole will celebrate the day when her sexual functions dry-up and wither away so that she can push all that messy business behind her. She wishes now that she never allowed Gideon to persuade her to have the breast implants or the brow-lift. She wants to be ugly and undesirable; she wants to look her age instead of trying so hard to be something she isn't. She will stop exercising and start eating real food again. She will steer clear of coke and crystal, E and K and absorb her vitamins from green vegetables and citrus fruit instead of from high potency vitamin pills. It's a well-known fact that chocolate and red wine are good for you so she will gorge on the finest cocoa beans and full-bodied cabernets until her body is saturated with anti-carcinogenics and anti-oxidants.

Flapjack

Nicole is watching TV when there is a timid knock at the front door of Brown Bread Cottage. For a moment she is frozen to the spot; rooted to the sofa with her heart suddenly knocking wildly in the side of her throat like a trapped bird. This is ridiculous! There is no way that Gideon could have found her here and yet she is terrified to answer the door. She sits tight and waits to see if the person goes away but there is a second knock, slightly more aggressive this time and a woman's voice calls out "Miss Nichols?" from the doorstep. There is a rattling of keys and Nicole finally leaps up from her seat and unlocks the door to peer round in to the gloom of the evening.

A small woman with large glasses and neatly styled hair smiles warmly in the pink light from the cottage and repeats her question, "Miss. Nichols?" When Nicole opens the cottage door a little further, sensing that she is in no danger, the woman in the long beige coat and incongruously high heels juts her head forward and smiles brightly, "I'm Mrs. Harris, the owner of the cottage. I just wanted to check that everything is to your liking."

"Oh, Mrs. Harris, I'm so sorry, I was dozing on the sofa and you caught me by surprise. Yes, hello, I'm Veron…*Nicole* Harvey. Pleased to meet you. Would you like to come in?"

"Thank you, love, I can't stop but I thought I'd better check up on you. Have you got everything you need? Is everything comfortable?"

"Everything is wonderful, thank you. The cottage is charming!"

"Oh good," smiles Mrs. Harris who appears to be expertly made-up and immaculately groomed for such an informal visit. She has dainty hands and a couple of rather impressive looking diamonds. Nicole puts her down for somewhere around sixty-five but she isn't the kind of sixty-five year old one might expect in the middle of the Derbyshire countryside.

"I've brought you some flapjack," she presents Nicole with a biscuit tin; "I made it this morning and thought you might enjoy some. I usually leave something in the kitchen for my guests but I didn't have time yesterday to bring anything over."

"Oh that's so kind, Mrs. Harris, thanks so much! I'll have a piece this evening with a cup of tea." Nicole accepts the tin and is genuinely touched by the gesture. She can't remember the last time anyone actually baked her something.

"Well, I'll leave you to your evening, love, but I just wanted to introduce myself. If you need anything – anything at all – I live at High View Grange. Turn right at the bottom of the lane and then the first left, we're the only house up there, you can't miss us."

"Thanks very much," smiles Nicole, holding up the biscuit tin; "and thanks for the flapjack."

"You're welcome, love. I usually come over on Monday afternoons to change the sheets but I'll let myself in if you're out somewhere."

"Great, well, thanks again. Good night." And Nicole closes the door and shoots the bolt across immediately. As she turns to face the rose-pink living room where the TV is gabbling to itself in the corner and her copy of *Frenchman's Creek* is face-down on the coffee table Nicole feels thrilled to be here. The simplest gesture of human kindness, a few polite words on the doorstep and the prospect of another serendipitous day tomorrow wrap her in a warm blanket of contentment.

She takes the tin through to the kitchen and eases off the lid to peep inside. Wrapped in a layer of waxproof paper she finds two layers of thick, treacly flapjack. The sweet delicious scent of oats and golden syrup take her back to a time and place she thought she had forgotten; her grandmother's kitchen. There was a time when Nicole had nothing more dreadful to contemplate than the end of the summer holidays and the occasional dental appointment and now – oh God, now! – there is scant refuge inside the waxproof lining of a biscuit tin.

Maybe tomorrow she should think about going in to Manchester? She isn't at all thrilled by the thought and immediately dismisses it as hasty. Perhaps she could go to a library somewhere and see if they have access to the internet. Do they have such things as Cyber-Cafés in Derbyshire? A Manchester area phone book would be sufficient for her needs and if she makes an appointment then she won't have to hang around in the city for longer than is necessary. Quite honestly she would rather not think about it just now. She would prefer to make herself a cup of tea and sit down with a piece of Mrs. Harris's flapjack and her Daphne du Maurier. There's plenty of time to worry about going in to Manchester and, for now at least, she would rather gather her wits about her and spend the weekend in the general vicinity of Castleton, becoming acquainted with the area.

Unfortunately the weather forecast for tomorrow is not so good. They're predicting heavy rain in the afternoon, through in to Saturday, and Nicole doesn't have a raincoat or an umbrella so maybe that should be her priority tomorrow morning? Buxton isn't far away and she is certain that there must be a few mainstream shops over there. With that thought in mind she feels calmer; a morning of shopping and a rainy afternoon is infinitely more appealing than a trip in to Manchester to fight with the crowds and the busy roads.

She puts the kettle on (an *electric* kettle; something she hasn't used in fifteen years) and spoons some of the tea she bought at the farm shop in to the small brown teapot. There are no curtains at the kitchen window and she can see her own reflection in the glass. It is slightly unsettling to think that out there, across the fields, she is visible and exposed. For all she knows there could be somebody standing in the back garden right now looking directly in at her and she would never know. Nicole suppresses a shudder and turns her back on the window to lean against the sink while she waits for the kettle to boil. She breaks a piece of flapjack in to two pieces and nibbles at the sticky chunk of oats and raisins mindlessly. There are adverts on the TV and the wall above the living room sofa is splashed with the shifting colours from the screen.

A Small Island

Nicole's phone starts to ring. It can only be one person. Nobody but Daphne knows the number.

"Daph?"

"Hi sweetie, how's it going?"

"Actually not so bad. I'm making myself a cup of tea and eating some flapjack that my landlady just brought over."

"Oh my God! It sounds like something from the last century!" Daphne laughs from four thousand miles away and Nicole tries to imagine her somewhere in the afternoon heat of Miami. As if reading her friend's mind Daphne explains to Nicole that she's out on the balcony of their condo while Jake, her boyfriend, is down by the pool. "It's, like, ninety degrees today," she says, "humid as fuck."

"Hard to imagine, darling. I've got the electric radiator on full-blast and I'm thinking of lighting a fire tonight." The kettle comes to a boil and Nicole balances the phone between her ear and her shoulder as she pours the water over the loose tea leaves. "Have you got any more news for me?"

"Well he's still fuming, of course, and swearing vengeance. Now that he knows how much money you took from his account he has been on to his lawyers and is ranting on about coming to England to hunt you down."

"Fuck!" Nicole places the lid on the teapot and closes her eyes. Despite the fact she is almost certain Gideon would never find her here she is sickened by the idea of him being in the same country. England is a small island, London is only two hours away and suddenly Brown Bread Cottage feels as exposed as a raft in the middle of shark infested waters. "Maybe I should go to Paris or somewhere? I could take the Eurostar from London and hide out on the continent for the next couple of weeks."

"Ronnie, don't panic. I seriously doubt that he'll actually come over there and even if he did he's never going to find you out there in the wilds. You know what he's like; he'll hang around London until he gets bored and then he'll probably come back to Miami after a few days and it'll all blow over. It's just bravado on his part right now; he feels that he's got to do *something* but he's too lazy to actually conduct an intelligent search for you. It's all about saving-face at the moment. If I were you I'd be more worried about this private investigator guy he employed than Gideon. Apparently he's already on the case."

Nicole feels nauseous. Her plans of just a few minutes ago suddenly seem ridiculously frivolous and shopping for a raincoat and umbrella is about as relevant as running from a burning building with nothing but a jar of moisturizer and a pair of roller-skates. It is probably best if she just locks herself away in the cottage for the next two weeks and stays in bed.

"I don't feel good about this, Daph. You don't know what he's capable of when he's angry. It was bad enough when he found out that I spent the week with James in Savannah and that was a minor blip on the radar compared to running away with three quarters of a million dollars. It's not as though his finances are particularly healthy these days; he hasn't worked in five years and his fucking gyms are losing money every day. He was such a jerk to sell off his shares in CompEx, but we've been through that *ad nauseam.*"

"Gideon is a jerk, period. It's this place, Ronnie; everybody who comes to Miami ends up losing everything. The only people who make a success down here are the people who know how to manipulate the corruption to their own advantage; why do you think Jake does so well? We wouldn't be living in a three million dollar condo if we had to rely on the income Jake makes from the club. You *know* where the real money comes from. Gideon came here looking for a way to escape and that's what he found. Unfortunately he dragged you here with him and ruined both your lives at the same time, so now it's up to you to get on with your life and stop worrying about Gideon. What's the worst he can do to you?"

Nicole doesn't want to consider that question. Is it illegal for a wife to steal money from her husband? Under the circumstances wouldn't any judge be lenient and dismiss the case as insubstantial? The fact is, Nicole isn't concerned about the money aspect, she's more worried about Gideon and what he might do to her. There was a time when she wouldn't have thought of him as a violent person but when they moved to Miami and he became mired in the drug scene his personality changed, along with his friends and his lifestyle. The mild-mannered computer nerd with the surprisingly artistic sophistication no longer exists and his crumpled cargo pants and plastic Swatch have been replaced by leather trousers and an Oyster Rolex. He drinks tequila instead of beer; he wears a diamond in his ear and got liposuction on his love-handles. He isn't the person Nicole married.

"Daph, look at some of the people he mixes with these days. If Gideon really wanted to he could track me down and have me 'disappear' mysteriously and without a trace. Remember what happened to Tyrone Daly? If Gideon can harbour that kind of malice towards a guy who nicked ten grand from him then what is he capable of when it comes to seven hundred and fifty *thousand?*"

"Listen, honey, I'll keep my ear to the ground and I'll let you know anything that I think might help you. Quite honestly I don't think you've got anything to worry about but I can understand your concern. I think you should be worrying more about yourself than about Gideon right now. Have you made an appointment to see a doctor yet?"

"Not yet. I am thinking about going in to Manchester next week. I'm not sure I can cope with that just yet."

Daphne sighs. "Sweetie, you need to get tested. From what I hear Courtney has been positive for at least two years and Gideon has never concerned himself with safe sex, has he? How many times did you have sex with him during the past seven months? You've got to stop pretending that this can't happen to you. The test two weeks ago may have been negative but that doesn't prove anything; Gideon fucked you just last month; he didn't use a condom. I know you don't want to hear any of this but you've got to keep having those tests until you're in the clear."

"And if I'm positive?"

"Then you'll deal with it, Ronnie, just like the thousands of other people who live with HIV. You know as well as I do that it's not a death sentence any more; the medications work as long as you stick to the regime and these days it's just a couple of pills each day; hell you take enough vitamins and anti-depressants, what's two more pills?"

Nicole places the palm of her free hand against the side of the little brown teapot and absorbs the warmth from the brewing tea. In the tiny kitchen with the cat-lovers wall calendar and the framed watercolour of Pevril Castle Nicole feels totally disconnected from reality. She knows this isn't a dream so pinching herself won't help.

How could Gideon do this to her?

"If Gideon is positive he deserves to die a long and painful death but, right now, that's not much consolation to me. Are you sure he doesn't know about Courtney yet?"

"Apparently not. He's still screwing around, according to Jake. Gideon only cares about himself and you aren't the only woman in Miami who should be worrying about their health. Gideon is like a little boy; he can't keep his dick in his pants."

When Nicole ends the conversation with Daphne she forgets her tea, abandons her flapjack and walks slowly through in to the living room to turn off the TV. Without the sound of the television voices the cottage falls silent and the ceiling seems to be a little lower than before. A few minutes ago everything seemed so cosy and relaxing but now the atmosphere has changed and the cottage is closing in around her. The ugly flowered curtains with the uneven Rufflette tape, the lifeless silk flower arrangement and the one-bar electric fire sitting in the gaping hole of the fireplace all conspire to make Nicole feel worse.

Maybe if it were summer she might feel different? She could go for a long walk across the fields or maybe sit in the garden of a pub somewhere and have a couple of drinks but in October the nights are long and lonely and there's the whole winter ahead. It might make more sense to go to the south of France or the Algarve but the thought of coping with a different language as well as a totally alien culture does little to appease Nicole's state of panic. She is trapped here for the foreseeable future and every day for the next six months she is going to live with the terror that the next blood test could be positive.

The duty-free vodka sits idly on the dresser. Nicole reaches for it and takes it through to the kitchen where she finds a glass. Room temperature vodka isn't particularly palatable but she isn't drinking it for the taste. What Nicole needs right now is anaesthetic and with a couple of pills she makes her way up the narrow staircase and buries herself beneath the mound of quilt and blankets.

An owl, screaming like a fractious baby, pierces the silence and then falls silent. The thermostat on the electric radiator clicks in to position and the tick, tick, tick of the warming metal beats in time to the gentle thud of Nicole's heartbeat inside the filling of her pillow.

She reaches over and turns off the bedside lamp plunging the room in to a dense impenetrable darkness and the cottage folds itself inwards like an origami box around her.

Friendly Greetings

Saturday.

The bus only goes as far as Castleton and Tallulah has to walk the extra mile and a half to Robert's house. It isn't raining yet but the glowering sky is pressing down on the craggy hillside ahead, a swirling mass of dark grey cloud approaching rapidly on a down-draught of damp, chilly air. Most of the trees are stripped bare and the road is scattered with fallen leaves. There is no pavement so Tallulah has to walk along the side of the narrow road, her inadequate shoes soaking up moisture every time she has to step gingerly on to the unkempt grass to avoid being hit by a passing vehicle. There is a smell in the air that is at once fresh and clean and yet dank with mould and the decomposition of autumn.

The directions are basic but clear; walk one mile out of Castleton, turn left at the first lane and continue up the lane until it turns right in to a small driveway leading to the house. Auntie June and Uncle Ted gave Tallulah the keys that were recovered from Robert's car after the accident and they are burning a hole in the palm of Tallulah's hand as she keeps them clasped tightly inside her coat pocket. Touching the keys is the closest thing Tallulah has ever come to touching death and she feels unsettled and nervous as she trudges wearily up the road. Auntie June explained that they had removed the leather key fob from the ring because it was charred from the heat of the burning car.

It is a long time since Tallulah was last in the countryside and she feels slightly incongruous surrounded by so much nature. This is a very beautiful part of the Peak District and a popular tourist spot because of the Blue John mines and the underground caverns where entire communities of rope-makers used to dwell. Tallulah hasn't been here since she was a kid but she can still remember the claustrophobia she experienced as their tour guide led them between narrow fissures to reach a mysterious underground lake. At certain times of the year the caves flood and that fact followed her around the mines, dampening her enthusiasm for the stalactites and stalagmites that were pointed out to them as they passed through the underground caves and corridors.

A couple of hikers, togged out in waterproof gear and heavy boots, stride gainfully towards her and offer a friendly greeting as they pass. Things are different in the countryside; strangers say hello and acknowledge your presence whereas in the city you can pass unnoticed for days on end. Tallulah isn't sure if she prefers the anonymity to this feeling of being totally exposed, especially as she is unsuitably attired in her electric blue wool-blend coat and suede court shoes. It's like one of those humiliating dreams where you suddenly find yourself walking naked down the high street.

She comes to the lane where she has to turn off the main road and she finds herself dwarfed between flanks of tall, dense hedgerows and partially canopied by a tangle of overhanging branches. It is darker here and there is an eerie silence where only the occasional bird calls a warning from a faraway tree. There is a narrow strip of uneven tarmac but it seems barely wide enough to accommodate a small car. Tallulah derives a small amount of reassurance from the bright colours of a discarded crisp bag under the hedge; it is a connection with civilization and makes her feel less alone. She tries to imagine how many times her cousin drove or walked up this lane but she still can't gather together a coherent picture of him in her mind. She has invented a kind of photo-fit composite that has more to do with the teenage boy she once knew than the man he had become before he died.

A couple of hundred yards up the lane there is a break between the hedgerow and Tallulah pauses to look out across the field, resting her hands against the damp grey wood of a rickety gate. There is a stile to one side of the gate with a worn-down stone platform and on the other side of the gate she can just make out a winding trail through the meadow where feet have trampled down the grass and weeds. And there, over to the far side of the field, is a house partially surrounded by tall, crooked trees. Tallulah assumes that this must be Robert's house and she watches it for a few moments,

Simon Temprell

capturing a sense of what she might expect when she
finally reaches the front door.

Number Two

It is a pair of grey semi-detached houses and they stand
alone as though stranded in a sea of fields and
woodland. A pair of hooded front-porches bend
furtively together like old women whispering secrets,
their tiled gables sloping inward as though in a state of
semi-collapse. Part of the façade is tangled with some
kind of green creeper and smoke drifts from one of the
chimneys. It is an unremarkable looking building; quite
small and lacking in rustic charm, but it stands alone and
abandoned in the middle of nowhere and there is
something sad about it. The roof sags and the fences are
broken and it looks, from here, as though the houses
have some kind of lean-to hastily added to the back.

Tallulah continues up to where the lane turns off
and then she finds herself walking along the muddy ruts
of a makeshift driveway where shallow puddles reflect
the ominous colour of the sky and tyre-tracks remain
visible in the reddish clay. She finds it impossible to stop
the dirt from squishing up around her impractical shoes
and realizes with dismay that they are probably ruined.
A magpie flaps with wings like a pair of fluttering black
gloves and comes to rest on a nearby tree stump, staring
inquisitively at her with bright beady eyes. Tallulah
instinctively salutes the bird with one hand; a superstition
passed down to her from generations past.

One for sorrow.

She looks around for a second magpie but there
doesn't seem to be another bird anywhere in the vicinity.

No sound right now but a slight clattering of twigs like teething rings as a gust of wind scurries across the meadow.

The house is in full view from the driveway; a rectangular pebble-dashed box with a wrinkled, sun-bleached asphalt roof that reminds Tallulah of flaky pastry. The windows are dirty and the front doors, shielded beneath the shadow of their rickety porches, are painted a faded turquoise like the bottom of an abandoned swimming pool. There is a small pane of patterned glass in each door and as she gets closer to the house she can read the hand-painted signs nailed to the identical garden gates: Number One and Number Two.

She takes the keys from her pocket and approaches the door of Number Two. There are three keys but only one of them looks like a front door key; it is large and heavy with a storybook shape. It is the kind of key that opens secret gardens and buried treasure and it turns easily in the lock.

The first thing that greets her is the smell.

It is the smell of a living person and it is warm. Robert has only been gone for a few days but Tallulah had somehow imagined that the house would smell damp and neglected. It is a smell of meals once eaten, clothes once worn and apples left too long in a barn full of hay. She stands on the threshold for a moment or two, acclimatizing herself with the unfamiliar surroundings and experiencing a strange sensation that she isn't alone. She calls out in to the entrance hall but her voice is swallowed by the shadows and there is no reply.

Several jackets hang from hooks on the wall by the door and beneath them there is a pair of green wellingtons and some mud-caked Timberland boots with yellow laces. The stairs rise to the right of the doorway and she can see through to the back kitchen where light is struggling to push through the cloudy windows. The floorboards are bare and dull. There is no carpet. The walls are papered with blistering anaglypta and painted a dull pinkish tone like the colour of a dirty plaster.

Tallulah closes the door behind her and reaching for the light switch she removes her muddy shoes. A pair of wall lights with amber glass shades alters the colour of the walls to a dusky orange and from here Tallulah can see through the door to her left where a fireplace filled with grey ash and pieces of charred wood dominates the living room. It isn't a grand fireplace; it is tiled and functional with a narrow mantel that holds nothing more than a box of matches and two heavily melted pillar candles, stuck directly to the tile, dripping coloured wax down the front of the fireplace. It appears that many candles have been burnt in the same place because there are numerous coloured drips and a dusty puddle of wax on the hearth next to the companion set.

The heating must be on; Tallulah unbuttons her coat. The living room is small but cosy. Bookshelves have been built in to the alcoves on either side of the fireplace and they are groaning with the weight of too many books. Some of the shelves have warped and others are propped up with hefty leather-bound volumes. A stack of old newspapers sits on the floor by the side of a corduroy wing chair and in the chair there is a burgundy velvet cushion, squashed and moulded by the shape of somebody's – presumably Robert's – back. It strikes Tallulah as unutterably sad to see the imprint of a person who could never have imagined that upon leaving his house he would never return. The lump in her breast suddenly weighs more heavily than before.

A Friend of Rob's

She removes her coat and drapes it over the large scroll arm of an oversized sofa, one end of which is covered with a sheepskin rug. The flowered curtains are pulled back clumsily from the bay window and hanging from the ceiling there are several multi-coloured glass balls, like Christmas ornaments, glinting dimly in the weak light from outside. It has just started to rain and the first drops splatter against the glass. The sky has turned an obstinate shade of charcoal and the room is almost in total shadow now.

Tallulah reaches across the sofa to turn on a table lamp but no sooner has the lamp come on than the bulb burns out with a pop. She has to switch on the main light, flooding the room with a harsh brightness that immediately banishes all shadows to a space somewhere beyond the walls. The room looks dirty; the rug is covered with bits of fluff and crumbs, the coffee table is strewn with magazines, coffee cups and there is a funny little glass vase half full of dirty greenish-brown water. It looks as though Robert was burning something in the little bowl that protrudes from the side of the vase and when Tallulah sniffs at it she recognizes the smell she encountered at Auntie June and Uncle Ted's. It is marijuana.

She puts the glass vase down quickly and sniffs her fingers.

Next-door is a dining room with a small hatch that opens in to the kitchen beyond. This room is relatively empty; just a rather scratched old table and six uncomfortable-looking chairs and in the middle of the table there is a large wooden bowl filled with apples, most of which are badly bruised and rotting. It is the apples Tallulah could smell when she first came in to the house and the dining room is almost suffocating with the over-ripe sweetness of them. There is another (unused) fireplace in here and above it a picture of a nymph-like woman (naked but for a transparent swirl of chiffon) being pulled towards some rocks by a barely visible man with horns and the legs of an animal. It could be Pan but Tallulah isn't sure because she doesn't see any pipes in his hand.

The kitchen is fairly large and lighter than the rest of the house. The windows look out across the fields and she can see a ramshackle shed from here. Old painted cupboards, lino on the floor and a metal shelf unit crowded with plants and herbs occupies one entire wall by the back door. Tallulah opens the fridge. There is milk, cheese, eggs, orange squash and some bacon wrapped in greaseproof paper. In the small freezer compartment there is a plastic bag filled with something that looks like dried parsley. Instinctively Tallulah opens the bag and sniffs. Yes, it is more marijuana. She pushes it hastily back in to the ice-choked freezer and closes the door.

The rain is coming down harder now and the presence of it surrounds the house, rattling against the windows and bouncing off the roof. There is a portable radio by the kettle and Tallulah turns it on. It is tuned to a classical station and the sound of music somehow humanizes the kitchen. Tallulah leaves it switched on.

She is desperate for a cup of tea but first she wants to check out the upstairs. She unplugs the kettle and fills it at the tap, plugging it back in and switching it on before she goes back through to the hallway, checking inside the cupboard under the stairs to find nothing but cleaning equipment and a rail of old clothing.

The unexpected sound of the phone startles Tallulah and she gasps. There is a part of her that seems to be on red alert and her nerves are stretched quite tightly. It's not that she really believes in ghosts but there is something unmistakably spooky about this house and it's not just because Robert lived here. She feels as though she's being watched from all directions and she has clichéd visions of old family portraits suddenly moving their eyes when somebody passes on the stairs.

The phone is in the kitchen. It is an old-fashioned dial phone in two-tone brown and cream, mounted on the wall by the fridge. It's probably Auntie June calling to see if everything's all right.

"Hello?"

"Oh," (pause) "hello, love, is Rob there?"

"I'm sorry, he's not," says Tallulah, "this is his cousin."

"Ah, OK. Well, can I leave a message for him, love? I'm supposed to be seeing him tonight but something's come up and I can't make it."

Tallulah hesitates. She doesn't know who this person is but obviously he's a friend of Rob's so she should really break the news to him, even though she dislikes doing it over the phone.

"Erm, well, I'm afraid I've got some rather bad news. You're a friend of Rob's, are you?"

"Yes, love, my name's Jeff, I live in the village. What's up? Nothing bad I hope?"

"Well, the thing is, our Rob was killed in a car accident on Wednesday."

"No! *Rob?* I only spoke to him Wednesday morning. He's supposed to be having a bit of a party tonight. Bloody hell."

"I'm really sorry," placates Tallulah, "It's been a real shock to us all, especially his mum and dad. They've asked me to come to the house to start sorting out some of his things. It's all a bit sudden but they want to get the house on the market before they have to pay the next couple of mortgage payments."

"Crikey!" exclaims Jeff with disbelief, "have you been in touch with some of his friends to let them know? I think there were about eight people coming over this evening for Halloween."

"Actually, I'm going to need as many phone numbers as I can get so that I can let everyone know about the funeral and everything, but I haven't got an idea who his friends are. Do you have any of the names or numbers?" Tallulah notices the magnetic calendar stuck to the side of the fridge. October 31st is ringed with a scribble of red biro.

"I'm sorry, love, I can't help you with that. Rob's friends were mainly from the college and I've only met a couple of them before. You might want to try Ursula next-door, she knows Rob's friends better than I do. You ought to leave a note on the front door with your phone number so anyone who turns up can give you a ring. The only person I really know is Rob's old university mate, Julian; he was supposed to be coming tonight. I can give him a call if you like, tell him what's happened."

"That would be great, if you wouldn't mind. Erm, can I take your number so I can let you know about the funeral and everything?"

Tallulah hunts around the kitchen and finally alights on a blunt orange crayon. She writes Jeff's number on the side of a box of sugar cubes.

"I live above my shop in the village," explains Jeff, "just on the other side of the little stone bridge. It's not much of a place really; more of a junk shop but I'm usually there most days if you need me. I honestly don't know what to say, love. Rob was a good bloke. You've knocked me for six."

"I still can't believe it myself," admits Tallulah, fiddling with the wax crayon between her fingers and making a mental note that Jeff has a junk shop; maybe he can help her with some of Rob's stuff? "I'll give you a ring in the next couple of days, Jeff."

"All right, love. And if there's anything I can do to help…"

"Thanks a lot, that's very nice of you. Bye."

The rain is coming down in buckets now and the sound of it hitting the house from all directions is almost drowning out the symphony on the radio. The kettle has boiled so Tallulah finds herself a mug and a tea bag (no *normal* tea to be found so she chooses Earl Grey) and she sits down at the small kitchen table. There are some biscuits in a Tupperware box and Tallulah nibbles on the corner of a Rich Tea.

A drink's too wet without one…

A Certain Degree of Novelty

There is going to be a huge amount of stuff to do. Auntie June and Uncle Ted probably never realized what a job this is going to be. Tallulah could do with a fortnight off work to get this stuff sorted out. She looks around the kitchen in dismay; every available surface is crammed with pots and pans, books and jars. None of it looks worth saving but shouldn't she at least go through it all to make sure she's not missing something important? It would be wrong to just chuck everything away without checking first.

It is only four o'clock but it is almost dark. The rain seems to be slanting from the sky in solid sheets, bouncing upwards as it hits the ground. If she hadn't been on the early shift today she could have made it over here sooner but she didn't knock-off until one. She's got the morning off tomorrow so, if the worst comes to the worst, she could stay here tonight and hope the rain's stopped by tomorrow. Or she could call a taxi but that would cost a bomb and Tallulah never uses taxis unless it is absolutely necessary. The thing is; she doesn't really *want* to spend the night in this house. It feels strange. It's a dead man's house.

She stirs her tea, removes the teabag and puts in a couple of drops of milk. Taking the mug with her, Tallulah heads for the stairs. The stairs are also carpet-less and the pine boards have worn away in the centre. There must have been a carpet at some time because the outside edges of the steps are painted black and Tallulah can see the holes where carpet rods would have been installed. Every step creaks ominously. Tallulah clings on to the hand rail as she makes her way up to the landing.

The bathroom is straight ahead; small, unremarkable and smelling slightly of damp. Then there is a small bedroom that Robert obviously used as his office. There is a pine desk pushed up against the window so that he could look out over hills to the ruins of Peveril Castle perched high above Castleton and now virtually obscured by low cloud and pouring rain. The computer is turned on and there is a coloured block turning around and around in the centre of the blue screen. It's a fairly old computer; even Tallulah with her scant knowledge of technology can see that much. In here too there are a lot of books; most of them stacked in little piles around the room.

Orbitally Rearranged Monoatomic Elements.
The Chemistry of Precious Metals.
Hyperdimensional Physics & Other Spatial Dimensions

Tallulah takes a sip of her tea but it tastes horrible. She drinks it because she's thirsty but she can't say that she enjoys it.

Robert's bedroom is large and square and the curtains are drawn so it's dark. Tallulah fumbles for the light switch but when the light comes on it is so dim that it barely makes much of a difference. The walls seem to be painted a very dark colour, which isn't helping matters, and Tallulah has to shuffle along the wall until she finds a bedside lamp. The bulb in the lamp is red so it's not much help but Tallulah can just about make out the layout of the room.

The bed is unmade and the duvet has been pushed on to the floor. There are a lot of candles on the dressing table; carelessly placed so that wax has dripped everywhere. A couple of small drawers are open, revealing bundles of socks and underwear. Tallulah pulls back the curtains but there is no light left to come in. For a split second she catches a glimpse of her reflection in the glass and her face is an unearthly crimson against the blackness outside.

This room has a smell that Tallulah can only attribute to the fact that a man slept here. Tallulah isn't sure what a man's room is supposed to smell like (it's not as though she's been in many men's rooms in her life) but she would know that this was a man's bedroom even if she had no idea whose house she was in. It's not that it smells unclean or nasty, it's just that the carpet, the curtains and the sheets are probably imbued with months of inhaling Robert and there are joss sticks on the bedside table so maybe they have something to do with the woodsy fragrance she can smell?

A large patchwork quilt hangs on the wall behind the bed and opposite there is another small fireplace containing remnants of firewood and more puddles of dried wax. There is a small portable TV and video player and beside it there are two coffee mugs and a bottle of cough medicine standing in its own sticky ring. It is the kind of room that is never meant to be seen by the light of day.

It's not very often that Tallulah is left alone in someone else's bedroom and she has to resist the urge to start rifling through the bedside drawers. Of course, inevitably, she will have to go through everything at some point but she still feels like an intruder and she can't quite bring herself to violate Robert's privacy just yet. This bedroom has a particularly strong atmosphere and she almost gets the impression that it was only recently vacated; as though Robert's sheets might still be warm to the touch, that the towel draped over the radiator might still be damp.

There are no more rooms upstairs, just an airing cupboard on the landing and some more built-in bookshelves crammed with paperback novels, jam jars filled with loose change and a collection of old Matchbox cars, some of them still in their original boxes. Tallulah stands at the top of the stairs for a moment, listening to the rain and wondering how she is going to tackle this momentous task. She decides, here and now, that she will have to forfeit her ten days of holiday and devote herself to this project. It's not as though she has any other plans and if she doesn't take the days before the end of the year she will lose them.

She goes down to the kitchen, rinses out her tea mug and calls work. Junie answers the phone and because she is already aware of the circumstances she agrees to talk with Mr. B this evening. It's possible they could re-arrange the schedule to accommodate Tallulah's absence as long as she could wait until Wednesday to take the time off. Tallulah says that's fine and puts down the phone.

An unexpected holiday.

Actually the thought is quite exciting! OK, so it's not a fortnight in Greece but a change is as good as a rest and if she stays here at Robert's house she will be able to organize everything efficiently and with a certain degree of novelty. Maybe she'll even have time to go to a couple of the underground caverns before they close for the winter? Castleton is, after all, a tourist spot.

Feeling buoyed by her sudden decision Tallulah goes through to the living room, turning off the harsh central light, and she falls back gratefully against the sheepskin rug draped over the far end of the sofa. The warm light from the hallway spills in to the room and the sound of the radio in the kitchen is distant but comforting. The rain hits the windows like handfuls of pebbles and Tallulah closes her eyes for a few moments. She can pretend that this is her house, that she's the kind of adventurous spirit who might live out here in the middle of the countryside. She imagines a couple of cats and maybe even a puppy. It's almost as though she can see herself pegging out her washing in the back garden and picking blackberries for Bramble Jam.

The rain is comforting, hypnotic. Tallulah draws her feet up in to the capacious cushions of the sofa and takes a deep breath. Suddenly the house doesn't feel so intimidating and if it doesn't stop raining by six she will throw caution to the wind and call for a taxi to take her all the way back to Chesterfield: Sod the extravagance!

Fear of Living

Nicole is bored to tears and she's only been here for three days. It's been raining all afternoon and it doesn't look as though it is going to stop any time soon. She's lit a fire and started on her second book but she feels agitated and restless, trapped in this silent little cottage with nothing but her own imagination to keep her company. There's nothing on TV worth watching and the constant sound of rain against the windows has lulled her in to a kind of trance. She may as well be in prison.

Doubt, like dry-rot, has started to set in and the foundations of Nicole's plan are beginning to crumble. She is no longer sure why she ran away from Miami like she did when it might have been more sensible to confront Gideon face-to-face instead of fleeing the country as though it is she who is in the wrong. She should have shamed him publicly; she had the sympathy of her audience behind her and nobody could possibly have blamed Nicole for hating her husband and taking him for every cent he's got. But the panic of discovering Courtney's HIV status had twisted Nicole's rationale and her immediate instinct was to get as far away from Gideon as possible, as quickly as possible. The money was a secondary consideration and was taken more out of spite than out of any need for survival.

But Gideon still has no idea why Nicole absconded from their marriage and, as far as he's concerned, she just up and left with seven hundred and fifty thousand dollars and she didn't even leave him a note of explanation. Wouldn't it have made more sense if she had at least let him know why she was taking such extreme action against him? Perhaps if he knew why she had gone he might not bother to pursue her? He might chalk it up to his own irresponsibility and leave her alone. But Nicole knows Gideon better than that; she knows how the drugs have changed him, making him greedy and self-indulgent, aggressive and lacking in compassion. Over the past few years Gideon has traded in his old personality for something vaguely resembling that of a monster and Nicole is scared of what he is capable of. That is why she ran away like she did.

For the first time in months she thinks about James and wishes that he was here with her now. If she had James by her side she could achieve anything and she could feel safe. When he was killed in the boating accident she was left with a gaping wound inside her heart and it has never healed. It was James's death that seeded the *real* demise of Nicole and Gideon's marriage; it was the cement that helped build the wall between them and neither Nicole nor Gideon had the strength or the desire to knock that wall down once it was built. The past couple of years have been lived in a kind of emotional vacuum and if Nicole is really honest with herself she can see that most of her time with Gideon – once they moved to Miami – was nothing more than a kind of glamorous fog that obscured the emptiness around them. What a waste of fifteen years. What a waste of her prime.

The more she thinks about these things the angrier she becomes. Gideon's reckless hedonism has wrecked not only his own life but also the life of his wife and it appears that he really doesn't care. If he was busy screwing around with other women then why didn't he just stop having sex with Nicole completely? It's not as though they had much of a sex-life anyway so why did he have to continue going through the motions when it was obvious that Nicole was no longer interested? Nicole now wonders if Gideon had some kind of sick intention to drag her down with him; like a man floundering in a quicksand of his own creation he was terrified of suffocating alone and so he grabbed the closest thing to him. Perhaps fear is easier to swallow when shared with someone else? Or maybe he just didn't give a fuck about anyone but himself? That seems a more likely answer.

Suddenly Nicole can't breathe properly. She presses the palm of her hand against her chest and she can feel her heart racing. She has to drag open the cottage door and stand in the driving rain, gasping from the shock of the chill and gulping down huge mouthfuls of air as though surfacing from several fathoms below sea level. Her face, hair and clothes are drenched within minutes and there is a kind of perverse pleasure in this re-acquaintance with her senses. She takes a few steps forward, out on to the pathway where puddles swallow her bare feet, icy cold but somehow refreshing. The wind lashes her with stinging arrows of rain and she closes her eyes, raising her face to the sky as though receiving some kind of holy benefaction. How can she be so terrified of dying when she has spent most of her life in mortal fear of living?

In a moment of blinding clarity she turns around and goes back indoors where the blazing fire and the unhealthy heat of the living room greet her with a greedy kind of lust. It is as though the cottage is waiting to re-claim her but Nicole is saturated with the cleansing rain and she refuses to succumb to the hermetically-sealed misery that she has created. Leaving the door wide open so that the rain sweeps in across the wooden floor behind her she drips across the rug and reaches for her phone. His number is etched across her brain like scar-tissue and she presses the numbers without having to think about what she is doing. She picked up this phone at the airport in Vienna; even if he traces the call there is no way he could know where she is right now. She has a pre-paid rental agreement and she can throw this phone away and get another.

She almost expects to get his voice mail but it is Gideon at the other end of the line; he sounds bored or tired and it is obvious that Nicole is the last person he expects to hear.

"Gideon?"

There is a split second of silence before he asks her, "where are you?" His question is not one of idle curiosity, it is a command and roughly translated it means 'I'm coming to get you'. Nicole's immediate reaction is to disconnect the call; the mere sound of his voice is like a slap across her cheek and it wakes her to the reality of the situation. She has to pull on her reserve of anger in order to bolster her courage and her response is equally pugnacious.

"You don't need to know where I am, Gideon, all you need to know is how much I loathe you."

And he laughs. He laughs without humour; he laughs like a man who is about to pull the safety-catch on a guillotine and his words are as sharp as the blade he intends to release. "Sweetheart, I don't care what you think about me. You're already dead to me, Ronnie."

"That's probably true," admits Nicole, swallowing hard and wiping the rain from her brow with the back of her free hand, "and if I die it'll be your filthy, infected cock that's killed me. You're a fucking murderer, Gideon. I hope you can live with that."

"What the fuck are you talking about? Are you high or something?"

"Ask that slut, Courtney. Ask her when she was going to get around to telling you that she's HIV positive."

He obviously finds that statement as amusing as her first because he continues to snigger and his words are curled with the heat of his malice. "Oh, that. Don't believe everything you hear, Ronnie, this town is crammed full of vicious lies and rumours and there's nothing wrong with Courtney. Quite honestly if there was any chance of me being positive I'd have pinned you down every night so that my filthy cock, as you so delicately put it, could shoot a few satisfying bullets. You have no idea just how much satisfaction I would derive filling you up with my poison night after night. You're a fucking dead-weight, Ronnie, you've been hanging round my neck like a millstone for years and I couldn't wait to get rid of you. You fucked-around with that British jerk behind my back and made a fool of me and even after I'd taken care of him you still came skulking back to me with your fucking tail between your legs. How pathetic is that?"

"Taken care of him? What do you mean?" Nicole doesn't have to ask what Gideon means but she is stunned by his statement and suddenly the heat from the fireplace is insufficient to stop her from shivering.

"Oh Ronnie, you *know* what happened to that motherfucker Tyrone Daly? You *know* I have my resources, sweetheart. How difficult do you think it was for me to get that fucker's speedboat tampered with? Christ! I nearly *came* when I heard how little of his body was left for recovery after the explosion. And I jerked-off just listening to you sobbing over his goddamned photograph every night in the other room. Some things are priceless!"

Nicole attempts to respond but her words are momentarily swallowed in a huge intake of breath that brings hot blinding tears to her eyes. She allows the phone to fall away from her ear and she presses it against her shoulder, still able to hear the echo of Gideon's laughter like an insect trapped inside a bottle. When she brings the phone back to her ear she is hoarse with emotion.

"You are despicable, Gideon. You deserve everything that's coming to you and if you think you're ever going to get your money back you need to get your head examined. That money was *ours* and it strikes me as a pittance for the fifteen years of hell I had to live through with you. There isn't a court, judge or jury who would condemn me for taking what is rightfully mine. I hope you end up with nothing, Gideon. I hope you rot in hell."

"What a way you have with words, Ronnie. You should have been a novelist."

"Fuck you!" And Nicole hurls the mobile phone in to the heart of the fireplace where it sends a shower of orange sparks up the roaring chimney.

Ursula

Somebody is knocking at the front door and Tallulah sits up with a start. She immediately feels guilty as though she is an intruder and for a moment she sits tight, wondering if the person at the door might go away. But the knocking continues, persistent this time, and somebody tries the door knob. They are probably getting soaked in this torrential rain.

Without considering the consequences Tallulah opens the door without first asking who is there. It is dark outside but beneath the dim illumination of the front porch lantern stands a woman of indeterminate age in a knee-length afghan coat with flowers embroidered on the large patch pockets. Beneath the coat she is wearing a black polo-neck and her pale, moon-like face appears to be suspended in mid-air between two slabs of mousy-brown hair that hang like curtains from a rigid centre-parting. Tallulah's immediate reaction is one of apprehension. Is this a gypsy come to flog her some ribbons or clothes pegs?

"Hello, duck," smiles the pasty woman with a lop-sided grin that reveals the sad fact that childhood braces might have improved her appearance. "I'm sorry to disturb you but Jeff from the junk shop called me earlier and said you were here. I'm Ursula, the next-door-neighbour."

"Oh, hello," smiles back Tallulah, shaking Ursula's rather bony hand and noticing the array of heavy silver rings she wears on almost every finger. "I'm Rob's cousin, Tallulah."

"Listen, duck, I am so sorry about poor Rob. I only found out yesterday when I read the *Derbyshire Times*. I was right upset, I can tell you. Rob was a really lovely bloke and he'd become a good friend of mine since he moved in here. It's a bloody shame."

Tallulah nods, growing accustomed to these awkward condolences and finding it easier not to struggle for words of mindless regret at this stage. She's never been one for coping with emotion of any kind and she prefers to brush uncomfortable declarations of pity or concern under the rug, along with her own inability to respond to such platitudes. "You're getting soaked," she observes, "would you like to come in for a minute?"

Ursula glances over her shoulder at a car parked in her driveway. The interior light is on and Tallulah can make out a figure sitting in the passenger seat. "I can't stop, duck, I'm just on my way out. That's my nephew, Tye. He's right cut-up about your Rob an' all. I think he looked at Rob as a bit of a father-figure seeing as how his own dad's scarpered. Teenage boys can be funny, you know, they don't say much but you can tell when something's got under their skin."

"I'm going to be stopping here for a couple of weeks while I sort out our Rob's stuff," explains Tallulah. "You'll have to come round when you've got a bit more time and we'll have a cup of tea and a chat."

"All right, duck. My door's right here if you want me," and Ursula indicates the door alongside the one Tallulah is currently holding open. "With the fence down you don't have to trawl all the way down the path. Rob talked about fixing it but it was more convenient to leave it as it is so we never bothered with it. Knock any time; I go to bed late so don't be worried about disturbing me."

"Thanks," smiles Tallulah and she watches Ursula scuttle down the pathway through the pouring rain, her head pulled down inside the collar of her bulky coat like a turtle retreating from an inquisitive finger.

Closing the door Tallulah checks her watch and is surprised to see that it is almost half-past seven. There's no way she's going to attempt to get a bus back to Chesterfield now so she will just have to splash-out on a taxi. She is hungry and wonders if there's anything worth eating in Rob's kitchen. She remembers the bacon and eggs in the fridge and decides to prepare some dinner before she goes home. Then, just as she's looking around for a frying pan, she remembers the party that Rob had planned for tonight and the last thing she wants is to be faced by a load of his friends; all of them coming over expecting food and drink and festivities. It's probably better to write a note for the front door and call a taxi as soon as possible so she can make a quick get-away. She can get some fish and chips from the corner when she gets home.

A Filthy Night

Now that Nicole has calmed down a little she is angry with herself for calling Gideon. All she has succeeded in doing is giving him more ammunition against her and she worries that he was somehow able to trace her call, even though they barely spoke for more than a couple of minutes. She doesn't know how easy it is to trace a mobile phone, especially one rented in Vienna, but any small possibility of him finding her is enough to jeopardize her plan to escape from him forever.

She has stripped off her wet things and taken a hot bath. Both bottles of elderflower wine are long-gone so she's finishing off the vodka and it is helping to blur the edges of her distress. The fire has died down to nothing more than crumbling embers and she doesn't want to go outside to fetch some more logs. She has switched on the TV again for company and they're showing a horror film; something with Jamie Lee Curtis running from house-to-house screaming her head off. It's only a quarter past eight and Nicole needs more than a tumbler of vodka to get through the evening. She remembers seeing an off-license connected to one of the village pubs and decides to drive over to buy more provisions.

It's a filthy night and the lane is muddy. Nicole's new walking shoes are immediately caked with dirt and her inadequate jacket does little to protect her from the deluge. She sprints down the path to the car but fumbles with the key, trying to get it in to the lock. The sound of the rain is deafening; it pelts from the impenetrable sky and drips heavily from the trees and bushes. If there is a moon it isn't visible on a night like this. The inside of the car smells of vinyl and cheap polish. The dashboard lights-up fluorescent green. Nicole almost changes her mind and sits for a moment wondering what to do but the stuffy interior of the cottage holds little allure and she feels grateful for the clean, rain-swept clarity of being outside. She releases the hand-brake and turns the car slowly in to the lane.

The car park at the pub is full so she has to drive around the corner until she finds an empty spot beside a row of houses by the church. Somebody has lit a jack o lantern and placed it in an upstairs window and its devilish grin flickers uncertainly from behind the darkened glass. Nicole remembers that tonight is Halloween. In America the neighbourhood kids would be trailing from house to house in their costumes, knocking on doors and demanding 'trick or treat' but here in Castleton the streets are deserted and Nicole suspects that most kids are tucked up safely in their living rooms watching the telly or messing around with their computer games. The foul weather would dissuade even the most adventurous child to stay indoors by the fire.

The door to the off-license is locked so she has to go round to the main entrance of the pub. The windows are brightly lit and she can hear the sound of voices and music from within. She doesn't feel up to facing a pub full of strangers and she considers turning back but then the door flies open and two men in waxed jackets and tweed caps come hurrying out and one of them holds the door for her. "Here you go, love." Nicole thanks him and goes through in to the smoky atmosphere of the main bar. She almost expects the crowd to fall silent and for every face to turn towards the door but nobody appears to notice her arrival and the noise continues unabated. She is able to slip through the crowd unnoticed, wondering if she can buy some wine or a bottle of vodka from one of the bar tenders.

Somebody has strung up orange paper decorations in the shape of pumpkins and there are fake cobwebs drifting from the light fixtures. One of the barmaids is wearing devil's horns and another a witch's hat. The area around the bar is crammed with people and Nicole pushes herself as close as possible and then stands waiting her turn. People shout and jostle for attention and drinks slop messily across the beer mats as the staff rush from one customer to another. Women in Saturday-night clothes and too much make-up sit on bar stools, laughing over their drinks and bags of crisps. Men in less thoughtful attire stand around in groups with their pints of beer and their cigarettes. One or two of them give Nicole a casual glance as she waits and finally somebody moves out of the way so she can lean up against the bar to attract the attention of a man who appears to be the landlord.

"Yes, love?"

"Is it possible for me to buy a bottle of wine of vodka to go?"

"Sorry, love?"

Nicole repeats her question above the raucous voices of the crowd and hopes that nobody is listening to her and putting her down as a sad old alcoholic.

"Of course, love. What is it you want?"

"Vodka will be fine. I don't care what brand. Whatever you've got."

"Will Smirnoff do you?"

"Fine, thanks."

The landlord disappears through a doorway and returns with a bottle of vodka. "It's bloody Bedlam in here tonight," he grins, taking Nicole's money and ringing it up. "We've got a live band in the other room starting at nine if you're interested. Here, have this one on me," and he fills a glass with a shot of vodka from one of the optics and places it on the bar. "You want a mixer with that?"

"Just some ice, please."

Nicole is amused to see that she gets two cubes of ice and a quarter slice of lemon with her minute shot of vodka. It must cost a fortune to get drunk in England!

She edges around the bar and there are posters advertising a band called Twankydillo. She can see through to the second room where there is a small stage set up with spotlights and microphones. There are tables and chairs set up and all of them appear to be full. The room is large and heavily beamed with thick chunks of ancient timber. The interior of a capacious inglenook fireplace is illuminated with red light bulbs and gas coals burn brightly in the hearth. Nicole feels strangely alone in the middle of this rabble so she swallows her vodka in a single gulp and looks for a place to put down her glass. As she does so the lights start to dim and the landlord appears on the stage to announce to band.

Folk

Three women walk on to the stage, all of them dressed as though they've just arrived from the Glastonbury festival. One of them carries a guitar and another has a violin. A man with a thick red beard takes his place at the drums and gives a thumbs-up sign to somebody in the audience. There is a riotous round of applause and the band offer self-conscious bows as they take their positions. The youngest of the three women takes centre stage and clasps her hand around the microphone.

"Ey up you lot!" she shouts with a cheeky grin, obviously making fun of the local dialect. "From ghoulies and ghosties and long-legged beasties and things that go bump in the night may the Goddess deliver us!"

Somebody whistles loudly and there is more applause as the musicians tune up their instruments. The lights go down completely and the stage is bathed in coloured light. The spiky-haired girl with the cheeky grin thanks the landlord of the pub and the audience for braving the weather and then she announces their first song of the evening. It is a folk song that Nicole recognizes and she is surprised by the sweet voice that floats from the young girl's mouth when she begins to sing. Three-part harmonies and some lilting melodies keep Nicole rooted to the spot, amazed that the band is so professional for such a rural venue. By the time they stop for a break and 'a couple of pints' Nicole is still clutching her bottle of vodka over by the fag machine and she decides to stay for the second half.

The band abandons their instruments and climb down from the stage to approach the bar. The lead singer looks at the bottle of vodka in Nicole's hand as she passes and makes a ribald comment about 'a woman who knows how to drink' while the guitarist with the lanky hair goes over to a table in the corner to join a couple of women and a young boy who smiles up at her as she places the palm of her hand against the back of his neck.

Nicole decides to get another drink but there has been something of a surge and it is impossible to get anywhere close to the bar. The lead singer of the band catches her eye again and indicates her own proximity to the bar maid with an inclination of her head and eyebrows raised in a question. Nicole pushes through the throng and the young singer asks her what she's drinking.

"Vodka on the rocks. Better make it a double," shouts Nicole, holding up her bottle with a smile. She produces a crumpled fiver from her pocket and passes it through to the girl.

"Here you go, love," she says as she hands the glass to Nicole. "I'm Petra and you must be…American?"

"American? No, I'm English, actually." Nicole looks down at her clothing to see if she's wearing something ridiculously inappropriate for Halloween in an English pub but her mud-splattered running shoes, her lemon-coloured slacks and Burberry bomber-jacket seem perfectly in order. "What makes you think I'm American?"

"Oh, you know…" mocks Petra with a calculating eye, "the tan, the hair, the teeth. Oh, don't get me wrong; you look *brilliant,* it's just that, well, look around at the women in here and, well, just look round…"

Nicole scans the room, peering between the heads of those closest to her, and she looks at some of the women in the pub. Admittedly she can't see anyone particularly pretty or sophisticated but could it be that during the past fifteen years she's somehow become *Americanized?*

"Is it the Burberry?" she asks, looking down at the sleeve of her checked jacket.

"Partly," smiles Petra, wiping the beer foam from her upper lip with the back of her hand. "I'm assuming it's *real* and not a knock-off; I wouldn't put you down as a Chav."

"A Chav?"

"Oh my God, where have you been hiding? Don't you read the tabloids?" Petra laughs at Nicole's quizzical expression. "It's a derogatory term for the kind of under-educated louts who are obsessed with knock-off designer clothing and cheap gold jewellery. If you hang around the Arndale Centre on a Saturday afternoon you'll soon become acquainted."

"Black kids?" asks Nicole, immediately thinking about the hip-hop generation in Miami.

"Funnily enough they're mainly white kids but they get their inspiration from the American 'Bling Bling' generation. The only problem is that these acne-ridden British kids just don't sit well in oversized sportswear with their baseball caps turned the wrong way round. I'm supposed to appreciate all of that – being so young – but I hate rap music and prefer to think for myself rather than following the trends like everybody else of my generation."

"My name's Nicole Harvey. It's nice to meet you Petra." The two women shake hands between a tangle of bodies and Petra indicates the table where her fellow musicians are now gathered. "Come on over and join us," she offers.

"Nicole, these are my partners in crime; Jack, Lynne and Ursula. Oh, and this is Ursula's adorable nephew, Tye. This is Nicole who *isn't* American, she just looks it."

Nicole nods and smiles at the gathered company, sheepishly hiding behind another swig of her vodka. "You sounded great!" she enthuses, "really professional."

"We *are* professional," gasps Petra with a mocking expression of horror.

"Oh, I didn't mean that to sound like it did," apologizes Nicole with embarrassment, "I just meant that you sound so good."

"You should buy a CD," suggests Tye opening his messenger bag and producing a handful of them. "They're nine pounds ninety-nine each."

"Tye!" admonishes his aunt with a fond smile of disapproval.

"I'd love to buy one!" And Nicole fishes through the crumpled notes in her pocket to produce a ten. She hands the money to the young boy and he, in turn, passes her one of the CD's.

Twankydillo: Warm Toast for Tea

"Is this your first CD?" asks Nicole, studying the back of the jewel case.

"It's our *latest* CD," replies Ursula. "If you like it there's four more for you to choose from."

"Great!" And Nicole salutes them with her glass, shrugging her shoulders in the attitude of someone who suddenly feels completely lost for words.

"We've got to go back on, Nicole; why don't you hang around and have another drink with us afterwards?" Petra drains her pint and slams the empty glass on the table. "You can sit here and keep Tye company."

And so Nicole remains through the second half of the gig and, whether it's the vodka or the charming music, she actually finds herself enjoying it.

A Means to an End

When the cab driver drops Tallulah off at the end of her road she is somewhat relieved to be back on familiar territory. She hurries in to the Tasty Plaice to get a savaloy and chips (she couldn't be bothered to wait for the next batch of cod to finish frying) and then rushes through the rain towards her little house.

Most of the street lights on her street have been smashed so there isn't as much light as there should be. Somebody has dumped a bag of chips unceremoniously by the side of the pavement and further along it looks as though somebody else (or maybe the same person?) might have been sick but the rain has washed most of it away. The curtains are open at Sue and Nick's place and their telly makes flickering blue shadows across their ceiling and walls.

When Tallulah reaches her own front door she is already soaked to the skin so there seems little point in shielding herself from the rain as she searches for her keys. She can hear one of the kids from next-door screaming and through the chink in their curtains she can see a purple balloon being swatted back and forth across the room.

Her hallway smells of paint and it feels chilly. She forgets that the bulb at the bottom of the stairs has gone so she flicks the light switch and nothing happens. She has to fumble her way to the living room to turn on the light in there. Oh God, it all looks so shabby. How come she never noticed it before now? Has Tallulah been blind to the miserable little room with its duck-egg blue walls and papered chimney-breast? Was she previously impervious to the threadbare, uncomfortable furniture clustered around the gas fire like a huddle of impoverished beggars trying to keep warm?

The house has been this way for years. It is a dilapidated shrine to her parents, complete with the wonky standard lamp and the fairground ornaments lined up along the curtain pelmet. She turns off the light, dumps her dinner in the half-painted kitchen and heads straight upstairs to her bedroom where at least she knows things will be a little less depressing. It is the only room in the house that has been re-decorated since her parents died and the furniture, though second-hand from the classifieds, is fairly modern looking.

But tonight Tallulah's bedroom looks dejected when she turns on the light and she stands for a moment in the doorway surveying the sad, impersonal environment she has created. Maybe it is something to do with having been over at Robert's eccentric little house but Tallulah suddenly feels disillusioned with everything around her. The apricot walls with the basket-weave border look bilious in this light and the duvet cover that was once the height of fashion is now a washed-out, faded terracotta colour that doesn't match the co-ordinating skirt any longer. Although the colours are warm the effect is distinctly depressing and the cheap self-assembly furniture is circa 1985. Blond veneered chipboard with doors that no longer close properly and the kind of plastic handles you might find on children's furniture.

Tallulah sits on the edge of her three-quarter size bed and pushes off her ruined shoes. She feels tired and wet and disgruntled. What had earlier seemed like a bit of an adventure is now turning back in to a chore and the thought of spending the next fortnight sorting through all of Robert's stuff is daunting. This is a huge sacrifice Tallulah is making for her aunt and uncle and she decides that she should take them up on their offer to let her take whatever she wants from Robert's house. His fridge, his cooker, his computer etc could all make a difference to her life and maybe she will even spend a bit of her savings on doing something with the kitchen cabinets?

When you have lived all your life achieving very little there comes a point when you start to wonder what it's all about. Every morning you get up at the same time, you brush your teeth, wash your face and eat the same breakfast cereal you've been eating since you were a child. Work is uninspiring and nothing more than a means to an end and every evening you get home at exactly the same time and watch the same television programmes before the news and then bed again at eleven. There are no surprises, no deviations from the norm and the reason Tallulah has never bothered to keep a diary is because she would write the same thing every day.

At forty-five years old, Tallulah the spinster in her soggy electric blue coat, sits on the corner of her faded bedspread and realizes that time is running out.

Things have got to change.

Robert

I had lost touch with our Tally, quite honestly. When I divorced Julie and moved to Castleton I cut myself off from everybody. I wanted solitude and that's what I got. I mainly think of Tally as she was when we were kids; kind of shy and quiet. She used to come over to our house sometimes and we'd play marbles or conkers and sometimes we'd ride our bikes over to Gran's house.

I was there, in my house, watching her when she first went to look around. I didn't want to scare her so I kept as quiet as possible but it was weird seeing her there. The light bulb in the living room lamp blew; something that seems to happen quite often when I'm around. Don't ask me why.

One of the great things about being dead is you can go wherever you want and it's as easy as changing channels on the telly. Earlier that afternoon I'd been over at Julie's house – the one she shares with that new bloke of hers – knocking their wedding picture off the wall and putting the willies up their stupid little poodle. Don't ever let it be said that ghosts don't have a sense of humour!

I spend quite a lot of time at Mum and Dad's house; mainly at night so I can watch over Mum while Dad's asleep. I know she's terrified about the cancer and I wish I could reassure her that there's nothing to be scared of, but that would be breaking the rules. You have to learn these things for yourself; that's what life's all about. I'll be here for her when she comes, but until then all I can do is hope she doesn't have to suffer too much.

Discarded Lingerie

It was difficult to concentrate on bras and pants when she was thinking about other things but Tallulah had to make the effort today because Mr. B has reluctantly allowed her to take the next two weeks off to sort out Robert's things. He let it be known what an inconvenience it is for her to take the holiday at such short notice and yesterday he made her work through her lunch hour and she didn't have the guts to complain about it. She was reduced to gobbling a Pot Noodle round the back between customers and she burnt the roof of her mouth on the scalding beef-flavoured slime.

Tallulah sits in the back of a mini-cab watching the lights of the city recede as they head out in to the Peak District. She brought her suitcase with her to the boutique so that she could go directly to Rob's house this evening after work. Uncle Ted coughed-up for the cab fare because he didn't want Tallulah struggling up that dark lane with her bags. The cab driver is Arabic but Tallulah has no idea which country he comes from;

they all look the same to her. He is silent in the front, listening to his CD, turned down very low so all Tallulah can hear is some kind of belly-dancing music. She imagines sand dunes and mosques and women with strings of jangling gold coins strewn around their hips.

Mrs. Delray was one of the customers this afternoon, parading around brazenly with her bra off and nothing but a red silk g-string covering her privates. She's a regular customer and according to Junie she's married to a much younger man.

"I saw him once when he came in to the shop with her and he's barely out of nappies."

But Mrs. Delray was alone today, being fitted for a new corset. A lot of the trendy women are wearing Mr. B's corsets these days; ever since they did an article in one of the Sunday supplements about the dying art of corsetry. Madonna was photographed wearing something specially designed by Mr. B and since then they've been run off their feet with special orders from all over the country. It seems that women are no longer hiding their corsets underneath slinky dresses, but exposing the undergarments for all to see. It's become something of a fashion statement; something that Posh might be seen out in. Ridiculous! Tallulah can only imagine what the folks round her way would say if they saw her parading down the street in a whale boned corset and a pair of skinny jeans!

"What do you think of this colour?" Mrs. Delray asked Junie this afternoon, holding up a pair of lavender silk cammy knickers with a triumphant flourish.

"It suits you, Mrs. Delray," simpered Junie, "it goes well with your colouring," and the boutique manager appraised her customer in the full-length mirror of the changing room. "There's a beautiful peignoir that goes with it if you'd like to take a look. It would make a charming ensemble; very romantic!"

That's the kind of thing Junie comes out with when she's trying to get a sale. It's something that Tallulah hasn't mastered herself and she prefers to keep her mouth buttoned rather than utter a load of nonsense. She has heard Junie come out with some incredible rubbish when faced with a size eighteen squashed and trussed in to an unsuitable garment like a Christmas turkey. Junie is the kind of woman who brings deli-sandwiches for her lunch and laments the fact that there isn't a Costa in the neighbourhood.

"There's nothing like a nice caramel cappuccino in the afternoon," she reflects wistfully whenever Tallulah passes her a mug of Nescafe. But Tallulah isn't fooled. She knows that Junie's husband ran off with a hair stylist and left her with bills up to her eyeballs.

Tallulah thinks about Mrs. Delray: Enviable Mrs. Delray with her pretty eyes and long blonde hair. She has the kind of body that only comes from years of gruelling exercise at the gym. For a woman in her forties she could easily pass for thirty-five. She is certainly not ashamed of showing-off her tight little bum, trim waist and nicely proportioned breasts and even when Mr. B is around she struts in front of him as though it's perfectly normal to be naked in front of strangers. Of course Mr. B is a nancy-boy so he couldn't care less about seeing a pair of tits or a tuft of minge but, even so, it's not very ladylike is it? The funny thing is; it's the wealthy ones who seem less concerned about nudity. Perhaps it's got something to do with the fact that they sunbathe topless in the south of France, get pummelled by personal masseurs on a regular basis and swan around in the sauna without a towel after their yoga classes. People like Tallulah prefer to remain under wraps at all times, even when visiting the doctor for a check-up. Not that Tallulah goes to see her doctor very often. She has, however, made an appointment at the health clinic to get the lump in her breast examined.

It is the first step towards a new start for Tallulah. She is going to be more assertive, more adventurous and less intimidated by her insecurities. She will attack Rob's house and belongings with gusto, taking anything that she thinks will work to replace all the ancient crap that her mum and dad left behind. No more turning on the gas jets with a pair of pliers. No more faffing about with the twin-tub when she's got a stackable washer and dryer from Rob's kitchen. And who knows what kind of future awaits when she's connected to the internet and the world wide web!

What must it be like to live the kind of life that Mrs. Delray lives? Tallulah can only imagine the posh dinner parties with candles and champagne that Mrs. Delray must give for her rich friends. Her house probably has a swimming pool and one of those huge flat-screen TV's that hang on the wall. And people like Mrs. Delray don't wonder if there's enough hot water for a bath or carry their shopping home with plastic bags cutting off the circulation in their fingers. It's all continental chocolates and pedicures for women like Mrs. Delray.

Outside the window of the cab all has become blanketed in darkness and only the faraway glitter of orange street lamps through the trees remind her that the city isn't far behind. Before it grew dark the sky was a flat wintry grey and the sun never appeared through its dense streaky clouds.

Mr. B came down from his workshop this afternoon holding Mrs. Delray's exquisite black satin corset in his hands. He presented it to her as though it was a sacrificial offering with both hands outstretched. "Here eet is," he announced in his heavy French accent. "You will try on the prototype so that we can get zee correct measurements for alteration."

"Gorgeous!" exclaimed Mrs. Delray, running her manicured fingers across the garment as though appraising a work of art, "you really are a genius Mr. B." And she allowed him to wrap the corset around her middle, one hand holding up her luxuriously conditioned hair and the other hand glittering with diamonds. In the mirror Tallulah caught a glimpse of herself, like a dark shadow in the background, watching the beautiful woman as she breathed in slightly to allow the tiny pearl-like buttons to be fastened with the deft jab of a silver hook. Mrs. Delray's breasts were suddenly transformed in to a mountain of creamy white flesh above the rigid contours of the black satin and her waist looked even smaller than before. She twisted and turned in the mirror, admiring her reflection and commending Mr. B on his fine workmanship. By comparison Tallulah looked like a drudge in her nylon blouse and pleated skirt; a farmer's wife dolled up for a country wedding; a shop assistant with unmanageable hair and too much foundation. Tallulah looked away and busied herself with the folding of discarded lingerie.

How would it feel to look like Mrs. Delray? What must it be like to have men gawping at you wherever you go? Tallulah can't imagine how powerful it must feel to use one's sex as a way to achieve goals and aspirations. Fluttering eyelashes, wet lips and hair that looks perpetually tousled and wind-swept. Even Mr. B looks impressed when he's with Mrs. Delray and he's usually more interested in the boys who hang around outside the Crown & Anchor in the summer. He probably envies Mrs. Delray's narrow waist for although

Mr. B has squashed his own form down to 24" he suffers agonies at night when he pulls the stays on his corset just a fraction tighter. He lives for his art, you see. It's not often you see a fifty year old Frenchman with an hour-glass figure and tattooed eye-liner around these parts. Not unless the circus is in town.

The Black Hole of Calcutta

"Are you going right in to the village?' asks the cabbie, turning his head slightly so that Tallulah catches a glimpse of gold in his ear.

"Just on the other side," she replies, "about a mile or so."

Somewhere in the dark night sky a rocket splits the blackness and sends out a shower of coloured sparks. Tomorrow is Bonfire Night.

> *Bonfire night, the stars shine bright*
> *Three little angels dressed in white*
> *One with a fiddle, one with a drum*
> *One with a pancake stuck to its bum!*

Tallulah hasn't been to an organized firework display since she was a kid. They used to go to the communal bonfire at the colliery where her dad worked; a huge affair with a bonfire as high as a house. She can conjure up the burnt sugar taste of the bonfire toffee they sold in little wax-proof bags and the tubs of virulent green mushy peas with mint sauce. Dad used to take her to the newsagent's to buy fireworks from behind a protective glass shield; she would point to the various brightly coloured tubes and packets, each one promising something far more fantastic than they ever delivered.

Light up the sky with Standard fireworks!
She wonders if kids today still feel the same kind of naïve excitement when they open the firework box and smell the gunpowder. She suspects that computer games have taken over and most children would turn up their noses at a few coloured sparks and a whiz-bang or two. Tallulah feels a familiar pang of nostalgia for an era that has all but disappeared and she wonders what the children of today will remember and pass on to *their* children. If the programme she saw the other night is anything to go by there will *be* no future, it will be nothing but a vast expanse of wasteland covered with ice. Hopefully Tallulah will be long gone before that happens.

As they pass through Castleton she leans forward to tap the cabbie on his shoulder, "turn left up here," she says, pointing ahead in to the darkness where the only thing visible is the subterranean glow of the driver's face reflected in the windscreen. The cab turns off the main road and the branches of trees and bushes close in around them as though bending and peering in through the windows to see who is coming.

"It's like the bloody black hole of Calcutta up here," mutters the cabbie, shifting gears and leaning forward to see in to the gloom. Through the window Tallulah can barely make out the formidable shape of the two houses crouching side-by-side, they are merely a denser shade of black than the sky behind them. Ursula's windows are dark and there appears to be no sign of life *anywhere*.

"Would you mind waiting until I go inside?" she asks as she hands over her money to the cabbie and he mutters something back at her as he climbs out to retrieve her suitcase from the boot. The night is silent and cloying. There are no stars, there is no moon and the air is strangely warm and humid; not at all like November. The cabbie dumps Tallulah's heavy suitcase unceremoniously on the ground, climbs back in to his car and speeds away down the rutted cart track leaving her alone in the darkness with her foot in a puddle. The keys to the house are in her shoulder bag and she has to fumble around beneath the paper hankies, lip-salve, purse, sweets etc to find them. She has an unsettling sensation that at any moment somebody will grab her from behind; one hand over her mouth to silence her and the other pushing the cold butt of a gun in the small of her back. But she's in the middle of the countryside. What would a robber be doing out here?

Miraculously the first key she tries is the right one and she falls in to the warmth of Rob's hallway with a certain degree of relief. She switches on the wall lights and breathes in the now familiar rotten-apple smell, deriving from it the same kind of comfort that one gets from sinking in to one's own sheets after a particularly horrible day. Her case stands in the light from the doorway and she hurries out to get it, childishly keeping her eyes focused on the case and not the surrounding darkness. She is so glad to drag the case in to the house, shut the door and slide the bolt across. One of the wall lights flickers and burns out.

The door to the cupboard under the stairs is wide open and Tallulah has to pass it on her way to the kitchen. When she was a child Tallulah would avert her eyes every time she had to pass an open bedroom door at night, for fear of what might be lurking in the shadows beyond. Darkened mirrors frightened her because she though the Devil might be standing right behind. In the winter she hated being sent upstairs to turn on her electric blanket because of the 'faces' she saw in the icy windows; watching her maliciously with glittering, frosty eyes. Seeing this dark, gaping entrance to the cupboard fills her with the same kind of fear and she hurries past as quickly as possible, reaching out to slam the door shut as she goes.

The house stands silently around her. No rain like last time; no neighbours, cars or drunks in the street like back at home. Tallulah is very aware that on three sides of the house there is nothing but darkness and beyond that, more darkness. Underground caverns, the ruins of an ancient castle and miles of barren moorland beyond the craggy hills surround this house completely and the closest McDonald's is a forty minute drive away!

Mirror Image

She takes her suitcase up to Rob's bedroom and strips the bed. She turns on the TV for company, closes the curtains and takes the dirty linens down to the washing machine in the kitchen. Under the sink she finds some Pledge and a couple of dusters so she goes back upstairs and starts to clean the dusty, wax-splattered surfaces of the bedside tables and the chest of drawers. There are old candles and burnt-down joss sticks everywhere and under the bed she finds books, crisp packets and screwed up tissues. Tallulah wonders if the fireplace works but it looks too small to hold much more than four or five chunks of coal and the chimney seems to be blocked-off. How romantic it would be to sleep by firelight.

She is just returning to the kitchen when there is a knock at the door and Tallulah finds Ursula standing on the doorstep again, this time draped in an enormous fringed shawl made from very fine dark purple velvet.

"I saw the lights on, duck," explains Ursula, "and thought you might like to come round for a cuppa."

Quite honestly Tallulah would rather not be disturbed in the middle of her cleaning frenzy but she should make an effort to be friendly with Rob's neighbour as they'll be living side-by-side for the next fortnight. Out here in the middle of nowhere it makes sense to stick together. "Lovely!" she says, "can you give me five minutes to finish this load of washing and I'll pop round."

"All right, duck. No need to knock, I'll leave the door off the latch."

And so Tallulah pops the sheets in to the dryer and goes next-door to visit her neighbour.

It is the mirror-image of Rob's house but that is where the resemblance ends. The hallway is painted dark red; a much darker red than the colour Tallulah has chosen for her own unfortunate kitchen re-decoration. This red is the colour Tallulah had hoped for but failed to achieve. The wall-lights are shaped like bronze snakes wrapped around red glass bowls and the floors have been painted black. Tallulah shouts a cheery 'hello' as she lets herself in and she catches a glimpse of purple velvet in the kitchen ahead. Ursula is brewing the tea.

"Come on in, duck," she calls. Ursula's kitchen is pine with ceramic tile in cobalt blue. She has a wooden clothes rack hanging from the ceiling and it is strung with bunches of drying herbs and flowers. There is a smell reminiscent of warm wine and cloves.

"I'm making my Christmas tea," she announces without turning to face Tallulah. "I know we're a bit *previous* but on a chilly night like this I always think it's nice."

Ursula has bare feet and when she lifts one of them to scratch at the back of her leg her sole is dirty. She wears a toe-ring and an anklet.

"Shall we take this through in to the living room?" suggests Ursula, raising the tea tray in both hands and indicating the living room with a jut of her chin.

Tallulah leads the way. The living room fire is lit and the leaping flames cause the deep mustard walls to shrink and swell. The sofa is swathed with shawls and throws; paisley over stripe, check over floral and it is heaped with squashy pillows of all shape and colour. A coloured scarf has been tossed over a lampshade to create a warm puddle of amber in the corner by the window and the wall behind the sofa is obliterated behind a heavy woollen tapestry depicting Flemish ladies in wimples chasing unicorns through a thorny forest.

"What a lovely room!" exclaims Tallulah, even before she's had the chance to properly look around. It is lovely in the fact that it is *different.* It is a room that gathers dust and perfumes and Tallulah suspects that by daylight it probably looks like a student squat.

Headlamps from outside send a shivery streak of light across the lining of the curtains and then they're gone.

Ursula places the tea tray on the coffee table and squats down on the shaggy hearth-rug to assume a yoga-like position with her voluminous skirts gathered up around her knees. She reminds Tallulah of the woman who works in the heath food shop in town and she wouldn't be surprised if Ursula's kitchen cabinets aren't crammed with all manner of chopped nuts, millet and unbleached flour.

The Witch the Refugee & the Virgin

"Sit down, duck, you're making me uncomfortable."

So Tallulah sinks back amidst the cushions and the shawls. She recognizes the same joss-stick smell that she's noticed in Rob's bedroom and looks around to see where it's coming from. She notices there are three cups on the tray. Somebody knocks at the door.

"Come in!" screams Ursula, "door's open!"

Tallulah wasn't expecting anyone else and she takes an immediately inventory of what she's wearing. She should have at least pulled a comb through her hair before she came round.

The woman who enters the room is like a Barbie doll. She is tall and skinny with big boobs, a lot of fake tan and very blonde hair.

"Hello!" The woman steps over towards the sagging sofa and extends her manicured fingers towards Tallulah like a bundle of diamond-encrusted twigs. "Nicole Harvey, nice to meet you."

Tallulah attempts to struggle up from her mound of cushions but the sofa is too deep and all she manages is an ungainly rocking motion as she takes Nicole's hand. "Tallulah, hello."

"Nicole is a *writer,*" announces Ursula, proudly. "She's here for a few weeks doing research for her latest novel; a murder mystery!"

Blonde Nicole with her scooped-out neckline steps past Tallulah with a gasp of self-deprecating laughter and plonks herself down at the other end of the sofa. "I'm not published in Europe, just in the States." There is no practical method of sitting *demurely* in this monstrous piece of furniture. Nicole's shapely legs don't reach the floor and her skirt rides up.

"Are you *from* American, then?" asks Tallulah, taking in the gold sandals and the French manicure.

"No, London," nods Nicole with a brilliant smile. "I live in London but I'm renting a cottage for the month up here. What a gorgeous part of the world this is."

"London must be really exciting," muses Tallulah with a faraway look in her eye. She is picturing elegant dinner parties and flocked wallpaper. She can almost taste the abundant champagne and raw Japanese seafood. She's never been to London in her life.

"Yes, it is," agrees Nicole, stroking the arm of the sofa with her nervous fingers.

Ursula leans forward to lift the lid of her teapot. Steam rises and she presses her face in to it; eyes closed. "Mm, lovely," she murmers as the flames of the fire dance wildly behind her head.

"I've been listening to your CD non-stop today, Ursula," interjects Nicole, wriggling to set herself in a more upright position, "I went in to Buxton and bought myself a cheap little CD player. I *love* it!"

"I'm in a little local folk group," explains Ursula to Tallulah, "Nicole happened to be in the pub on Saturday night when we were playing and she got talking to Petra, the lead-singer. That's how we met."

Tallulah smiles but doesn't say anything. She's thinking about the time and she wants to get those sheets aired before she puts them back on the bed.

The tea is poured. There is no milk but there is honey instead of sugar. The tea is the colour of beetroot juice but smells invitingly aromatic.

"I wanted to ask you if there's anywhere around here I can get access to the internet?" asks Nicole as she accepts her mug of tea and balances it precariously against her knee.

"Not that I know of, duck, not unless you go in to one of the bigger places like Buxton or Sheffield. I don't use a computer myself, I prefer the old-fashioned way of finding things out."

"There's a computer in Rob's house you are welcome to use," chirps in Tallulah, feeling rather chuffed that she can offer up some kind of service to a real live author from London. "Rob's my cousin," she explains, "next-door. I'm clearing out the house for his parents."

"Tallulah's cousin was killed in a car accident last week," fills-in Ursula with a reverent expression of regret.

"Oh, I'm so sorry, honey." And kindly Nicole reaches across to press her hand against Tallulah's arm. Her perfume is intoxicating. There is something about her that reminds Tallulah of the elegant Mrs. Delray in her custom-made corset; but a bit more tarty.

"Rob was a fab friend to me," mulls Ursula over the steaming rim of her mug. "He only lived next-door for a couple of years but he was interested in some of the things I dabble in myself; herbology, aromatherapy; that kind of stuff. I think he was intrigued to live next-door to a witch."

The word is spoken with calculated ease but it falls to the ground with a deep resounding thud and both Nicole and Tallulah stiffen before it.

"You're a witch?" This is Nicole, being polite but her expression has just stiffened, "You practice Wicca?"

"Not so much Wicca as my own brand of witchcraft. I can't be doing with all those rules and laws and recipes for spells so I make up my own magic. My grandmother was a witch before me and they say it skips a generation so I suppose I inherited my gifts from her."

Tallulah looks down in to her teacup and thinks twice about a second sip. She notices for the first time the little bronze statue on the mantelpiece; a horned man sitting cross-legged on a rock. There's probably an upturned crucifix in here somewhere if she looks hard enough.

"But you're going to Rob's funeral on Friday. Isn't that kind of strange if you don't believe in Christianity?"

Ursula pauses for a moment, as though assembling her thoughts before she answers. "The funeral is in memory of your cousin, duck; it hasn't got anything to do with spirituality. The people who go to funerals come from all different faiths and some of them believe in an afterlife while others think of eternal damnation." Ursula sips her tea, wrinkling her nose against the steam.

"Most *pagans* believe in some variation of reincarnation or transmigration. A lot of witches believe we cross over to 'Summerland', a place of rest and peace where we get reunited with ancestors and friends who've passed before us, but haven't travelled on. It's what the Christians call Limbo. At Summerland we're supposed to renew bonds, review our past lives, and set out lessons to experience and learn in the next life. To put it simply, in keeping with the Wheel of the Year, we start life in darkness, grow to the peak of maturity, and decline until we greet the darkness before rebirth. Death, therefore, isn't an end. It's simply a transition between births; a change of form. Does that make sense?"

"So we just keep coming back as a different person over and over again?" Asks Nicole, sounding dubious.

"Or you might decide to come back as an animal," suggests Ursula with a smile, "it all depends on what life lessons you want to learn next time around. Some people just come back as cats or dogs to have a good time; being reincarnated as an animal doesn't usually involve the same kinds of lessons we have to learn as human beings."

It sounds like a load of old clap-trap to Tallulah but she is too polite to contradict. She can't help admitting that it's going to be quite exciting having a real-live witch next-door; it's like spotting a unicorn in the mist at dawn or finding pixies under the toadstools at the bottom of the garden. She's always wanted exotic friends; the kinds who don't need special occasions to drink wine; the kinds who eat snails and watch sub-titled films.

"Well I can't believe in anything," admits pouty-lipped Nicole with a wistful sigh, "I believe that when I die I'm finished. All this presumption that we actually *mean* enough to deserve an after-life, well, quite frankly I think we're no more significant that a speck of dust. It's not very cheerful and it keeps me awake at night sometimes but I really think you should just live every day as though it's your last and bugger the consequences."

"Life is definitely for living," nods Ursula, sagely "look at poor Rob; he got up last Wednesday thinking it was going to be just another ordinary day and – wham – end of story." She shoots an apologetic look at Tallulah, "sorry, duck, I wasn't thinking."

"It's all right, Ursula, I know what you mean. I was thinking the same thing just the other day."

Tallulah doesn't bring up the subject of the lump. After all, she barely knows these women.

"Another cup of tea, either of you?"

"Lovely," says Nicole, holding out her mug.

"If I'd thought about it I'd have popped in some eye of newt with this Christmas tea," jokes Ursula with a playful smile.

And the three women chuckle in the firelight; the witch, the refugee and the virgin facing each other across a tangle of misconceptions.

Insufficient Funds

"I'm sorry, love, but I've run your card through twice now and there are insufficient funds available."

Nicole stares dumbly at the shop assistant as if she's been accused of shop-lifting.

"But it can't be," she stammers, "I've got *thousands* of pounds in that account."

"I'm sorry, love, but you'll have to call your bank. It's so annoying when this happens, isn't it?" smiles the friendly girl with the charm-bracelet and dragonfly earrings. She probably says the same thing to every customer who is overdrawn at the bank, just to make them feel less humiliated.

Nicole leaves the shop feeling irritated. The bank is in Miami, it is too early to call them and she doesn't have access to the internet. Damn! She's only got twenty-five quid in her purse and the debit card is her only access to the money she and Daphne secreted away from Gideon's business account two weeks ago. She curses herself for not opening a British bank account immediately and transferring the funds but, quite honestly, it was the last thing on her mind.

It is ten o clock on a misty November morning and Nicole is in Castleton high street with her shopping bag ready to be filled. A team of local workers are putting up Christmas lights along the main streets of the village and there is a pick-up truck filled with real Christmas trees outside one of the pubs. For a village with a population of just 1,200 there are an awful lot of pubs, thinks Nicole absently as she crosses the street to enter the car park.

She drives to Tallulah's house, remembering her offer of two days ago. She will ask to use the computer for a few minutes, just to check up on her bank account. Normally she wouldn't take a stranger up on such a casual offer but Nicole is worried that something might have gone wrong and without that money she has nothing.

"Sure, no problem," says friendly Tallulah, answering the door in a shabby pinafore dress, "it's upstairs." And she leads Nicole up to the guest bedroom where Rob keeps his computer. "Don't ask me how to turn it back on or anything, I haven't got a clue about computers," she admits with a shrug.

But Nicole is computer literate. In America you have to know how to use a computer otherwise you're not part of the human race. Old age pensioners go surfing for cheaper medications, children research on-line encyclopaedias and hope to catch a glimpse of something forbidden, and frustrated housewives have affairs with married men from distant states with whom they'll never meet. Nicole doesn't come from the so-called 'computer generation' but she is young enough to know the rudiments essential to everyday living. She is self-taught and internet savvy.

Your current balance is $3.67.

Nicole stares at the computer screen and momentarily loses her focus. Rob's desk is piled high with books and papers and his computer is hideously misinformed. It's just not possible! When Nicole left

Miami last week there was seven hundred and fifty thousand dollars in this account and she can't have spent more than a couple of thousand – at the most – since she came to England. She goes to the account activity and there it is, right at the top of the page; a funds transfer of seven hundred and fifty dollars on October 24th. This is followed by a few debits such as the hydrofoil fare, hotel rooms, the car rental place and the Chatsworth farm shop but, until yesterday, there was a balance of seven hundred and forty-one thousand dollars so why is there an ominous-looking asterisk crouching impudently beside this princely sum of money?

Nicole scans to the bottom of the statement page and finds a note explaining that a balance followed by an asterisk represents credits and debits not yet posted to the account. What does this mean? Where did seven hundred and forty-one thousand dollars go overnight?

Panic closes Nicole's throat and she has to swallow hard to stop herself from choking. She wonders if Gideon somehow got wind of the convoluted banking process Nicole devised with Daphne to get the money from his bank accounts in to an anonymous account set up under the assumed name of Nicole Harvey. Could he have reclaimed the money or found a way to put a block on her spending? Or maybe he has alerted the authorities that money was embezzled and the funds have been traced back to her?

Tallulah pops her head around the bedroom door and asks Nicole if she'd like a cup of tea. Nicole is too stunned to answer but she nods her head and conjures up a watery smile as though nothing is the matter. While Tallulah is downstairs boiling water for the tea Nicole goes to her e-mail account; she has eighty-three unread messages. One of the messages is from Gideon and it reads, quite simply; "You're going to suffer for this, cunt." It was sent on Saturday evening, a few minutes after Nicole had talked to him on the phone.

She immediately sends an urgent message to Daphne, asking her to look in to the dilemma with the money. She explains that she no longer has a phone and, obviously, is now unable to purchase a new one. 'Please, please respond to this e-mail as quickly as possible,' she writes, 'if this is fucked-up I'm totally in the shit.'

She hears voices downstairs in the hallway; it sounds like somebody has arrived and the last thing Nicole needs at this moment is idle conversation with strangers. She hopes that whoever is downstairs will go away but somebody is calling her name and it appears that she is expected to go down there to get her tea.

A Cold Flannel

Ursula and Petra are in the kitchen with Tallulah. They've come to help with some of the packing. It is difficult for Nicole to force a convincing smile on her face as she sits at the table with the other women but her only link to the internet is here so it is impetrative that she remains as friendly as possible with these people. They are discussing yesterday's funeral and Nicole has to apologize; she had forgotten that Tallulah's cousin was cremated the day before.

"It wasn't much of a funeral, actually," says Tallulah as she fills up the teapot (Nicole had forgotten just how much tea the Brits consume every day as compared to the cups of coffee in America). "Only a handful of people there and then Rob's ex-wife, Julie, turning up like a bad penny and setting Auntie June off outside the crematorium like that."

"She's a hard-face cow," comments Petra as she runs a black-painted finger-nail around a closed packet of digestive biscuits to slit them open. "I can't imagine Rob married to somebody like that. She's the type who gave up her virginity for a bag of chips."

"Petra!" admonishes Ursula, "you don't even know the poor woman! You're only scathing because you thought Rob should have been with somebody like you." She explains to Tallulah and Nicole that Petra had a bit of a 'thing' for Rob, despite the fact he was twenty years her senior.

"He was very youthful," defends Petra, "and he was very open-minded, unlike most people his age." She points this mild jibe at Ursula but Ursula just shakes her head and makes a face.

"Rob was a latent hippie," Ursula observes, "he moved here to get away from all the crap out there in the real world and thought he could escape from modern life by smoking pot all day and writing his articles on global warming and straw-bale houses. What he really needed was a realistic grasp on life and a solid plan for his future but he was drifting and he thought he could re-capture his youth by hanging out with people *years* younger than himself. Total mid-life crisis! Blokes get to that age when they start questioning the meaning of the universe, they go out and get a tattoo, buy a sports car and shag a few birds and then they settle back down again. Rob was just depressed."

Nicole thinks about Gideon and almost joins in with the conversation, but it is best if she keeps her thoughts to herself. Gideon has two tattoos, a pierced nipple, a bright red Ferrari and a girlfriend who dances on the tables of nightclubs when she's drunk or tweaking on drugs.

"Our Rob was always a bit of a hippie," remembers Tallulah, "you should have seen his bedroom when he was a teenager; candles, peacock feathers and mobiles all over his ceiling. He used to listen to weird music and cut his hair with a razor blade. Nobody thought he'd go to university."

"What's so wrong with being a hippie?" asks Petra, pulling lightly on her pierced eyebrow, "everybody's so freaked out by unconventional behaviour because they're so fucking insecure themselves. Why are people so scared of people who break the mould?"

"Folks like to peg you as one thing or another; they don't like it when they can't fit you in to a box. Look at the way people treat me." Ursula's pocked, greasy complexion shines with an unhealthy pallor between the lank veils of hair.

Although Nicole, by Derbyshire standards, is somewhat unconventional in appearance she is most definitely not a hippie. She loathes the smell of joss sticks; preferring expensively perfumed candles that come in heavy glass jars with silver lids. She detests ethnic-print skirts with bits of mirror sewn in to the hem and the kind of clunky jewellery that both Ursula and Petra are wearing in abundance.

Nicole is thinking about seven hundred and forty-one thousand dollars so she doesn't join in with the conversation. Instead she fiddles with her platinum and diamond rings and struggles to keep her heartbeat regular. Her breathing is constricted. She is suffocating. She could do with a couple of Ativan but they're back at the cottage.

What will she do if the money has gone? She knows a few people here in England but she has lost touch over the years and her father is widowed and living on his pension in a one-bedroomed council flat in Margate. She hasn't worked in fifteen years and her past work experience is mainly based on self-employment so she has no references. The idea of trying to start a new business, especially in a country where things have changed so much since she last lived here, is daunting. Nicole has no idea how much people get paid for doing unskilled jobs these days but she is certain it wouldn't be enough to live on and can she really imagine herself setting the alarm for seven every morning and going to work on the bus?

"I'm sorry, will you excuse me for a minute, I need a breath of fresh air," she gasps, pushing her chair back from the table and staggering towards the back door.

"Are you all right?" asks Tallulah, jumping up to unlock the door.

"I just feel a bit faint, that's all; I'll be fine in a minute."

Ursula and Petra exchange a glance that Nicole catches just before she lurches forward in to the garden and throws up her breakfast all over the wood pile. Her vomit steams in the misty air. Tallulah holds her arm and gently rubs her back as though she is a nurse. The rooks caw with delight from their untidy tree-top nests as they peer down at her with black beady eyes.

"I'm sorry about that," groans Nicole, coughing and spluttering as she attempts to clear her throat of bile, "it must be something I ate."

"Come back inside, you're sweating. I'll get you a cold flannel."

"I'll pop next door and get you some chamomile and peppermint tea, it'll help to settle your stomach," suggests Ursula, sweeping through the kitchen in her voluminous black skirt.

Nicole allows herself to be fussed-over for a few minutes, sitting in the chair with a wet face-cloth pressed against the back of her neck. Petra dunks a digestive in to her mug. "Better out than in," she observes, dryly as she observes Nicole. The wet biscuit flops over and falls with a splash in to her tea.

Something Fishy

"Something's not right there," says Ursula as soon as Nicole is gone. "There's something fishy about that woman and I can't put my finger on it. She's in some kind of trouble."

Ursula doesn't bring up the subject of auras but the sulphurous shade surrounding Nicole suggests uneasiness and emotional pain. And then there's Tallulah who appears to be shimmering with a worrying white halo of light which usually indicates serious disease. Petra, as usual, is glowing with the luminous yellow of freedom and vitality.

"I don't think she's a writer," suggests Petra, "she doesn't *look* like a writer."

"What do writers look like, then? Does Jackie Collins look like a writer?"

"If she was that kind of writer she'd be published all over the world and not just in the States. She reckons she writes murder mysteries but she looks more like she should be judging a bloody ballroom dancing competition in Blackpool. Don't get me wrong, she's nice enough, but there's more to her than meets the eye."

"She seems very nervous," says Tallulah, mopping up a splash of spilled tea with a dishcloth, "it's as though she doesn't really listen to what she's saying. And she's wearing a wedding ring."

"So there must be a husband tucked away in London, then. It's not like we've actually asked her much about her personal life."

"She looks like she's got money."

"She looks like she's got *problems,*" concludes Ursula with a raised eyebrow.

Still in Credit

Nicole buys a phone card and calls the bank in Miami. It takes a while for them to check her account but when they confirm that the money was transferred back in to Gideon's bank account Nicole doesn't wait for an explanation. She leaves the phone card in the slot with one pound twenty-nine pence still in credit and she sits in the car and cries. How can this have happened?

Bread

"She's found out about the money," says Daphne as she checks her e-mail messages from Gideon's computer.

"Man, I wish I was a fly on the wall right now," grins Gideon, wiping the syrup from his breakfast waffle on to the corner of a napkin.

"I almost feel sorry for her, poor bitch; all alone in the middle of the English countryside with no money, no job and nobody to turn to." Daphne lights a cigarette and blows the smoke over her shoulder.

"Not to mention the criminal charges for embezzling money from a corporate account if she ever tries to come back to the States," adds Gideon as one might add a cube of sugar to enliven a glass of cheap champagne. "She'll be lucky if she can buy herself a loaf of fucking bread!"

Daphne smiles, viciously; *"bread,* darling? Let the bitch eat *cake!"*

And they laugh because it's always so gratifying when something goes exactly as you planned.

State of Mind

With only nineteen pounds to her name what is Nicole Harvey going to do? It is going to take more than Ativan and vodka to calm her down today. She is experiencing a panic attack following an altercation with a woman in a multi-storey car park in Sheffield.

The underground section of the car park had a traffic light at the entrance to prevent too many vehicles from racing down the ramp at one time. Nicole was waiting at the red light, her foot resting lightly on the accelerator, ready to go. The woman in the car behind her honked her horn impatiently. Nicole glared in to her rear-view mirror with contempt and the woman rammed the palm of her hand down on her steering wheel once again. Nicole could feel anger blurring her vision and she was just about to pull on her hand brake and get out of the car when the bitch in the red beetle revved up her engine and pulled out around Nicole's car and down the ramp ahead of her.

This was just too much for Nicole's nerves and, ignoring the stop light, she sped after the red car with a vengeance. With tyres screaming against polished concrete and headlamps on full beam Nicole sped up to within a couple of inches of the bumper in front of her, all the while yelling obscenities through her windscreen. She continued to follow the red car despite the fact that they were passing empty parking spaces and when the beetle finally pulled in to a spot (presumably because there were several people getting in and out of their cars in that section of the concourse and the driver felt somehow protected) Nicole continued around the corner. She parked a few rows away and she watched the ugly, fat bitch get out of her car.

When the coast was clear, and wantonly ignoring the security cameras placed all around the area, Nicole marched over to the offending car and whacked the side window with a brick that she found propping open the fire exit. It didn't offer her the satisfaction of shattering but a single crack shot from one corner to the other upon impact and it was as though every last drop of her bile and anger went in to that act of violence. Immediately after the glass cracked Nicole became acutely aware of where she was and what she had just done. She dropped the brick and hurried back to her car; humiliation and shame burning the back of her neck. This was the act of a fucking crazy woman! This was totally inappropriate behaviour for a woman who was once on the committee of her neighbourhood watch association. Nicole left the garage immediately and returned to Brown Bread Cottage without visiting the Job Centre as she had planned. Now she is wondering if the management company of the car park or the police will come to find her after identifying her registration plate on the video tape.

She will claim acute depression and she can show them the various bottles of anti-depressants and anti-anxiety pills in her toiletry bag if they don't believe her. She will use the 'Prozac Defence' and say that she's been having suicidal thoughts following the rejection and persecution of her husband.

It is probably best if Nicole hides indoors for a few days until her state of mind improves. The outside world is just too unpredictable and aggressive to cope with.

Just reliving the experience in the car park is making Nicole uncomfortable again and she can taste the anger in the back of her throat as though a recently formed scab has just been torn away to reveal the seething wound. Who did that fucking cow think she was, anyway? What right did she have to honk her horn at Nicole like that; didn't she see that Nicole was in a state of shock for God's sake? People like her should be rammed off the road and left to die, they should be sent back to their fucking council houses and barricaded in!

Oh dear, Nicole, time for another Ativan maybe?

Jeff

And while Veronica swallows another pill Tallulah swallows the final piece of her Bakewell Tart at Rose Cottage tearoom. She walked in to the village this afternoon to pick up a few groceries at the tiny grocery shop and because the day was so dreary and foggy she stopped in at the quaint little cottage café for a cup of tea and a piece of homemade cake. It is quite exciting playing the Lady of Leisure and she feels light-headed and giddy with the idea that, for these two weeks at least, she can pretend to be somebody other than her own dreary self.

The women who lunch at Rose Cottage wear clothing from Marks & Spencer's and sensible shoes; they use pastry forks and add hot water to their individual teapots to make the tea go further. Snippets of conversation tell of gymkhanas and bring-and-buy sales and the breeze from the open doorway is awash with a fragrant blend of Yardley lily-of-the-valley and egg mayonnaise sandwiches. If these women had any idea that last night Tallulah was discussing female circumcision with a witch and a homosexual aromatherapist from Hull they would probably not be offering her friendly smiles over the rims of their china teacups.

Ursula's friend, Martin, is the first 'real' homosexual Tallulah has met. Oh yes, she's seen plenty of them on the television but in real life the only gay men she has come across are those with limp wrists and speech impediments. Mr. B is a prime example in his Chinese slippers and whale-boned corset. Ursula invited Tallulah round for dinner and they ate some peculiar concoction made from chick peas and cauliflower, drinking several bottles of homemade blackberry wine. Martin rubbed Tallulah's feet with neroli oil while Ursula read poetry aloud from a leather-bound book. It was preposterous but strangely comforting.

Tallulah pays her bill and emerges in to the swirling cape of fog. There are a couple of jewellery shops on the opposite side of the street where they sell all manner of things made from the famous Blue John stone found only in this part of the country. A few weekday browsers litter the narrow main street, most of them kitted out in hiking boots and practical weatherproof jackets. It is so different here from the neighbourhood where Tallulah lives and she pauses to breathe in the scent of it. Fields fertilized with manure, leaves rotting under hedgerows and ancient mossy stone damp from the fog make a pleasant change from the petrol fumes and chip shop grease that lurks perpetually around the streets of Chesterfield.

On the way back towards Rob's house there is a picturesque little bridge that arches over a fast-running brook and on either side of the water there are cottages and a few little shops. Soaring up behind the cottages, partially submerged by fog and low cloud, there is a sheer craggy rock-face topped with the shadowy silhouette of trees. Tallulah takes a diversion over the bridge and tucked around the corner she discovers a small square of grass in the middle of which stands an enormous oak tree and a stone Celtic cross. She wishes she had a camera.

"Afternoon!" Tallulah turns towards a man who is standing in the doorway of a small junk shop. He is holding a mug in one hand and a small dog is peeping out from behind his legs. "Oh, hello!" calls back Tallulah when she realizes that he is talking to her.

"Miserable day, isn't it?"

"Yes," she responds, glancing up through the oppressive layers of fog. "I'm presuming there's only one junk shop in Castleton. You must be Jeff? We talked on the phone?"

"Ah, yes, Rob's cousin, isn't it?"

Tallulah nods. "You know I never realized that Castleton is such a lovely place. Even in this weather it's got a sort of magic about it. I've only been here once before and that was with a school trip when I was eleven. One of the draw-backs of not having a car, I suppose."

"You should buy an old banger," suggests Jeff, barricading his little dog from running out in to the street. "There's so many lovely places round here to see but you need a car to get to them."

"I'm not sure I'd know how to drive," admits Tallulah, "I passed my test when I was eighteen but I've never driven since."

"Oh, a few refresher lessons would soon have you finding your feet. It's like riding a bike, once you've learned you never forget."

"Rob's mum and dad offered to lend me their car but I'd be mortified if I scratched it or something."

"How's your auntie doing? She's been having chemotherapy hasn't she?"

"Oh, not so bad. They think they've caught the cancer before it spread so we're keeping our fingers crossed."

"That's good," nods the man, "I just lost my sister last year to lung cancer."

"Oh, I'm sorry," offers Tallulah with sympathy. She is unused to this kind of intimacy with strangers; where she lives the neighbours might nod in recognition and mutter 'all right?' as they pass by on the pavement but very few of them stop to make real conversation. Tallulah doesn't even know the names of the people who live next door and they've been living there for two years now.

"This is Barney, by the way," and Jeff indicates his little dog, "he's ready for his dinner. Would you like to come in for a cuppa? I've just mashed a pot."

"Oh, thank you, but I just had some tea at the café." Tallulah isn't the kind of woman who accepts invitations of tea from complete strangers. Jeff seems nice enough but she wouldn't know what to say to him and it would be awkward having to sit down and make small-talk.

"Fair enough, you'll just have to come round another day. You did say your name is Tallulah didn't you? As in Tallulah Bankhead?"

She nods resignedly, wishing for the umpteenth time that her mother had just called her Jane or Betty.

"Well that's quite a name to live up to," grins Jeff, "she was quite a character by all accounts."

"That's what everybody says, but the only film I've ever seen her in is *Lifeboat;* it was one of my mum's favourite films."

"Ah, Hitchcock; that is one of his most underrated films, I think. I'm a bit of a Hitchcock fan, you see; I've seen them all a hundred times."

"Well I've only seen it once and I didn't think it was much cop. I prefer *The Birds.*"

"Ah, yes; his second attempt at making a true horror film after he did *Psycho.* I have to say that *Psycho* holds up better in the long run." Jeff turns towards the inside of his shop and places his mug on a shelf he then picks up Barney and allows the dog to lick his chin enthusiastically.

"Well, listen, if you want any help clearing out Rob's stuff I've got a van and I'd be happy to take your rubbish to the tip in return for any unwanted bits and bobs for my shop. And you can borrow my copy of *Lifeboat* if you want to study your namesake in greater detail."

"Thanks a lot," grins Tallulah, "Rob's got a lot of stuff and his mum and dad aren't interested in saving much of it so it would be great if you could take some of it off our hands. They want to put the house on the market as soon as they can."

"That's a shame, it's a decent little house and it's got quite a bit of land attached to it. If they could afford to hold on to it for a bit longer, do it up a bit, they'd probably get more money."

Tallulah knows nothing about house prices, she just knows that Auntie June and Uncle Ted need to get rid of the place as soon as possible and they don't care what she does with the furniture or Rob's things.

"Well, thanks, Jeff. I'll definitely take you up on the offer to get shut of some stuff. The sooner the better, actually. I'm already filling up skips with stuff to be thrown away."

Jeff looks at his watch. "I'm free in about an hour if that's not too soon; I'd hate to think of you throwing something good away. You know what they say; one man's rubbish is another man's treasure."

"OK," says Tallulah, "that's fine, I'm not going anywhere." And she raises her free hand in a friendly wave and turns back towards the bridge. There is a large sign that reads 'Welcome to the Devil's Arse'; a tongue-in-cheek reference to the underground caverns that lie just beyond the row of terraced cottages.

The sky is totally obscured by the fog and although she can't actually see them Tallulah can hear birds making a racket from a nearby tree. Tallulah tries to imagine Rob making this journey from the village and she wonders if, like her, he walked or if he usually took his car. It's only about a mile and the scenery (on clear days) is beautiful but Tallulah has no idea if her cousin was the type of person who appreciated such things.

Robert was a freelance writer. He was also a teacher at the Poly in Sheffield; something to do with ecology and things like the polar icecaps and the rain forests. Auntie June mentioned that he was writing a book but Tallulah presumes it will be about the kinds of things that go way above her head. She saw part of a documentary on the deforestation of the Mexican jungle a couple of weeks ago but she changed channels because *Casualty* was on the other side.

A Remedy

When Nicole knocks on Tallulah's front door there is no answer so she tries Ursula instead. Ursula doesn't have a computer but she does have a warm kitchen and a huge selection of herbal teas so Nicole sits at the battered pine table with her hands wrapped around a hand-thrown pottery mug of dandelion tisane.

"Something's bothering you, Nicole. You don't have to tell me what it is but I can see that you're worked-up and fretting about something." Ursula screws the lid on to the large jar of dried petals and puts it back on a shelf. "Remember I'm a witch; I know these things." And she smiles kindly, displaying her frighteningly uneven teeth. With the right lighting and a crack of thunder Ursula could easily scare little children at the pantomime.

"Oh, it's nothing," sighs Nicole, "I'm just a bit tired. I didn't sleep much last night."

"That cottage is haunted, you know; perhaps it's the ghosts that are keeping you awake?"

"Ghosts? Oh, I don't think so. I haven't seen or heard anything untoward while I've been there. Anyway, I don't believe in ghosts."

Ursula was busy when Nicole knocked at the door and the table is strewn with pieces of bark, dried fungi and seed pods. On the cooker top there is a large cast iron pot bubbling and steaming, the lid chattering quietly against the sides as a pungent smell like wet straw escapes.

"What are you making?"

"It's a remedy for gout. Tom Willow, one of the local farmers, buys it from me. He refuses to give up the booze and so he drinks my potion in equal quantities and swears it helps to reduce the swelling in his joints. I've tried telling him it would do him a hell of a lot more good if he stopped propping up the bar at The George but you can't teach an old dog new tricks."

"I've never met a witch before," admits Nicole, realizing as she makes this observation how odd it sounds. "I suppose I always thought of witches as something in fairytales or people looking for an excuse to abuse kids and animals. If you really do have the ability to cast spells and make magic how come you're not living the high-life in a mansion with more money than you know what to do with? I know if I could make magic spells I'd be wishing for all kinds of lovely things."

Ursula chuckles, "that's probably why you're not a witch. We don't *choose* to do this, as though it's a profession; we're born in to it and with these gifts comes a certain code of ethics. Of course there'll always be those who abuse their powers but, on the whole, most modern witches live their lives modestly and quietly. I like helping other people with their aches and pains, their trouble and strife. I've got a comfortable life and I don't wish for anything more than that."

Nicole sighs. "I wish I could say the same thing."

"What about your life in London? Aren't you happy with what you've got down there? I should have thought that writing books would be a peaceful and rewarding kind of occupation as long as you can make enough money to live on. What does your husband do?"

Nicole looks up from her mug. "My husband?"

"I couldn't help but notice the ring."

"Oh, yes, my ring. Well, my husband and I are separated; he's been having an affair with somebody else and that's one of the reasons why I came up here, to get away from it all for a while."

"And is it working?" asks Ursula, "this separation?"

"Oh, it's all so complicated, Ursula. I don't want to go in to it but things are getting very ugly. Quite honestly, I'm in a bit of a mess."

Ursula nods but says nothing. Nicole isn't enjoying the taste of her tea so she puts down the mug and pushes it to one side. She would love to spill out the entire truth to Ursula, just to see the sordid details scattered across the table along with the herbs and seeds. It would be a relief to get some of it out of her system but she is still scared that Gideon might come looking for her. Money isn't his only motivation for revenge and she knows how vindictive he can be when somebody crosses him.

"You've got some money problems, haven't you? I'm not trying to pry in to your personal business but I saw something in your aura the first time I met you."

"Big time," admits Nicole with a wry smile. "I'm in the shit, to put it bluntly."

Ursula reaches out to place her hand over Nicole's and she offers it a gentle squeeze. "I know you don't believe in my mumbo-jumbo but can I do something for you? I'm not promising to make you a millionaire or to help you win the lottery but I might be able to ease your situation slightly."

"Right now, Ursula, I'll take whatever help I can get, even if it means resorting to witchcraft."

"Hang on a minute," says Ursula, rising from her seat, "let me pop down to the cellar to see if I've got some corn husks."

A Gristly Word

Next door Tallulah has just arrived home and the phone was ringing as she opened the front door.

"Hello, duck, how are things going?" It is Tallulah's grandmother again.

"Well, not as fast as I'd like, Gran. Our Rob's got loads of stuff to get rid of and I'm scared to just throw any of it away without going through everything first. I've already filled two skips with rubbish."

"You want to set up a big bonfire and burn it all if it's rubbish. June and Ted don't want any of it. Of course there are all kinds of rules and regulations these days about bonfires; people phoning up the council to complain if you so much as burn a few leaves. I was telling Ted this morning about the bloody council but he's up to his neck with June and her vomiting. She's nothing but skin and bones and the doctors don't seem to know what they're doing, making her wait around all day at the hospital without so much as a cup of tea."

Tallulah sits at the kitchen table with the telephone jammed between her ear and her shoulder and the fog presses up against the windows; solid and impenetrable as a sheet of blotting paper. It wraps the house like a layer of insulating foam, absorbing sound and vision to create an eerie atmosphere of isolation.

"…nothing but grey skies and rain and rain and more rain. Every day it's the same and according to the forecast there's to be no let up. It's so depressing, duck, I've not been out for a week now and I'm feeling so low and miserable. I've been here sixty years and I've never known weather like it. Did you have that thunder last Wednesday? I was having a perm and the lights went out and the lightning was terrible; it was like a tube going horizontally across the sky instead of the normal upwards. A thunderbolt dropped at the back of where the old gas tanks used to be. It seemed to stretch all the way from Newbold to where Mrs. Buckeritis lives and of course all the lights went off and I was shivering with fright. There I was, huddled up in the chair with my hair dripping wet, and the hairdresser was sat with me drinking tea and brandy. I had to laugh after but at the time it was terrible. I've never know thunderstorms in November and there's more to come according to today's weather warning. I'm wondering if Christmas will bring a heat-wave; I wouldn't be surprised!"

"We didn't have thunder here, Gran, but its thick fog today." Tallulah drains her mug and rolls up the open end of the biscuits.

"Aye, I saw that on the weather today; all over the moors apparently. Just you stay indoors with the doors locked and don't answer if anybody knocks; you don't know what nutcases are roaming around out there these days. I was telling our Linda the other day about the new neighbours at the top of the crescent; I'm fed up with them. All they need is a red-light put up outside the house and it'd be a bloody knocking-shop! They live worse than animals; filthy both in themselves and the house. Bad language, living over the brush, as they say, I think they're all doolallie and all the brains he has are in his bloody trousers! They're a load of bloody wazzocks of the first degree and I don't know whose kids are whose. I feel like I could do with a 'ha'apeth of God help me', as they say."

"Well I'll be back home next week; I've got to go back to work the following Monday. I can't say I'm looking forward to it," admits Tallulah as she sweeps biscuit crumbs from the Formica table in to the palm of her hand.

"Well, you've got to earn a living, duck. I would have thought you'd be happy to get back home after being stuck out there on your own."

"I like the quiet here, Gran, and Rob's friends have been ever so helpful. Back at home I don't know nobody and the neighbours are all strangers to me. At least out here the people in the village are friendly and there isn't a day goes by without somebody phoning or calling round to give me a hand." What Tallulah doesn't tell her grandmother is that she's actually *dreading* the return home. Thoughts of that soulless house with the half-painted kitchen and the chilly bedrooms make her anxious and unsettled. She feels as though she's been exposed to something better and she doesn't want to go back to the empty life she left behind just a week ago.

"I'd better go, Gran, there's somebody at the door. I think it's Rob's friend Jeff from the junk shop; he said he'd come and help me shift some of the old furniture out and take it to the Salvation Army."

"Well don't you go putting your back out trying to lift furniture; the last thing you need is a stint in the hospital with an injury."

"I'll talk to you later, Gran. Bye." And Tallulah puts down the phone while Gran is still saying goodbye.

There isn't anyone at the door. She just said that because she didn't want to listen to any more mindless rubbish about the weather and Gran's neighbours. You see, despite what her gran says about the National Health Service they can be remarkably efficient and swift if they need to be. The doctor called Tallulah this morning to

135

give her the results of the mammogram. They want to perform a biopsy on the lump in her breast. And they want to do it as soon as possible.

Cancer: It's a gristly word; difficult to chew and dry like a piece of overcooked mutton. Tallulah has known it would come to her at some point, she just wasn't sure when. Ever since her mum died she's been aware of the terrible C word and she knew then; on the day they took her mother's body away to the morgue, that the cancer wasn't gone; it was merely waiting to find another host. Tallulah suspected that she had probably inhaled the disease while spending so much time by her mother's sick bed. She felt the weight of it in her lungs as she left the hospital that day and it's taken all this time to come back to tap her on the shoulder and reintroduce itself. "All right, Tal? How's it been going? Remember me; Cancer?"

How come everything has suddenly changed for Tallulah after all these years of solitary confinement? Some kind of cosmic shift must have displaced the magnetic forces surrounding Tallulah's fate because she has been ripped from the roots of her humdrum existence and tossed in to the eye of a storm. What with Rob's death and the clearing out of this house and now breast cancer! Where's the justice in that? Surely if she was due some kind of surprise then it should have been something pleasant? If, supposedly, you reap what you sow, what the hell has Tallulah done that is so terrible that it deserves this?

Vacant Patches

The sound of Jeff's van outside jolts Tallulah from her unhappy thoughts. When she pulls open the door she sets the fog in motion and it swirls in to the porch like smoke. The headlamps of Jeff's van look jaundiced in the murky afternoon light and Tallulah can hear music until Jeff switches off the ignition and then it falls silent except for the ticking of the van's engine as it starts to cool down. A huddle of spindly birch trees creak gently like a row of old rocking chairs in an imperceptible draught.

"Hi!" calls Jeff as his legs appear from the van. His jeans are torn at the knees and his boots are caked with dry mud. Tallulah wonders if he tore the jeans on purpose or if he bought them like that; why else would anyone wear clothing that is so obviously beyond repair? She isn't so behind the times that she isn't aware that 'distressed' jeans are all the rage but isn't Jeff too old to be concerned with such vanities?

"I haven't seen fog like this for years. I can remember when I was a kid going in to Sheffield when they still had the old trams and the smog used to be terrible. All the cars had fog lights in those days."

Jeff must be older than he looks. Tallulah is pretty sure the old-fashioned trams stopped running in Sheffield at the end of the 1950's. It's difficult to gauge his age because of the way he dresses. His torn jeans, sheepskin jacket and longish hair make him look a bit like a hippie but he doesn't seem to be much older than Tallulah. Maybe that's just because Tallulah has always looked older than she is.

"According to my gran it's all to do with global warming. I think she just watches too much telly. A few years ago it was sending men to the moon and atomic explosions that caused the weather to change but now she's got the melting icecaps to blame for everything! Come on in, Jeff, it's chilly out here."

"Actually I've met your gran," explains Jeff, exhaling smoke as he approaches the house; flicking his cigarette butt in to a puddle. "I went over to her house with Rob once when we were in Chesterfield. A lovely old lady. She had me in stitches talking about the war."

"Oh she can talk about the war all day if you let her. I think she misses it. She's always saying that life was better back then."

"Let me take my boots off," suggests Jeff as he reaches the door, "they're filthy. I took Barney up to the castle this morning and the mud is terrible." He squats down to untie the dirty yellow work boots. He is wearing a bracelet made from small shiny shells; the kind they used to use in infant school for counting. Tallulah can smell the cigarette smoke that hangs around him, mingling with the dampness of the fog. It's a smell that Tallulah associates with her father and she is one of the few people who actually like it.

"The floors are a mess anyway, so it won't make much difference. I've not bothered to Hoover round because every time I clear out another cupboard I just make more mess so it doesn't seem worth it. I've packed away all of the things that I want to keep myself so you're welcome to take whatever you think you can sell in your shop. You can root around in those skips out back if you feel like it. Most of the big pieces of furniture are going to a second-hand shop in Bakewell and they're going to pick them up on Friday."

"What about the Matchbox cars and the old board games that Rob keeps up on the landing? Any interest in getting shut of those?" asks Jeff, standing up and closing the door behind him.

"I've put them in to boxes upstairs. You can have the lot if you want them. Ursula from next-door was saying that some of them might be quite valuable, especially those that are still in their original boxes. Maybe you can make a few bob on them."

"More than a few bob," says Jeff with a smile, "some of those old toys sell for hundreds of quid. I might put some of them on e-bay. There are collectors all over the world looking for that kind of stuff. I'd be happy to split the profits with you fifty-fifty."

"Oh no, that's all right, Jeff. I would probably just have thrown them all away if you didn't want them; I haven't got time to faff around trying to sell any of this stuff. Come on through, I'll put the kettle on."

It is strange how the dynamic of the house changes when there is someone else here besides Tallulah. It is as though the house needs company to bring it to life and although Tallulah has grown used to being here alone she is very aware of how easy it would be to hide away from the world in this house. In her own house there is a constant awareness of neighbours and traffic and the tight clutch of the town surrounding her, but here in Rob's house there is a silence that is almost a presence in itself.

"It looks like you've done a pretty good job of clearing most of the stuff out already," comments Jeff as they enter the kitchen. Tallulah has left most of the cupboard doors open so she can see where she has been; most of them are now completely empty and she has just kept a few essential items aside for her own personal use. Most of the kitchen stuff she has packed in to boxes and these are stacked up neatly by the back door. On the walls there are vacant patches surrounded by accumulated grease and dirt where pictures, calendars and ornamental plates have been removed. There is a sharp smell of ammonia and bleach.

"It's starting to feel impersonal now that most of Rob's things are gone," observes Tallulah as she fills the kettle, "even the *smell* of the house is changing. It makes me feel sad to think of other people moving in here."

"Why don't you buy the place yourself?" suggests Jeff, pulling out a chair.

"Oh it's too far away from work and, like I said, I don't drive," explains Tallulah, rinsing out two mugs under the tap, "anyway, it'd be too expensive for me. Auntie June told me they've got to get at least ten thousand more than what Rob paid for it just to pay the estate agent and solicitor's bills."

"What's your house like in Chesterfield?"

"Oh, you know; a typical terraced house. It belonged to my parents and they left it to me when they died so it's the only house I've ever known. It's a bit old-fashioned and I haven't got the money to do it up but some of the neighbours have put in new kitchens and bathrooms; some have even added extensions at the back. I don't see the point myself; it doesn't matter what you do to them, they're still the same grimy old houses."

"I couldn't move back in to town," admits Jeff, pushing up the sleeves of his jumper, "I used to live in Sheffield in a flat and it was fun when I was younger but I've been in Castleton for ten years now and I can't think of living anywhere else. Of course the village mentality gets to me sometimes and you have to be careful not to give out too much information about your personal life, but, on the whole, everyone here is pretty decent. Fortunately the house is paid for and my bills are really low so with the shop and the auctioneering I do I can just about keep my head above water."

"Auctioneering?"

"Yeah, I work the local estate sales; house clearances, that kind of thing."

"That must be interesting."

"No, it's a load of old tat most of the time. Every now and then I get to work on a nice old place with lots of antiques but then the dealers from London and Manchester descend like a swarm of flies to pick the stuff over before the auction and most of it is shipped off to be sold at ridiculously inflated prices to people with more money than sense. I end up with the stuff that nobody else wants."

For a moment, as Tallulah stares out of the kitchen window, waiting for the kettle to boil, she thinks about her tedious little job at Mr. B's. What would it be like to have the kind of independence that Jeff has? How lovely to wake up in the morning and not know what the day has in store for you; the luxury of making your own schedule and taking a day off whenever you feel like it. Tallulah has spent her entire adult life waking to an alarm-clock, catching the same bus every day and doing what she is told by people who hardly even notice that she's there. Three weeks holiday a year plus the usual long weekends at Easter and Christmas and Sundays reserved for bacon butties, cleaning the bathroom and hoovering the threadbare carpets.

"Was Rob happy here?" Tallulah's question emerges from her private musing and she is barely aware of having spoken it out loud.

"Yes, I think so," answers Jeff. "He was a bit lonely, like all of us, but I think he enjoyed being out here on his own with all this privacy for his writing. To be perfectly honest I think he liked keeping himself to himself and he wasn't even that fussed about seeing his family very often."

"I was just talking to my gran on the phone and apparently Auntie June is pretty sick. I think it's the chemo more than anything but she can't seem to keep her food down."

"She ought to ask her doctor for some pills. There's something made from cannabis that's that supposed to be good for post-chemo nausea; I think it's called Marinol. My sister's doctor prescribed some for her when she was sick and it was the only thing that helped her to gain some weight. It made her high as a kite as well, but she didn't mind that!"

"Actually, Rob gave Auntie June some marijuana to smoke and she reckons it helps a lot. I was a bit shocked when I found out she was smoking the stuff – Uncle Ted as well and he's not even ill – but if it makes her feel better then what's the harm in it?"

"Precisely! I've never understood the hoo-hah that surrounds pot smoking. I keep hoping that they'll de-criminalize it like they have in Holland. Personally I've been smoking it since I was at college and it's never done me much harm."

Tallulah pauses for a moment as she dries the mugs on a tea-towel. She looks at Jeff, and then at the fridge. "Actually, there's a whole bag of it in Rob's freezer compartment. Would you like it?"

Jeff laughs. "I'd be an idiot to refuse an offer like that, but let me pay you for it. Rob always got good stuff."

"Oh, I don't want any money for it," says Tallulah as she opens the fridge and reaches inside the freezer compartment for the zip-lock bag containing the marijuana. She hands it to Jeff and he places it on the table next to the bobble-hatted teapot.

"Are you sure you don't want to keep it for yourself, or give it to your Auntie?"

"Oh, I don't smoke," explains Tallulah, "and I'd feel funny giving Auntie June a bag of drugs, even though I know she's already using it. Maybe I'll need a puff or two at some point soon, though."

"How do you mean? Have you got problems on the horizon?"

Tallulah sits opposite Jeff at the small table and clasps her hands in front of her. There is something very liberating about having these intimate conversations with total strangers. The simple fact that she probably won't see any of these people again is enough to encourage her revelations, as though whispering to a faceless priest through the grille of a confessional.

"I've got to have a biopsy next week. I've got a lump in my breast." Tallulah doesn't look directly at Jeff; instead she focuses on her clasped fingers and waits for his response.

"It's probably benign," he says, reaching across the table to place the palm of his hand over her clenched knuckles. "A lot of the time it's nothing more than a cyst."

"Yeah, you're right," smiles Tallulah, "there's no point in getting my knickers in a twist until I know what's going on. The thing is I've never been in hospital before and I'm more terrified of *that* than the actual lump."

"Is somebody going with you to the hospital?"

"No, it's more-or-less an in-and-out doctor's appointment. I'm having what they call a core needle biopsy; just a local anaesthetic and a needle inserted in to the lump. I don't want to involve Uncle Ted or Auntie June; they've got enough on their plate. I'd rather not tell anybody until I know if it's anything serious."

Jeff removes the tea cosy and the lid of the teapot. He peers inside and reaches for the teaspoon to poke at the teabags. "Why don't you let me take you to the hospital? I hate to think of you going through it all on your own."

"Oh no!" exclaims Tallulah hurriedly, "I'll be fine." The last thing she wants is to be fussed over, especially by somebody she barely even knows.

"I insist," says Jeff with a determined tone to his voice, "after all, you've just given me a couple of hundred quid's worth of weed so I *owe* you."

And he pops the lid back on to the pot and pours out two mugs of strong, dark tea.

The Sweetest Little Twist

"We should *really* go to London," suggests Daphne, finishing off her third sour apple martini. "I've never been and I'd love to see what it's like."

"It's grey and cold and drab," says Gideon wearily. He has just taken some ketamine to bring him down from the excess of coke he snorted earlier and his brain isn't quite in synch with his mouth. "The Brits are all uptight and repressed and ugly as shit and everybody's poor. Why do you think they all come here?"

"But I'm tired of Miami, sweetheart," whines Daphne, pulling her little girl face and sighing. "It'll be the same old, same old all through the winter; I'll be forced to work the parties and the clubs and I'm getting real tired of having to deal with all those dirty old men who think that twenty bucks shoved under my garter belt will buy them a lot more than a fucking lap-dance. You're rich, sweetheart! It's degrading having to go out to work every night when everybody knows I'm your girlfriend. Let's go to London and torment Ronnie!"

Gideon shifts slightly to reposition himself amidst the mound of white cushions that have been strewn across the shaded balcony to create a kind of Morocco-meets-Florida ambiance. He doesn't want to talk about Veronica at this precise moment in time, he just wants to kick-back and enjoy the high. "She managed to get away with a measly ten thousand bucks, Daph; that's all. I think the least I owe her is *that* after fifteen years of marriage."

"I thought you hated her, Gid, I thought you despised her and wanted to see her dead?"

"I never said *dead.*"

"You said you wanted her to rot in hell. Isn't that the same thing?"

"Listen, Daphne, I've cut her off. She's got no money and no home and no work and if she tries to come back to the States I'll have the fucking feds on her as soon as she steps through customs."

"But that could get *me* in deep shit, Gideon. It was me who orchestrated that entire fraudulent bank transfer for Ronnie, it was me who pushed her to do it; she was all ready to run off with nothing just because she thought you were screwing around with an HIV positive whore."

Gideon laughs. "Man, that was the sweetest little *twist* you came up with, Daph, you are one nasty bitch! I would never have thought of that one. I hope I never get on the wrong side of you, that's for sure!"

"She cheated on you, Gideon! She was fucking that guy James for nearly two years behind your back; they were talking about running off together."

"And James conveniently disappeared leaving our poor, broken-hearted Ronnie in a state of total collapse for six fucking months! You don't think I derived *some* quantity of satisfaction from that? The thing is, Daphne, you've always been jealous as hell of Ronnie and you've been looking to get in to my pants since the first day you laid eyes on me. Don't you think it's time to let go and move on?"

"Sometimes I think you're still in love with her," pouts sultry Daphne, tugging on the narrow strap that holds up her bathing suit.

"And sometimes I think you're fucking crazier than she is."

Quagmire

The money spell hangs above the door of Brown Bread Cottage; a five pound note wrapped in a corn husk and bound-up with green wool. Ursula has sprinkled oils and herbs around and muttered an incantation and now Nicole's future prosperity is suspended on a rusty nail just beneath the sign that reads 'duck or grouse'. She now has eight pounds forty-nine pence in her purse (not including the five pound note she reluctantly gave-up for Ursula's spell) and poverty stares her in the face every time she looks in the bathroom mirror. Her tan is fading and she's got a spot right in the crease of her nose. Dark circles and puffiness, open-pores and frown-lines seem magnified since she came to Brown Bread Cottage and she is almost certain that her Buns of Steel are turning in to yesterday's dough.

There is a reason why prison sentences are usually more lenient for wealthy, educated criminals than they are for the poor and stupid; the judges believe that someone accustomed to luxury and privilege will suffer so much more than somebody who is unfazed by a dirty toilet and cockroaches. It is just another example of how unfair the class system is, underlining the simple fact that the more money you have the easier life invariably is. So now that poor Nicole is down to her last few pounds she is beginning to envy people like Tallulah and Ursula who appear to be perfectly happy with their meagre earnings and their unspectacular lives.

She is down to the final phial of oxygenated skin serum that costs $200.00 from her Miami Beach dermatologist. Yesterday she was forced to wash her hair with the Vosene somebody had left behind in the bathroom cabinet and without conditioner Nicole's hair is now stringy and dull. No more leek and walnut sausages from the farm shop for Nicole, no more Duchy of Cornwall biscuits; it's Walls' bangers and Asda's own-brand ginger nuts from now on.

As she sits in the oak-beamed living room of the cottage Nicole's brain is tumbling round and round like a washing machine and the colours of her thoughts are dirty grey and nicotine yellow. Her main concern is how to get her hands on some cash because she realizes that the search for a job, no matter how menial it might be, will take time and then she'll have to wait at least a week before she receives any pay. Eight pounds forty-nine pence isn't going to last her very long and her rental car is almost on empty. She left all of her credit cards behind in Miami, assuming, foolishly, that she would never need them again; that Veronica Rustin and her excellent credit record would fail to exist upon the creation of her new persona. American Express, Visa and Mastercard must be wondering what's happened; not a single charge on any of her accounts in the past week. Stocks will fall, interest rates will rise and the state of the American economy is at risk without people like Veronica to keep things afloat with their excessive and extravagant spending.

It will be impossible to get credit here in England with her bank account empty, no job, no home equity and absolutely no financial prospects. She can't borrow money from friends she hasn't spoken to in years and her father barely gets enough money each month to pay his gas bill so she can't go running to him. Nicole never thought that she could be in such an impossible situation; people who have always been reasonably wealthy can't imagine life without money. Unlike the impoverished citizens of fifty years ago most people in the twenty-first century have wallets stuffed with plastic cards; flexible friends that will help them to live above their means when times are tough. There is no such thing as 'penniless' in today's world and yet that is what Nicole is facing; a life of penury, something that went out with work-houses and child labour.

Nicole twists her fingers together until her knuckles turn white and her rings cut in to her flesh. And suddenly, like a sky-diver plummeting to certain death she feels the upward tug as her emergency parachute unfurls and she is dragged from danger just before she hits the ground. Her stomach flips over, turning a single somersault.

Her rings! She can sell her rings!

The sheer panic of her situation had temporarily blinded Nicole to the fact that she is wearing enough jewellery to feed an average family of four for five years. Her platinum and diamond wedding ring is from Tiffany and cost somewhere in the region of twelve thousand dollars. Her emerald-cut engagement ring is probably worth about five thousand and combining that with the two David Yurman *pavé* diamond rings Nicole bought for herself she must have somewhere in the region of twenty thousand dollars worth of bling on her hands alone. Then there's the Cartier watch, the diamond and white gold tennis bracelet, the diamond studs and the necklace Gideon gave to her for Valentine's Day three years ago; all of these things combined could easily total another ten thousand so even if Nicole can only get fifty percent of their worth she could still have a substantial amount of money to work with until she sorts herself out.

The rich, as opposed to the poor, somehow always find a way to claw their way out of the quagmire. If somebody like Tallulah ever found herself in a similar dilemma she wouldn't get very far trying to pawn her nine karat gold sleepers or her Argos love-heart pendant.

Suddenly energized and enthusiastic, Nicole rushes upstairs to change in to something more presentable. She will spend her last few pounds on some petrol for the car and she will drive in to Manchester where there must be some reputable jewellers who will be more than happy to buy her treasures at a substantial discount. It is important that she presents herself as intelligent and sophisticated; she doesn't want the disdainful staff of snooty jewellery shops to look down their noses at her as though she's standing at their door with a begging bowl in her hands. She will think of a suitable sob-story involving an errant husband or an unexpected tax debt that is threatening to bankrupt her; it shouldn't be difficult for a woman like Nicole; she's been using her manipulative charm on people for years.

1:7

And while Nicole prepares to sell her jewels Tallulah sits at Rob's computer and exposes herself to the amazing scope of the World Wide Web. Jeff has shown her how to log on to the internet and how to utilize the search engines. It is like having a complete set of Encyclopaedia Britannica spread out across the desk in front of her but without any of the complicated cross-referencing or shuffling of pages.

Breast cancer is the most common malignancy in women and the second leading cause of cancer death (exceeded by lung cancer in 1985). Breast cancer is three times more common than all gynaecologic malignancies put together. The incidence of breast cancer has been increasing steadily from an incidence of 1:20 in 1960 to 1:7 women today.

There are thousands of entries for Tallulah to read and each one seems to be more frightening than the last. There are clinical studies, statistics and personal accounts of symptoms, treatments and preventative measures. There are photos of malignancies, mis-shaped breasts and inverted nipples to turn Tallulah's stomach and she has to avert her eyes to stare out of Rob's bedroom window otherwise she might be sick.

One woman writes:

The first doctor I saw diagnosed it as a subcutaneous cyst and declared it was nothing to worry about. I was flooded with relief. She gave me a choice---leave it alone or have it surgically removed, if I was uncomfortable with it. Fortunately for me, I didn't want to have a lump on my chest, so I opted to have it removed. The biopsy report showed that it was a malignant tumour. The surgeon who removed it told me he recommended a radical mastectomy and a partial mastectomy of the unaffected breast, as a preventive measure because lobular invasive carcinoma has a higher risk of being bilateral and/or recurrent. I was shocked and numb. I left the doctor's office with very little information about the disease and no idea what I was gong to do about it. I felt like I had just been given a death sentence.

And another:

It's hard to imagine, until it happens to you, what if feels like to be told you have a malignant tumour growing inside you. I imagined the worst. I immediately pictured a black, spongy substance like mould creeping around inside me where healthy pink tissue should be instead. It was particularly hard for me to hear this diagnosis and the recommended treatment because my father and brother-in-law were having chemotherapy treatments at the time for aggressive lung and brain cancers. Their prognosis was not good and I felt mine would be just as bleak.

Tallulah tries to imagine what she would do if the doctor gave her six months to live. It is the kind of frivolous speculation that schoolgirls whisper about when they're sleeping over at friends' houses. Tallulah has never spent the night at a friend's house but she remembers the conversations they used to have huddled together at the back of the art room during lunch break.

"Would you rather be blind or deaf?"

And the unanimous answer was always 'deaf'.

"What would you do for a thousand pounds?"

Tallulah still remembers that Alison Wetherall, the slag of the upper fifth, said she'd do *anything* for a thousand quid except murder somebody. Tallulah was more fussy and said that she would consider kissing the chemistry teacher, Mr. Wapplington, but she wouldn't eat a lump of poo.

"Not even for a thousand quid?" asked Alison incredulously.

"Ugh! No. I couldn't eat even a *teaspoon* of poo," replied Tallulah, screwing up her nose at the mere thought of such a disgusting act.

"For a thousand quid I'd eat poo that was still warm."

And Tallulah had no reason to disbelieve her reckless friend.

Tallulah has spent forty-five years doing nothing with her life. Her childhood aspirations were predictable and boring; to meet a nice boy, to get married and to have children. When those dreams failed to materialize she spent her time looking forward to holidays, weekends, sunny days and Christmas bonuses but Tallulah has never been on an aeroplane, visited another country or sat out in the sun for more than fifteen minutes without coming out in a heat rash. Her Christmas bonus last year was a twenty pound note and a box of Terry's All Gold.

So what would she really do with her final few months on Earth? Well, for starters she'd definitely sell her house or, if that wasn't fast enough, she'd get one of those home equity loans and go on a world cruise. But would she feel happy travelling around from country to country with a load of strangers when she could be at home, surrounded by familiar objects and waking up every morning in her own bed? It might be preferable to just pack-in her job, spend her days lunching and shopping and going to the pictures every afternoon. She could buy a second television for her bedroom, a satellite dish, groceries from Waitrose and get her hair done in one of the fancy salons. She might even consider having a reckless love affair with the bloke from the chip shop who always gives her the biggest piece of cod. Sex! Yes sex! She can't possibly think about dying without knowing what it's like to get shagged. She might even *pay* for it and get herself a man who looks like a movie star.

But the thought of sex isn't quite as appealing as it ought to be and Tallulah quickly crosses that off her mental list. When you're worried that the lump in your breast might be cancerous the last thing you feel like doing is ripping your bra off in front of a total stranger and expecting him to arouse your passions. Maybe she really is better off not knowing about sex; what you've never had you never miss. It's probably messy and humiliating and – at her time of life – painful. Her vagina is probably nothing more than a dried-up impenetrable prune; shrunken and shrivelled with all the juice sucked out of it by years of neglect.

No matter how big a prune may be
He's always full of wrinkles
A baby prune is like his dad
But he's not wrinkled half so bad
You may have wrinkles on your face
But a prune he has them every place
So, no matter how big a prune may be
He's always full of wrinkles.

Tallulah watches Ursula as she steps in to her garden to peg out some washing on the line. A breeze catches the hem of her skirt and sends it billowing around her ankles. From a distance Ursula looks much younger than she does close-up. With her long hair hanging loose she could be a young girl; you don't see many women over forty with hair that long these days. If Tallulah had hair like that she would put it up in a bun or learn how to fashion one of those French-plaits that look so smart with a fabric bow tied at the nape of the neck. But Tallulah doesn't have the patience for long hair; she prefers to maintain the same style she's had since she was at school. Her hairdresser, Shirley, reckons she'd look nice with a bit of curl but Tallulah prefers to keep her centre parting and lacquered 'wings'. She looks like she ought to be snogging Tucker in the playground at *Grange Hill* but she's not thirteen any more! The only time she ever tried something different was in 1979 when she decided to get an Afro. She can still remember the broken combs and the gallons of Silvikrin conditioner it took to stop it looking like a Brillo pad on top of her head.

At one o clock the estate agent comes round to take a look at the house. Most of the rooms have been stripped bare of their knick-knacks, pictures and clutter but instead of making the house look larger and cleaner the lack of personal items merely makes everything look shabby and neglected. Tallulah assumes that Rob never did any decorating himself and merely moved in to the house and kept the existing wallpaper, paint and curtains. The carpets are cheap and heavily patterned and now that the rugs are gone you can see where the weave has worn thin or become stained. The wallpaper in the bedrooms is faded and scuffed, in patterns that are more suited to an old lady than a man in his forties. On the stairs and landing the heavily over-painted woodchip is coming apart at the seams like the rind of an old grapefruit and most of the curtains are the ready-made kind manufactured from thick, coarse-textured fabric (except for the kitchen where the curtains are made from rose-patterned fibreglass).

"Is it all electric?" asks Darren, the young estate agent in his Prince of Wales check as he twists the knobs on the cooker, "no gas?"

Tallulah makes him a cup of tea while he goes down to the cellar. She can hear him banging around down there; tapping on walls and messing around with the electrical box.

"Got a bit of damp down there," he says as he comes back in to the kitchen, making notes on his clipboard. "Mind if I have a nosy about upstairs?"

It strikes Tallulah as sad that Rob's home has been reduced to nothing more than a collection of empty, dilapidated rooms. She wishes that the house looked a bit more promising for potential buyers but, unfortunately, Auntie June and Uncle Ted don't have the resources to tart the place up for re-sale. There are those programmes on the telly where experts come in and show you what you can do to improve your chances of selling and they use hidden cameras to listen in on what prospective buyers say about the place as they wander round. It's embarrassing to watch the owners' expressions when somebody wrinkles up their faces and says there's a funny smell or makes a snide remark about the choice of paint colour. She can hear Darren running the bath taps and flushing the toilet and he's probably wishing he was in a nice clean Barrett house with leaded windows and beige carpets.

"It's a shame," he comments as he comes back down to get his mug of tea, "this is a fabulous location; very desirable for city folk who want a weekend place or somebody who works in Manchester or Sheffield and wants to play at living in the country. But it needs a lot of work to bring it up to standard and there's not much in the way of character, is there?"

Tallulah glances around the kitchen and has to agree. These days people want stainless steel appliances and granite countertops, they prefer gas central heating and double-glazing. It's not a big house and it's all straight-lines with no surprises. But the view across the fields from the kitchen window is priceless and Tallulah can imagine a nice conservatory instead of this cheap little lean-to. The living room and dining room could be knocked-through to make a decent-sized lounge and there's plenty of space in the cellar for storing things or even for making a utility room. But these things cost money and it's probably not worth the investment on a place like this.

"What're the neighbours like?" asks Darren, making conversation as he sips his tea and burns his top lip.

"Very nice," answers Tallulah, tempted to tell him that Ursula is a witch. "She lives on her own, she's very friendly."

"You've had quite a job sorting all this stuff out. Mr. Clegg tells me you're their niece; it must have been quite a shock when your cousin got killed like that. Lucky for Mr. and Mrs. Clegg they've got you to help out. You live in Chesterfield, don't you?"

"Yes, up by the spire; Grey Street."

"Oh yes, I know that area. We just sold a house round there a couple of weeks ago. Sturdy little houses, those are, and very convenient for the town centre and the station. You own or rent?"

"I own it. I've lived there all my life. I inherited it when my mum and dad passed away." Tallulah scratches at some congealed food on the draining board with her fingernail.

"We got a hundred and forty-nine grand for the one on Winsdale Street and it hadn't had anything done to it since it was built. Old lady lived there but she had to go in to a home, poor dear. Nice sized kitchens and three decent bedrooms; perfect for a young couple just starting out or a little family."

"How much do you think you can get for this place, then?"

"Hrm," speculates Darren with a cursory glance down the hallway, "I'd say somewhere in the region of one-thirty, one-thirty-five tops. It needs twenty or thirty grand spending on it to bring it up to scratch and there's not many round here can afford that kind of money when they're stretching themselves thin with a mortgage. If you were right in Castleton you'd have a better chance but this is a bit of a no-man's land. It'd be different if it was Manchester or Leeds; folk don't mind investing in the city but when they're buying in the country they want something quaint; something *old* with beams and roses round the door."

"Well I hope it doesn't take too long to sell," worries Tallulah, "the mortgage payments are too much for Auntie June and Uncle Ted to keep up and our Rob only put a small down-payment on the place."

"We might have to price it accordingly," says Darren as he scribbles in the margin of his notes. "Anyway, I'll take a quick look round the outside and then I'll be off. Thanks for the tea, love. I'll be in touch with Mr. & Mrs. Clegg later this afternoon."

And as Tallulah sees him out Ursula pops her head out of her own front door and invites Tallulah round for a chat.

"Estate agent?" she asks, in a stage whisper as the two women watch Darren disappear round the side of the house. Tallulah nods.

"Thought so; you can spot 'em a mile off." And she pulls the broken fence a little bit wider so that Tallulah can squeeze through without dirtying her skirt.

The Fusty Smell of Charity

Nicole is fuming.

She has spent the entire day trailing from one jeweller to another and not one of them showed the slightest interest in buying anything from her. She is exhausted and hungry but her purse is empty and she wasted her last few pounds on buying petrol to get to Manchester. Gold sandals are not the most practical footwear in the middle of November and she has rubbed a blister on the heel of her foot. Her Burberry jacket is not thick enough to keep out the keen northern wind and without sustenance she feels light-headed and fragile.

It is five o' clock and the shops will be closing soon. The last jeweller she visited recommended a pawnbroker on Church Street and although Nicole knows she will get only a fraction of what her jewellery is worth she can't return to Castleton without *something*. She hurries through the evening streets, pushing her way irritably between the jostling crowds. It is dark and windy; pedestrians are bundled-up in hats and scarves while Nicole looks as though she's dressed for a garden party. Her nose is running and she doesn't have a tissue, her eyes are smarting from the wind and it feels as though her ear lobes are burning scarlet.

"For God's sake!" she snaps at a dawdling girl who stops dead at the corner of the street, blocking Nicole's passage.

"Excuse *me!*" responds the girl caustically and she stands on the pavement, hands on hips, glaring defiantly as Nicole manoeuvres herself past.

"Oh fuck off!" yells Nicole, all decorum lost as she hurries down the street, soliciting startled glances from passers-by.

"We're closing in ten minutes," announces the pawnbroker as soon as Nicole steps in to his shop on a gust of November wind. It is an old-fashioned establishment and there is a brass bell on a spring that tinkles as she closes the door behind her. The shop is crammed with all manner of miscellanea from bicycles to bird cages, suitcases to fur coats. The man stands behind a glass counter filled with jewellery, watches and ornaments and his expression is one of serious irritation. His sagging cardigan is fastened over his thin chest and the pockets are stuffed and gaping. He is wearing a tie but there appears to be something spilled down the front of it and he doesn't look as though he's shaved in a couple of days. The fusty smell of charity hangs in the air and Nicole feels sullied by mere proximity to this wretched place. The thought of her Tiffany rings vying for space with all this cheap tat beneath the smeared glass is enough to send her scurrying back out in to the street but this is her final chance before closing time and desperate times call for desperate measures.

"Can I help you, Madam?"

"Yes, I was wondering how much you could give me for these," and Nicole removes the two David Yurman rings from her fingers and places them on the disreputable counter in front of the equally disreputable pawnbroker. She has already decided to start with the least valuable items, hoping that maybe she can find a more respectable dealer to purchase the other things at a later date.

"Let's have a look," says the grimy little man, wiping the palms of his hands down the sides of his polyester trousers. He removes a small magnifying glass from his trouser pocket and raises it to his eye like a monocle, squinting against the glass and bringing the first ring up to his face to investigate.

"Nice piece," he concedes with a sniff. He turns the ring around between his fingers and peers inside to find the hallmark. "Platinum. Pavé diamonds," he mutters under his breath as he weighs the ring in the palm of his hand before dropping it on to a small scale.

"It's David Yurman," explains Nicole but this information doesn't appear to impress the pawnbroker as he picks up the second ring and repeats his scrutiny without saying another word.

"How much were you hoping to get for these, Madam?" He looks up at Nicole through his wire-rimmed glasses and she can see the hairs curling out of his nostrils like the legs of an insect.

"Well, they cost me a couple of thousand dollars each when I bought them two years ago."

"You bought them in America?"

Nicole nods.

"Hrm, well I might know somebody who would take these off my hands. I doubt that I'd be able to sell them here. I can offer you two hundred a piece."

"Two hundred pounds?" Nicole is dismayed.

"With today's exchange rates that's about four hundred dollars. That's the best I can do." He pushes the rings back across the counter dismissively and turns away from Nicole as though he has already lost interest.

"How about five hundred for both of them?" she asks.

"Two hundred a piece, take it or leave it."

Nicole has no alternative but to take it. The pawnbroker counts out the crumpled bank notes and places them in an untidy heap on the counter.

"Now, if you don't mind, I'm closing."

Nicole picks up the cash, stuffs it in to her bag and leaves the shop without saying goodbye or thank you. The brass bell tinkles merrily as she steps out in to the street and a sudden gust of wind scatters paper bags and sheets of newspaper across the pavement. Nicole can't wait to get back to the car and to hurry out of Manchester as quickly as possible. She feels tawdry and cheap and she can't wait to get home to soak in a nice hot bath. The city feels threatening, as though the buildings and the traffic conspire to surround her with malicious intent. The faces of the passers-by are pinched and indifferent and they hurry forward, propelled by the wind and their desire to get home to the fireplace and a nice cup of tea. Nicole is invisible to them.

She stops at a coffee shop to get a latté and an oat-bran muffin. The warmth and the aroma surround her like the arms of an old friend and she looks around at the crowded tables where friends meet to exchange gossip, where lovers share confidences. There was a time when she was one of them but now she feels like an intruder and paranoia is setting in. She feels as though the server is looking at her with suspicion when she places her order and she almost expects him to lift up the twenty pound note to the light to make sure it is real.

There is a seat at the long counter by the window so Nicole squeezes in beside the wall, removes an unfolded newspaper from the stool and positions herself so she can stare straight out in to the street. Her reflection is superimposed against a background of stationery traffic and every time another person enters the café there is a ripple of cold air that follows them, nipping at their heels like a hungry dog.

She notices that there is a computer with a sign offering free internet access. Nobody is using it so Nicole gets up and takes her coffee and muffin over to the desk and logs in to her e-mail account.

There is no response from Daphne and nothing more from Gideon but there is a message from a superficial acquaintance called Fleur; one of the many sycophants who hang around on the Miami scene with nothing better to do than gossip.

Hi Doll! Haven't heard from you in a while, what're you up to? Thought I'd see you at Nico's place on Saturday night; it was wild! Jordan saw Gideon the other night on Lincoln Road having dinner with Daphne and a couple of other people; apparently they were all off their heads on something or other. I've heard rumours that Daphne and Jake are splitting-up, is that true?

If you want to meet up for a cocktail at the Sky Bar next Friday there's a promotion for the agency. Jessica Simpson's on the guest list!

Hope you're not too pissed about Courtney. I doubt that she'll go through with it and she's not bright enough to follow through with a paternity suit so Gideon's probably off the hook. Scandal, scandal! Don't you just love The Beach! Rumour has it that she's going to marry Shawn and move back to LA where she belongs. Out of sight, out of mind, sweetie!

Kisses, Fleur x

Courtney pregnant? Nicole stares at the computer screen and her vision blurs with angry tears. How many more indignities is she supposed to bear? Nicole can imagine them all – the entire mindless Miami crowd – whispering and speculating with gleeful abandon in every VIP lounge across the beach. Gideon has made her the laughing stock of Miami.

Nicole decides to throw caution to the wind and she replies to Fleur's e-mail, informing her that she has left Gideon and moved away from Florida. She also drops in a few unsubtle suggestions that he may be playing with some of the local rent boys. 'I couldn't continue to live with his cheating and his lies,' she writes, 'he's always been bisexual but his obsession with under-age boys was becoming too much for me to handle and I just couldn't take any more so I had to leave.' Nicole adds, at the end of her message, 'please keep this to yourself, darling, you know how quickly malicious talk gets around.'

Press Send. Message Delivered.

That will set the rumour-mills aflame. Nicole breaks off another piece of her muffin and washes it down with the remains of her coffee. If she is a 'woman scorned' then watch out Gideon because her fury has only just started to bubble to the surface.

Ripped Asunder

Somebody has broken in to Number Two.
Tallulah returns from the shops to find the kitchen door forced open and a small pane of glass is broken. Floorboards have been prised up to expose gaping foundations filled with rubble, furniture has been turned over; empty drawers scattered violently across the room. The sofa has been ripped asunder with sharp knives so that the foam and stuffing oozes out from the slashed fabric like the intestines of an upholstered beast. Most of the boxes so carefully packed by Tallulah have been emptied across the floor, scattering the contents, shattering glass, breaking china.

Who could have done all this in such a short space of time? Tallulah was only gone for an hour or so. Admittedly she hadn't intended on walking home in the dark but she forgot to look at the time when she went out and she doesn't wear a watch.

She looks around at the chaotic mess and destruction and she bursts in to tears, sinking down on the bottom landing to bury her face in her hands. All her hard work destroyed. The house violated and vandalized by mindless yobs – most probably – for who else would cause such wanton havoc in a house that has nothing to steal.

Ursula's car isn't in the drive so she must be out. The cold wind whips around the corner of the house and rattles the loose fence between the houses. The tops of the trees sway and groan against an impenetrably dark sky. There are no stars tonight.

Tallulah calls the police and they say they'll have somebody round within the hour.

Pulp

At Brown Bread Cottage Nicole is listening to her Twankydillo CD. She has lit a fire and the wind creates hollow sounds in the chimney as the heat begins to rise. With four hundred pounds in her bag she feels an enormous sense of relief; it's amazing what money can do for a person's sense of wellbeing. She wonders if Ursula's money-spell hanging above the doorway had anything to do with her change of luck? OK, so it wasn't exactly a change of luck or a miracle wind-fall but surely spells should be open for interpretation? It was Ursula who said that a spell is merely an intention that must be visualized and if that intention is strong enough then anything is possible. This morning she had eight pounds forty-nine pence and this evening she has four hundred; the spell worked!

Of course she has to formulate some kind of plan otherwise the cash in her bag will quickly disappear before she has time to flog her other jewellery. The cottage is paid up until the end of the month so her only necessity – for now at least – is food and petrol. She will have to continue rinsing her knickers through and alternating between the yellow trousers and the calf-length summer dress that can be scrunched in a ball and left un-ironed. If her tan continues to fade she will soon have to start wearing pantyhose (she still can't get back in to the hang of calling them 'tights'; there's just something so *parsimonious* about that generic term used by all and sundry to describe everything from 5 denier sheers to those thick woollen things that schoolgirls in

1930's comic books were forced to wear under their gymslips.) Clothing, at this stage in the game, is a luxury and if the worst comes to the worst Nicole will have to swallow her pride and pop in to a local branch of H&M.

Menial work is out of the question. There is no way a woman of Nicole's social standing can consider serving Whoppers in a paper hat at Burger King or scrubbing the toilets of women whose homes reek of New Money and Ambi-Pur. Minimal wage is not an option for Nicole. She must patch together some kind of *curriculum vitae* and print it up on nice paper, hoping that no one will bother to get in touch with the fictional employers she lists in the United States. She knows her strengths and her weaknesses so there's no point in pretending to be something she's not; but a little elaboration can't hurt. Party-planner, visual merchandiser, set designer, photographic stylist, organizer of corporate events; these are all distinct possibilities. At a push she might consider retail work (designer-label fashion or up-market home furnishings ONLY!) but it is notoriously under-paid and she's not really in a position to take advantage of the staff discount. She will pop over to use Tallulah's computer again tomorrow and see what she can find on-line.

This evening she is celebrating the end of her taxing day with a Cornish pasty and baked beans. There's a reality show on TV; minor British celebrities she's never heard of battling to stay alive in the middle of Dartmoor with nothing more than a barn full of 1920's farming equipment. What she would really enjoy right now is a glass or two of champagne but, of course, when you're on a tight budget champagne is one of the luxuries of life that must fall by the wayside. Gideon always kept at least half a dozen bottles of champagne in the fridge and they drank it like most other people drink cheap chardonnay. *Veuve Clicquot* was their label of choice; not because they preferred the taste any more than, say, Möet or Bollinger, but because it was trendier. Fashionable labels apply to more than just clothing when you're wealthy; the masses stick to their annual bottles of cheap plonk at Christmas or anniversaries and bugger the indignity.

Nicole dwells for a moment on some of the privileges she left behind in Miami; those little extravagances that somehow became 'necessities'. They had 'people' come in to their condominium once a week to change the flower arrangements and water the plants. They had a maid service for cleaning, ironing and changing the bed linens. They bought their weekly groceries at the gourmet store and used a catering company for formal dinners. Shopping, for Nicole, was arranged for recreation rather than from any sense of need and she thought nothing of spending the afternoon at Bal Harbor, idly trailing the floors of Neiman Marcus clutching an array of tiny shopping bags filled with 'scientifically proven' face creams and body scrubs.

Now she wishes she had been a little more thoughtful in her preparations when she fled for England. It's true; she imagined that she would be able to buy whatever she needed once she got here, but it would have made sense to at least pack some of her old photograph albums, souvenirs and keepsakes. Some things can never be replaced. There is an art – a mind-set – to leaving behind materialism and it is something that Nicole finds difficult. If she wanted to live a life of austerity she would have dedicated her life to Christ or retired to a cave in Tibet but she never imagined that a country cottage in the middle of the English countryside would become her hermitage.

Bring out the cat o' nine tails, let the flagellation begin.

There is one very worrying aspect to Nicole's current situation (besides the financial concerns) and that is the simple fact that if Gideon knows about her secret bank account then he is also aware of her pseudonym and, presumably, her whereabouts. It doesn't take a rocket scientist to follow her paper-trail once they know the name on her travel papers. Will the retrieval of Gideon's money absolve Nicole of her crimes against him or will he continue to pursue her just for the sport of it? And is it possible that Daphne is in personal danger, since it was she who helped Nicole to organize her escape route? How else could Gideon have discovered the details of Nicole's camouflaged banking system? Without a phone Nicole is unable to check up on her friend and, as yet, there is no response to her e-mail messages. Would it be wise to contact the Miami police (anonymously, of course) and ask them to check up on Daphne's well-being?

Nicole checks her watch; it isn't yet nine o' clock. She wonders if Tallulah would mind her dropping by to use the computer for half an hour. It's not as though somebody like Tallulah will be actually be *doing* anything and she probably eats her 'tea' at five-thirty like most working-class people in this part of the world. If she could just send an e-mail message to some division of the Miami Beach police or a reporter at the *Miami Herald,* tipping them off that Daphne is in danger, it would make her feel better. She would never forgive herself if Daphne was hurt or, worse yet, dead. Oh yes, Nicole is very aware of the lengths Gideon will go to when crossed. She thinks of Tyrone Daly; found strangled in a dumpster in the Arts District and her mind turns to

James, the love of her life, killed in a speed boat accident that wasn't an accident at all.

Gideon the bastard! Gideon the vindictive, drug-crazed, egocentric slimebucket who surely deserves to wither and perish under hideous circumstances. Nicole's anger is fermenting inside; it bubbles and fizzes as though alive with yeast and sugar and she can feel it turning to hate and loathing. She no longer recalls the sweet, romantic, funny young man she met all those years ago when life seemed so uncomplicated and joyful. That person no longer exists; he has been swallowed whole by the manipulative, lazy, self-destructive sleazeball manufactured and corrupted by the kind of lifestyle Miami is famous for. Life is too short for regret but, at this moment in time, Nicole regrets bitterly her wasted life with Gideon. She was independent, successful, young and beautiful when she met him and now, fifteen years later, she is nothing more than the squeezed-out pulp of her former self.

She puts on her sturdy walking shoes, brushing off the bits of dried mud and grass in to the hearth. She grabs her Burberry jacket and car keys and she hurries out of Brown Bread Cottage. The wind has grown stronger and it whips up small cyclones of air as Nicole hurries down the path. Leaves and debris rustle and swirl through the garden and down the dark lane as though pursued by something wild and uncontrolled.

It only takes a few minutes for Nicole to reach Tallulah's house and when she gets there she is alarmed to see a police car parked in the driveway alongside a pick-up truck. Every window of the house is brightly illuminated. Nicole's immediate reaction is to turn her car around and to leave as quickly as possible. As unlikely as it might seem she is worried that this might have something to do with her and she wonders if

Gideon's private detective has somehow traced her e-mail message to Daphne from Tallulah's computer. Nicole committed a crime, albeit a thwarted one, and it is possible that Gideon wants full retribution for her betrayal.

As she pauses in the lane with the engine running and her foot hovering above the gas pedal the door to Number Two opens and the guy from the junk shop comes out. She recognizes him because he is wearing the same fringed jacket he had on when Nicole bought the silver-plated tea strainer from his shop. She is just about to speed away when headlights flood her rear-view mirror and Ursula's Citroën comes rattling around the corner to stop beside Nicole's car. She has no alternative but to wind down her window.

"What's going on here?" shouts Ursula.

"I don't know, I've only just arrived," replies Nicole.

Jeff walks down the pathway and leans over to peer in to Nicole's car. She opens the driver's side window and the night air gusts in to, whipping Nicole's untidy hair in to her eyes.

"What's happened?" she asks Jeff, holding her hair back and looking over at the house.

"There's been a break-in," he explains. "Vandals, maybe. They didn't take anything but they've messed up the house.

"What's that?" shouts Ursula.

"Tallulah's house has been broken in to," relays Nicole across the interior of her car.

Ursula raises her eyes in an expression of 'whatever next?' and pulls her car in to her own driveway. Nicole winds up her windows and turns off the engine. She has no alternative now but to get out of the car and join the support group.

Mindless vandalism in the middle of nowhere? Nicole is unsettled by this unlikely situation and she can't help but believe that Gideon is behind it. She should have thought twice before she jeopardized Tallulah's safety by using her computer to send messages to Miami and yet it never entered her mind that the connection would be made. And if the thugs are already here in Castleton then surely it is only a matter of time (hours?) before they get to Brown Bread Cottage.

She gets out of the car and joins Ursula and Jeff beneath the porch of Tallulah's front door. She catches a glimpse of torn-up floorboards and scattered belongings. Somebody is kneeling on the staircase, dusting the banister for fingerprints. Tallulah is visible in the kitchen, talking to a police woman with a notebook.

"I don't believe it," gasps Ursula, "there hasn't been a burglary round here for years."

"They didn't take anything," repeats Jeff. "The police are wondering if the burglars were actually looking for something specific; hence the hacked-up floorboards and the holes in the walls. This wasn't an ordinary run-of-the-mill burglary otherwise they would have grabbed the telly, the computer and the stereo system and scarpered as quickly as possible. It would have been easy; everything was already un-plugged and packed-up ready to go but they didn't take any of it."

Nicole suppresses a shiver and folds her arms across the front of her inadequate jacket.

"Come on," nudges Ursula, "let's go in to my place and put the kettle on. Jeff, tell Tallulah to come round when she's done with the police. She can sleep in the spare room tonight. She won't want to sleep in *there* on her own."

"I already offered to spend the night," says Jeff. "Tomorrow I'll fetch some hardboard and timber from the DIY place and patch up the floorboards."

Ursula turns down the corners of her mouth and raises an eyebrow but declines from comment. Nicole wonders if there is something going on between Tallulah and Jeff that she doesn't know about, but that's their business. Right now she would like to get away from the crime scene and hide in the sagging confines of Ursula's sofa with a cup of tea. Maybe it's time to tell Ursula the whole story. Maybe tonight she, Nicole, could sleep in Ursula's spare bedroom and then, tomorrow get as far away from here as possible.

Robert

If there's one thing I've learned from my many lives it's that you cannot run away from your problems. Even when you transition from one life to the next you carry the sins of your former existence with you. In a spiritual sense you can run but you can't hide and there'd be a huge amount of money saved on psychotherapy if everyone could remember what they did wrong in their past life to explain the problems they're having in their current life.

Oh yes; I suffered from depression just like thousands of other people. I took pills and sat around in group-therapy circles listening to people blather on about their petty grievances and concerns. I smoked pot and drank alcohol to try and blot out the self-doubt and lack of self-respect but I never really got to the root of my problems. Maybe if I'd tried past-life regression or hypnotherapy I might have had more success but I admit that I was a sceptic and even Ursula couldn't convince me that a crystal placed on the corresponding chakra would open my mind. But when I'm here – between lives – I can see quite clearly why I preferred rainy weather to sunshine; why I was claustrophobic; why I had an unnatural fear of horses. Learn to interpret your dreams and you're half-way to understanding.

Everyone is born with a sixth sense but very few of us are encouraged to nurture it; quite the opposite, in fact. Remember the ghosts and monsters that lurked in your childhood bedroom at night? And remember how your parents would tell you not to be silly; that ghosts and monsters don't exist? Well they do. And I'm here to prove it.

Straddling a Fault Line

Tallulah is back in Chesterfield, back at work and feeling strangely disconnected from everything that was once so familiar. The tins of red paint remain by the draining board in the kitchen and the roller has gone hard in its tray where she left it. Mr. B is feeling the pressure of his Christmas obligations and consequently Tallulah and the rest of the staff are very conscious that even when there is a momentary lull in the day's business they must endeavour to appear occupied. Sometimes Tallulah resorts to mindless tactics such as purposefully emptying a box of dressmaker's pins on the floor just so she can spend five minutes picking them up again. Time passes slowly when you're straddling a fault-line, never quite sure when a sudden seismic shift could swallow you whole.

Uncle Ted has paid Jeff a nominal amount to fix the damage caused by the burglars at Rob's house and Jeff, true to his word, accompanied Tallulah to the hospital for her biopsy. It was a simple, painless procedure but the implications run deep and Tallulah is anxious to see the doctor for the results. Everyone keeps reminding her that no news is good news but she doesn't see it that way; knowing, as she does, how busy health professionals are these days and how a patient's notes can be left unattended for many days while emergencies are dealt with elsewhere.

She has decided that if the lump is malignant she will ask them to remove both her breasts immediately. Even if there is no sign of secondary cancer elsewhere she would rather be safe than sorry and a lumpectomy, although much less traumatic, would only leave her feeling vulnerable to future problems. It would be like gouging the eye out of a peeled potato only to find upon dissection that the entire core is rotten. It's not as though she has much use for her breasts, anyway. There is no man in her life to appreciate them, no baby to suckle, and as far as Tallulah is concerned they're obsolete. She is terrified, of course, but it is the thought of the surgery and the recovery that frightens her more than the cancer. She is scared of the anaesthetic; of not waking up or of being conscious while they slice in to her flesh but finding herself unable to cry out or open her eyes. She's seen documentaries about that.

Jeff brought Rob's cooker, washing machine, tumble dryer, fridge/freezer and computer over and took away the old appliances for the dump. There are boxes of china and kitchen stuff lining Tallulah's hallway but she hasn't had the time to start unpacking any of it yet. The house feels overwhelmingly dingy and she hasn't the enthusiasm to start putting things away due to the fact that the cupboards are already filled with rubbish. It's not like you can just throw stuff in the dustbin; there are phone calls to be made and special arrangements with the council if you want them to take away anything other than the usual weekly bin-bags.

The simple fact is; the house feels dead since her sojourn at Number Two. She is ashamed of the shabbiness as though really seeing it for the first time and every evening when she gets home from work she has taken to a new routine. She microwaves something for dinner as quickly as possible in the disorganized kitchen, attempting to ignore the half-painted walls, the mounds of boxes and disrupted appliances, and takes her meal through to the living room where she eats it on her lap in front of the gas fire. With the living room door firmly closed and the lights off she can almost imagine that she isn't in the middle of Chesterfield until voices break the silence as somebody walks directly past the window or a car goes roaring down the street. The heating is on but when she emerges from her little cocoon to make her way up to bed the rest of the house feels chilled and damp.

This evening she stands in the middle of the kitchen waiting for her Cumberland pie to beep. It was a particularly tiresome day at work because Mrs. Delray came in and demanded attention for the entire afternoon while she was being fitted for an all-in-one. As much as Tallulah envies Mrs. Delray she also secretly despises her. Tallulah's indisposition towards Mr. B's privileged clients has become increasingly apparent since she returned from her fortnight's holiday. Yesterday she told a particularly irritating customer to 'calm down for heaven's sake' when she flew off the handle over an uneven hem. And just this morning she purposefully stabbed a needle in to the shoulder blade of a whining cow who refused to keep still while being adjusted from behind. It is as though Tallulah no longer has the patience to pander to the whims and foibles of these spoilt rich old bags since she experienced life as a lady of leisure in Castleton. Do any of these women care that Tallulah might have cancer? Would any of them give a toss about her welfare if they thought they might not get their stupid corsets in time for their Christmas parties?

When your health is jeopardised and mortality rears its ugly head there is a distortion of perspective and suddenly the trivial aspects of life buzz around your head like an annoying bluebottle. When the alarm goes off at seven every morning you feel like hurling the clock at the wall and pulling the duvet up over your head. When you miss the bus by thirty seconds and the driver refuses to acknowledge your ungainly sprint in his rear-view mirror you feel like prostrating yourself across the pavement and hammering your fists against the concrete until they bleed. And when a customer refuses to say please or thank you after you've just presented her with the entire stock of black lace cami-knickers you have to stop yourself from picking up a pair and swatting her across the face with them. Is it worth it for nine thousand a year?

A plan has been formulating itself in the back of Tallulah's mind these past few days and as she watches her Cumberland pie turning listlessly inside the microwave she wonders if she dare consider acting upon it. Rob's house has gone on the market and Uncle Ted reckons they'll consider taking two thousand less if somebody without contingencies makes an offer. If Tallulah was to sell this house, by the time she'd paid all the relevant fees and taxes she'd still be able to buy Rob's house with a few thousand to spare. The main drawback is the location of Rob's house and the lack of public transport. Jeff has offered to give her a few refresher lessons in his van but she'd still have to buy a second-hand car and there wouldn't be any money left to do-up the house once she moved in.

There is nothing worse than having a dream just inches away from your grasp; it is worse than having an itch in the middle of your back and nothing to reach it with. Tallulah has lain awake at night trying to figure out a solution but, so far, her mind just continues to turn around and around like the bubbling cheesy crust of her Cumberland pie. She has never wanted anything as much as she wants this and the taste of it is bitter at the back of her tongue. The last time she was so het-up about anything was when she begged her mum to buy her a Raleigh Chopper when she was twelve. Unfortunately Choppers were considered too expensive and too vigorously masculine for a little girl and so she ended up with a pink bicycle with a basket on the front and streamers dangling from the hand-grips.

The microwave pings and the Cumberland pie is ready. Tallulah levers it out with the aid of a tea-towel and dumps it unceremoniously on to a plate. The smell of minced beef and onion straggles through the chilled air of the kitchen and Tallulah realizes that she has lost her appetite. The prospect of another ready-made dinner in front of the gas fire fills her with misery and she feels on the verge of tears. She feels unaccountably trapped and alone and the house seems to hum with complacency around her. Without Mum and Dad to keep this place alive it has become nothing more than a wounded memory. Tallulah can no longer associate these rooms with her childhood and she would rather live in Rob's empty house with no curtains, no carpets and no telly than continue this motionless existence alone. At least in Castleton she would have Ursula and Jeff for company and even Nicole, although somewhat stuck-up, was more fun than the people who live round here.

She calls Jeff but gets no reply. She calls Ursula
and is envious when she hears the sound of music and
laughter in the background when the phone is picked-up.
She can envision Ursula's comfy-cosy living room
flickering by firelight and candles; cushions and shawls
tossed from the sofa to the floor and the coffee table
littered with coffee mugs, wine glasses and books. The
thought of all that disorganized richness strikes a harsh
chord in Tallulah's heart and she realizes that she is in
danger of sobbing down the phone.

"Is everything all right, duck?" asks Ursula,
picking up on Tallulah's tremulous 'hello'.

"Not really," sighs Tallulah, clenching her jaw to
staunch the emotion that threatens to burst forth at any
moment, "I really miss you."

"Aw, well we miss you as well, duck. It's not the
same having the house standing empty right next-door. I
got used to hearing your telly through my bedroom wall
at night. Jeff's here with Petra and Martin; it's a kind of
spontaneous birthday party for Petra, she's reached the
grand old age of twenty-two."

"I wish I was there with you all. It's my day off
tomorrow and I've got bugger-all to do. I suppose I
should start unpacking some of these boxes but I haven't
got the inclination at the moment. I think I'm
depressed."

"Why don't you come over here? You can spend
the night and go back to Chesterfield tomorrow after
tea."

"Oh no, Ursula, it's already half-past seven,"
argues Tallulah, although she's desperately tempted to
hop in a cab and head right over.

"The night is young!" announces Ursula with a
trill in her voice, "get your arse in to gear, call a taxi and

you'll be here in time for Chinese; we've only just ordered it."

"Well, if you're sure…" But Tallulah needs no further persuasion. She calls the taxi firm, dashes upstairs to throw a few things in to a carrier bag and just has time to change in to her denim skirt before the cabbie is pipping outside in the street. It's an extravagance she can ill afford but it's not as though she throws her money around on a regular basis and the lure of an evening at Ursula's house is better than any pill the doctor could prescribe.

Good Shit

"I refuse to keep calling you Tallulah," announces Petra across the debris of Chinese take-away on Ursula's coffee table. "It makes you sound like a second-rate showgirl in a Charlie Chaplin film." She is drunk and quite possibly stoned because Jeff is passing around a joint. "Don't you have any nicknames? What did they call you at school?"

Tallulah shakes her hand at the joint as it is proffered to her by Martin and smiles to show that she's not prudish, just not partial. He hands it to Ursula.

"My mum always called me by my full name, but my dad used to call me Tally. It's stuck with my relatives but at school the kids used to call me Tar."

"Tar sounds too much like Shell or Shaz," laughs Petra, swigging back more red wine, "I vote for Tally."

"Tally," says Jeff, trying the name on for size, "it's got a nice ring to it, kind of like Sally."

"Tally Ho!" jokes Martin, mimicking the riding of a horse and slapping his backside.

"Personally I like Tallulah," chimes in Ursula, "it's got a kind of faded grandeur to it. I've never met another Tallulah in my life before."

"It sounds like a *drag* name," exhales Martin on a pungent stream of smoke.

"Well I'm named after the fucking dog on Blue Peter," groans Petra, "so I can't really pass judgement on *anyone's* name!"

"Tally, Tally, Tally..." repeats Jeff. His has sunk down amidst the cushions on the sofa and he is slurring his words slightly.

"You're stoned, mate," laughs Petra.

"This is good shit," nods Ursula, appraising the joint between her fingers before taking another drag.

"Your Robs'," mumbles Jeff, glancing at Tallulah with bleary eyes, "bloody good shit."

"I haven't smoked pot in yonks," grins Martin, leaning back against the arm of the sofa and pulling his feet up under him, "it's so sixties!"

"Well it's better than doing all that other crap," rebukes Ursula, "all that E and G and K. Toxic poison that stuff is."

"A bit of E now and then is fun and the occasional snort of Charlie but that's my lot."

"I know what you get up to, Martin" jokes Ursula, flipping her hair over one shoulder and reaching for her wine glass, "you'll take whatever's offered you."

"Hey, listen to the original Acid Queen over there! Wasn't it you who spent most of your art college years tripping on LSD?"

"Oh everybody was doing it back then," laughs Ursula, "it was practically mandatory. Anyway, I'm a witch so I'm supposed to take mind-altering substances."

"I've never taken anything," admits Tallulah with a shake of her head, "nobody at school ever even *talked* about drugs, it was thought *bad* just to smoke and drink cider back then."

"You should have gone to college, duck. That's when things start to get more interesting."

"College…" croaks Jeff from beneath his mound of cushions, "best years of my life."

"I was expected to go straight to work when I was sixteen," says Tallulah, "all us working-class kids did the same thing, only the posh kids went to college and university."

"Well there was none more working-class than my family," reflects Ursula wistfully, "but thankfully my mother was a bit of a thwarted artist and she pushed me to go to college. I wasn't that fussed myself but I was glad when I realized how *not* like school it was. You could call the lecturers by their first names and hang out with them at the pub at lunchtime and you could dye your hair and listen to Tangerine Dream while you were tripping on 'shrooms. Brilliant!"

"What course did you take at Art College?" asks Tallulah.

"I did a foundation course and then went on to do two years of pottery."

"Do you do any pottery now?"

"No. The only things I mould from clay these days are bits and pieces for my spells."

"Like voodoo dolls?" asks Tallulah uneasily.

"Oh yes, duck, *voodoo* dolls!" And Ursula widens her eyes in mock horror.

The conversation is interrupted by a sudden knock at the front door. Ursula looks up at the clock and says "who the hell can that be at this time of night?" She levers herself up from the chair and goes in to the hallway to answer the door. They hear Nicole's voice apologizing for calling so late but could she use the phone?

"I thought she'd gone back to London?" whispers Petra.

"No, she came back," informs Tallulah, up-to-date with the gossip thanks to daily phone calls from Ursula. "Apparently she was worried that whoever broke in to Rob's place might have been looking for *her.*"

"Sounds a bit far fetched," shrugs Petra, "why would her husband want to do something like that?"

"According to Ursula her husband's a right bastard. Apparently he killed this bloke Nicole was carrying-on with; made it look like a boating accident."

Ursula brings Nicole in to the living room to say hello. Nicole is wearing the same yellow trousers and Burberry jacket she always wears. For somebody so posh she doesn't seem to bother much with her clothes. Actually, thinks Tallulah, she's not looking too great this evening; her hair is lank and pulled roughly back in a greasy pony-tail and she's not wearing any make-up.

"Are you guys smoking pot?" she asks; her eyes widening with interest.

"Yep," grins Martin, holding the joint, "you want some?" And he holds the joint out towards Nicole.

"Brilliant!" she says, leaning forward to take it from him, "if I'd known you lot were in to this stuff I'd have begged a few tokes off you before now." She inhales deeply and closes her eyes, holding the smoke in her lungs before letting it out in a long, elegant stream. She opens her eyes. "Fantastic!"

"You know where the phone is," says Ursula, settling back in the chair. Nicole nods and goes through to the kitchen, pulling the door closed behind her.

"She's got to call America," explains Ursula; "wants to speak to that husband of hers."

"He's in *America?*"

"Oh, didn't I tell you? She's not from London, she's from *Miami;* been living over there for the past fifteen years. And she's not a novelist either; that was all made-up as a cover. She ran off with a load of her hubbie's money when she found out he was having an affair and thought she'd hide out up here for a bit until it blew over. Unfortunately he somehow got wind of what she was up to and managed to get his money back from her account so now she's high and dry with nothing to her name, poor cow."

"He sounds like a right one to me," says Tallulah, "I think she's scared of him by all accounts."

"Quite honestly I'm not sure how much to believe," whispers Ursula, leaning forward to share her confidences, "I mean, she told me that he knocked-off this bloke she was shagging; arranged some kind of fake boat accident. Come on! I wasn't born yesterday!"

"Sounds a bit far-fetched," agrees Martin, "she's probably just bored and wants to create a bit of excitement in her life; you know how these middle-aged women get when their hormones start drying-up."

"Oh come on, Martin, Nicole's not *that* old," argues Petra, picking strands of greasy noodle from a cardboard container and tipping back her head to wind them on to her tongue.

"Forty-six," divulges Ursula, "but she's had work done."

"Blimey! I thought she was in her thirties."

"She's been living in America too long. You know how scared they are of getting old over there; she's got the tits of a twenty-five year old."

Tallulah is surprised. She had pegged Nicole as somewhere around the mid-thirties but perhaps that's just because she usually looks so glamorous with all that streaky blonde hair and the tan. Maybe she doesn't come from Miami at all; maybe that's made up as well? She's seen films with characters like that; women who go a bit doolallie and start having delusions. There used to be a girl who worked at Trebor who was like that; they called her Fibbing Frida because she made up the most outrageous lies about herself. She once told Tallulah that she was flying to Australia on holiday when the wing of her plane caught on fire and they had to crash-land on a deserted island. Now that story was particularly unlikely because Frida was only nineteen, came from a council estate and left school at fifteen to have a baby so what would she be doing on a plane, let alone going to Australia?

The thing is; Nicole doesn't strike her as the kind of woman who would make up stupid stories just to garner attention. She's obviously posh and well educated and where did all her expensive jewellery come from if she isn't rich? She wouldn't be forced to sell everything if she wasn't in some kind of trouble.

How exciting! This is one of the reasons why Tallulah likes coming to Ursula's house; there's always something unusual happening. These past few weeks have really opened her eyes and now that they're open it's hard to shut them again. Here she is, sitting in a cosy living room with a glass of red wine in her hand, having eaten her very first Chinese take-away (yes, it's true!) and mixing with the kind of people she's only ever seen on the telly. Ursula, the witch, Jeff the junk shop man, Martin the homosexual aromatherapist, Petra the art student with her pierced eyebrow and tattoos and Nicole the sophisticated runaway wife from Miami being hounded by her drug-addicted husband: All this while sitting in a haze of marijuana smoke. Whatever next!

Nicole comes back in to the living room looking distracted. "Pass me that joint," she says to Jeff, "I need to get stoned." She throws herself down on the sofa next to him, upsetting more cushions and causing Jeff to slump in to an even more ungainly position. He hands her the joint and Nicole inhales deeply. "Is there any more wine in that bottle?" she asks. Ursula pours her a glass.

"So, did you talk to him?"

Nicole offers them a strangely plaintive smile and blows smoke high in to the air. "No, I didn't speak to Gideon but I did get hold of my friend, Daphne."

"That's the one who helped you get away?" prompts Ursula.

Nicole nods. "Yes, my so-called best friend. The fucking bitch double-crossed me! She's been screwing Gideon behind my back for months, apparently, and the two of them invented this entire fucking scenario to get rid of me. She helped me devise this plan where we transferred money from Gideon's business account in to another account under a false name – *my* false name. She even organized the fake ID, travel documents and tickets for me to get away and all the while she was in cahoots with Gideon; the two of them laughing behind my back all the fucking time." Nicole takes a final drag on the now depleted joint and stubs it out in the ashtray, reaching for the wine glass.

Tallulah sees Ursula shoot a look of incredulity at Martin. Petra sits up from her lounging position and reaches for the bag of pot to start rolling another joint. Her nail varnish is black and her knobbly fingers tremble slightly as she removes a cigarette paper from the packet. "Couldn't he just have dumped you, straight-off, without going to all that trouble?" she asks.

"He didn't want me getting my hands on any of his money," explains Nicole, "so he thought that if they could trap me in to doing something illegal – embezzlement – that I wouldn't have a leg to stand on. If I go back to the States now they'll arrest me so, you see, I'm completely fucked."

"What a bastard!" gasps Petra, obviously enthralled by all this drama.

"It all sounds a bit John Grisham to me," admits Ursula, "do people really go around doing stuff like that in real life?"

"Darling," smiles Martin, "you just have to pick up the paper and you'll see the kinds of lengths people will go to these days. It's not that unusual."

"So what are you going to do?" asks Jeff, raised suddenly from his lethargy.

"Well first I've got to get my hands on some money, so I need to find a buyer for these," says Nicole, holding up her hand causing her diamonds to catch the light from the fireplace. "I've not had much luck so far but there must be somebody who wants a heavily discounted Tiffany ring or a Cartier watch."

"I could help you flog them on eBay if you like," suggests Jeff, "I could take some digital photos and see if we get any offers. You can put a reserve on them so you don't *give* them away and if we don't have any luck I know a few dealers in Leeds I can take you to."

"Great, thanks Jeff. Woo, that weed is pretty strong! I'm flying!"

"When all else fails, get high!" jokes Ursula and she raises her wine glass to Nicole.

"So where's my birthday cake, then?" asks Petra, after a moment of silence, "I've got the munchies."

"Oh God! I forgot all about that! Hang on a minute, I'll go and fetch it," and Ursula gets up and goes through to the kitchen, staggering slightly so that she has to steady herself against the sideboard.

Tallulah smiles to herself. There's no way she can go back to the humdrum life she was living before she met these people. She will call Uncle Ted tomorrow and talk to him about it; perhaps he'll let her move in to Rob's house while the estate agents are dealing with the sale of her own house in Chesterfield? Now that she's made up her mind she doesn't want to dither any longer; cancer or no cancer, what difference does it make if she's in one house or the other?

Ursula returns with a huge chocolate cake complete with twenty-two burning candles and the assembled group break in to a discordant rendition of Happy Birthday before Petra extinguishes the flames with one deft blow.

Drastic Measures

The lump in Tallulah's breast is malignant.

And today she walked out on her job at Mr. B's following an altercation with a customer who insisted that Tallulah was trying to catch a glimpse of her fanny in the changing room mirror. It wasn't so much the indignity of the accusation as it was to do with Mr. B's very public tongue-lashing in the middle of the shop. He wanted Tallulah to apologize to the customer in front of Junie and Sue but Tallulah refused; calling the customer a 'fat bitch' and going on to say that she'd rather look at an appendix scar than *her* wizened old bits.

Tallulah's spontaneous insult, referring to the customer's vagina as a scar, could well have sprung from her subconscious fear of the malignancy in her own breast but she failed to link the two things together and merely blurted out the first thing that came to mind. Her doctor had told her that a lumpectomy would probably suffice, followed by six weeks of radiotherapy – as long as the surgeon doesn't find anything more sinister when he operates. The surgery is scheduled for next week (they don't waste time when it comes to malignant tumours) and if Tallulah had thought things through before she insulted Mr. B's customer she could have taken two months off work with sick-pay. Unfortunately her mind was elsewhere and so she walked out of the shop without so much as a by-your-leave and cried all the way home on the bus.

Stage one cancer means that it hasn't spread to the lymph nodes and the tumour, in Tallulah's case, is less than 2cms in diameter so the doctor reckons they should be able to cut it out without losing the entire breast. Tallulah asked about having both her breasts removed immediately but the doctor dissuaded her from such drastic measures and tried to reassure her that a lumpectomy would be sufficient for the time-being.

The time-being: Tallulah isn't comfortable hearing that dubious phrase. The time-being means 'not today but probably tomorrow'; it means 'let's wait and see' or 'take this one step at a time'. It is a phrase used to placate fractious children when forced to accept a disagreeable situation such as starting a new school or watching Daddy leave with a suitcase in his hand. What Tallulah wants to hear from her doctor is: 'Don't worry, we'll remove the lump and the cancer will be gone.' But, of course, she knows that no doctor worth his salt would be able to offer that kind of reassurance.

She has already started to pack some boxes with things to take to Rob's house. She still refers to it as Rob's house even though the papers have already been signed and soon it'll be *her* house. Uncle Ted and Auntie

June are only too happy for Tallulah to move in as soon as possible and Darren, the estate agent, has arranged to put Tallulah's house on the market. He reckons it'll be easier to start showing it to prospective buyers once all her things are gone. "People like to see the space empty," he told her, "unless it's decorated to professional standards and then they like to see it looking like a picture in a magazine." Tallulah has no delusions regarding the general disrepair of her interior decoration.

She isn't unduly worried about being temporarily unemployed. She doesn't have a mortgage and the sale of her house will add a few thousand to her savings account so she can live off that for a while. Her monthly bills are minimal due to the fact that unlike most people in this day-and-age she has no need for modern trappings such as satellite television, mobile phones, car payments, credit cards or health club memberships. Tallulah can survive on a hundred quid a week if she's careful. She will take just a few essential pieces of furniture to Number Two and Jeff has offered to take her to a few estate auctions to buy anything she doesn't already have. Rob's home insurance is paying for the repairs to the broken floorboards and damaged walls and they've even agreed to install new stair carpet. Jeff has a mate who is in the building trade and he's going to write up an invoice for the insurance company; meanwhile Jeff has offered to do most of the work for free.

It's easy to push the thought of cancer to the back of her mind when there's so much else to think about. She has been worrying about the lump for so long that the dreaded confirmation is actually something of a relief. At least now she knows what she's up against and something is being *done*. The monster in the dark has come out of the shadows and Tallulah can see its face. Its name is Cancer and she has been waiting for it to come and get her.

Sour Grapes

And light-years away on the other side of the Atlantic Gideon is hanging out with his dealer, Lyle. The midday sun is high and the shades are drawn. There is an unhealthy gloom in Lyle's living room and the air is stagnant from lack of ventilation.

Lyle lives in a small apartment that he rents from a friend of a friend; month-to-month basis, cash only, no questions asked. It is a reasonably new place overlooking Biscayne Bay with an open-plan kitchen, a tiny bedroom and a bathroom just big enough for a shower cubicle, a toilet and a miniature wash basin. Designed for style-conscious first-time-buyers the apartments at Belhaven Court have hardwood floors, stainless steel kitchen appliances and tall ceilings to lend a more spacious feeling to the compact 450 square feet of living space. Unfortunately Lyle isn't very style conscious and his apartment resembles more of a dumping ground, filled as it is with a jumble of second-hand furniture and trash.

The main room is dominated by an oversized L-shaped sofa of pale tan leather. It is the kind of sofa that sags and flops over the rigid framework in a misguided attempt to appear contemporary and one of the arm pillows is split at the seam, revealing tufts of something that resembles loft insulation. Most of the sofa is piled high with discarded clothing, dirty plates caked with dry spaghetti sauce and then utilized as ashtrays. Several pizza boxes, McDonald's bags and cookie wrappers litter the coffee table and in the middle of this mess, propped up on a stack of video cases, there is a laptop computer connected to the internet.

Lyle sprawls on the sofa with his legs stretched out in front of him, slouching down amidst the piles of junk wearing nothing but a pair of partially unbuttoned jeans. He was once firm and muscular but as he approaches his fiftieth birthday his body is suffering from lack of attention and his stomach bulges over the creased waistband of his 501's. One nipple is pierced with a silver ring and his belly button is tattooed with a primitive sunburst. His sagging muscles are testament to his real age but his handsome face remains mostly unlined and he prides himself on the fact that people still glance furtively at him when he's out and about. In one hand he holds the TV remote and in the other he grasps a small glass pipe which is stained with thick brown tar.

"Fucking can's blocked again!" Gideon emerges from the bathroom wielding a bent wire coat hanger. He is wearing long baggy shorts with bulging cargo pockets and a tee shirt that has ridden up to expose his stomach. "You need to get a plunger, Lyle."

"No, Gid, you need to use less fucking paper when you take a dump. You're the only one who blocks up the john every time you come over here. What the fuck are you eating?"

Gideon tosses the wire hanger in to the corner of the room where it clatters against the wooden floor and he throws himself down on the opposite end of the sofa, dislodging a pile of magazines and credit card bills. "I eat a hell of a lot better than you do, buddy."

Lyle raises the pipe to his lips and flicks a plastic lighter. A small puff of smoke drifts upwards as he inhales and he holds the smoke in his lungs, his eyes squinting with the effort, as he offers it to Robbie. The acrid, chemical smell of the crystal meth drifts in a thin haze around them as they smoke. Lyle is watching VH1

"She is so fucking lame," complains Gideon, one eye on Jennifer Lopez as he takes a second hit.

"I think she's hot."

"She's a fucking whore," states Gideon without emotion and then he coughs violently, bending forward to place the pipe and the lighter on the edge of the crowded coffee table.

"And talking of whores, what's up with Ronnie? Any word from her?" asks Lyle without taking his eyes from the TV screen.

"I've stitched her up well and good; vanquished in England with diddly squat in her pocket-book. Daph can be a vindictive bitch when she sets her mind to something and she helped Ronnie dig her own fucking grave. I hope she rots."

"You know everybody's saying that she left you because you've been screwing around with other guys. They were making wise-cracks at the Sky Bar last week about you and some underage hustlers. I told 'em it was a load of crap but you know how those jerks eat up that kind of shit."

Gideon snorts with derision and slumps further in to the sofa. "Yeah, Ronnie sent an e-mail to that big-mouthed cunt, Fleur. Sour grapes, man; nothing but sour grapes."

"Gideon, you are one son-of-a-bitch!"

"Don't I know it, man! Nobody fucks with me and gets away with it."

And Gideon pushes his head back against the torn leather of Lyle's sofa and closes his eyes. Right now, he just wants to get fried.

A Normal Life

"Positive?"

"Yes, I'm afraid so Miss Harvey."

The doctor is younger than Nicole, she is Indian and on her forehead, at the point of her sixth chakra (concealed wisdom), she has painted a vermilion bindi that draws Nicole's attention away from her dark-rimmed eyes.

Nicole's immediate reaction is disbelief followed by a conviction that there must be a mistake. She had the blood test just last week, before she discovered that Daphne and Gideon had concocted their heinous lie regarding Courtney's HIV status. She only returned to the hospital today for the follow-up because she wanted a prescription for sleeping pills and she couldn't be bothered to go through the rigmarole of finding a local GP who would treat her.

"It's not a mistake, Miss Harvey, I'm sorry," apologizes the doctor, "when the laboratory gets a positive result they test it several more times to make sure that they're not getting a false positive."

"But maybe they mixed up my blood with somebody else?"

"It is very rare that something like that happens, but we will take more blood today for further tests and that will confirm the result."

Nicole feels very calm. There is none of the expected panic or hysteria, she merely looks at the doctor and wonders how much longer she will have to spend at the hospital because she's hungry and could do with a sandwich. So she's HIV positive; what's the big deal? Thousands of people are positive these days and they live perfectly normal lives, controlling the disease with highly effective medications. Nicole has several friends in Miami who have been positive for years and they have never had any symptoms or treatment.

"Your CD-4 count is rather low," explains the doctor, reading from the notes in front of her, "this indicates that your immune system has already been compromised quite severely by the virus. A normal range of T-cells is between five hundred and fifteen hundred per cubic millimetre of blood and yours are down to two hundred and forty which puts you at risk of developing full-blown AIDS unless you start treatment as soon as possible. This, combined with a viral load of almost three hundred thousand copies suggests that the virus is rapidly multiplying and systematically destroying your T-cells to a level where you will start to develop opportunist infections."

"So does that mean I've been positive for a long time?" asks Nicole, suddenly feeling less complacent, "I know people who have been positive for years and they've never gotten sick or had to take any medications."

"That depends on the individual, Miss. Harvey. When was your last HIV test?"

"Oh, years ago," admits Nicole, shamefacedly, "I didn't think I was particularly at risk."

"Well it could be that you've been positive but asymptomatic for a long time; some people never develop the early symptoms of infection and can continue a normal life for many years before their immune system reaches a point of collapse. There are other people, however, who progress from infection to full-blown AIDS within twelve months or less and it can depend on how virulent the particular strain of HIV is that they've contracted."

"There's more than one kind of HIV?" questions Nicole, wiping the palms of her hands down the front of her trousers. This is beginning to sound a lot more burdensome than she had initially imagined and she wishes the doctor would just give her a prescription for the pills and let her go.

"There are several mutations of the HIV virus and we would have to run a genotype resistance test to find out if your particular strain is resistant to any of the medications currently available for treatment. Hopefully you will not have any resistance to medications and we can start you on a regime that will control the replication of the virus and allow your immune system to recover. Most people experience good recovery within just a few months of starting the regime."

"And do I have to start taking pills straight away?"

"We recommend that anyone with a viral load as high as yours, especially combined with a low T-cell count, should start treatment before the immune system becomes irreparably damaged. Without the medications you are at immediate risk of becoming sick. Do you have any idea where you might have contracted the virus? Is there a husband or partner involved?"

"I have a husband," explains Nicole, attempting to keep the vitriol out of her voice, "but we're separated. He lives in Miami."

"And what about other sexual partners?"

"Well, there have been others but I'm not seeing anyone at the moment."

"You should contact your husband and suggest that he gets tested and we recommend that you get in touch with anyone with whom you have had unprotected sex. We can offer you counselling if you'd like and we have social workers who can answer any questions you might have. From a medical point of view we would like to take some more blood today for the genotype test and we will also test you for tuberculosis and give you a pneumonia shot. Once we have the results of the genotype we will be able to prescribe a suitable course of medications."

Nicole is no longer listening to the doctor. She is staring straight past her, through the slats of the aluminium blinds where the wind is stirring the naked branches of a tree. Against the late afternoon sky the branches spread like arteries and Nicole perceives the course of the virus, pulsing vigorously through her veins; tiny computer pacmans gobbling up T-cells with voracious ease.

The Rule of Three

If Nicole's life had once been a sumptuous Jacuzzi filled with richly perfumed bubbles surrounded by mounds of triple-milled soaps flown in from France it is now a scummy enamelled bathtub with a squirt of Palmolive and a shrivelled bar of Imperial Leather.

From the penthouse to the pavement.

From riches to rags.

She sits on the uncomfortable sofa at Brown Bread Cottage with only two more days before the end of her rental agreement and seven pounds fifty-three pence to her name. Jeff has photographed her remaining jewellery and watch but so far the offers on eBay have fallen way below the reserve. Tomorrow he is taking her to meet a dealer in Leeds who might be interested but Nicole is beginning to think her luck has run out. And the person responsible for Nicole's calamitous fall from providence is Gideon.

As puerile as it may be, Nicole would find great satisfaction in shredding photos of Gideon in to tiny pieces or watching them blister and burn over the flames of the fire. Unformed acts of vengeance blossom in her mind, ranging from harmless pranks such as mailing him dead birds or dog turds to more serious deeds such as arson or castration with a blunt instrument. She pictures Gideon and Daphne lying side-by-side on a pristine bedspread having inhaled a lethal amount of toxic fumes or the two of them tangled over the glass-splintered dashboard of a crumpled car by the side of a busy highway. And suddenly she thinks of Ursula.

"A *voodoo* doll? That's pretty strong stuff," warns Ursula, leading Nicole in to her kitchen where she appears to be anointing coloured candles with various essential oils. "I wouldn't recommend it, even in the most execrable circumstances. I usually only resort to poppet magic for binding spells or for healing, it's considered bad form for a modern day witch to cast curses on people and there's a popular belief that the ill-wishes can come back on the spell-caster threefold; it's called the Rule of Three. I used to dabble in that darker stuff when I was a teenager; I was a bit of a Goth when I was at college and thought it was cool to burn black candles and wear an inverted pentagram round my neck. These days the only poppets I make are for local women who want to lose some weight or for folks who think they're already under some kind of curse themselves."

Nicole wanders over to Ursula's big stone sink and watches some birds pecking at the berries of a holly bush. The sink is piled with dirty plates and coffee mugs and on the draining board there is an open packet of sugar and a glass jar filled with bits of pale crumbled bark labelled 'angelica root'. "I want to fucking murder them," she hisses through clenched teeth, banging the heels of her clenched hands down against the edge of the sink and leaning forward slightly as though she might vomit over the dirty dishes.

Ursula crosses the room and touches Nicole's shoulder gently. "Listen, duck, people do some really shitty things in this life but it won't help matters if you take the same attitude. Ignore them; let them go; if my experience has taught me anything it's that people like Gideon and Daphne will get their come-uppance without any help from you or me."

"I've got AIDS, Ursula." Nicole doesn't turn around as she makes this simple statement but her words seem to reverberate around the room as though they have a life of their own. "I saw the doctor yesterday afternoon and if I don't get treatment as soon as possible I'm going to start getting really sick."

"But I thought you said they'd made all of that up to scare you? I thought it was their ploy to push you in to taking the money from Gideon's account?"

"Well that's what Daphne told me but now I don't believe a word either of them has ever said to me. The doctor in Manchester gave me the results of my blood test yesterday and I was astounded."

"Oh, love, I'm so sorry; come on, let's sit down." Ursula pulls out a chair at the kitchen table and touches Nicole's elbow to move her away from the sink. Nicole sits down as though in a dream and places her hands against the rough pine of the table, spreading her fingers to display the worn-down, chipped remains of her once immaculate manicure.

"Let me make you some fennel tea; it's very calming," offers Ursula, running her finger along an array of spice jars until she finds the requisite one.

"I've hit rock-bottom," sighs Nicole, "I honestly don't know what I'm going to do. I've got to vacate the cottage in two days time and I've only got seven quid in my purse and no prospect of work on the horizon. Jeff's trying to sell my jewellery but so far he's not had much luck and I've not even got enough gas in the car to take me back to Manchester to see the doctor next week. I can't believe that everything's gone so wrong practically overnight. My life was so *easy* up until a few months ago and then all hell broke loose."

"Perhaps it was *too* easy, duck. There's not many folk who can sail through life without a few hiccups and it sounds like you had a pretty long run of it. I always get nervous myself when things seem to be going too well and I get that feeling in my gut that I associate with the calm before a thunder storm." Ursula places her old-fashioned kettle on to the Aga and rattles through a cupboard to find some cups.

"Funnily enough I'm not that upset about the HIV; not yet anyway. I think I'm still kind of in shock and I can't believe that it's really true. I'm more angry about the way those two have stitched me up with no apparent conscience. I can't even go back to Miami to have it out with them because I'll be arrested at the bloody passport control but if I don't do *something* I think I'll go mad. I know revenge isn't very adult or intelligent but when it's the only thing left you start to obsess about it."

"It would make more sense for you to protect yourself against further attacks than to retaliate. I can certainly help you with *that* if you like? And I'll be happy to do some healing on you if you're open to the idea."

"I'm open to anything right now," admits Nicole with a wan smile, "what have I got to lose?"

"And you can stay here until you get yourself sorted out, the spare room isn't much but it's better than wandering the streets or sleeping in your car."

"I hope it won't come to that, Ursula, but thanks for the offer. If Jeff's mate buys my jewellery tomorrow I'll be fine and it'll give me a breathing space to get myself sorted out."

"Well the invitation is always there if you need it, duck. And in the meantime perhaps I should do some work on your chakras, see if we can't open up those channels and get some positive energy flowing."

Tea & Sympathy

There must be something in the air. Illness and disease is all around, fogging up the atmosphere like the smell from an overflowing flip-top bin. "Things happen in threes" Tallulah's mother always used to say when faced with a succession of bad luck and it's true; you hear of one plane crash and then there are two more; you hear news of a tsunami in Sri Lanka, a volcano erupts and completely obliterates an Indonesian village while mudslides threaten entire Californian communities. As Nicole copes with the news of her deadly viral infection and Tallulah anticipates the removal of her malignant tumour there is a phone call from Gran to say that the doctors have discovered secondary cancer in Auntie June's ovaries. It's all doom and gloom on the health front and to top it all Uncle Ted's piles are still playing-up, despite his recent surgery.

Let's indulge in some more tea and sympathy.

Tallulah is over at Jeff's place enjoying a ham and cheese sandwich and a cup of tea for lunch. He moved a van-load of her stuff over to Number Two this morning, including all the appliances he only recently relocated to Chesterfield. Most of Tallulah's old furniture is not worth saving so it will all go to the dump and much of her mother's ancient kitchen equipment, china and glassware is already on display in Jeff's shop vying for space with the H.R Pufnstuf lunch boxes, the 'magic' drinking birds and the Boy George dolls. Jeff's little shop is crammed to the ceiling with such miscellanea and Tallulah suspects that the browsers are more interested in a temporary nostalgia-rush than in actually buying anything. "Oh my God, Kev, do you remember these things?" they say as they point out the kitchen canisters that used to come free with every ten gallons of petrol. "Crikey! I've not seen one of these in years," they trill at the discovery of a Goblin teasmade.

"I make more money selling this stuff on the internet than I do in the shop," admits Jeff, "but there's no rent to pay seeing as how it's all part and parcel with the house and it's a great tax write-off."

The shop occupies most of the ground floor of the house but there's a little kitchen at the back practically overhanging the fast-flowing current of Peakshole Water and it is here that Tallulah sits with Jeff, nibbling the corner of her sandwich. The kitchen has an antiquated water heater above the sink decorated with self-adhesive vinyl flowers in day-glo colours and the small fridge is almost obliterated beneath a plethora of decorative plastic magnets. It is the kind of damp, peeling kitchen that harbours silverfish under the sink and attracts flies in the summer. There isn't room for a table so they are perched on bar stools and the gas jets are turned on for warmth.

"I *like* your shop," confesses Tallulah with a shy smile. "It's a bit like going in to somebody's lumber room and being left to have a poke around; you never know what you might find."

Barney, Jeff's little dog, is sitting patiently between them, staring up with an expectant expression as he watches every bite they take. Occasionally Jeff breaks off a piece of ham and hands it down to be swallowed whole and Barney shifts to a more advantageous position in the hope of procuring another morsel. He looks expectantly from Jeff to Tallulah and then back again.

"I make most of my money from selling stuff on eBay these days; there are collectors of just about everything all over the country and they'll pay a lot more than the casual browsers who happen to drop in on their way round the village. I sold some old *Beano* comics to a guy in Sunderland a few weeks ago for three hundred quid; that's why you shouldn't throw any of Rob's stuff out until I've had a look at it first. I couldn't believe what I found in that skip of yours!"

"Oh, I'm just trying to get the house emptied out. I haven't got the time to mess about selling stuff unless it's really worth a lot of money. It was hard enough finding somebody to take all the furniture away without me having to pay *them*. Nobody wants second-hand furniture these days." Tallulah picks up her tea and blows on the surface before taking a sip.

"I've already got a couple of collectors bidding on some of Rob's Matchbox and Dinky toys. There's a 1935 Oxo van that's up to four hundred quid already and a Golden Shred delivery van that's probably going to sell for about three hundred. We'll probably make a couple of thousand on those alone."

"Really?" Tallulah is astonished that anyone would want to buy those tatty little metal cars with their peeling paint and blistered tyres. If Jeff hadn't expressed an interest in them she'd have thrown them away with the rest of the 'rubbish'.

"Yep! And some of those old Rupert Bear annuals are worth about a hundred quid a piece."

"Crikey! Wouldn't it be lovely to give a cheque to Auntie June and Uncle Ted as a surprise when you've sold everything? You'll have to take your share, of course, I'm not having you do all this work for nothing."

"It's my pleasure, Tally. Rob was a good guy and he did me a few favours so I'm happy to help. It's not like I've got anything else to do at the moment and I get a buzz from seeing how much I can get for this stuff; it's addictive."

"Are you having any luck with Nicole's jewellery?"

"Not really. The problem is it's worth too much and people who are shopping on eBay aren't looking for fine jewellery. I think we'll do better with my mate Julian in Leeds; he buys and sells expensive stuff like that and he won't try to diddle us like a lot of those dealers. Actually he's a friend of your Rob's, that's how I met him; I think they were at university together. I'm taking her over there tomorrow to meet him."

"She's in a right state," nods Tallulah, compressing her lips in an expression of concern. "Fancy running all the way from Miami to get away from your husband only to find out that he's been knocking-off your best friend behind your back and then – on top of all that – to be stranded without any money, no job and no possibility of going back to America."

"Oh she'll be all right," says Jeff confidently, "people like her always land on their feet. You should be more worried about yourself, Tally. I know you're putting a brave face on it but it can't be easy trying to move house and think about that operation you've got to have."

Tallulah holds her mug between the palms of her hands but there is very little warmth left inside. "I'm going to postpone the operation until after Christmas. I just want to enjoy my first Christmas in the house and then face up to everything else after the New Year. The doctor reckons it won't do much harm to leave it for another month; apparently it's a slow-growing tumour. I'm trying not to think about it at the moment."

"I'm sure you'll be fine," reassures Jeff, leaning forward to place his hand on Tallulah's knee, "it sounds like they've caught it very early and it's only stage one so it's not spread anywhere else."

"That's what they told Auntie June and now look at her," sighs Tallulah with a frown.

"You can't think like that. Positive thinking is the best way to cope with these things; it's been medically proven that people with a positive attitude towards illness have a much higher rate of recovery than those who give-in to it."

Tallulah knows that people have to say these things; that it's an automatic response to anyone who is facing the possibility of a life-threatening illness. But she's grateful for Jeff's kind words and glad that there are people in her life who seem genuinely concerned for her welfare. Irrespective of that thought, she would rather change the subject to something more interesting. There is probably some connection in her mind between Jeff's concern and her own speculations about his private life but her next question tumbles out of her mouth before she's had a chance to analyse it.

"So how come you never got married, Jeff?"

"Married? Me? Oh, I suppose the stock answer would be 'I've never met the right woman' but that's not really the case. Actually I've met several promising candidates for marriage over the years but I think I've got what they call commitment phobia; I'm terrified of giving up my independence. I got very close to it about fifteen years ago but I chickened out when I started thinking about looking at engagement rings. She was a lovely girl – Sam, her name was – but she ended up marrying a car mechanic from Macclesfield and now, by all accounts, she's as happy as Larry. What about you? You've never met the right bloke?"

Tallulah snorts air down her nostrils and raises her eyebrows in exasperation, "I've never met *any* bloke, full-stop. The last boyfriend I had was Danny Hodges in junior school and at eleven years old there's not much to get worked-up about unless you count peeping at each other's privates under the desk at milk break!"

Jeff splutters on his tea, laughing. "Tally, you little tart! I didn't have you down as a flasher!"

"You'd be surprised what little girls get up to, given half the chance!" jokes Tallulah. "If our Rob was here now he'd tell you a few stories about me that would have you rolling on the floor. He used to egg me on to do all sorts of daring stuff and it was always *me* who got in to trouble for it. You'd have thought butter wouldn't melt in his mouth."

"He was a bit of a rogue was Rob," agrees Jeff with a grin, "but he was a laugh and never seemed to take things too seriously. I've met blokes who sell pot before and they're usually head-cases or total stoners; Rob just did it because he enjoyed meeting people, I think."

"He *sold* pot to other people?" This is the first Tallulah has heard about Rob being a dealer.

"Oh, you know, just an eighth here and there; he had his regular customers round here and he'd go up to Manchester and buy for everybody, adding on a bit of commission for his time and trouble, of course. I don't think he was in to it Big Time."

Barney suddenly cocks his head to one side and the bell above the door jangles as somebody enters the shop. Jeff puts down his mug and ruffles Barney's fur. "I'd better go through and see if I can flog somebody something they don't want. Why don't you pour yourself another cup of tea and then I'll give you a hand sorting through those boxes of records you were going to throw out."

Tallulah slides off her stool and watches Jeff and Barney disappear in to the shop. A few dusty rays of sunshine slant through the filthy kitchen window and, for a second or two, everything is transformed by the brightness. With the gas jets hissing and the brook rushing over the rocks outside Tallulah knows what it must feel like to be a cat; curled up and dozing on a window sill, dreaming of mice.

Julian

Jeff's friend Julian Smythe is a floppy-haired, pin-striped ex public schoolboy who took early retirement following a series of spectacularly good returns on the stock market. He now spends his days buying and selling diamonds with a sideline in antique jewellery and watches. He lives in a Grade II listed mansion outside Leeds called Longfield Hall with three Great Danes, a live-in housekeeper, a cook and two full-time gardeners. No wife.

Nicole is wearing her grubby yellow trousers, her scuffed gold sandals (displaying toes with chipped red nail varnish) and her ubiquitous Burberry bomber jacket that appears to have ketchup spilled down one sleeve. She tried valiantly to do something with her hair this morning but there's only so much you can do without conditioner, hairdryer or mousse. She had to use the stub of her lipstick as blusher and, without deodorant, she is hoping that the last few squirts of her Bulgari White Tea hold up long enough to disguise the fact that she hasn't shaved her armpits for a month.

"Jolly nice to meet you, Nicole," blusters Julian Smythe as he pumps Nicole's hand furiously in the entrance hall of his spectacular home. Honed flagstone floors stretch away in to the distance like a slightly rumpled quilt and an enormous arrangement of autumn flowers and berries cascades ebulliently beneath a crystal chandelier the size of a small spaceship. "I'm afraid I haven't been up for long so I'm still finishing my breakfast, would you like to come through and join me?"

Nicole counts each individual chime as a clock strikes eleven somewhere beyond the velvet curtains to one side of the sweeping Jacobean oak balustrade. She follows Jeff and Julian through a pair of open doors to the left of the entrance hall and finds herself in a capacious oak panelled room with an ornate coffered ceiling and mullioned windows looking out across an expanse of elegantly appointed gardens. There are two fireplaces; one at each end of the room and both are blazing with logs. The room smells of woodsmoke, coffee and furniture polish.

"Please take a seat, Nicole," volunteers Julian, pulling out a tapestry-upholstered chair at the table and ushering her towards it. "Can I interest you in some coffee, tea...kedgeree?" He indicates a series of silver urns and serving dishes on a huge sideboard frowned upon by a life-size portrait of a censorious gentleman in pantaloons and knee garters.

"Some coffee would be lovely, thank you."

"I'll get it, Jules," offers Jeff, already approaching the sideboard with insouciance as though perfectly comfortable playing the country squire.

"I hope you don't mind," says Julian, taking a seat opposite Nicole and indicating his plate of half-finished breakfast with a sweep of his hand, "I hate to waste this rather scrumptious kedgeree; the smoked haddock came from Whitby this morning and it is absolutely first rate. Are you sure I can't tempt you, my dear?"

"No, I'm fine, thanks," smiles Nicole, despite the fact she had nothing for breakfast but a cup of Nescafé (without milk or sugar) and a slice of pork pie with the mouldy part of the crust cut off. She feels totally degraded and ashamed sitting here surrounded by such splendour and she feels certain that Julian is looking at her with barely disguised horror. If she had known it was going to be anything like this she would never have agreed to come.

"I have to apologise for my appearance," she laments with a self-deprecating sigh, "I'm not sure if Jeff explained my situation to you but I've been reduced to living in penury for the past month due to the fact that my husband has exiled me without a penny to my name. I hope you don't imagine that I would normally leave the house looking like this."

"My dear," gushes Julian, flapping a large white napkin across his lap, "you really don't have to apologize; you look positively radiant. Just half an hour ago I was still in my disreputable old jim-jams stinking of Ralgex so there's really no cause for concern on your part. I can assure you that the only reason I'm dressed at this hour is because I was made aware of your imminent arrival by my inimitable housekeeper, Mrs. Moon."

Jeff brings two cups of coffee to the table and takes a seat next to Nicole. He leans forward and reaches for the milk and sugar. "Don't listen to him,

Nicole," he quips with a smile, "Julian is the only bloke I know who wears polka-dot pyjamas to bed every night."

"How reassuring to know that there are still some men out there who have a keen sense of propriety," commends Nicole. "I was beginning to worry that the art of sartorial elegance was something relegated to the realms of gay men and Italians."

Julian chortles through a mouthful of kedgeree and swipes his heavy fringe away from his forehead with a spade-like hand. Nicole notices the heavy signet ring on his pinkie; another affectation that would look foppish on anyone less dignified than a man like Julian.

"So, Jules, we're hoping you can help Nicole out," broaches Jeff, pulling his chair further under the table. "As you know, she's experiencing hard times and would like to sell her jewellery."

Nicole removes a suede pouch from her jacket pocket and pulls open the drawstrings. She empties out her booty on to the white damask tablecloth and it falls in a nonchalant, tangled heap of gold, platinum and diamonds. "My worldly goods," she scoffs with derision.

"It could be a lot worse, my dear," says Julian as he reaches across to pick up her watch. "A Pasha de Cartier eighteen karat white gold with round-cut diamonds; retails at around nine thousand. It's in excellent condition. Probably pretty easy to find a buyer for this; somewhere in the region of six or seven thousand." He reaches out to pick up the Tiffany rings, turning them around between his fingers, inspecting the hallmark, bringing them up close to his face to scrutinize the stones. "No problem getting somewhere in the region of five for the wedding band and about three for the solitaire."

"A pretty good haul," Jeff says as he stirs milk in to his coffee.

"The bracelet and necklace aren't so great but they're probably worth a couple of thousand," suggests Nicole, pushing them towards Julian.

"Most definitely," agrees Julian, running the chains across the palm of his hand. "Let's see; how would you feel about twelve thousand for the lot and if I sell them for more than expected I'll split the difference?"

"That would be brilliant!" gushes Nicole with a sigh of gratification and relief. "I don't want to sound too desperate but how soon do you think you could give me the money?"

"I can give you a cheque today or, if you prefer cash, I could get it for you by tomorrow."

"I don't have a bank account over here yet but I'm not sure I want to carry twelve thousand pounds around in my handbag."

"Well how about I give you a thousand in cash and a cheque for the rest? That way you will have some flexibility until you get yourself sorted with a bank account."

"Oh my God! You don't know what a relief this is," beams Nicole. "I've been living on instant coffee and stale bread for the past week."

"How ghastly! We'll have to something about that. Are you absolutely certain you don't want to try some of this delicious kedgeree?" asks Julian, "it's practically lunchtime."

"You know," she replies, "I've suddenly found my appetite." And she pushes back her chair to walk around to the richly encumbered sideboard.

Hiroshima

Tallulah makes herself a cup of Maxwell House and pops the heel of yesterday's loaf in to the microwave to soften it up a bit before spreading it with margarine. The back door of the house is still boarded-up and the kitchen is piled with cardboard boxes and bin bags but the sun slants through the streaky window and out there she can see nothing but fields and trees against a sky mottled with white cloud.

She went to the hospital this morning to visit Auntie June and she is feeling unsettled by the experience. It wasn't easy to appear cheerful and optimistic in the face of all those tubes and machines and it was particularly difficult to ignore the rapid deterioration of her aunt's physical condition. Her hair is falling out in large clumps, leaving wispy bald-patches in several places on her scalp. Her eyebrows have disappeared and as her face grows increasingly sunken and sallow her eyes appear to protrude as though somebody is gradually tightening a rope around her neck. Her mouth is filled with ulcers and the only thing she can eat with any degree of comfort is ice lollies.

"No chance of smoking marijuana in here," she joked with Tallulah when the nurse was out of earshot. But Tallulah doubts that even marijuana could comfort Auntie June at this stage.

It was so difficult not to think about her own health while she was sitting by the hospital bed holding her aunt's hand this morning. As much as she wanted to offer reassurances and sympathy she couldn't help but wonder who would be sitting by *her* side should the situation ever get to this stage. There were three other women in the neighbouring beds, all of them cancer patients. The stifling heat of the hospital room combined with the antiseptic smell of sickness made Tallulah feel light-headed and nauseous. She was shamefully relieved when she stepped out through the automatic doors of the hospital and emerged in to the fresh, clean November air; it was like waking from a horrible dream. Knowing that she was leaving Auntie June inside that place, sealed-up and suffocating like a fairground goldfish in a plastic bag, Tallulah returned to Castleton in a fog of apprehension.

She can remember feeling like this as a child whenever there was a looming dental appointment. She would try to focus on something nice that would take her mind off the inevitable terror of gas and needles but the fear was always there, blighting everything that she did. An episode of the *Liver Girls* or a bag of Thornton's special toffee (probably not the best way to placate a child who lives in fear of deep-root fillings) could blind her temporarily from the truth that the following morning she would be dragged to the local dental office. The interminable wait by the fish tank while the whine of the drill shrieked from behind closed doors; the dental hygiene posters and the fake plants all conspired to make Tallulah feel defenceless and terrified.

She has a month to bury her head in the sand. She has a month to organize her new home, to anticipate Christmas and to pretend that January might never come. A month is a long time and there's no point in spending it worrying about what might happen later. The house in Chesterfield is empty and ready to be sold. When Tallulah closed the door on her old life she left without regret, which was surprising because she spent her entire life living in that house. There was no lingering perusal of the empty rooms, no final goodbyes to the ghosts of her childhood or the memory of her parents; it was an unsentimental departure and Tallulah climbed in to Jeff's van without so much as a backward glance.

If Tallulah had known she was going to buy this house she might have been tempted to keep most of Rob's old furniture; at least for the interim period, but everything was taken away or dumped and so the house is now empty. She brought her bed and a few occasional pieces of furniture but the living room and dining room are stripped and bare. For the time being Tallulah intends to live in the bedroom, she can't really think ahead just yet and the prospect of buying new furniture is beyond her comprehension. Without a job or a substantial savings account she must live parsimoniously but, fortunately, an unfurnished life doesn't worry Tallulah and if she closed off the empty rooms through the winter she can save on the heating bills as well.

The sound of the telephone is magnified by the emptiness and it is so unexpected that it makes Tallulah jump. She pushes a couple of boxes to one side to reach the phone and isn't surprised to hear Gran's voice wavering at the other end of the line, she is shouting instructions to somebody and Tallulah hears the tail-end of the conversation; "…and shift that manky buddleia while you're at it, it's on its last legs!"

"Gran?"

"Oh, ey-up duck! I've got young Brian over giving me a hand with the garden. He's put some bulbs in the front for me and now he's cleaning up the back where those railings came down in the gales. Did you go to see your Auntie June this morning?"

"Yes, I just got back half an hour ago. She doesn't look very good, Gran; they've got her hooked up to all sorts of tubes and stuff and they're not sure that's she's strong enough to survive another operation."

"Oh dear," sighs Gran, "I don't know what our Ted's going to do if anything happens to June; he idolizes her, you know. It'll be their fiftieth anniversary next August – their golden anniversary – and I'm beginning to think she's not going to make it. I can still remember the day they got married as though it was yesterday, duck. August the sixth. I always remember that date because it was the day we dropped the bomb on Hiroshima. Not the year they got married, but the same date."

"Well from the look of her today I'm not sure she'll even make it to Christmas."

"Oh dear, oh dear. And then there's folks round here who live off the dole and vandalize the phone boxes and they've never had a day's illness in their lives. It just doesn't seem right, does it? Mind you, old Mrs. Belfit is having her ninetieth birthday next week and she's as fit as a fiddle. I wish I was half as active as she is, duck. They invited me to the do in Dinnington but I don't feel like travelling all that way. To me it's like going to the moon."

"You should go, Gran, it'd be nice for you to get out." Tallulah fiddles with the flaps of a cardboard box, tearing off the tape to see what's inside.

"Oh I can't be doing with all that fuss at my age, duck. They said their Derek would come and pick me up and bring me home again but I'm not very fond of that Chinese wife of his. Whatever he sees in her I'll never know. I think he had blinkers on when he married that one. She stout and short and she's got a face like the back end of a tram smash; slitty eyes, typical Chinese. I think Maureen thought she'd be like a little orange blossom so she was very disappointed. Their Derek is nearly a millionaire and nothing but a stuck up snob. He wanted to take Maureen and the family down to London for two nights at the Dorchester with lunch at Harrods then an evening at the philharmonic something or other at a hundred and fifty quid a pop. I told her he should save his money and buy Maureen a new bungalow but she keeps quiet where their Derek's concerned."

"Well, I'm in the new house, Gran. I moved the last of my stuff yesterday and the old place is going on the market this weekend."

"I'm never going to see you now. It'll be like when our Rob moved out there. I don't know why you wanted to leave Grey Street; it was so convenient for the shops. How are you going to find a new job stuck out there?"

"I'm going to get a little second-hand car, Gran. Jeff's going to give me some refresher lessons in his van."

"Jeff eh? It's Jeff this and Jeff that these days; you're not courting are you, lass?"

"Don't be daft, Gran! He's just a friend of Rob's giving me a hand, that's all."

"Well you just be careful out there on your own. You're not too old to get yourself in to trouble and the last thing you need is a baby at your time of life."

"Gran, I'm forty-five."

"All the more reason to be sensible. Annette Johnson had their Kylie when she was forty-nine and she'd had her tubes tied, so think on!"

Intents & Purposes

It's alarming how money can alter your attitude from one of utter despair to one of enthusiastic optimism and although Nicole is well aware that twelve thousand pounds won't go very far unless she exercises a certain degree of frugality she can't control her natural cravings. She has paid for another month at Brown Bread Cottage and is now on a shopping spree in Manchester. A few hours are all it takes to restore her faith in retail therapy. Any sensible person with a more realistic grasp on reality might have confined themselves to high street chain stores but Nicole's recent brush with destitution appears not to have dulled her yearning for extravagance.

She may only have a thousand pounds in her purse but Jeff had a brilliant idea and told her to go straight in to the American Express office and get herself a replacement card. With her British passport as identification and her account details conveniently stored on the website Nicole had no problem convincing the clerk in the travel office that she is, indeed, Veronica Rustin. With a limitless credit line and the bills being sent to Gideon there must be some unscrupulous way of escaping payment. But for the moment the sheer exuberance of having a platinum card back in her wallet makes Nicole feel impervious and bugger the consequences!

Harvey Nichols has just about everything she could possibly want. She flits from department to department, piling up her purchases with the aloofness of one unfamiliar with the purpose of price tags. In the changing room she stuffs the filthy yellow trousers and her scrappy old Burberry jacket in a waste bin and the assistant very kindly arranges for her to change in to a new outfit. And while she waits for an appointment in the beauty salon she takes lunch in the café and tinkers with her new mobile phone.

The woman who walked in to Harvey Nichols is not the woman who walks out. Restored to her former glory, Nicole feels reunited with a person she thought was gone forever. She goes to a coffee shop and dials Gideon's number.

"Hey, it's Gideon. I've probably lost my phone again so leave me a message and I'll call you back when I find it." Beeeep.

"Hi Gideon, it's me, Ronnie. I just wanted to let you know that your spiteful lie has boomeranged back with poetic justice; it's just unfortunate that I had to be in its flight path on the return journey. I'm HIV positive, darling. You'd better get tested otherwise your unfailing ignorance could kill you sooner than we all anticipated. Oh, and you'd better tell Daphne to do the same thing; maybe the two of you can get tested together; very cosy. Oh, and this is my new cell phone number so put me on speed dial. I'd love to hear from you. Bye!"

A woman at the next table averts her eyes as Nicole closes her phone and it's obvious from her demeanour that she was listening to Nicole's conversation. As Nicole stands up to retrieve her new coat from the back of her chair she leans in towards the woman and fakes a violent sneeze. "Oh, I'm so sorry," simpers Nicole, brushing at the woman's sleeve with her hand, "I must be coming down with something." And she leaves the coffee shop in a flurry of expensive carrier bags.

It is dark by the time she gets back to Brown Bread Cottage. With her boot crammed with bags it takes several trips before Nicole has emptied the car. She had a field day in the supermarket, piling her trolley so high that she had to steady her purchases as she wobbled dangerously to the check-out. She has bought a new lap top with wireless connectivity, easily convincing herself that it is a piece of equipment that no self-respecting person can live without these days. A representative from American Express already called her on her new cell phone to make sure that the card hadn't been stolen; so concerned were they that this sudden spending-spree might be fraudulent. It feels like Christmas has come early for Nicole Harvey.

She lights a fire, takes a fragrant bath and wraps herself up in a gorgeous cashmere-lined bath robe before preparing a delectable feast of giant prawns, rocket salad and crusty artisan bread washed down with several glasses of not-quite-chilled champagne. There is a half-wheel of oozing Brie and some plump Muscat grapes for later and while she settles down to digest she empties out a plastic bag of 'notions' she bought from a little haberdashery shop in York.

A meter of pink felt, a bag of buttons, some reels of cotton, a pack of darning needles and a mound of kapok may seem to be incongruous purchases for a woman like Nicole but, don't worry, she's not taking-up handicrafts. She is taking up *witch* crafts. If Ursula refuses to jeopardise her magical scruples then Nicole will take it upon herself to solicit revenge on Gideon and Daphne. She has bought a book on ancient conjurations and it has all the information she needs to activate her intents and purposes.

The intent; to cause as much misery and suffering to the people who ruined her life. The purpose; to wreak havoc and satisfy her craving for retribution.

Snip, snip, snip go her scissors as they slice through the baby-pink felt. There is no requirement for accuracy or precision, these little dolls are merely the receptacle for Nicole's hatred and vengeance. The power is in her hands as they stitch and sew; weaving and scheming as she imbues her handiwork with all manner of evil thoughts and petitions. She purchased some knotweed from Culpepper's and she crumbles it between her fingers to mix with the kapok for stuffing the effigies. And in a measuring jug she mixes equal parts of linseed oil, almond oil, cooking oil along with some balsam, nine pinches of ash from the fireplace and three black peppercorns. This is her Destruction Oil as outlined in the book of spells and curses.

As she concentrates on her project she refills her glass of champagne and between lukewarm swigs she mumbles her curse over and over again.

> *"Before the night is over,*
> *Before the day is through,*
> *Whatever you have done to me,*
> *Will come right back at you."*

She fashions a tiny penis for Gideon and a pair of breasts for Daphne. She threads coloured wool for hair and stitches buttons for eyes and then, when the dolls are complete, she sprinkles them liberally with the oil she has made.

She looks at the clock. It is almost eleven. The night is silent save for the crackling of the fire and the shifting of the embers. Nicole feels more than a little drunk and the champagne bottle is drained. The walk in to the village will sober her up, she thinks as she goes upstairs to change in to something practical for her purposes. The black designer jeans and the black roll-neck jumper will be perfect under her charcoal grey pashmina. She will be the epitome of designer chic as she carries out her diabolical acts. Maybe it really is true; the Devil *does* wear Prada!

In to her tote bag go the dolls along with a small hammer, a bag of nails, a black candle and a box of matches. She throws in a bottle of Ashbourne water and a packet of mints along with her cell phone for good measure. Fortunately the night is clear and mild so she doesn't have to worry about the elements hindering her intentions.

It's not easy navigating a country lane at night when the moon is nowhere to be seen. Things rustle menacingly in the hedgerows and strange animals scurry from view as Nicole advances towards the village. She is counting on the pubs to be closed and the villagers to be in their beds by the time she gets to the church yard but a couple of cars swish past her, headlamps flaring, as she stumbles uneasily along the main road in to Castleton. Thankfully the main street is deserted, incongruously strung with Christmas lights and decorated with fir trees; a picturesque tableau that somehow seems at odds with Nicole's mission.

She vanishes up a side street and wends her way to the church where everything is thankfully under shadow. A dog barks and somebody shouts out, calling it back indoors. A light goes out in an upstairs window and the flicker of a television screen illuminates the curtains of another. Nicole glances up at the church clock; it is five minutes to twelve.

Hidden from view behind a leaning gravestone she empties her bag on to the grass. It takes several attempts to light the candle and stick it firmly to an upturned urn and Nicole is thankful that there is no breeze tonight. She watches the clock and waits for the hands to overlap at twelve and then, without pausing to consider her actions, Nicole takes the dolls she has made and with a single nail she hammers them (Gideon face-down on top of Daphne, a position Nicole thinks is an appropriate adaptation of her own) to the gnarled trunk of an ancient tree while whispering "I beat you, I break you, I curse you." And then, as outlined in the book, she extinguishes the candle, picks up her bag, and walks away from the church yard without looking back.

The curse is complete.

Robert

The last time I died was in 1952. It was the twenty-fifth of November and we had just returned home from the opening night of Agatha Christie's *Mousetrap* at the Ambassadors Theatre. I was seventy-two years old. I lived with my brother in Islington and I died of food poisoning. Bad oysters.

The time before that was in 1847; crushed to death in a German coal mining accident. I was twenty-seven years old. And before that was in 1769; I was a French prostitute and I died of syphilis at the age of thirty-two.

My lives so far have been fairly mundane; I have never been famous or significantly involved in any historic events. I have lived through wars, natural disasters and the bubonic plague. I visited Crystal Palace before it burned down in 1936 and I witnessed cannibalism in New Zealand over a hundred years before the Europeans arrived.

It's too early for me to decide who to come back as next time but I think I'll wait several decades; I'm not in much of a hurry. With the state of the world at the moment I'll be interested to see what develops before I throw myself back in to the *mêlée*. There are a lot more lessons to learn and, as comfortable as things are here, I know that I will feel compelled to gain more knowledge at some point in time.

There's no hurry. I have all the time in the universe.

Black Magic

Only eighteen shopping days left to Christmas; that's what the advertisers are telling everyone. Tallulah hasn't really given much thought to Christmas, mainly because there's been too much going on but also because she hasn't got the money to waste on presents and cards and decorations. The usual tin of Quality Street for Gran and maybe some flowers for Auntie June, that's the extent of Tallulah's gift-giving this year. She hasn't bothered with a tree for years; not since the old aluminium monstrosity finally died a natural death and had to be thrown away. All through her childhood Christmases Tallulah would stare with innocent wonder at that three foot silver tree on top of the telly; each spindly branch weighed down with ancient ornaments and jerry-rigged fairy lights with half the bulbs missing. It seems amazing to her now that such an ignominious piece of tat could appear so magical but maybe it had something to do with the fact that there was so little enchantment in her every-day life that a few coloured lights and a bit of tinsel were enough to satisfy her low expectations.

She has stripped the wallpaper off the master bedroom walls (with Jeff's help) and Petra came over one afternoon to help her paint. She used a colour called Lilac Spring which looks exactly as it sounds. Ursula is making her some curtains from some old bed sheets in a bright apple-green and although she can't afford a carpet the floorboards are in decent condition and Jeff has given them a new coat of varnish. Unfortunately the little bedroom fireplace doesn't work (the chimney is bricked-up) so Tallulah's romantic dream of bedtime firelight had to be squashed but a pair of bedside lamps rescued from Jeff's shop and topped with new shades create a warm and inviting atmosphere at night.

When you live in the country the seasons play a much more prominent role than they do in the city. It has turned colder and there has been a heavy frost the last few mornings. Tallulah wakes to the sound of the birds and she likes to snuggle down beneath her quilt for half an hour, enjoying the fact that she doesn't have to get up for work. The absence of traffic and neighbours make it easy to forget that there's a world of commerce continuing out there; a whirl of buses and cars, trains and aeroplanes transporting thousands of people to their jobs. She likes to stand at the kitchen sink, munching her toast and sipping her tea while looking over the fields behind the house. It doesn't matter what the weather is like, the view is always beautiful.

This particular afternoon Ursula is helping Tallulah clean the windows. They have buckets of hot soapy water from which steam evaporates in to the cold December air. Jeff told them not to attempt the upstairs windows; he will bring his ladder at the weekend and tackle that task personally. Ursula jokes that he fancies Tallulah but Tallulah refuses to believe such an outlandish suggestion. She hasn't had a bloke fancying her since she eighteen when one of the factory foremen wanted to take her out to a pea and pie supper at the church hall. Tallulah didn't go; the bloke in question was twenty years her senior and recently divorced with custody of three kids and an Alsatian.

"He doesn't fancy me," she protests, "he's just a really nice bloke and we have a laugh. Jeff's not the courting kind, he's a confirmed bachelor."

"Isn't that a euphemism for being gay?" quips Ursula, dunking her squeegee.

"Jeff's not gay!" declares Tallulah adamantly. "If he was he'd be after Martin, not me."

"Well a chap of his age who's never been married is a bit suspicious to me. He probably wears women's underwear or goes up to Manchester to get beaten by a sadistic prostitute!" Ursula cackles at her own joke, pausing to wipe soap suds from her cheek with the back of her hand.

"Ursula! You're terrible! *You've* never been married and you're about the same age as Jeff so does that make you a lesbian?"

"Actually I *was* married, for twelve years, but not your idea of a marriage. We had a handfasting, which is the Wiccan equivalent of a Christian marriage. He was a witch, you see. He died in 1987; asphyxiated in a chemical fire at Coalite." Ursula rubs at the window pane without looking at Tallulah as she imparts this piece of information without emotion. "I don't talk about it much because I'd rather keep it to myself. Jim was a very special person to me and I like to keep him private, in here," and she indicates her heart with a thump of her fist against her chest.

"I'm sorry, Ursula, I didn't mean to pry."

"Don't worry about it, duck, that was all a long time ago and, anyway, you weren't to know."

As Tallulah wrings out her cloth a car crunches around the bend and pulls up outside the house. Both women look over their shoulders to see who it is but Tallulah doesn't know the man who gets out of the white Escort. He is middle-aged with a moustache and a flat cap and he's wearing green Wellingtons and carrying a plastic bag.

"Afternoon Ursula!" he calls out as he makes his way up the garden path.

"All right, Arthur. We don't often see you up here, what's up?"

"Well," he puffs, coming to rest by the broken fencing between the two houses, "I was hoping you might be able to shed some light on these," and he opens the plastic bag and produces what look like two oddly shaped dolls made from felt. He offers them to Ursula and she drops her squeegee and wipes her hands down the front of her dress before taking them from him.

"Where did you get these, Arthur?" she asks, turning the strange little objects around in her hands.

"Mrs. Jacobs found them nailed to the cedar round the back of the church. Looks like somebody was burning black candles an' all; we found a stub on one of the gravestones."

"Well, the fact that you've brought them up to me means you know what these things are but they're nothing to do with me. I don't go in for black magic."

"We didn't think it'd be you, duck, we were just wondering if you might be able to shed some light. It could've been kids, of course, but we've never had anything like this happen in the village before so we're a bit flummoxed."

Ursula examines the dolls more closely and hands them back to Arthur. "Probably somebody mucking about," she says dismissively. "Or a tourist, perhaps."

"What'll I do with 'em, then?" asks Arthur, looking down at the offending articles.

"It's best if you bury them somewhere. Poppets can be powerful magic and you don't want to go messing with somebody else's spells."

He grunts uneasily, "can I leave 'em with you?"

"Go on then, I'll make sure they're disposed off in the correct manner."

"Grand," smiles Arthur with relief and he drops the dolls back in to the plastic bag and props it up against the fence amongst the weeds. "And how's the practicing going for the carol concert?"

"Oh, you know; it'll be all right on the night, as they say."

Arthur chuckles, doffs his cap and bids his farewells before plodding back to his car.

"That's creepy," shudders Tallulah, staring at the plastic carrier bag with agitation, "who do you think could have made them?"

"I've got a bloody good idea," replies Ursula sternly, "and she's playing with fire."

"Not Nicole?"

"Silly cow. I told her not to meddle with poppets but she obviously took it in to her own hands. And to top it all she did it in *our* churchyard. You know what they say about shitting on your own doorstep…"

"But does that stuff really do anything?"

"It does if you believe in it and Nicole's current state of mind is not what you'd call stable. Intention can be a very powerful thing and that's what poppets are; they're made with intentions and it's those intentions that cause the damage. Most witches these days don't muck about with curses and the like because we believe that a curse can turn back on you and cause three times the amount of bad luck as you wished on your enemy. It's what we call the Rule of Three. Unfortunately most people find it more convenient to blame all their problems on an outside force instead of looking within. The answer to every question and the root of all evil is inside each and every one of us."

"Do you think Nicole really hates her husband *that* much?" asks Tallulah, frowning.

"You don't know the half of it," replies Ursula, "if that woman was a stick of Blackpool rock she'd have 'vindictive' written all the way through her."

Wake-Up Call

"This is the second test, Mr. Rustin, and they're both negative. There's no indication that you're HIV positive but come back in three months and we'll test you again."

Gideon stares at the incomprehensible list in front of him. Lymphocytes, basophils, neutrophils and everything appears to be within the normal range. Even if he *is* HIV positive and it isn't yet showing in his blood tests there's no way he could have passed it on to Veronica because she is obviously in the advanced stages of the infection and must have been positive for at least six months or more; maybe even years. On the one hand it is a huge relief to know that he isn't carrying the virus but he can't help but torment himself with the fact that he has had unprotected sex with Veronica on several occasions during the past few months. She could have infected *him*.

Daphne's tests are negative too and Gideon did the right thing and called Courtney advising her to take the test as well. The fabrication that Courtney was already positive is something that Daphne cooked-up to convince Veronica that she was in danger and all of this seems suddenly to have taken on a life of its own. Gideon can't help but think that they have tempted fate by making up such monstrous lies and he won't rest until he has had the final definitive test.

"What about the symptoms I've been noticing?" asks Gideon, referring to the blisters and sores that have recently started to appear around his mouth and nose and the creepy-crawly sensation under his skin."

"How long have you been using crystal meth?" The doctor asks this question with a bluntness that surprises Gideon; he has never discussed his drug use with anyone but his closest friends.

"I'm sorry?" Stalling for time, Gideon feels immediately paranoid. Is this some kind of police sting operation? Is he being filmed for an NBC documentary investigation?

"You are displaying several classic signs of chronic meth usage; the sores on your face, the susceptibility to chest infection and prolonged bouts of flu-like symptoms and the descriptions you gave me of ants or insects crawling under your skin; a condition known as formication."

"I don't use drugs," lies Gideon but he is unable to meet the doctor's eye, "well nothing more than the occasional joint."

"I see," responds the doctor patiently. "Let me just advise you that if you wish your HIV status to remain negative you should be extremely conscientious when it comes to protecting yourself during sexual activity. Miami is saturated with drug users and HIV infection and there's an epidemic of new infections that shows little sign of abating. Let your wife's situation be a warning to you, Mr. Rustin and please be careful because you've had your wake-up call."

Gideon leaves the hospital with a copy of his test results and his tail firmly between his legs. His only thought is to get back home and to smoke up so that he can put today's humiliating experience behind him. Who the fuck does that doctor think he is anyway? Pompous prick!

Chequered Past

Nicole is on the pill so when Julian Smythe fails to unearth a condom in his bedside drawer she assures him that there's no problem.

"What about AIDS?" asks Julian, floundering naked across his king-sized four-poster bed. His face is red and sweaty with exertion and excitement. His once muscular bottom is showing signs of enervation and Nicole has to avoid recalling some of the rock hard buns she has clutched on to in her lifetime.

She laughs blithely, "AIDS? I don't think there's much chance of that Julian, not unless you've been screwing around with a load of old tarts!"

"My last girlfriend was a duchess," stammers Julian.

"And my husband is a multi-millionaire so I think we're pretty safe, don't you?"

How simple-minded some people can be, thinks Nicole as she reaches forward to pull Julian back in to the missionary position he seems to favour. There are some opportunities that a woman should not miss and this is one of them. If she can seduce Julian successfully – ensnare him with her feminine guile – she could be made for life. No more worrying about careers and poverty, no more making-nice with witches and dowdy shop-assistants in an attempt to scrape together some kind of social life. Longfield Hall is a far cry from Brown Bread Cottage and Nicole fancies herself in the role of Lady of the Manor.

She is already aware of Julian's chequered past and if he were to become HIV positive she could merely pass it off as sad testament to his former misdemeanours and lament the fact that he has passed on his deadly legacy to her; thus sealing their fate together as a couple. He would be devastated, of course, and she would be the picture of decorum and understanding; uttering her reassurances that love has no bounds and rushing him down the aisle as quickly as possible.

The e-mailed copy of Gideon's test result, although mildly surprising, isn't completely inconceivable. You see Nicole (or rather, Veronica) has been a bit of a slut these past few years and she puts it all down to depression and disillusionment with her life and marriage in Miami. Her therapist told her she was a sexual compulsive; using sex as a way to salve her insecurity and lack of self-esteem. Her husband told her she was a wanton whore and yet wasn't he the one who introduced Nicole to a life of sexual freedom and depravity in the first place? Gideon is the one to blame, Gideon is the perpetrator of the sin and therefore it is easy for Nicole to absolve herself of all responsibility. She could have picked up the virus from any one of those men she bedded; she never used condoms, she never practiced safe sex, she viewed herself invincible. It was probably one of those bisexual guys who gave it to her; one of those bum-boys trying oh so hard to be 'normal' when really all they wanted was to be pinned down on all-fours by a Latino with a ten inch cock. Thank God for the cocktail! If she'd contracted this disease ten years ago she'd be shitting herself but now; just two pills a day and she'll be right as rain.

"You've got a lovely pair of tits, Nicole," gasps Julian as he pounds in to her with all the misguided bravado of an overgrown schoolboy.

"Be careful with them," warns Nicole as she checks out the hand-stitching on his linen bed sheets, "they cost me a bloody fortune."

Cold Moon

Diamond rings and pearls
Might suit other girls,
I think they may be sham.
Don't we all discover
Stars above may shimmer
But nothing sparkles like a Babycham.

Tallulah is treating herself to a glass of bubbly. She bought a four-pack of Babycham this morning, intending to save it for Christmas Eve, but Ursula has invited her to join the full moon circle tonight and Tallulah feels in need of a little Dutch courage.

She is wearing her black pleated skirt and a black polyester blouse with a huge floppy bow at the neck; something she's had in her wardrobe since Mother's funeral. It's a bit tight under the armpits but if she doesn't stretch forward too far the seams should hold. Black seemed to be the most appropriate colour for a gathering of witches.

Ursula has a sacred sanctuary in her cellar where she holds her rituals. Tallulah has never been down there but she is familiar with Rob's cellar so she knows the layout. She can't imagine anyone wanting to sit down there in the chilly dampness under a sixty watt bulb but maybe that's what witches feel most comfortable with? Tallulah imagines a circle of folding chairs – the kind they have in doctor's waiting rooms – and maybe a candle or two. Everything she knows about witchcraft is from films and Arthur Miller's *The Crucible* which they had to study for O-Level English so, in Tallulah's mind, it's all sacrifices and accusations.

The moon, when it appears through the rawboned branches of the winter trees, is corpulent and ringed with a haze of frost. Ursula refers to it as the Cold Moon, explaining to Tallulah that every full moon of the year has a name. There are very few people who aren't attracted to the mysterious beauty of the moon and in a sky untainted by the orange glow of the city it appears watchful and sentient. Tallulah stands in the darkness of the kitchen and stares at it through the window, sipping her Babycham and trying to visualize the view of Earth from up there. She feels very small.

Tallulah was instructed to let herself in at Ursula's house. "We don't stand on ceremony here," explained Ursula, "the door is unlocked, just take your shoes off in the hallway and take a piece of parchment from the hall table. With a pencil; write down something you would like to wish for and bring this petition down to the cellar with you."

There are already several cars parked outside the house and four pairs of shoes lined up against the wall when she lets herself in. The hallway is dimly lit and there is a strong smell of incense. She removes her shoes and takes a piece of paper from the stack on the table but she has to ponder for a few moments, wondering what she should wish for. When she has scribbled her petition she follows the smell of the incense under the stairs and down in to the cellar where she can hear some kind of simple pipe music. On every stone step there is a single votive candle in a red glass cup and at the bottom of the steps there is the small ante room where Rob kept his bulk cartons of toilet paper and baked beans and where Ursula stores her jars of herbs on metal shelving.

Through the archway she can see the main cellar. The brick walls and vaulted ceiling have been whitewashed and from the centre of the room there is a circle of glass suspended on strong wire ropes; this forms

Ursula's altar upon which she has laid the tools of her craft. Beneath the altar there is a circular rug with a woven pentacle. The flagstone floor is scattered with large cushions and there are several people already seated. Nobody is talking; they appear to be meditating. Ursula stands by the archway and she smiles at Tallulah, beckoning her forward but putting her finger to her lips. She is holding a small metal cup in to which she dips her finger and she traces some kind of symbol with the perfumed oil on Tallulah's forehead before drawing her in to an embrace. "Welcome," she whispers and guides Tallulah clockwise to a vacant cushion where she is instructed to sit.

The cellar is bright with candlelight. It flickers on the ceiling and undulates across the walls. In each corner of the room there is a small altar decorated with candles and statues, crystals and amulets, everything dusty and dribbled with wax as though having lain there, undisturbed, for many years. Tallulah glances covertly around the room. There is a young man, probably not much older than his mid-twenties, with dyed black shoulder-length hair and a metal spike protruding from below his bottom lip. His forearms are tattooed and his clothing is loose and black. There is a middle aged woman with a conventional grey-white hairdo and dark purple lipstick who appears to be wearing some kind of elaborate necklace of intertwined serpents and next to her sits Petra who offers Tallulah a friendly smile. The fourth person is dressed as a woman but is most obviously a man; tall and lanky with long stringy hair the colour of cornflakes. He/she is dressed in a long flowing robe with a hood and has a silver ring on every finger, including both thumbs.

The mystical pipe music is coming from a small portable CD player in the corner and the rhythmic droning soon lulls Tallulah in to a state of dreamy contemplation. Five more people arrive; two men and three women and the circle is complete. Ursula approaches the central altar, picks up a small brass bell and moves around the room, ringing the bell and lighting a candle on each of the four peripheral altars. At each altar she welcomes a deity ("hail and welcome!" chant the congregation at each stage) and then she returns to the centre of the room and produces water and salt, the 'giver' and 'preserver' of life. She mixes them together in a silver goblet, using what looks like a jewelled letter-opener and then she proceeds to circle the room sprinkling the salt water on each person's head. This is followed by a second circumnavigation with a censor of incense, the smoke of which is wafted around the circle.

Tallulah feels as though she is part of something ancient and covert. She is excited to be part of something so outlandish and she pictures herself as though watching from the outside. Drab, ordinary little Tallulah Clegg is sitting here in a sacred circle surrounded by the kind of people she would once have described as 'weird'. Ursula, as High Priestess, dominates the room with her presence; dressed in a trailing robe of black chiffon with a plunging neckline she looks almost stately. Although far from beautiful her waxy complexion appears to radiate light and her face looks softer and less timeworn than usual as she asks the group to deposit their petitions in to a small cauldron of burning oil.

As the scraps of parchment flare up in the cauldron the assembled group starts to chant; quietly at first but with increasing vigour until they are shouting the words, aiming their energy in to the flames;

Fire! Fire! Burning higher!
Making music like a choir!

Bring to us our heart's desire!

And then, when the flames finally abate, the chanting comes to an abrupt stop and the cellar is plunged in to a resonant silence where the solid walls seem to absorb the incantation and reflect it back at the congregation as a silent echo.

Tallulah watches Ursula reach for a plaited loaf and a large silver goblet and these are passed around the circle so that each person can break off a chunk of bread, dip it into the goblet and then thank the Lord and Lady for something they feel thankful for. This is probably the most humiliating part of the ritual for somebody as timid and shy as Tallulah; watching the bread and wine approach her she knows that she must speak out-loud in front of these strangers. Some people offer generic thanks for good health and prosperity while others mention loved ones and personal triumphs. When the goblet arrives in Tallulah's hands she stares at the floor and mumbles her thanks for 'new friends' and as she quickly passes the wine to the next person there is a general response of "and so mote it be." The worst is over.

The ritual only lasts about forty-five minutes and afterwards they all file upstairs where there is food and drink laid out on the kitchen table. The group suddenly transforms itself in to a regular babble of voices and laughter; people hugging each other and wandering around the house as though it is their own. Ursula introduces Tallulah to several people and everyone is so friendly that Tallulah can't believe that this is what witchcraft is all about. She never imagined that witches would sit around drinking wine and eating sausage rolls, exchanging stories about the terrible road works on the M1 and the shocking price of petrol.

"Two hundred calories in this little slice," complains one woman, holding up a narrow wedge of quiche.

"Orchids are not as difficult to grow as you'd think," says another.

"So what did you think to your first Full Moon?" asks Petra, coming to sit alongside Tallulah on the capacious sofa.

"I liked it," she admits. "It wasn't at all scary."

"So are you going to become a witch?" Petra bites in to a chunk of fruit cake, spilling crumbs down the front of her jumper.

Tallulah laughs, "Maybe," she replies.

"Listen, I've got a question for you. There's no obligation for you to say yes, I won't be offended if you think it's a bad idea but my flatmates have decided not to renew the lease on our place and I'm going to be out on my heels at the end of the month. I was wondering if you'd be interested in renting out your second bedroom. I can't pay more than a couple of hundred a month but it's better than a kick up the arse and I know you're a bit strapped until you get another job."

Tallulah is startled by this suggestion but not averse to the idea. She likes Petra and, it's true, she could do with some help with the bills. Number Two is virtually empty and Tallulah is going to be rattling around in there for years until she can afford to start buying furniture so renting one of the rooms to Petra could be a convenient and sociable thing to do. It would be the communal living that Tallulah never got to experience when she was younger and she's always fancied the idea of being the kind of person who shares late-night confidences over mugs of drinking chocolate.

"I think that'd be great," she says, "as long as you don't mind sharing with an old woman."

Petra grabs Tallulah in a sudden bear-hug, squeezing the breath right out of her body and upsetting her plate of pasta salad. "Brilliant! Can I move in before Christmas?"

"I don't see why not," laughs Tallulah, scraping the mayonnaise off her pleated skirt, "as long as you don't expect me to decorate your bedroom."

"I'm an art student," declares Petra with a grin, "that's my job!"

And then Ursula enters the living room with her guitar and Petra gets up to join her in a few jovial verses of *The Saucy Sailor.*

Apparitions

Nicole has the flu. Her head throbs, her throat is sore and her body aches all over. When she attempted to go down the stairs this morning she tripped and banged her shoulder as she fell. She doesn't have any aspirin or Lemsip and she left the milk out last night so it has gone sour. She makes a cup of tea and carries it carefully back upstairs, placing it on the bedside table and climbing gingerly back under the quit, dressing gown and all. Her skin hurts. Even her *hair* hurts.

It is seven-fifteen but the morning is still dark. A cold wind gusts against the outside walls of Brown Bread Cottage and it shrieks between the gaps in the ill-fitting bedroom window. Nicole feel wretched and she wonders if she should call Julian and ask him to bring her some supplies. Maybe he will come and fetch her; bundle her up in a nice thick blanket and carry her off to Longfield Hall where Mrs. Moon might make her homemade chicken soup and mop her fevered brow.

But Julian doesn't get up until after ten so Nicole will have to wait a few hours before she bothers him.

In her present state Nicole doesn't want to think too deeply about Julian. He is a convenient crutch for her at the moment but he irritates her with his blustery cheerfulness and British reserve. Compared to the men Nicole knows in Miami Julian is a poor substitute but she suspects that her choice is limited. He is wealthy and emotionally unsophisticated but he has a child-like fascination with beautiful women and Nicole suspects that he is the kind of man who never quite recovered from the shock of being weaned from the breast. He is putty in her expert hands but Nicole needs something more than a malleable lump of grey to stimulate her exacting nature and a man who has a nursery-book name for his penis is slightly sickening.

When he kisses her his lips are hard and dry; his tongue curls in and out of Nicole's mouth like the prodding of an inquisitive slug. And he has the ugliest feet she has ever seen. They are calloused and flaky and his toenails are thick and yellowed. He had the decency to apologize for them but Nicole doesn't understand why a man of his social standing doesn't see a chiropodist. And then there is his blue-white skin and oversized nipples, his skinny, hairless legs and the protruding mole in the small of his back. For a man who appears so dapper in his country gentleman clothing he is remarkably loathsome when naked. Compared to Julian Gideon is a film star and with a pang of bitter regret Nicole turns away from these thoughts and concentrates instead on Julian's bank account.

She needs financial stability and she's not going to find it with a cleverly worded CV or a forty hour week at minimum wage. Her age and the fact that she hasn't worked in England for over fifteen years weight heavily against her and she honestly doesn't know if she has the fortitude to consider full-time employment again after years of sybaritic luxury with Gideon. She has become soft, she has lost her edge and she doesn't even know if she still has the right to work in England. Maybe her social security has expired? Maybe she no longer has National Insurance? And how do any of these Brits survive on twelve thousand a year when petrol costs a pound a litre?

The simple fact is Nicole is spoilt. She has forgotten how to look after herself and her priorities are skewed. She is dysfunctional to the point of naiveté and she still can't grasp the simple fact that in her present position she should be prepared to take any kind of job as long as it doesn't involve hard physical labour or getting her hands dirty. Instead she has been spending her time shopping and sending vitriolic e-mail messages to Gideon and Daphne (to which she no longer receives any response). The majority of her energy has been expended courting Julian and although it appears to be working she isn't sure that she can go through with it, even for the sake of a manor house and a well-stocked wine cellar. Julian is only in his early fifties so it's not even likely that he'll pop his clogs any time soon so she can't rely on an early demise and a vast inheritance to save her.

At nine o' clock the phone rings. It is Ursula and Nicole is so pleased to hear her voice that she almost starts to cry. "I've got the flu," she whines, "and I can't get out of bed."

"Quite frankly it's not surprising that you're feeling lousy," admonishes Ursula over the phone, "if you meddle with voodoo dolls and black magic what do you expect?"

"I've already told you that had nothing to do with me, Ursula," lies Nicole, "I wouldn't know where to start with something like that." She sniffs and it feels as though there is a wad of cotton wool pressing against her sinuses. "Do you think you could bring me some medicine? I'd go to the store myself but I've fallen down the stairs and I don't think I can drive."

Ursula sighs heavily and it sounds as though she is stirring a cup of something. "I'll mix you up some of my own cold remedy and bring it over in a couple of hours," she promises.

Thank God for Good Samaritans!

But Nicole is worried. She's been reading about HIV on the internet and she is well aware that the initial signs of a compromised immune system are flu-like symptoms and swollen lymph nodes. The glands below her ears are definitely swollen and there are strange lumps under her armpits. It's not so easy to be blasé about things when you're feeling like shit and Nicole is anxious now to start on the medications. She has a doctor's appointment next week for the results of the genotype test and then they'll be able to prescribe a suitable course of tablets for her to take. She feels resentful that Gideon and Daphne have somehow escaped the calamity, not just because she wants vengeance but also because she would feel less alone if she knew they were going through the same experience. She has considered calling her friend Tony in Miami (he has been positive for several years now and is the picture of good-health and vitality) but she doesn't want to toss any more ammunition to the Gossip Vultures, she is certain that they're already having a field-day over there.

You might think that Nicole would be humbled by this recent turn of events; that she could possibly begin to empathise with Third World countries and the plight of the Africans, but Nicole's inherent selfishness is unaffected by her glimpse of mortality and she just thanks her lucky stars that she has access to Western medicine and indoor plumbing. It's fine for philanthropists such as Oprah and Angelina Jolie to swan off to these places; building schools and adopting babies while being followed by a battery of cameramen, but Nicole doubts that any of those do-gooders are compromising their own safety and comfort for the benefit of the cause. It's easy to toss a hundred quid in to a blind man's violin case if you've got money to throw away but how much of a sacrifice is that?

The simple truth of the matter is that Nicole feels invincible. The news about her health was surprising but it hasn't knocked her down in the way she imagined it might and even now, feeling so lousy, she can't grasp the idea that she has a fatal disease. When AIDS first entered the headlines in the early eighties it was a fascinating topic but it was confined to a close-knit community of gay men in America. There were a few documentaries on TV and a lot of tabloid speculation but Nicole didn't really take much notice of it. It wasn't until several years later, when the epidemic reached catastrophic proportions and started to infiltrate the heterosexual community that Nicole began to pay more attention.

Nocturnal apparitions of living skeletons with bulging eyes haunted her. She was convinced on several occasions that she was positive; usually following yet another risky sexual encounter. A sore throat, a mouth ulcer or an unidentifiable mark on her body would plunge her in to abject fear and she would dash to the Middlesex hospital in London for another anonymous test.

During the past twenty years Nicole has been treated for gonorrhoea three times, she has been exposed to syphilis (but did not contract the disease), has suffered the indignity of crabs on several occasions and endured a series of painful laser treatment for genital warts. It's a miracle she never contracted herpes or hepatitis B. It's hardly surprising that a woman with this kind of medical history would eventually become HIV positive and yet she fails to acknowledge the severity of her condition. They are calling it a 'manageable disease' these days, more a chronic illness than a death sentence; so why should she get her knickers in a twist about something that can be controlled? AIDS is the new diabetes.

When she staggers out from beneath the quilt to go to the toilet she barely makes it across the hall before her bowels turn to water. There is no warning, it just happens, catching Nicole off-guard as she reaches for the toilet seat. The mess is unimaginably gross and for a moment she remains in a bending position, clutching the rim of the toilet in stunned disbelief. She hasn't shit herself since she was seven years old! The overpowering stench sends her reeling in to the hallway where she steadies herself against the wall and then she feels the floor slipping away from beneath her feet.

A few seconds later she regains consciousness and finds herself sprawled across the landing carpet with her filthy cashmere-lined dressing gown tangled up around her thighs. Her mouth feels parched and her head is throbbing. There is a grainy light filtering in through the downstairs windows and it textures everything with a monochromatic hue. The wind worries at the front door, whistling and moaning between the bricks and mortar of the cottage and it has started to rain. Nicole doesn't have the energy to sit upright so she crawls across to the bedroom door and props herself up against the door frame. Her face is greasy with cold sweat. She is scared.

And then, in the corner of the bedroom, barely concealed by the shadow of the large ugly wardrobe, Nicole sees a figure. It is a woman and she is wearing what looks like a long black coat, fitted at the waist and with a high collar. She doesn't move, she doesn't speak, she just stands silently and stares intently at Nicole with eyes that catch the light from the little bedside lamp. Her expression is inscrutable but there is an atmosphere in the room; an atmosphere of chilled suspense like the gap between a flash of lighting and the first rumble of thunder. And then she is gone.

Nicole blinks and the room is empty again. The wind dashes the rain against the windows and the house shudders against the assault but there is nothing in the corner of the bedroom but an elongated crack from floor to ceiling where the plaster has started to separate and the wallpaper has split.

Cake

Gideon is well informed of Nicole's every move and her unfolding story is worthy of a Latin *telenovella*. The private detective he recently hired reports back to him from England at the end of every day and it would appear that Nicole is now a regular overnight visitor to a large country house that belongs to a diamond broker/antique dealer called Julian Smythe. The connection between Nicole and Julian is vague at this stage but the detective has informed Gideon that the introduction was made by a junk shop owner called Jeff Pike, a friend of the dead college lecturer, Robert Clegg. Nicole is regularly sighted going in and out of the house of the former lecturer (now inhabited by his cousin, Tallulah Clegg) and the next-door-neighbour, a Ms. Ursula Colefax who is reputed to be a witch!

Gideon reads his daily e-mails with interest. He derives a great amount of satisfaction from the simple fact that Veronica appears to be making something of a mess of her life over there in England. He isn't sure what he is going to do with all this information but he knows one thing for sure; it will come in handy as ammunition at some point in the future.

The twelve foot Christmas tree in Gideon's living room is a sterile, department-store affair created by the florists who come in to look after his plants. It is white with blue lights and silver balls and it creates an aquarium-like glow at night. It stands in front of the floor-to-ceiling windows and is reflected in the dark glass beyond which the expansive ocean stretches darkly to the horizon.

It is after two in the morning and Daphne was supposed to be back from work by one. Gideon has called her cell phone several times but gets nothing but her voice mail. If the bitch isn't here by two-thirty he's informing the concierge to turn her away and he's going to bed.

The TV is switched on but the volume is down and Gideon is listening to music. He has been high since this afternoon and his eyes feel gritty and sore. He grinds his teeth and clenches his fists in an attempt to ease the tension of withdrawal but knows that he will have to take something if he wants to get some sleep. Smoking pot doesn't seem to work for him any more and sleeping pills just seem to make him feel even more jittery and disorientated.

He hates Christmas! If he wasn't having a party on Christmas Eve he wouldn't have bothered with the tree or the decorations on the balcony but it's become something of an annual event. It will be strange this year without Ronnie to organize everything; if there is one thing she's good at it's arranging parties. Daphne doesn't have a clue. Her idea of a good get-together is a trip to the liquor store, a local DJ and some party platters from Publix so Gideon had to rely on the PR girl from the gym to pull everything together this year.

What is Ronnie doing hanging around with this jerk in Leeds? They've only just met; surely they can't be *that* close already? And Ronnie must be keeping her HIV status close to her chest otherwise she'd never get a man to come near her. Maybe an informative Christmas card sent to this Julian guy will throw a spanner in the works and see Ronnie out on her ass for the holidays? Or maybe desperate old guys have to take what they can get and are willing to risk their health for the sake of a decent fuck?

Gideon's cell phone rings. It is Daphne. He flips open the phone; "where the fuck are you? I've been calling you for the past hour."

"Gideon, it's not Daphne, it's me, Tiffany. I'm using her phone because I don't have your number and you're not listed."

"Well where the fuck is she?" demands Gideon in his usual charming manner.

"She's at Mercy Hospital. They've just taken her in an ambulance."

"What? She's at the hospital? Why? What's happened?"

"It's awful, Gideon. The presentation was delayed because somebody from the bachelor party OD'd on heroin and in the panic they forgot that Daph was inside the cake. She was trapped in there for over an hour and when they opened it up…" Tiffany breaks off abruptly and Gideon can hear her crying.

"Tiffany! What the fuck? How is she?"

"She's dead, Gideon. She suffocated. The lid of the cake got jammed and she couldn't get out."

Flora and Fauna

"You can sip it if you like," suggests Ursula, "but I find it goes down easier if you just gulp it all down in one go." She hands the mug of brownish liquid to Nicole who is now cleaned-up and sitting in her bed supported by a mound of freshly-plumped pillows.

"What is it?" asks Nicole suspiciously, sniffing the warm concoction and recoiling from the foul smell.

"Mainly yarrow with a little elderflower and peppermint to sweeten the taste," replies Ursula, sitting on the edge of the bed, causing the mattress to creak and dip dangerously. "It tastes revolting but I find it usually does the trick, especially when you've got a fever. When the doctor gets here he will be able to tell you if you need something stronger."

Nicole holds her breath and swallows the lukewarm liquid as quickly as she can but it makes her retch all the same. She shudders and hands the empty mug back to Ursula with a grimace.

"How are you feeling now?" asks Ursula, placing the empty mug on the bedside table, craning her neck to look out the bedroom window across the rain-swept garden.

"I feel lousy," admits Nicole. "Thanks for cleaning up the mess; there was no need to do that, but thanks all the same." It is a long time since Nicole thanked anyone for anything so the words don't form easily on her lips.

"I'll take those things and dump them in my machine," says Ursula, indicating the bin-bag crammed with Nicole's soiled clothing. "That dressing gown should probably be dry-cleaned though."

"If you could just rinse it through with some cold water I'll take it to be cleaned later." Nicole doesn't divulge how much the dressing gown cost, it would probably shock somebody like Ursula who appears to buy most of her own clothing from jumble sales and charity shops.

"You need to talk to your doctor in Manchester. This could be connected to your HIV infection, you know. When Doctor Rice gets here he'll probably suggest that you see a specialist as soon as possible. I doubt that he has much experience with HIV round here; probably more familiar with Mad Cow disease!"

Nicole smiles weakly. She doesn't want to contemplate the possibility that her body is under attack from enemy fire. That's how she envisions the virus; a marauding army of killer micro-organisms advancing upon the depleted trenches of her poor defeated T-cells.

"Ursula, you mentioned a week or so ago that this place is haunted, did you mean it or were you just having me on?"

"Why? Have you seen something?" Ursula's question is almost too nonchalant, as though she knows something but doesn't want to reveal too much too soon.

"Well, I'm not sure if I was delirious or hallucinating, but this morning, after I'd fainted, I thought I saw a woman standing over there by the side of the wardrobe. It was only a few seconds and the room was pretty dark but it was unmistakable."

Ursula glances over to the corner of the bedroom where the cracked plaster has torn the flowered wallpaper. With the curtains open and with Ursula sitting on the edge of the bed the suggestion of a ghost suddenly seems ridiculously fanciful and Nicole is ready to trivialize her experience.

"A woman in a black coat?" asks Ursula, without looking at Nicole.

"Yes!" declares Nicole with enthusiasm, "a long black coat."

"That'd be old Flora Dakin, then. I've seen her a couple of times myself; both times out there in the garden at twilight. I sometimes walk round this way in the summer when the nights are light and I've seen her standing out back by the wheelbarrow, just staring out across the fields as though she's waiting for somebody to come home."

"Who is she? What happened to her?"

"Oh she was a rope-maker, used to live up in Peak Cavern when there was an entire village clustered just inside the mouth of the caves. Apparently she was carrying-on with the bloke who lived here, a young botanist called William Drinkwater. She got knocked-up, young William scarpered and poor old Flora swallowed a fatal amount of Cowbane. She was only nineteen."

"When did it happen?" asks Nicole, pushing herself further under the quilt.

"Oh, sometime back in the early eighteen hundreds, I think. You should ask Mrs. Harris about it, she's seen Flora umpteen times since she bought this place."

"I've never seen a ghost before," proclaims Nicole with a certain degree of pride, "it happened so quickly that I wasn't even sure if I'd seen her or not."

"Nothing to be scared of – ghosts – they can't hurt you. It's the *living* you want to be worried about."

"Tell me about it!" quips Nicole. "If it wasn't for the living I wouldn't be in the state I'm in now, would I?"

There is a knock at the front door causing Nicole to jump slightly.

"That'll be Doctor Rice," says Ursula, "I'll go down and let him in." The bed-springs complain noisily as Ursula stands up and Nicole lists to one side as the mattress levels out.

Smoke without Fire

Someone has been watching the house.

Tallulah doesn't know who or why but three times now she has seen the same dark blue car outside. It is unnerving because nobody comes up this lane unless they're visiting Ursula or Tallulah.

"Probably an estate agent or something," suggests Petra as she carries another box upstairs to her room. Today she has her hair tied in little knots all over her head and she's wearing black lipstick.

They've taken up the bedroom carpet and Jeff helped Petra to give the floorboards a quick sanding and a coat of polyurethane. She's painted over the wallpaper with bright white paint and pinned white cotton sheets over the windows like sails, tacked-back at the corners. An enormous white paper globe hangs from the centre of the room like a full moon wrapped in twine. Nothing more than a mattress tossed on the floorboards, covered with a white fluffy duvet and a clothes-rail on wheels – the industrial kind that they use in shops – hung with

Petra's clothes. She has a large poster of Che Guevara on the chimney breast and a bright red pop-art mobile dangling from the ceiling in one corner. It's all very minimal. Very Art Studenty.

"I thought about it being an estate agent," says Tallulah as she stands at the bottom of the stairs, "but I just don't think it is… it feels, what's the word? Clandestine."

"So tell the cops about it if you're so worried," says Petra, reappearing at the top of the stairs in a pair of ridiculously heavy black pit-boots.

"I've not got anything to tell them," admits Tallulah, "it just makes me feel a bit uncomfortable, especially after the burglary."

"We've got an alarm system now, Tally, and anyway, there's nothing left to nick; this place is empty!"

"You're right! I'm being silly. I suppose the burglar has just put me a bit on edge, that's all. I keep listening at night because I think I can hear footsteps round the back of the house and I've been keeping my light on at night. It'll be nice having you around to keep me company; knowing that you're on the other side of the wall."

"You probably won't think it's nice when I'm up till three in the morning playing Aphex Twin at full blast because I'm stoned!"

"You've got your headphones; I've seen them."

Petra clomps down the stairs and as she passes Tallulah she thumps her shoulder playfully and says, "Have you been peeping at my stuff already?"

"No, I saw you carrying them up yesterday."

Petra laughs and goes outside to get the last of her things from the back of Jeff's van. It is raining and the path is flooded in several places. Jeff comes round from behind the van holding a couple of bulging bin bags. He is wearing his suede fringed jacket and ripped jeans. "That's it!" he calls as he splashes towards the front door, squinting through the rain.

"I'd better put the kettle on, then," smiles Tallulah, retreating in to the kitchen.

With just nine days to Christmas there is a tangible atmosphere of anticipation in the air and Tallulah finds herself caught-up in the reckless mood of the season. She doesn't have the money to waste on the usual frivolities and she's not the type to run up a huge credit card bill that takes the next year to pay-off so she finds her enjoyment in simple pleasures instead. Holly berries crystallized with early morning frost and robins perched on the clothes line are the real-life Christmas cards on Tallulah's window sill. Tijuana Brass and Mantovani on the cassette player cheer the late afternoons with recognizable carols as she butters her toast and sips her tea, and in the fridge, alongside her miniature bottles of Babycham, she has carefully collected a small cache of treats to be saved for Christmas Day. Ferrero Rocher, a bag of tangerines and a box of dates sit temptingly on the top shelf of the pantry.

"Are we going to have a tree?" asks Petra as she swings in to the kitchen carrying a small box of glasses and china. "We could stand it in the living room window and throw a few cushions on the floor and then we can light a fire and look at the lights." Jeff follows Petra in to the kitchen, wiping his hands on a piece of kitchen paper.

"I can get you one cheap from my mate in Hope," he offers.

"I've got to watch my money," informs Tallulah, "I don't think I can run to a tree this year, let alone lights and decorations."

"Aw," complains Petra with an exaggerated frown, "we've *got* to have a tree!" She turns her attention to Jeff who smiles and says he will see what he can do.

"Jeff, you've already done way too much for me already," remonstrates Tallulah, "I don't want you putting yourself out on our account."

"It'll be my Christmas present to the two of you," he states with a grin. "But you have to promise that you'll invite me over one evening to share it with you."

"I was thinking of doing Christmas dinner here," says Tallulah. "With Ursula arranging her dinner on the twenty-first for Yule I thought I could arrange dinner here for Christmas. Nothing fancy; just the usual traditional stuff. I'm not a great cook but I think I can just about manage to roast a turkey and boil a few sprouts."

"Brilliant!" enthuses Petra, "I'll be in charge of the decorations."

"Oh, I've got something for you in the van," remembers Jeff and he disappears down the hall while Tallulah fills the teapot with boiling water and Petra empties her things in to a cupboard that Tallulah cleared-out for her.

"Ta dah!" trumpets Jeff, returning with an electric fireplace insert moulded to look like burning logs. "I thought this might work in your bedroom fireplace. Not the same as the real thing but it'll bring a bit of warmth to the room. I got it in a job lot a couple of days ago; three quid! It even flickers."

Tallulah still can't believe how nice people can be. She has never had friends like this before and on several occasions she finds tears standing in her eyes when somebody does something unexpected like this. "Oh, Jeff, that's lovely. I hope it fits. Thank you!"

"I'll pop up and see," enthuses Jeff, shrugging off his jacket and placing it over the back of a chair.

"Somebody's got a crush on you," sings Petra with an impish grin as soon as Jeff is out of earshot.

"Don't be daft," decries Tallulah, colour flushing her cheeks, "he's just a nice bloke. He'd do the same for anybody. Look at all that work he did in your bedroom."

"That's because I'm young and helpless," jokes Petra, "I need a father-figure in my life."

"Well I'm too long in the tooth for father-figures or boyfriends for that matter so you can get those romantic notions out of your head. Me and Jeff are just friends."

"Whatever!" replies Petra in the dismissive tone that insinuates she doesn't believe a word of it, "but, if you ask me, there's no smoke without fire and Jeff's kindling is ready to ignite!"

"You've got a vivid imagination, Petra. Is that something they teach you at Art College?" Tallulah sees Ursula hurrying across her back garden beneath a broken umbrella so she raps on the kitchen window and beckons for her to come over. She mimes the pouring of tea and Ursula raises her hand in acknowledgement. "Ursula's been round at Nicole's place this morning," informs Tallulah, "apparently she's got the flu."

"I'm not surprised; she never wears the right clothes. I saw her the other day traipsing through the village without a coat."

"She thinks she's still in Miami."

"Hello, hello!" Ursula comes in through the kitchen door and stamps her feet on the door mat. "Blimey, it's bitter out there."

"I wish it would snow," says Petra.

"It's too cold for snow," observes Ursula, flapping the rain off her umbrella and propping it up against the door frame, "and there'll be plenty of time for that in January and February."

"I want a white Christmas!"

"Well don't bet on it. The odds are 15/1 at Ladbrokes according to the BBC."

Ursula remains by the kitchen door rubbing her hands briskly together to restore the circulation. "I can't stop; I'm supposed to be in Macclesfield by three."

"Have you got time for a cuppa?" asks Tallulah, reaching for another mug.

"No, duck, I'm late already."

"So how's the patient at Brown Bread Cottage?" asks Tallulah.

"Oh God, she's in a right state," sighs Ursula, "Doctor Rice has asked me to keep an eye on her; she's got a temperature of a hundred and two and she's dehydrated. Poor cow didn't make it to the loo in time and messed herself on the landing; made a right mess, I can tell you."

"There's nothing worse than being ill when you're on your own in a strange place," observes Tallulah, although she's never been in that particular position herself so she is merely quoting from hearsay.

"The worrying thing is she reckons she's seen the ghost of Flora Dakin; the girl who haunts the cottage. I didn't say anything but Flora only usually appears before something bad happens. Mrs. Harris reckons she's a kind of barometer for misfortune. I've seen her twice now and both times were followed by calamities. The first time was back in eighty-seven just two days before Jim was killed in the fire at Coalite and the second time was a couple of years ago on the night before I fell and broke my collar-bone."

"Perhaps it's not flu she's got," suggests Petra with wide-eyed innocence, "perhaps it's something deadly."

Tallulah catches a glimpse of something in Ursula's expression as she turns to look at Petra but Ursula doesn't elaborate.

There is a hammering sound upstairs followed by a crumbling noise.

"What the hell is that!" yelps Ursula.

"Oh, I'm sorry," apologises Tallulah, "Jeff's upstairs mucking about with my bedroom fireplace. He's brought me an electric log-fire to put in the grate."

"ARE YOU ALL RIGHT UP THERE?" shouts Tallulah, raising her face to the kitchen ceiling.

"FINE!" shouts back Jeff.

"He'd make somebody a lovely husband," quips Ursula, grinning at Tallulah mischievously.

"What is it with you two? Can't a bloke help a woman out without being accused of ulterior motives? He's just a friend."

"Sounds like we've touched a raw nerve," coos Petra, "methinks the lady doth protest too much."

"And I think you two have got over-active imaginations," replies Tallulah, swiping the draining board with a damp J-cloth.

"So how's your aunt doing in hospital?" asks Ursula, changing the subject.

"Not too good. I spoke to Uncle Ted this morning and they've got her on some sedatives and pain-killers that knock her out. She's asleep most of the time but it doesn't look good. The doctors have given her a couple of months at the most."

"Oh dear," sighs Ursula, "your poor uncle."

"Yes, he's beside himself."

"Listen, I'd better be off. I'll call round later when I get back. Petra, don't forget we've got a rehearsal at seven." And Ursula grabs her flapping umbrella and slams the door behind her.

Tallulah is just about to start pouring the tea when Jeff calls out from the top of the stairs. "Tally? I think you'd better come up here and look at this."

"Come on, Petra; let's see what he's done to my fireplace."

The two women trail upstairs and Jeff is waiting for them at the bedroom door with a strange expression on his face. He has dust in his hair and his hands are dirty. There is a small pile of bricks and mortar in front of the fireplace.

"Oh my God, what happened?" asks Tallulah, looking at the mess.

"The chimney," explains Jeff, "some of the bricks up the chimney were loose so I poked around a bit and a couple of them just fell out. It seems it wasn't bricked-up at all, it was just superficial. And look what I found inside…" He points to two large plastic bin-liners on the floor.

"What are they?"

"Take a look for yourself."

Tallulah approaches the bags with caution. One of them is crammed with small zip-locks bags of fine white powder, each one apparently containing the same amount. The second bag is wrapped around several bundles of bank notes which Tallulah empties out on to the floorboards with a dull thud. Petra gasps.

"Oh my God! How much do you think's here?"

"Quick calculation," answers Jeff, "I'd say about five grand. It looks like we've found the skeleton in Rob's chimney and probably the motive behind the break-in."

255

"Cocaine," whispers Petra with awe, moving in for a closer look while Tallulah sinks back on her heels to gawp at her cousin's ill-gotten gains.

Getting the Cream

"I'll send a car to pick you up," says Julian, "you can stay at the house as long as you like but I'll be in Amsterdam for the next couple of days."

Nicole is talking to him by phone. She called as soon as Ursula left but he was in a meeting and she had to wait for him to call her back. It is now almost four in the afternoon and it is already dark; these short winter days in England are pretty depressing and it hasn't stopped raining all day. No wonder the Brits drink so much!

"I don't want to inconvenience anybody," wheedles Nicole, "but it's just that I don't have anybody here to look after me and the doctor said I need constant surveillance. I'm dehydrated."

"Well Mrs. Moon will take care of you; she's a marvellous nurse. I feel jolly sick that I can't be there to see you, my dear, but this trip is important. This is a big time of the year for diamonds, you know."

"That's OK, Julian, I look terrible and I feel lousy so I wouldn't be much fun. Anyway, I don't want you to catch whatever it is I've picked up."

Little does he know, thinks Nicole. Thank God he's going to be away; she'll be able to luxuriate in that huge manor house all on her own and she won't have to put up with Julian bumbling around her with that stupid expression on his face. It'll be like a little spa retreat.

"You're amazing, Julian, thanks so much."

"Oh, please…" Nicole can practically hear him blushing with pleasure, "it's nothing. I'll send the car over at six; is that OK with you?"

"That's perfect," purrs pussycat Nicole, licking her lips in anticipation of getting the cream.

Money for Nothing

"So what are we going to do with it?" asks Petra, staring excitedly at the mound of cocaine and cash on the bedroom floor.

"Well it'll have to go the police, obviously," says Tallulah, looking to Jeff for confirmation.

"The cops!" exclaims Petra with indignation, "Why would you want to call the cops? They'll just pocket the money and sell the coke and Hey Presto; Money for nothing!"

"Petra, we can't keep it," insists Tallulah, "it's not ours and it probably wasn't Rob's either. It's *drug* money and it's illegal."

"I'm surprised at Rob," says Jeff, "I mean; I knew he flogged the odd bit of dope here and there but I had no idea he was mixed up in the hard stuff."

"Yeah, me neither," agrees Petra, sitting down on the edge of Tallulah's bed. "It's not like he was throwing money around or anything and I never saw him use anything other than pot. He did get Martin some ecstasy once but that was just a one-off."

"Bloody hell!" sighs Tallulah, "this is *all* we need."

"Well just think about it before you contact the police," continues Petra. "Just think how this money could help out your auntie and uncle right now. If you want to give the coke to the cops then, fine…but don't give them the cash as well."

"Look," explains Tallulah, "this house was broken in to by somebody who was obviously keen to get their hands on this little lot. Somebody knows that it's here and they're going to be well pissed-off if they find out that *we've* kept the money. I want to sleep safe in my bed at night, all right? It's *got* to go to the police; let *them* sort it out."

"OK, OK," surrenders Petra, holding the palms of her hands up towards Tallulah, "it's your house, do whatever you like."

"Tally's right, Petra, it's too dangerous to hold on to this stuff." Jeff speaks with conviction but his expression is ambiguous. Tallulah wonders if he agrees with Petra; after all; who *wouldn't* be tempted to keep it to themselves? "However…I'm trying to imagine the shit hitting the fan if the papers get hold of this; they'll drag Rob's name through the mud and that's not going to be very nice for his mum and dad, is it?"

"I didn't think about that," admits Tallulah, "but what option do we have? I'll talk to Uncle Ted first and ask him what he wants to do; after all, theoretically it's still his house so this is his decision. They thought the world of Rob; this is going to gut them."

Rhubarb

Nicole doesn't feel any better despite the expert ministrations of Mrs. Moon. The guest suite at Longfield Hall is expansive but heavily decorated in the style of a Victorian mausoleum and Nicole finds it oppressive and impersonal after the relative cosiness of Brown Bread Cottage. She is propped-up against a mound of frilly white pillows and surrounded by acres of floral chintz. The four-poster bed dominates the room but there is still plenty of space for a sofa, two armchairs, an enormous, ugly black marble fireplace and several oil portraits that seem to watch Nicole with censorious eyes.

She feels as though she is clutching at straws and her grip is loosening. Being here in this strange house all alone she has too much time to dwell on her unhappy situation and she feels lost and desolate. Julian hasn't called once since she got here and she isn't even sure that she cares. Her body aches all over and she wakes in the middle of the night drenched in an uncomfortable cold sweat that soaks the sheets and pillows. She has no appetite and can't even manage the scrambled eggs and thin slices of toast that Mrs. Moon brings up for her on a tray. Orange juice stings her throat and upsets her stomach and mouth ulcers make it painful to chew even the softest of food. She can't concentrate on books or magazines and there is no TV in her room so she watches the clock as it passes the time of day and she listens to the silence of the house. She may as well be dead.

Miami, Gideon and the superficial lifestyle to which she had grown accustomed now seem light years away and she aches to be back in their beautiful condominium overlooking the ocean. She ponders with regret the walk-in closets filled with designer clothing, the state-of-the-art kitchen gleaming like a hospital morgue, the expansive rooftop terrace complete with lap-pool and striped cabanas. And she remembers Gideon; as he used to be. She thinks longingly of the early days of their marriage before they moved to Miami when Gideon was loving and attentive towards her. His baggy jeans, his ruffled hair and the geeky spectacles he wore when he was reading or using the computer; his *charm*. Where did that person go?

Nicole has to brush tears from her eyes as she contemplates her current situation. Reduced to leeching off a man she has only just met; a man who irritates and annoys her despite his hospitality. She knows there is no future with Julian but, right now, what are her options? The small amount of money she has won't last forever and in her current physical state she can't even contemplate the idea of finding a job. She checks her e-mail every few hours but there are no new messages. It seems that everybody has forgotten about her. She browses idly on the internet, checking the weather reports, reading her horoscope and depressing herself with more and more information about AIDS.

She clicks on the *Miami Herald* website to see what the weather is like in Miami today and she is immediately assaulted by a photograph of Daphne on the main page beneath the headline; *Model Asphyxiated in Freak Accident*. She reads the accompanying story with mounting trepidation, her stomach twisted in to knots, her emotions pulled in opposite directions. Daphne was Nicole's closest friend for the last five or six years and despite her evil machinations to oust Nicole from Gideon's life it is difficult to remain indifferent when faced with her former friend's tragic death. Does anyone – even a calculating bitch like Daphne – really deserve to die for their sins?

I beat you, I break you ,I curse you.

Does Black Magic really work? Was it the ritual with the voodoo dolls in the church graveyard that caused Daphne's sudden demise or is it mere coincidence? Nicole, who has always thought herself unsusceptible to superstition, is now beginning to doubt her convictions and what, at the time, had seemed like a symbolic gesture of hatred, seems to be far more potent than she ever thought possible. And if it is powerful enough to kill Daphne then what kind of fate awaits Gideon? And, for that matter, what might happen to Nicole if Ursula's warning about the Rule of Three comes to fruition?

Nicole checks her watch; it is almost eleven o' clock in the evening and Mrs. Moon has already paid her final visit before retiring to her quarters. Nicole decides to call Ursula despite the late hour. She must admit her culpability with the voodoo fiasco and ask for Ursula's help in reversing the curse she has cast over Gideon. A broken leg or a tax audit is the kind of misfortune Nicole had hoped to generate from her novitiate's magic but maybe she underestimated the strength of her emotions that night in the graveyard? The thought of Daphne scrabbling wildly to be released from the toxic fumes of her freshly painted cake clutches at Nicole's throat, restricting her breathing.

"No, you didn't wake me up," says Ursula when Nicole expresses concern for the late hour of her call, "I've got Tally, Jeff and Petra round."

Nicole tells Ursula about Daphne.

"Well, of course I knew it was you, Nicole," admonish Ursula when informed of Nicole's deception, "and I'm not at all surprised at the outcome. Poppet magic is incredibly powerful if the intention behind it is real and there's no doubting the malevolence you were feeling at the time. Luckily I've still got the dolls; I was intending to bury them but haven't got round to it yet. Obviously there's not much we can do for your friend Daphne but we can break the curse on Gideon if that's what you want to do."

"Can you do it for me?" asks Nicole, anxious to implement the reversal as soon as possible.

"No, it's something that only you can do. The person who casts the spell is responsible for breaking it. It's probably best if you do it here because you'll need to cast a circle and that's something I can help you with. You'll also need something that is precious to you; any object will do but it has to be something that has personal value, something small like a piece of jewellery."

"Well I've sold all my jewellery except for my pearl earrings so I suppose they'll have to do."

"We can do it tomorrow night, if you like," suggests Ursula, "we've got a waning moon, which is preferable, and we'll have to perform the ritual after midnight. Why don't you come over to my place at around eleven?"

Nicole is pleased. She will ask Julian's driver to take her back to the cottage tomorrow afternoon and she will resume her independence. Coming here to Longfield Hall was a mistake and thinking that she could rely on the financial support of a man she doesn't respect – let alone love – was preposterous.

She feels hungry for the first time in days and the smoked salmon sandwiches on her supper tray are already dry and warped on their plate. She wonders if Mrs. Moon might still be around downstairs; perhaps she could beg a few biscuits or maybe some cheese on toast?

There is a woollen throw over the back of one of the bedroom armchairs so Nicole drapes it around her shoulders like a shawl and ventures out on to the darkened landing where nothing but the sonorous tick of a grandfather clock breaks the silence. She doesn't really know the layout of the house and she's never been in to the kitchen but it is situated somewhere adjacent to the dining room. The sweeping staircase is wide and impressive and on either side of the balustrade there are ornate iron lanterns that have been dimmed down for the night. After the suffocating warmth of her bedroom the hallway feels chilled and the ancient flagstone is cold beneath her bare feet.

The cavernous dining room is in complete darkness and Nicole has to weave her way carefully around the furniture. Only the faintest wash of grey light filters in through the windows and the room smells of soot and polish. There is a door over to the left of one of the fireplaces and that is where Mrs. Moon disappears between courses so Nicole assumes it must be the kitchen. The heavy panelled door creaks alarmingly as she pushes it open and she finds herself in a narrow corridor. The corridor is completely dark and Nicole can't find a light switch so she feels her way along the wall until she reaches a second door at the far end. This door seems to be upholstered with felt and it swings slightly as she pushes against it.

The kitchen is warm and smells of baking bread. Julian's three dogs are curled over each other in front of the Aga and they look up at Nicole as she enters; sighing and settling again once they ascertain that she is no threat. A lamp has been left on by the side of the sink and the dishwasher is churning through its cycle with a rhythmic watery sound. Everything is clean and organized and cosy. It is a huge kitchen with a massive scrubbed pine table dominating the centre and two of the walls are of exposed stone decorated with copper jelly moulds and a rack of saucepans. On the table there is a bowl of fruit, several newspapers opened to crossword puzzles and a coffee mug next to a scattering of crumbs.

Nicole is beginning to feel weak and her limbs are trembling from the exertion of coming downstairs. She grasps the edge of the table and stands for a moment, willing the dizzy spell to pass. Sweat dampens her forehead and she has to swallow painfully to clear her mouth of bile. She sinks down on to one of the chairs and rests her head against the uneven pine of the table to stop the room from spinning and she's worried that she's going to be sick. The dishwasher rumbles and clatters and water gurgles in the drains. Biscuits and cheese on toast have suddenly become much less desirable and Nicole wishes that she had remained safely in bed. She isn't sure that she'll be able to make it back upstairs without vomiting or fainting.

A telephone starts to ring in another room beyond the kitchen and Nicole is surprised to hear it being answered. She can hear a voice talking very quietly; a man's voice and she feels suddenly intrusive. The dogs flap their tails against the floor and prick up their ears but they don't get up. The last thing Nicole wants is to be discovered sprawled across the kitchen table wrapped in a throw so she forces herself to stagger up from the chair. The voice in the other room grows louder, more agitated, and she pauses to listen. It is Julian! He must be back from Amsterdam.

Making her way unsteadily across the kitchen, using the edge of the table as a support, Nicole advances towards the door at the other end of the room. If she thought she could make it back upstairs without passing-out she would probably avoid Julian until the morning but she is shaking and feverish and the cold floor is making her ankles throb. She leans up against the frame of the door and wipes her face with the back of her hand. Julian is reassuring someone that all Christmas deliveries will be met but Nicole only catches every word or two; if she were one of the *Famous Five* she might be hearing something like: *"rhubarb, rhubarb,* delivery, *rhubarb,* on-time, *rhubarb,* don't worry…"* and even in her current state of semi-collapse this strikes her as amusing.

She pushes open the door and enters what is obviously a library or a study. Dark panelled walls, heavy tartan curtains and a blazing fireplace set the scene. Julian's tie is loosened, his shirt collar open and he is sitting at a large leather-topped desk with the phone in one hand and a cut-glass tumbler of whisky in the other. His suitcase sits by the side of the desk.

"I'd better go, Richard, I'll call you tomorrow, OK?" Julian places his cell phone on the desk and smiles brightly at Nicole as she clutches on to the door frame for support. "Nicole!" he exclaims, "I thought you were tucked up in bed with a hot water bottle?"

"I feel terrible," admits Nicole. Her mouth and lips feel dry; her vision blurs slightly and all she wants to do is collapse across the carpet and stay there. "I came down looking for something to eat but I've gone off the idea now."

"Well you look as though you'd be better off in bed. This house is draughty and you shouldn't be poddling about in your bare feet you silly old sausage! Come on; let's get you back up the wooden hill to Bedfordshire."

Nicole attempts a smile but her head is spinning. As Julian gets up to come around from behind the desk Nicole notices him casually lean across to push a hinged oil painting closed on the opening of a wall safe. Before the portrait of the buxom lady clicks neatly in to position Nicole catches a glimpse what looks like a huge amount of cash. And there's nothing unusual about a man of Julian's profession having a safe full of money, it's just that Nicole's wavering gaze meanders down to the wing chair where there are several bulging packages of something that looks suspiciously like cocaine.

She faints. It's not a very romantic kind of faint; she doesn't raise the back of one delicate hand to her forehead before sinking in to a ladylike curtsey on the floor. No; Nicole moans, reaches out for the back of the sofa, misses her target and thumps to the ground, banging the side of her head on the corner of the coffee table. She doesn't really lose consciousness but for a few moments the fall jars her in to a state of bewilderment and she can't quite work out why she's on the floor.

"Nicole, are you all right?" Julian comes to kneel beside her and he lifts her head from the carpet.

"Oh God, I must have fainted," says Nicole as though some explanation for her ungainly position must be offered.

"I'm getting you back upstairs, pronto, madam. And I'm calling the doctor, you're burning up."

Julian picks Nicole up in his arms and gently carries her out of the study and back through the kitchen. She is too weak and perplexed to really register what is happening but her teeth are chattering and she can't seem to unclench her jaw. She has to turn her head away from the scent of Julian's aftershave.

Out of the frying pan into the fire; it would seem that Nicole has abandoned one drug fiend for another and this one isn't even sexy! Julian isn't the type you'd expect to find dealing in narcotics but she's met enough of Gideon's friends to know that class and upbringing have very little relevance where drug-traffic is concerned. The small-time dealers who sell on the streets are usually brain-dead losers who need the money to support their own habits but the guys who run the large-scale operations need to be more sentient and sophisticated in order to control what is, in effect, a highly elaborate enterprise.

As Julian carries Nicole up the sweeping staircase of Longfield Hall her fever-addled mind turns over the rich soil of her imagination and she wonders – just wonders – if there could be some way of tapping in to this situation to her own advantage. After all, Nicole has been called a lot of names in her time but Opportunist was never an appellation she's been ashamed of.

Ghost Gold

Tallulah stifles a yawn with the palm of her hand and glances at Ursula's clock. It is almost twelve-thirty and she's been up since half-past six this morning. Petra is sitting cross-legged on the living room carpet staring at her laptop computer, tapping proficiently at the keys while Jeff and Ursula pass a smouldering joint from one end of the sofa to the other. They've been ensconced in here since Ursula and Petra returned from their carol concert rehearsal and the coffee table is a mess of wine glasses, crackers, cheese and pâté.

"Yuck!" mutters Petra as she reads from her computer screen. "It says here that it was also called the 'Spittle of God'. Others referred to it as the 'Semen of the Father in Heaven'. Apparently putting the white powder in water doesn't result in it dissolving. Instead, it forms a gelatinous suspension, and looks very much like a vial of spunk."

"Yeah, it's not very appetizing to look at," agrees Ursula, "but it doesn't have much of a taste and no smell at all. You just put a few drops under your tongue a couple of times a day."

"I'm sorry, Ursula; I know you believe in all this herbal mumbo-jumbo but I find it hard to believe that if this stuff is so powerful and effective how come I've never heard of it before?" This is Jeff, exhaling his words in a long stream of smoke. "All this crap about attaining a higher consciousness, self-healing and finding the path to spiritual transformation sounds like something I'd rant on about after a couple of these." He holds up the joint to illustrate his point and Petra wiggles her fingers in the air indicating that she'd like some spiritual enlightenment of her own. He passes it down to her.

"Most of this stuff is indecipherable," groans Petra, "it's worse than a physics lesson. *White Powder Gold positively affects the bioelectric patterns that move through the brain. Reports have indicated health benefits including: huge boosts in mental & physical energy, increased deep cellular health, improved nutritional assimilation, spiritual growth, elevated mood & anti-depression, strengthened immune system, vanished aches and pains, increased mental clarity and focus, greater strength & stamina, increased libido, fat loss & lean muscle gain, and more youthful appearance and vitality.'*"

Jeff laughs. "It's the bloody elixir of life! I don't understand why Rob was keeping it so quiet."

"He *wasn't* keeping it quiet," insists Ursula, "he was writing a *book* about it. He just wanted to make sure that he got his facts straight before he started spouting-off about it. Julian was the one exploiting the stuff; making money out of it. If it wasn't for Rob's research Julian would never have known about White Powder Gold."

"But it was Julian's money that paid for it, so it was only fair that he should be the one to benefit," remarks Tallulah. "Our Rob was getting his cut from Julian so it's not as though he was being exploited or anything."

"That's a matter of opinion," mutters Jeff.

Ursula reaches out to refill her wine glass. "The *book* was more important to Rob. He was fascinated by the subject and having a physician's background combined with an interest in spiritual enlightenment he got caught-up in the quest to prove the existence of the so-called Philosopher's Stone."

"A middle-aged Harry Potter," quips Jeff with a derisive snort.

"Look," interrupts Tallulah, "at least he wasn't dealing in drugs and that's a huge relief for me. I'm just glad I didn't call the police or Uncle Ted before Ursula came home otherwise we'd have been left with egg on our faces. This was pin-money for our Rob and a lucrative sideline for Julian so where's the harm in that? If there are people out there prepared to pay fifty quid for a tiny bag of the stuff then more fool them; it's not illegal."

"Except for the fact that the money was all handled under the table," responds Petra. "The reason he was so secretive about it, the reason he didn't put the money in a bank account, was all a way of avoiding the tax man. The part that still puzzles me is who broke in to the house and ransacked the place looking for it? I can't imagine that somebody as rich as this Julian bloke would be bothered about a measly five grand."

"Perhaps they were looking for something else?" suggests Ursula, pulling her bare feet further under the sofa cushions.

"Like what?"

"I don't know, but that wasn't an ordinary burglary. They didn't even take the computer or the telly."

"That's not surprising," cracks Jeff, "who'd want to nick a ten year old Sony Trinitron and a computer they couldn't even *give* away to a charity shop?"

"Hey, listen to this…" interjects Petra, peering closely at her computer screen. "There's more here about this stuff; it says that this unique white powder is something that alchemists have attempted to produce for centuries. Miners used to call it 'ghost gold' after finding it near what they considered more valuable deposits, and chose to ignore it. Modern day alchemists have studied White Powder Gold and find it contains rhodium and iridium which are both thought to be beneficial to AIDS and cancer patients. People taking the powder have experienced a variety of interesting and powerful effects. It was always said that the white powder of alchemy could cure illnesses, prolong life and revitalize the spirit." Petra pauses to look at Tallulah. "Maybe you should start taking the stuff, see if it has any effect. It can't do you any harm."

Ursula agrees, nodding her head enthusiastically and exhaling smoke in to the air. "I never thought about it but Petra's got a point; you've got a ton of the stuff next-door. I'm a great believer in fate and maybe this was Rob's legacy? I wonder if he ever gave any to his mother?"

"It goes on to say that Bristol-Meyers-Squibb Laboratories is doing cancer research using precious elements which are known to correct mutant DNA. This occurs by coupling these elements with the cells via light transfer or vibrational frequency. Electrons that flow through a superconductor are known to pair off and convert into a light frequency during the process. Some believe this could be what happens in human cells. So the idea that superconductors are at work in this research could well be right. White powder gold ash contains superconductors."

"OK, now you've lost me," says Jeff.

"You don't need to know all the technical stuff," asserts Ursula, "I've been treating people with herbal concoctions for most of my life and I still don't really know why some of them work on some people and not on others. The main thing is that you have to *believe* in them and Rob was sufficiently convinced about this stuff to dedicate two years on writing a book about it."

Tallulah has never been one for taking medicines of any kind. Her medicine cabinet contains nothing but aspirin, plasters and ear drops and before this current situation she hadn't been to see her doctor in years. She knows a bit about homeopathic medicines from one of the women she used to work with at the sweet factory; Sharon used to swear by some drops she put under her tongue to calm her claustrophobia and swore that her chronic psoriasis was completely cured by the regular application of sulphur ointment. What harm can come from swallowing a few drops of Rob's powdered gold every day?

"Do you really think it might work?" she asks.

"Listen, duck," replies Ursula, "you've got to have faith in things you don't understand sometimes. Believe me I've seen bloody miracles happen just from putting my hands on somebody and that's what you have to believe in these days; miracles. You're already walking around with magnets in your bra and drinking the burdock-root tea I gave you so why not try Rob's powder as well? We can perform some crystal therapy as well if you'll get over your prudish aversion to getting your khaks off in front of me!"

"Crystals are amazing," nods Petra, "when I started sleeping with an amethyst under my pillow I *totally* stopped having nightmares."

Jeff snorts derisively and levers himself up from the sofa. "OK, it's time for me to go home to bed. Amethysts under pillows, magnets in bras and powdered gold that cures all ailments; it's all getting just a bit too eccentric for me! I'm a great believer in chemicals of the prescription kind but if your girls want to believe in magic then good luck to you. Barney will be needing his walk otherwise I'll be waking up to a pile of shit by my bed in the morning."

"Eloquent as always, Jeff! I'll let you see yourself out, I'm not sure I can get up," smirks Ursula.

"I think I'll be off as well," says Tallulah, standing up to leave. "Are you coming, Petra; it's nearly one and you've got college in the morning."

"I'm not going tomorrow; it's the last day so nobody will get any work done. I'd rather stay in bed. Two whole weeks! Brilliant! I'll hang about here a bit longer if that's all right with you Ursula?"

"You know me; never in bed before three." Ursula sprawls out across the sofa and sighs contentedly. "Good night you two. Don't do anything I wouldn't do!" And she cackles at her own feeble joke.

Jeff puts on his coat and wraps a scarf around his neck. It is freezing outside and the puddles have turned to ice. The sky is cloudless and punctured with stars.

"Goodnight, love. Sleep tight." And he raises his hand in Tallulah's direction as he makes his way down the path towards his car.

Tallulah unlocks her front door and the burglar alarm beeps insistently. She keys in her code number and the house falls silent. She has taken to setting the alarm even when she's just next-door these days. The smell of Petra's butterbean casserole still lurks stodgily in the air and the heating has turned itself off so the hallway is chilly. Petra has strung-up homemade paper-chains, festooning them from one side of the hallway to the other and she has wrapped tinsel around the banister rails. The kitchen light is on and Tallulah goes through to make sure the back door is bolted.

Don't do anything I wouldn't do.

Tallulah is growing tired of the ribald comments regarding her and Jeff. She is embarrassed because she knows that Jeff isn't at all interested in her that way and she wishes that Petra and Ursula would just let them be friends. Jeff is a kind and thoughtful man but he has never shown the slightest bit of interest in Tallulah when it comes to the romance department and Tallulah isn't even sure if she's bothered with all that nonsense at her age. He is attractive in an unassuming kind of way and for a man of his age he has the personality of somebody much younger. In many ways he is lost in a similar kind of time-warp as Tallulah herself and she finds herself drawn to his nostalgic fondness for the past. A man who collects children's toys and old copies of the *Radio Times* can't be a bad person.

Boyfriends can be tricky things and Tallulah has listened to enough griping and moaning from the girls at the Trebor factory to know that courtship and marriage can make life one long round of rows and unhappiness. Men seem to be the root cause of all women's problems and Tallulah has watched enough *Eastenders* to know that no matter how much you love a man he usually turns nasty in the end. They have affairs and stay out drinking, they become abusive and leave the kids to their wives. Some of them even become violent or take up strange hobbies like train-spotting just to get them out of the house.

Of course there's the *romantic* ideal to consider; the heart-shaped boxes of chocolates, the dancing at Top Rank and snogging at the back of the pictures but then there's all the awkwardness and messiness of sex to consider and Tallulah has always shied away from those thoughts. What must it feel like to be naked next to a man with all his muscles and hairiness? And from what she's seen of men's genitals she doesn't know what all the fuss is about; a penis isn't the most attractive of bodily parts! And are men as clean as they should be?

These are all questions that have plagued Tallulah since she was old enough to think about such things and they still puzzle her now.

She checks the kitchen door and is satisfied that it is securely fastened. The bags of Rob's white powder are in a Debenhams carrier in the pantry and Tallulah takes one of them and empties the powder in to a drinking glass. She measures out some cold water from the tap in to a measuring jug and mixes it with the powder. It immediately turns to the consistency of wallpaper paste and it clings to the inside of the glass like the slimy substance left in the trail of a slug. How is she going to take a few drops from the glass without something to suck it up? She remembers her ear drops in the bathroom cabinet; they are stored in a bottle with a little rubber pipette and she figures she can use that if she rinses it out with hot water first.

In the bathroom Petra's coloured tights are strewn across the shower rail; scarlet, purple and black like discarded skins. Her makeup and lotions are stored in a metal basket on the window sill and the white hand towels are smeared with her foundation and lipstick. As messy as it might seem to an outsider Tallulah is glad of the disruption; it is a constant reminder that she is no longer living alone and she embraces the untidiness. Although Petra is half her age they seem to get on famously and she makes Tallulah laugh with her lurid stories about her boyfriend, Scott. Apparently they have sex in public places and just last week Scott managed to do it on the back of a double-decker between Sheffield and Renishaw! Having met Scott only once Tallulah finds it difficult to equate the mild-mannered lad with the randy sex-maniac who buys flavoured condoms and watches videos of lesbians with pierced vaginas.

Tallulah finds the ear drops and rinses out the little dropper under the hot water tap. In the bathroom mirror she appears as a smeary ghost; pale and tired-looking with hair the colour of stripped pine. It is a familiar face; one that she has seen staring back at her for forty-five years but tonight, as she leans further in to get a better look, she realizes that the little girl who used to stare back at her has been swallowed up by somebody who looks more like her mother. Age is a funny thing. It distorts and it wrinkles so that people, like photos left out in the sunlight, become faded and creased until they fail to exist at all.

She returns to the kitchen and sucks up some of the gelatinous white substance from the drinking glass in to her little ear-dropper. Following Ursula's instructions Tallulah drips a few splashes of the liquid under her tongue and closes her mouth, waiting to see if there is a bad taste or some kind of immediate reaction. But there is nothing. She rinses out the dropper again and puts some cling film over the glass, popping it in to the fridge next to Petra's tofu and bean sprouts. She breaks off a couple of grapes and pops them in her mouth before turning out the lights and heading up to bed.

That night, under her polycotton duvet, Tallulah dreams that Jeff is driving an electric lawnmower in the nude. He waves to Tallulah from across an expansive lawn and when she approaches him her climbs off the mower and takes her in his arms. There is no embarrassment or awkwardness and it feels perfectly natural to be standing in the middle of somebody's garden with a naked man pressed up against her. Sitting under the shade of a nearby tree she can see Petra and Ursula waving at them from a picnic blanket and when she looks down she finds she is wearing one of Mr. B's black satin corsets and a pair of skimpy lace pants.

"Look, it's barely open," murmers Jeff, holding a deep red rose to Tallulah's nose for her to smell.

"I wonder what it tastes like," contemplates Jeff. And he parts the delicate petals of the bloom with his fingers and burrows his tongue deep in to the heart of the flower, all the time keeping his eyes fixed firmly on Tallulah's face.

When she wakes up she has only been asleep for a couple of hours; Petra is running the water in the bathroom and Tallulah's knickers are decidedly damp.

An Inconvenient Truth

Julian's driver takes her in to Manchester for her doctor's appointment. She doesn't tell Julian the exact nature of her appointment; she just tells him that she prefers to see her own doctor rather than his. She doesn't feel much better than she did last night but she is desperate to get the results of her genotype test so that she can start on a regime of medications. With her pashmina wrapped snugly around her shoulders and wearing dark glasses she steps out of the car like a film star entering rehab. There are no flash bulbs and no paparazzi, just a reflection of the sun in the plate glass doors and two arthritic geriatrics on Zimmer frames.

Dr.Sukhwani with her vermilion bindi sits behind her desk and smiles sweetly at Nicole as she takes a seat. A garish chart of the human lymphatic system and an anatomic life-size model of a heart are the only decorations in Dr. Sukhwani's office.

"I have the results of your genotype here, Miss. Harvey and it appears that the strain of HIV you have contracted is a *mutant* form of the virus. HIV is notorious for its ability to change, or mutate, and thereby evade the effects of drugs. Many drugs used to treat HIV interfere with the virus' reverse transcriptase enzyme, slowing the viral growth rate and that's why they've been so successful. The drug 'cocktail' you have probably heard about is currently halting the progress of the disease in thousands of patients. However, mutations in HIV's RT gene produce an enzyme that is uninhibited by the drugs, allowing the virus to begin growing again. Now, in some cases, these mutations mean that the virus is resistant to some of the medications we currently have to offer our patients and it narrows the treatment options. This is called cross-resistance and about fifteen percent of HIV infected patients in the UK have some form of mutation."

Nicole shifts uneasily in her chair. She senses that what the doctor has to tell her is not good news.

"It appears that the strain you have contracted is resistant to two classes of HIV medications so we have a limited selection to play with at this stage. It's imperative that you start on some form of treatment as soon as possible to avoid further damage to your immune system."

"I guess I'll take whatever you suggest, doctor," replies Nicole, "I don't think I've got much choice in the matter at this stage. I've been feeling really lousy the past few days and the glands in my neck and groin are swollen. I want to start on the treatment as soon as possible."

"Well, we can get you started right away. I'm going to suggest a combination of two different types of drug; basically it will be three pills a day and we'll see how you respond after three months. There might be some side-effects with these drugs; they're very powerful and it takes some time for your body to adjust to the toxicity levels. You may experience nausea, weight-loss and loss of appetite as well as severe bouts of diarrhoea. Most of these side-effects should disappear after a few weeks. I'll give you some leaflets on what you can expect."

"And I have to take these drugs for the rest of my life, right?" asks Nicole.

The doctor nods her head. "Yes, as you know there is no cure for AIDS but the medications we have available today are very effective and can control the disease, making it a chronic condition rather than a death sentence. In many cases we can reduce the virus to undetectable levels but, of course, we can't eliminate it completely and you will remain infectious so it's important for you to observe safe sexual practices."

A brief pang of guilt twists in Nicole's gut as she thinks of Julian but she is too self-centred to worry about his irresponsibility for more than a couple of seconds. If he's stupid enough to fuck somebody without a condom – knowing all the risks involved – then that's his lookout. It's too late in life to start worrying about the welfare of others and for too long now Nicole has had nobody to care about. James was the last person she really loved and when he died he took a part of her with him; the part of her that was compassionate and humane. The woman who sits in the doctor's office is as hard and brittle as the polish on her nails and like a bitch running from the hounds she thinks only of her own survival.

Illness is not something that Nicole had planned for and it is such an inconvenient truth. Coming to England was supposed to be a new beginning, but not in the way it is turning out. Penniless, unemployed, loveless and now plagued by an incurable and possibly fatal disease there doesn't seem to be much to live for. So why should somebody in Nicole's position concern herself with the plight of others? She is the one who needs sympathy. She is the one who needs help and charity but she's not holding her breath. In her experience very few people offer themselves up for assistance unless there's something in it for them and after fifteen years living in Miami she has become immune to superficial kindnesses. Well-worn phrases like 'you scratch my back, I'll scratch yours' come to mind and at this stage in her life Nicole is not about to expose her back to anyone.

She collects her pills from the chemist; glancing briefly at the rattling containers in the white paper bag and acknowledging with a shudder that her life is now totally reliant on those three little canisters. The doctor has warned her that by missing just one or two doses of these pills she could render them useless and further compromise her list of available drugs so it is vitally important that she makes them as much a part of her daily routine as her three-step skin-care regime. She buys a bottle of water at the chemist and swallows her first three pills before she even steps back out in to the street where Julian's car is waiting for her.

Christmas is all around and yet Nicole feels strangely detached from the bustling crowds of festive shoppers and the sickening merriment of familiar carols being played in every store. A man dressed as Santa Claus stands on the street corner, ringing his bell and ho, ho, ho-ing in an attempt to seduce passers-by to throw some spare change in to his bucket. The streets are strung with coloured lights and giant illuminated snowflakes and there is a smell of bitter coffee and cinnamon buns in the air. Under different circumstances Nicole would be tempted to scurry in to Harvey Nichols but her stomach feels decidedly tricky and all she really wants to do is get back in to bed and close the curtains against the encroaching holiday season.

The traffic is heavy today and the journey back to Julian's house is painfully slow. There are roadworks and traffic jams to hinder their progress and all the way back to Longfield Hall Nicole thinks about her future. She has no firm plans beyond the next few days and she wonders if it will be convenient to stay with Julian through Christmas if she doesn't feel any better by the end of the weekend. It is Christmas Eve on Monday and she has no idea what his plans might be. In some respects she would prefer to spend the time alone at the cottage but she doesn't feel well enough to look after herself just yet. She wonders how quickly the pills will work.

"Mr. Smythe has gone down to London," informs Mrs. Moon when Nicole finally staggers in to the grand foyer of Longfield Hall. "He said to tell you that he won't be back until tomorrow. He will call you later."

That's a relief! She won't have to make pleasant conversation with him or attempt to appear grateful. She might ask Mrs. Moon if she can make herself a nest on the living room sofa and she can spend the day watching the TV in her dressing gown. Without Julian around she doesn't have to feel like she is a guest, she can pretend that she is the lady of the house and that is a role she is far more comfortable with. Fortunately Mrs. Moon isn't the stereotypical dour-faced housekeeper with a secret passion for her master; she is a jolly, round-featured Yorkshire woman with a passion for local gossip so Nicole doesn't have to worry about an 'atmosphere' due to resentment and jealousy. Thank God this isn't Manderley and she is not the second Mrs. DeWinter!

Her bed has been made and the sheets are turned-down. There is a fire in the grate and her magazines have been carefully fanned-out across the coffee table. Mrs. Moon has promised to bring up some tea and toast and Nicole is so exhausted by her outing that she can't even be bothered to remove her clothing before she slumps across the eiderdown, pressing her face in to the lavender-scented sheets. She feels wretched. She wonders how Gideon is feeling. Those ill-conceived little dolls are still with Ursula and Nicole is too weak to contemplate a trip to Castleton today as planned. Her fear of the consequences have little to do with Gideon's safety, she is now more concerned about her own fate and maybe, by reversing her intentions, she can escape the so-called Rule of Three. It would appear that Nicole is already cursed but maybe she can still redeem herself if she displays some kind of remorse? She isn't sure how magic works but there has to be some way of escaping the boomerang-effect of her ill-wishes.

She's never been one to pray but at this moment she whispers for forgiveness and hopes that someone or some*thing* will hear her above the weeping and wailing of humanity.

Hardly likely, Nicole!

There are far more deserving causes in this world than a bitter, selfish miscreant whose fate has been forged not by misfortune but by egotism and spite.

The Old-Fashioned Kind

The Christmas tree is so big they have to chop the top off to make it fit in to Tallulah's living room. Jeff screws the freshly-sawn trunk in to a special stand that keeps it upright and there is a reservoir in the bottom that they fill with warm water to feed the fragrant branches and to stop the needles from falling too quickly.

"We don't have any decorations or lights," laments Tallulah, standing back to admire the rich green foliage that springs out in lush symmetry when Jeff cuts the strings that bind it.

"Leave that to me," mitigates Petra from the living room doorway. Today she is wearing a pleated tartan mini-skirt and bottle-green tights and her pierced belly-button is exposed below a black mesh top that shows her bra. She seems impervious to the cold. "I'm a dab-hand with silver-foil and egg boxes!"

"I've brought some lights from the shop," says Jeff. "They're the old-fashioned kind, mind you, not the little white ones that people seem to prefer these days. "We'll have to use three different types because there's only twenty bulbs on each string."

The lights are still in their original boxes and from the faded out-dated graphics they look as though they were probably manufactured in the early sixties: Pifco Mini Lanterns, Rainbow Lights and a box of Vesta-Lights with a drawing of Father Christmas flying over the snowy rooftops in his sleigh piled high with presents.

"Do they still work?" asks Tallulah doubtfully.

"Yep! I plugged them in before I brought them over and I've bought some spare bulbs."

"It's a shame we don't have any furniture in here," observes Tallulah, casting a critical eye around the empty room. The bare floorboards are pitted with nail-heads and the cracks are filled with dust. The wallpaper on the chimney breast is turquoise and green and looks as though it was designed by somebody with a Spirograph.

"There are some deck chairs in the shed, we can bring those in and throw a few pillows on the floor," suggests Petra. "If we light a fire it'll be lovely. I'll take those spare tree branches round to Ursula's; she can use them for her Yule decorations. Did you see the log she brought back this morning for her fireplace? It's massive."

"She was making a table centrepiece with pine cones and holly when I went in earlier," says Tallulah. "It's quite exciting; I've never been to a Yule party before. It's like a really old-fashioned Christmas; the kind they used to have before electricity and television."

"There's quite a crowd coming, apparently. I'm not sure she's going to fit them all in to her cellar for the ritual."

"Well I'm just going to the party afterwards," says Tallulah, inspecting the tree lights, "so I've got some baking to do this afternoon. I haven't made pastry in years so I'm not sure what my mince pies will be like but I promised to try."

"If all else fails, there's always Mr. Kipling's!" jibes Petra. "Personally I've never been able to stick mincemeat; the idea of suet turns my stomach."

"I bought the vegetarian kind," informs Tallulah, proudly, "I didn't even know there was such a thing until Ursula told me. Most of her friends seem to be vegetarian."

The tree takes up most of the window and makes the living room dark with shadows. It is a sinister, monstrous thing without adornment and it seems oddly incongruous and sad; like a caged animal that should be running wild. Tallulah has never had a real tree before and she's not quite sure if she feels comfortable with the idea. As squalid and tacky as their little aluminium tree used to be, at least it wasn't torn from the ground and left to die in the central heating. Christmas trees are a strange idea when you think about it; trust the Germans to think-up such a brutal tradition! Perhaps if Queen Victoria had never married her beloved Albert the familiar sight of the Christmas tree might never have materialized and — like the swastika — would have faded in to obscurity.

"Do you want to go for a driving lesson?" Jeff asks Tallulah as he finishes with the tree.

"I haven't got time today, Jeff. Maybe tomorrow afternoon if you're free?"

Jeff has been giving Tallulah lessons in his van and she is surprised how much she still remembers from her lessons all those years ago. Of course she's only practiced on quiet country roads so far and the idea of the motorway or city ring roads fills her with secret dread. The hardest thing is remembering how to co ordinate all the actions; mirrors, clutch, gear-changes, signals and all the time having to be aware of the car in front of you. Jeff assures her that it will become second-nature but Tallulah wonders if she has the natural aptitude for driving; especially at her advanced age.

"OK, we'll I'll be off then. I've got to pop in to Leeds to pick up some stuff from an auction. I'll come back at around nine tonight and we can join the festivities next door."

The phone starts to ring so Jeff sees himself out and Tallulah hurries through to the kitchen. It is Darren, the estate agent. Apparently he's found an interested buyer for her house in Chesterfield and they're offering just two thousand below asking price. He suggests that they counter-offer at *one* thousand. It's a game that Tallulah has never understood but she realizes that people like to boast that they got a good deal and so she agrees to whatever Darren thinks is best.

"I can have a contract with you as soon as tomorrow," he promises. Obviously he is thinking of his generous commission and wants to get the ball rolling before everyone becomes too involved in their

Christmas plans. Tallulah is relieved. It will be one less thing to worry about if she can get the sale of the house sorted out before she has her operation in January and it'll be a weight off Uncle Ted's mind as well.

The phone rings again almost as soon as she puts it down. This time it is Gran calling to inform Tallulah that she got her Christmas card in this morning's post.

"A very touching verse," she says, "it brought a tear to my eye."

When she hears that Tallulah has a buyer for her house she immediately launches in to a critique of the 'astronomical' interest rates and how the current government are making a mess of the country.

"Things are going from bad to worse, duck. Two blokes robbed the bank opposite the Co-Op last week and burglaries are *rife* round here now. My door-chain is on even now in the middle of the day. I'd move out in to the countryside like you, duck, if I thought I could get to the shops but there's no point in somebody of my age thinking of flitting. Poor Carole Watson from number thirty-two moved down to a village outside Derby and they're not getting on at all well with the conversion. What with the terrible weather, then their joiner's had a nervous breakdown and now their plasterer can't come until after New Year so they're having to come up here to stop with Doris until January. It's shocking!"

"Any news about Auntie June?" asks Tallulah, for want of something to say.

"No, duck. Ted was over here the other night and he looked terrible. I told him he'll end up in Mickleover if he doesn't watch it. He took me to the doctor's and she said I've got dangerously high blood pressure and angina. Tell me something I don't know, I thought, but I didn't say owt. She gave me some tablets to put under my tongue but after the first one I hit the ground and everything went haywire: Sick, mess, sweat all on my newly cleaned suite. When I finally got up – what a mess! I sent for the emergency doctor because your Uncle Ted had already left. I told him how I'd been and how Dr. Cotton hadn't even examined my chest so *he* did and he tells me I haven't got angina and to stop the tablets immediately. So what sort of doctor is *she?* I'm scared to go to her any more in case she gives me the wrong medication. There aren't any good doctors round here any more so I suppose I'll just have to hope for the best. It's really knocked me for six, duck. At ninety-six I couldn't stand another of those. I couldn't get to the phone or knock the neighbours and with all the doors locked and bolted I was really scared my time had come. Have you found a job yet?"

"Not yet, Gran. I haven't really been looking. I'll wait until after Christmas because nobody's interested in interviewing at this time of the year."

"Well don't leave it too long otherwise you'll end up like that bloody layabout Kevin. Do you know he's still claiming the dole after all this time and back living with his mother. I'd have turfed him out months ago but Glenda's too soft."

"So are you still going to Mr. and Mrs. Turnbull's for Christmas dinner?" Tallulah pokes her finger in to the butter she's left out to soften on the draining board.

"Well, I'm not thrilled about that, duck, as you know but it'd be rude to turn them down. They don't eat their dinner until the middle of the afternoon and I'm used to sitting down by one. Are you having your friends round?"

"Yes; there'll be four of us. I'm doing the turkey and Petra's vegetarian so she's making a nut roast. I've got a Christmas pudding from Tesco's."

"Well make sure it's not got a coin in it," warns Gran, "I chipped my dentures a few years ago and they say it's supposed to be lucky!"

"All right, Gran. I'll be over to see you next week some time. Probably the day after Boxing Day. I'll give you a call on Tuesday."

"Ta-ra, duck. And tell that young girl lodging with you that she wants to get some meat down her; she'll be anaemic if she doesn't watch it. You want to fry her up some liver and onions."

Petra wanders in to the kitchen and pours herself a glass of milk from the fridge.

"All right, Gran. Talk to you later." And Tallulah ends the conversation with a smirk.

Petra likes to dunk her orange Penguins in to her milk and the brown residue that remains at the bottom disgusts Tallulah every time she finds an abandoned glass in the sink.

"Gran says I should feed you some liver and onions to stop you from becoming anaemic."

"Your Gran's a nutcase. She was eating tripe cooked in milk when I talked to her the other day. I didn't think *anybody* ate tripe any more."

Petra makes a disgusted face and removes the wrapper from her Penguin.

"I'm thinking of doing something different with my hair," announces Tallulah, suddenly. It is a thought that comes out of her mouth almost as soon as it pops in to her head and now that it's out it cannot be retracted. Petra's face lights-up and she pauses mid-bite with her chocolate biscuit dripping milk.

"Brilliant! It's about time you had a make-over. That hairstyle went out with midi-skirts and wedges! D'you want me to do it for you?" she suggests, hopefully.

"Well, as long as you don't do anything drastic," begs Tallulah, raising a nervous hand to her lacquered wings. "Do you think a coloured rinse might work?"

"Blimey! You've been watching too much Trinny and Suzanna!" jokes Petra with a grin. "What's brought this on?"

"Oh, I don't know," shrugs Tallulah, "I just thought it might be nice to get dressed up this evening for Ursula's party. I've got a frock that somebody at work gave me and I've never worn it; I think it'll be all right if I take the hem up a bit."

"I've got some bleach; we could give you a few highlights if you like? I don't think we'll have to cut it much, just blow-dry it differently and get rid of that awful centre-parting. You'd look so much better with a bit of a fringe."

"OK, I'll let you do it, but promise me you won't make me look like mutton dressed as lamb; I just want something simple and appropriate for my age. And perhaps you can help me with a bit of make-up as well? No panda-eyes or glitter but something that makes me look a bit less washed-out."

"Woo-hoo!" shrieks Petra, "a *project!*"

And like the subdued Christmas tree in the living room Tallulah spreads her branches and waits to be decorated.

Cause & Effect

Birds of a feather flock together and Gideon's feather's are every bit as oily and ruffled as Nicole's. Raven's feathers.

They scavenge and maraud through other people's lives, pecking holes in everything they encounter causing the trash to spill out in foul-smelling heaps, polluting the environment.

Here he crouches, unwashed and stinking in his penthouse condominium surrounded by the debris of his own making. For three days he has remained indoors, not answering the phone or checking his e-mail; locked in his master bedroom suite with the curtains pulled across the windows to block out the sunlight. The curtains are the kind with special blackout lining for malingerers who don't like to get up until lunchtime. The bedroom is a rancid cocoon of stale air and crumpled sheets. Thumping rock music reverberates from concealed speakers sending shock waves through the walls and floor.

There is vomit splashed half-way up the wall beside the bed and a bottle of ketchup has been hurled violently at the opposite wall creating a vivid crust of darkening red like blown-out brains in a movie. A hamburger and a handful of French fries smear the upholstery of the white leather chaise longue and the luxurious ivory coloured carpet is littered with empty bottles, food wrappers, discarded clothing and spilled puddles of various unspeakable fluids because Gideon can't even be bothered to make it to the bathroom.

He shakes uncontrollably and a cold, greasy sweat trickles down his temples and stings his bloodshot eyes. He looks like an animal; rabid and feral. When he tries to unclench his fists he finds his hands clawing at the carpet. He grabs at the pile of the carpet and – on all fours – he prowls the room with saliva hanging in threads from his clenched mouth. He is naked except for one filthy white sock and a pair of soiled boxer shorts.

He stares down at the shredded photographs of Veronica and he drools on to the scraps as thought they are appetizing and about to be devoured. When he retches his stomach is unable to produce anything more than a few more strands of bile but the contraction of the muscles is painful and his jaw snaps wide like the tortured yawn of a wolf as it contemplates the full moon. Gideon is poisoned inside and out. Poisoned with drugs and alcohol and poisoned with enmity and resentment.

Cause and effect.

He blames Veronica for everything. He blames her for the loss of his youth, for the loss of his fortune and for the loss of his sanity. She was once everything to him; lover, mother and friend and he gave her everything she ever wanted. But when they moved to Miami things started to change and Gideon detected a certain withdrawal from Veronica as though she was somehow *offended* by her surroundings and the people they were meeting. The more Gideon settled in to life on the beach the more Veronica disengaged. Oh yes, she went through the motions but Gideon knew that her heart wasn't in it. They stopped having sex as often and when they did screw it wasn't as intense. So Gideon sought his satisfaction elsewhere and consequently so did Veronica.

Then along came that smarmy British git, James, and Ronnie was lost. She fell hook, line and sinker for him and Gideon couldn't stand it. He was twisted with jealousy. It was a betrayal of the highest magnitude and Gideon isn't used to being betrayed. So he stalked revenge and he didn't care how much blood was spilled in the process just so long as Ronnie's life would be completely shattered by the experience.

After that Gideon lost all interest in her and he watched with some satisfaction as she fell from grace in a most degrading way. Using sex and drugs as a way to escape from her misery Ronnie floundered in a squalid mire of her own creation. She lost her dignity and

Gideon lost his respect for her. And then along came Daphne and the rest, as they say, is history...

He must clean up his act. He must clear his head and cleanse his body in order to get on that plane tomorrow. He will take some tranquillizers before he leaves for the airport and hopefully he can stave off the worst of his withdrawal until they land in London. He has already sent word to his old friend Ian to guarantee a decent supply of crystal. The sad truth is; Gideon would not be able to make this trip unless assured that his habit can be fed. He has become totally dependent on the chemicals he ingests and without them he believes that he may as well be dead.

Reaching out towards the chaise longue he scrapes the mashed hamburger away from the leather and starts to cram it in to his mouth despite the fact that it makes him gag. He is ravenous and repulsed at the same time but he has to feed his body in order to feed his mind. He grabs at the cold French fries and clutches them in his fist like a bunch of headless flowers.

He's going to take a cold shower, order room service and take a couple of sleeping pills... and tomorrow he's going to England.

A New Woman

You can't make a silk purse out of a sow's ear but pigskin can be very attractive if you accept it for what it is. Petra has done the best she can with the materials at hand and Tallulah could easily be the kind of woman who buys her groceries at Marks & Spencer instead of the kind found loitering under the fir tree logo of her local Spar. Her hair has been shagged (ironic, joked Petra, that Tallulah's hair should be shagged while the rest of her remains unmolested!) with a razor blade and streaked with blonde highlights. It's not as subtle as a salon treatment but it looks a hell of a lot better than the seventies evocation of a Bay City Roller's fan! The jagged fringe touches Tallulah's eyelashes and moves when she blinks but the effect softens her high forehead and frames her pretty eyes. It has been blown-dry in a haphazard style and tousled with mousse that smells of green apples.

Her skin tone has been evened out with foundation and powder and her high cheekbones accentuated with a soft blush. She shied away from lipstick because the only colours in Petra's make-up bag were far too dramatic so they opted for clear lip-gloss and just a smudge of copper eye-shadow. She looks a bit like Judy Finnigan says Petra when they're finished.

"I hope you mean twenty years ago and not the way she looks now," cringes Tallulah.

The dress is probably the most surprising aspect of Tallulah's new look; it is a chocolate brown jersey fabric with a plunging neckline that crosses beneath her breasts and ties in a bow at the back. It is simple but well-made and it has a beautiful silk lining that helps the fabric to slip and slide across her thighs as she walks. The only problem is Tallulah doesn't have any suitable shoes. The dress needs something high-heeled and strappy but Tallulah doesn't own anything that elegant so she has to make-do with her rather mumsy beige court shoes ('something the queen might wear' comments Petra disparagingly). All-in-all one might say she looks like a new woman and the effect is quite striking.

Petra, looking like the bride of Dracula in a black lace dress and kinky boots, leaves for the winter solstice ritual next-door and Tallulah sits self-consciously on the edge of her bed wondering what she's going to do with herself for the next hour before Jeff arrives. She keeps getting up to stare at herself in the bathroom mirror, poking at her hair with tentative fingers and adjusting the front of her frock so it doesn't show too much of her bargain bra from Mr. B's. The strange thing about dressing-up is that it not only changes the way you see yourself but also the way you *feel* about yourself. When you look like a bit of a go-er you feel like a bit of a go-er and Tallulah starts to understand why so many women spend a fortune on expensive lingerie. Maybe if she had realized the power of an up-lift bra and a leatherette g-string at a younger age she might not be standing here at the age of forty-five with her hymen still firmly intact!

Time for a Babycham.

She makes her way carefully down the stairs, turning sideways to avoid stumbling in her shoes and noticing the way her hands look against the banister with her nails painted metallic copper. How invigorating! She feels almost confident enough to tackle the perfumery hall in House of Fraser where the sales girls would rush forward to spray her wrists with exquisite designer scents instead of ushering her quickly through to Toiletries for a dab of Lentheric.

As she enters the kitchen she can hear raised voices and laughter from Ursula's house and the light from her kitchen window spills across the back garden in geometric slabs. There is an exciting atmosphere, a festive feeling in the air, and Tallulah's stomach is knotted with nervous anticipation. The last party she went to was a wedding reception for one of the Trebor girls where they had a cold buffet and a mobile disco. It was a horrible evening and Tallulah ended-up getting stuck with a lecherous uncle who tried to get his hand up her skirt during the Macarena. She has never been one for parties, always shying away from the more gregarious guests and hiding in corners with a plate of sandwiches. But tonight she feels more confident.

As she empties her bottle of Babycham in to a glass she notices a faint light coming from the old shed at the bottom of the garden. It looks like the flickering beam of a torch and it flashes across the broken window before dipping down and fading. There's nothing much in the shed apart from some rusty gardening equipment and a few old cans of paint but Tallulah is disturbed by the idea that somebody is out there. She turns off the kitchen light and stands to one side of the sink so she can watch the shed without being seen and she sees the shadow of a person pass behind the window. Then the silhouette of a second person appears and Tallulah instinctively grabs the telephone and calls Jeff.

"Don't go out there," he warns her, "I'll be there in a few minutes. Just keep watching and see if you can catch a glimpse of them if they leave."

She wonders if she should call Ursula's house but it is almost eight o' clock and they'll be starting their ritual so she decides to wait until Jeff arrives. She takes a gulp of her Babycham and keeps her eyes focused on the outline of the shed where the wavering light continues to bob up and down.

The voices from next-door have died-down so they must have gone down to the cellar. The TV in Tallulah's bedroom is still turned on and she can hear the Christmas adverts jingling away up there without an audience. Her mince pies sit proudly on a silver paper doily ready to be transported to the party and the patty tins are still soaking in the sink.

The garden is long and narrow so the shed is quite a way from the house and Tallulah doesn't feel too vulnerable. The back door is locked and bolted and if she sees anybody approaching the house she can run round the front and let herself in to Ursula's. She goes through to the living room to peer around the Christmas tree. She wondered if there might be a vehicle out there with a registration plate she could take down but, of course, with Ursula's gathering there are quite a lot of cars parked in the lane so the intruders could leave their car inconspicuously out there and nobody would notice. Jeff's van appears round the bend as she squints through the glass so she hurries to the front door and unlocks it for him.

"Are they still out there?" he asks as he rushes up the garden path.

Tallulah nods.

"OK, you stay here and I'll go out back."

"Jeff, I don't think it's safe for you to go out there on your own, you don't know who you're dealing with. Shouldn't we call the police?"

"Look, the cops won't get here for at least half an hour, by which time these buggers will be gone."

"Oh, Jeff, don't do anything silly. They're only in the shed, it's not as though they're going to nick anything valuable. Let's just call the police and let them deal with it."

"Tally, these are probably the same blokes who broke in to the house. I can't believe that it's unrelated to the burglary unless it's just somebody buggering about. Don't worry, I'll be careful."

So Jeff unlocks the kitchen door and makes his way slowly towards the garden shed while Tallulah stands in the darkened kitchen watching him with her heart in her mouth. He is just a few yards away from the shed when Tallulah notices the beam of the torch is extinguished and she sees the door swing open. Jeff ducks behind a large bush and disappears from view but Tallulah can see two figures climbing over the fence and making for the front of the house. She hears Jeff shout but the intruders don't stop. Jeff is suddenly leaping over the fence, chasing the figures through the field until he catches up with one of them and brings the person to the ground.

She doesn't hesitate any longer. She dials 999 and asks for the police.

Bitter Pill

"What are these?" Julian asks Nicole, emerging from her private bathroom having just popped in there to relieve himself. He holds up the three pill containers she got from the chemist.

"Pills," she answers dryly, turning her attention back to the magazine she is flipping through.

"What are they for?" he asks, approaching the bed.

"The doctor gave them to me for my nausea and diarrhoea," lies Nicole smoothly. "So, did you get everything you needed in London? You came home earlier than expected."

Julian places the pill containers on the bedside table and sits on the edge of the bed, loosening his tie. "Yes, it was very successful," he yawns.

"Diamonds?" suggests Nicole.

"Absolutely!" is his response. But Nicole wonders if his so-called business trip was connected with all that white powder she saw in his study last night. Her fever has dropped and she is feeling a little better, she has even eaten a few spoonfuls of chicken soup.

"Julian, I haven't asked you what your plans are for Christmas but I was thinking I should probably go back to the cottage tomorrow; I don't want to disrupt your plans."

"I don't really have any plans," admits Julian, "I usually go to my mother's on Christmas Eve and stay over until Boxing Day but you're more than welcome to stay here if you like. Mrs. Moon will be here and I'm sure she'll make sure that you're well cared for."

"Well I'm beginning to feel a bit better and I think I'd rather be on my own for a few days to recuperate. You've been really wonderful and Mrs. Moon is fantastic but I don't feel right sponging off you when I'm perfectly capable of looking after myself."

"My dear, you're hardly 'sponging' but if you'd prefer to be on your own for a while then I'll get Frank to drive you back to the cottage tomorrow. I'll have Mrs. Moon prepare some food for you to take and perhaps you can arrange for Jeff to look in on you; I'm sure he wouldn't mind. Are those other friends of yours going to be around for Christmas?"

"They're not really my friends, Julian. Ursula has been very kind but I've not got much in common with any of them and I'm sure they'll be busy with their own plans. No, I'll be fine on my own and I've got my mobile if I have to call anyone."

"Okie dokie. I think I'll go and change before dinner. I've got a couple of people coming over tonight so I hope you don't mind if I leave you on your own for the rest of the evening?"

"No, that's fine. I wasn't expecting you tonight anyway and I'm exhausted."

Julian reaches across the bedspread and squeezes Nicole's hand. "Get some rest and I'll see you in the morning, then. Mind the bed bugs don't bite." And he leaves the room, closing the door quietly behind him.

Shit!

She should have been more careful with those fucking pills! Nicole grabs her handbag and scoops the canisters inside. Tomorrow she will put them in to unmarked containers and make sure that they're secreted away from prying eyes. You never know who might go snooping through your medicine cabinet while they're washing their hands and she doesn't want to become a social pariah. It's one thing to be HIV positive in Miami Beach where most people understand that sharing a bottle of spring water won't put you at risk but here in the middle of the English countryside she would probably be relegated to a barbed-wire enclosed barn with a red cross painted on the door.

The fear of being a social outcast is a bitter pill for somebody like Nicole to swallow but there is absolutely no reason why she can't continue to hide her infection in the same way she has been hiding her working-class background and addiction to Cadbury's milk chocolate all these years! Who could possibly suspect that a woman in a pair of exquisite Ferragamo shoes could be infected with a Third World disease?

The packaging is much more important than the contents where Nicole is concerned and she believes that her worth is valued by the way she is perceived, not by substantial evidence. Having lived for so long in Miami where image is everything she has come to accept that the American Dream is the *only* dream worth pursuing. It doesn't matter how many degrees you have or how high your IQ; kindness is something you dole out only when there are cameras and reporters present to document it. A beautiful body, fabulous hair and a prestigious address with a walk-in closet jammed with designer clothing means more than a second language or political affiliation. The right car, the perfect partner and being seen in the hottest nightspots is paramount if you want respect and adulation so who cares if you read the foreign press or listen to Wagner while writing cheques to provide aid for Romanian orphans?

AIDS is something that Nicole would rather keep to the sidelines of her life; something to wear on her lapel at a charity fashion show or to sympathise with when she's dining out with influential gays. But AIDS is not something Nicole wants in her medicine cabinet and so she must do everything in her power to obscure the truth.

Clearing the Air

Ursula's Yule celebration has turned in to a frenzy of police activity and the area around the two houses is alive with flashing lights, walkie-talkies and an incongruous gathering of witches dressed in all manner of strange robes and adornments. The police are interviewing Jeff and Tallulah in the kitchen. It appears that the person Jeff pushed to the ground is a girl – a *young* girl – fortunately he didn't hurt her and was able to keep her in his grasp until the police arrived. The second person got away but it won't be difficult for the police to find him (and they know it is a male because the captured girl has already confessed everything in a sobbing babble of confused fear and regret.)

The two teenagers had visited Robert's house on several occasions in the past to buy pot. They are friends of one of Robert's students and when they discovered that Robert had been killed in the car accident they decided to raid his house for his cache of marijuana. They had watched him produce large bags of the stuff when he was weighing-out their quota so they felt fairly certain that he would have a substantial amount hidden somewhere in the house. Following the fruitless break-in they decided to return to check out his shed because their friend at the college had suggested to them that that was where Robert kept his stash.

According to the girl her boyfriend has the bag of pot that they found under a loose floorboard in the shed and the police are now hunting him down. They have his home address and it won't take long for them to find him. This is a huge relief for Tallulah because the thought that the burglars were still at large kept her awake at night and maybe now she can get a good eight hours sleep without jumping to attention every time she hears an owl hoot. The police need written statements from both Tallulah and Jeff but they agree that it can wait until tomorrow and by ten-thirty the drama is over. The witches have filtered back in to Ursula's house and the lane resumes its normal state of quietude. The grass is crystallised with a thin powdered frost and the air is still. When Tallulah closes her front door she shivers slightly and rubs her arms, turning to join Jeff who is still sitting at the kitchen table looking slightly stunned.

"What a night, eh?"

"Yeah," agrees Tallulah, "I never thought that moving out here would be so exciting. I thought country life was supposed to be all homemade jam and cow pats!"

"Believe me, I've lived here for ten years and absolutely nothing has happened in all that time. Excitement for me has been limited to the occasional fist-fight at the pub on a Saturday night and a run-in with some gypsies a few years back. Apart from that I've had to feed off local gossip like everybody else round here and there's only so much satisfaction you can derive from hearing about somebody's wife running away with a travelling salesman or one of the choirboys turning out to be queer."

"I suppose this is going to get in the papers," sighs Tallulah, sinking down opposite Jeff. "I feel bad for Uncle Ted and Auntie June but the police reckon Rob was only a small-time dealer. People don't seem to care much about marijuana these days since it was downgraded to a class C drug; there's too much publicity about heroin and crack for people to worry about something that has been legal in Amsterdam for years."

"Since when did you become the authority on marijuana legislation?" jokes Jeff.

"Since you introduced me to the internet," responds Tallulah, "it's amazing what you can learn once you know how to Google."

Jeff laughs. He looks different in his button-down collar and pleated trousers; more mature. "We should go next-door and join the party. I'm sure they're all talking about us."

"Tell me something new, they're always talking about us. Actually I meant to have a word with you about that, Jeff. I've been feeling awkward recently whenever Petra or Ursula makes one of their smart-arsed comments about me and you and I wanted to clear the air. I don't want you to think that I'm not grateful for everything you've done for me over the last few weeks – you've been brilliant – but I don't want you to get the wrong idea about me. I'd much rather have you as a friend than anything else and, correct me if I'm being presumptuous, but I don't want Petra or Ursula making you think there's anything else going on in the back of my mind. I've been single all my life and, at my age, I'm more comfortable that way." Tallulah fiddles with her nails and avoids Jeff's eye as she speaks, she can feel the colour rising in her cheeks but it's important to get this out. "I'm probably not putting this very well but I hope you understand what I'm getting at."

Jeff looks at Tallulah and his expression is serious. He cocks his head to one side and raises his eyebrows questioningly. "So, no shagging then?" he says. Tallulah starts to laugh; more with relief than humour.

"No shagging" she repeats with a grin.

"OK, well I will just say one thing, if I can…"

"All right."

"You look smashing tonight. I didn't have much chance to tell you earlier but when you first opened the door I thought you were somebody else. This new look has taken ten years off you."

"Did I look *that* bad?" questions Tallulah with a frown.

"I'm not falling for that one, Tally. I know how sensitive you women can get over the way you look. Let's just say the ingredients were all there, you just needed the right recipe to bring them all together. After all; a cake's just flour, eggs, butter and sugar until you create the batter and bake it."

"So you're comparing me to a Victoria Sandwich?"

"More of a Black Forest gateau," grins Jeff, "one of those multi-layered concoctions they bring to the table on a trolley in posh restaurants."

"I'll take that as a compliment," says Tallulah with uncharacteristic coyness.

"From a friend," emphasizes Jeff.

"From a friend," nods Tallulah with a smile.

And they make their way next-door to join the party; Jeff with his hands jingling the change in his pockets and Tallulah carrying her plate of mince pies as though they are offerings to a king.

Robert

Oh the strange little rituals that human beings follow in their misguided attempt to bring some sense of order and continuity to their self-important lives. It all seems so silly and useless to me now but I suppose routine is essential when there's so little security to grasp on to. Every morning millions of people get out of bed to stare at themselves in bathroom mirrors clouded with steam. They brush their teeth and gargle with Listerine, they shave and moisturize, pluck and groom in the certain knowledge that they will go through it all again day after day until they are too old or too infirm to do it for themselves. Who invented the weekend? Who decided that roast beef is for Sundays, that fish is for Fridays and school children should be tortured with semolina pudding at least once a month?

Christmas decorations go up, only to be taken down again a few weeks later. Cars drive from A to B and back to A again in mindless circles and soon every day feels just like the last. As I observe it all from my vantage point I can see the futility in it all and yet I can still understand the necessity for order. I used to wash my car on the first Sunday of every month. I used to eat at the Indian restaurant in Sheffield every Thursday evening after my late class at the college. I used to swallow my White Powder Gold every morning and every night in the hope that it might prolong my life and keep me healthy, and look what happened; I got drunk, got stoned and drove myself over the edge of a ravine.

O Come All Ye Faithful

When you're feeling under the weather and it's the Saturday before Christmas it's not a good idea to go to the supermarket. But poor Nicole gets back to Brown Bread Cottage in the middle of the afternoon and, like Old Mother Hubbard, finds that her cupboard is bare. Her fever has lifted but she still feels very weak and listless and she should probably have gone straight to bed but the empty silence of the little cottage scares her after the luxurious grandeur of Longfield Hall and she feels a desperate need to pamper herself. Loneliness manifests itself in many ways; some people stuff themselves with food until they have to stick their fingers down their throats and others drown their sorrows in booze. Nicole prefers the 'modern way' of coping with depression; it's called Retail Therapy and if somebody could bottle it and put it on the shelves of Boots they'd make a bundle!

Tesco seems to have changed its image since the days of Green Shield stamps and she is astonished at how many cars are parked in the expansive car park outside. She has to drive round several times before somebody pulls out to create a free space and then she has to walk what feels like miles to get to the store. As usual she is inappropriately dressed for the weather and a bitter wind cuts through the thin fabric of her flimsy jacket. She has tied her hair back in a jaunty pony tail and smeared on some lipstick but her pallor is deathly and the wind makes her eyes run.

The supermarket is mobbed with crazed Christmas shoppers who seem to be on a single-minded quest to beat their opponents to the check-out with the most amount of provisions in their trolleys. Manic Christmas music blares out of the sound system and a rush of hot air blasts Nicole on the back of her head as she enters the throng. She is glad of the support when she finally grabs hold of a trolley and eases herself forward through the crowd in a haze of bewilderment. Bright lights, vivid colours and an overwhelming smell of baked goods, cooked meats and flowers make her legs weak and she has to lean forward so that her elbows rest on the handle to guide her forward in a drunken fashion. The front wheels of the trolley have a mind of their own and lead her towards things she doesn't want; the more she attempts to steer the more they drag her in the opposite direction until she is literally staggering to maintain control.

"Excuse me, love!" persists a fat woman in a red anorak and ski-pants as she pushes by to reach for the furthest bunch of bananas.

"Can I just reach past?" asks a young mother with a chocolate-smeared child jammed in to the kiddie seat.

"Mind your back," mutters a surly skinhead with a basket full of trifle sponges and jelly as he elbows his way past Nicole to grab some double cream from the refrigerator cabinet.

She doesn't know what she wants and every time she pauses to scan the shelves somebody blocks her way or pushes past. Her head hurts, her throat is sore and somebody catches her heel painfully as they ram their trolley recklessly up the aisle. "Watch what you're doing!" she shouts after the woman with the Santa Claus hat but all Nicole gets in return is an ugly glare and two raised fingers.

At the delicatessen counter there is a milling horde of customers holding little white tickets and waiting for their turn. Nicole pulls a ticket from the machine; number fifty-six. She looks at the digital indicator and is dismayed to see that they're only now serving number twenty-three so she gives up on the idea of thin-sliced Bavarian ham and decides to buy the ready-packed stuff instead.

She has no list to follow, no menus planned in her head and so she throws whatever takes her fancy in to the trolley with nothing more than a frantic desire to get round this hideous obstacle course and back out to her car. Mince pies, a miniature Christmas cake decorated with royal icing and a plastic snowman, pre-cooked turkey complete with stuffing and bread sauce, pickled onions, mature cheddar, a box of Cadbury's Roses and four bottles of champagne vie for space amidst a jumble of randomly selected items. She remembers that she doesn't have a freezer and has to fling several frozen meals in to a free-standing display of selection boxes while nobody is looking.

The cash registers are swamped and the queues stretch in to the aisles so that people have to crash their way through the lines to get round the store. It takes almost twenty minutes to reach the conveyor belt and then the spotty cashier with the flashing deely boppers runs out of till roll and she has to wait for a supervisor to bring her some more, by which time Nicole is tempted to pop open a bottle of champagne and swig it straight from the bottle. She slumps over her trolley and doesn't realize that she is expected to bag her own groceries and so, when it is time to pay, the woman behind her huffs a beleaguered sigh of exasperation because the cashier has to help Nicole sort herself out before she can continue.

"WHAT?" yells Nicole, glaring at the woman in the horsy headscarf but the woman just averts her eyes and tuts sharply with a sympathetic neighbour who appears equally indignant. Damn the sodding Brits! They're so fucking passive aggressive!

"Merry Christmas!" sneers Nicole sarcastically as she steers her laden trolley away from the cashier with a backward glance, crashing in to a steel barrier and jarring the bones in her wrist. The thin, piercing scream of a child reverberates through Nicole's head as she makes for the doors and she narrowly misses a twenty-pound frozen turkey as it comes barrelling across the floor from an overloaded trolley with jammed wheels.

It is growing dark when she emerges from the supermarket and she is slapped rudely in the face by a sudden gust of icy wind. The early evening is clear and glacial with streaks of Arctic-rose along the horizon. The moon is already visible; a pale transparent impression like a frosty watermark embossed in to the vellum of the sky. Nicole adjusts the collar of her jacket and shivers, lurching out across the cluttered expanse of the car park with her errant trolley veering dangerously in all directions.

She is loading her shopping in to the back of her car when somebody calls out her name and she looks up, bangs her head on the open boot and drops a bag of groceries on to the ground. The plastic bag splits and the contents fall across the tarmac.

"Oh, I'm sorry!" gushes Tallulah, rushing forward to help Nicole pick up the packages and boxes. Jeff is following behind her with several carrier bags weighing him down. What has the woman done to her hair? It looks as though somebody has been hacking at it with a pair of blunt scissors! And those streaks!

"Hello Tallulah, hi Jeff!" Nicole adopts her bright and breezy public persona, smiling brightly and rubbing the crown of her head.

"Are you all right?" asks Tallulah, holding the packet of pre-cooked turkey in her hand and looking down at it as if it contains a turd.

"I'm fine, no problem," assures Nicole, taking the package from Tallulah and dumping it in to the boot with the rest of her things.

"How's the flu?" asks Jeff.

"Oh, finally I think I'm over the worst of it but I probably shouldn't have come out here today, it's made me feel a bit tired. I just didn't have any food in and I wanted to get my groceries before Christmas."

"Are you spending Christmas with Julian?" asks Jeff, placing his bags carefully around his feet.

"No, he's going to his mother's so I'll be at the cottage. Actually It'll be nice to have some quiet time to myself. Julian and his housekeeper have been brilliant but I feel more comfortable in my own space. Tallulah, your hair looks great! And you're wearing make-up as well! Fabulous!"

Tallulah smiles awkwardly and thanks Nicole but she is still staring mournfully at the packaged turkey in the back of Nicole's car.

"You know," she starts, "I'm having a little Christmas dinner at my place; just Jeff, Ursula and Petra but you're more than welcome to join us if you're not doing anything. I don't like to think of you being on your own at Christmas."

"Oh that's nice of you, but I'll be perfectly fine. I'm not that bothered about the holidays, actually and under the current circumstances – my first Christmas without Gideon and everything – I think I really wouldn't be very good company."

"Well if you change your mind just give me a call. You can always pop round later in the day for a drink if you get bored."

"Thanks a lot; I'll keep that in mind. Now, I think I'd better get home and back in to bed, I'm freezing!"

She slams the boot closed, offers them both her most dazzling smile and climbs in to her car, thankful to be rid of them. Oh, they mean well enough but, *please,* spend Christmas with a bunch of losers? I don't think so!

She backs out of the parking space and drives away as quickly as possible considering the mess of shoppers and trolleys meandering all over the place. She realizes that her tank is empty and she sees a petrol station on the other side of the roundabout so she heads over there, almost forgetting to turn left on to the roundabout instead of right and causing another motorist to blare his horn at her.

The pumps are all occupied so she has to stand in the forecourt waiting for somebody to pull away and she fiddles with the controls of the car radio to find some soothing music. Christmas carols and jarring pop music seem to be about all she can find so she settles for *O Come All Ye Faithful* and checks her hair in the rear-view mirror. She doesn't see that the car in front of her has pulled away until the driver behind honks his horn sharply and points through his windscreen with irritation.

"Jerk!" Nicole mutters as she pulls up to the pump and roots through her bag for her wallet. Oh Christ! Her wallet isn't there. She must have left it on the checkout counter in the supermarket. "Fuck, fuck, fuck!" she curses, turning the key in the ignition only to find that the engine won't start. The petrol tank signal is flashing empty. She tries again but the engine refuses to ignite and the twat behind her honks his horn again as though she's somehow doing this on purpose.

Nicole pushes the car door open so violently that it practically slams back in her face. She jumps out of the car and storms up to the car behind, rapping on the driver's window with her car keys. He winds down his window and stares at her arrogantly; "what the hell are you pissing about at?" he demands, placing his elbow on the open window ledge to lean closer to Nicole. She can smell alcohol on his breath.

"It's none of your fucking business, you ignorant prick! My car's out of gas and I left my wallet in the supermarket so I suggest that if you're in so much of a hurry that you choose a different pump because I'm likely to be here for quite some time."

"Bloody women drivers," he groans, "too busy tarting yourself up in the bloody mirror when you should be paying attention."

Nicole has just about had enough for one day. She can feel her anger fizzing up from deep in the pit of her stomach and her peripheral vision is flashing with coloured stars of indignation. "Listen, dick-head, why don't you back your lousy little car in to that empty bay over there and keep your bigoted comments to yourself. Cock-suckers like you should be castrated at birth, preferably with a blunt instrument. Now get the fuck out of my face and go home to your shitty little council house."

Nicole is practically shoved to the ground as the driver of the car jerks open his door and grabs her by the wrist. He brings his face within an inch of her own and his voice is low and menacing; spit forms at the corners of his mouth and his eyes blaze with hatred.

"Don't you dare speak to me like that you stuck-up cow. I don't know who you think you are but your registration number is easy to remember and I'll come after you – no fear – if you don't apologize right now."

"Let go of my wrist," hisses Nicole through bared teeth.

"Apologize, slag."

"Let go of my wrist or I'll have you for assault."

"Just try it," he snarls.

Nicole yanks her wrist upwards but he refuses to let go. His grip is tight and his nails are digging in to the delicate veins on the underside. She doesn't pause to consider the consequences of her actions; instead she sinks her teeth in to the fleshy part of his hand and chomps down until she tastes the salt of his blood on her tongue. He yelps like a wounded animal and immediately drops her wrist, staggering back against the bonnet of his car.

"You mad cow!" he yells and by now there is quite a crowd of onlookers gathered around the petrol pumps. One of the garage assistants is striding towards them from the office and Nicole wipes the blood from her lips with the back of her hand, shaking with the exertion of the skirmish.

"I might be mad," she spits, "but you just got bitten by a cow with HIV so I'd suggest you see a doctor as soon as possible."

And before she can be detained Nicole runs as fast as she can across the forecourt and through the hedge that surrounds the roundabout. She staggers across the road and in to the car park of the supermarket, weaving between the parked cars until she reaches the absurd normality of the store where shoppers continue to fill their trolleys and Christmas music blares out from the loudspeakers.

She hurries to the cashier where she left her wallet and interrupts the woman who is being served. "My wallet," she gasps, "I left my wallet here just now."

"Oh, yes," nods the cashier, it's right here," and she reaches under the counter to hand the wallet to Nicole.

"Shit! Oh Shit!" mumbles Nicole as she hurries out of the supermarket and takes a diversion around the back of the building in to some playing fields. It is dark now and the fields are deserted. She keeps running; stumbling over the coarse grass and flailing wildly as she attempts to keep her balance. When she finally comes to rest by a set of swings she falls to the ground with exhaustion and throws up across the scuffed asphalt.

This is like a crazy dream; she can't believe what just happened and now she's made things ten times worse by running away like a frightened school girl. She should have stood her ground; demanded that somebody call the police and stated her case against the arrogant dick-head who accosted her instead of fleeing in a panic. It won't take more than a few minutes for the cops to trace her from the registration of the rental car and although she's not sure what kind of criminal charges she might face she lacks the fortitude to withstand a run-in with the law. She wonders how long it will take the police to trail her to Brown Bread Cottage. If she could get there immediately she could grab her essential items; British passport and any other documents pertaining to Veronica Rustin, and she could run away from Nicole Harvey just like she ran away from Gideon. It's not as though she's murdered anyone (has she?); maybe by biting the man at the garage she could be accused of *attempted* murder? She doesn't even know if you can infect somebody with HIV through a superficial wound but the intention was there.

Her mobile phone is clipped to the waist of her jeans. She will call Julian and make up some cock-and-bull story about her car breaking down in the middle of nowhere. Perhaps he will send Frank to pick her up but even Longfield Hall is no refuge to her now because too many people know about her connection with Julian. She calls him anyway, thinking that at least she could get a lift back to the cottage.

"Julian? It's Nicole."

"Yes?" Julian sounds strange; not his usual jocular self.

"My car's broken down and I'm stranded about five miles outside Castleton. I was wondering if Frank might be able to come and get me."

"You've got a nerve," states Julian coldly.

"I'm sorry?" Nicole is confused. Surely he couldn't have heard about the altercation at the garage already?

"I don't know what to say to you, Nicole. You're an abominable, deceitful worthless piece of shit. I can't believe that anyone could be so totally evil."

"Julian, I don't know what you're talking about," stammers Nicole, leaning against the cold metal support of the swings with a sinking feeling of desperation creeping up from her stomach.

"I looked up those pills," states Julian icily, "and they're not for nausea and diarrhoea at all, are they? And you haven't got the flu either, have you? You've been conning me from the first moment we met."

"Julian, look…"

"If you've infected me, I'll make sure you rot in a prison cell for the rest of your life, and presumably that won't be a lengthy sentence. You've fucked with the wrong person this time, Nicole."

Nicole clips her phone shut and drops it to the ground as though it has burnt her fingers. This is a nightmare. She doesn't pause to consider her options; instead she runs towards the main road on the opposite side of the field and hopes that somebody will be kind enough to give her a lift as far as the next village. It is imperative that she gets to the cottage as soon as possible but beyond that objective she has no idea what her game-plan should be.

The News at 4:40 pm

A *heated altercation broke out this afternoon in the forecourt of a local petrol station between two drivers waiting to use the pumps. Eye-witnesses say that Kevin Thompson of Macclesfield grew impatient with a female driver, sounding his horn to move her forward at the Hibel Road branch of Tesco at approximately four-fifteen this afternoon. The unidentified driver of the second car, a woman in her late-thirties driving a dark blue Toyota Avensis, apparently got out of her car and approached Mr. Thompson. An argument broke-out between the two drivers and Mr. Thompson stepped out of his car and grabbed the unidentified woman by the wrist. The woman then bit Mr. Thompson's hand, drawing blood, and warned him that she is HIV positive before she abandoned her car and ran in the direction of the Tesco supermarket. Police are currently investigating the abandoned car which appears to be a rental and they are confident that the driver will be apprehended shortly. Video tape of the incident is being studied by the police; meanwhile Mr. Thompson is being treated for the wound to his hand. Experts tell us that HIV transmission through human bites can only be caused by blood-to-blood contact and it is unlikely that saliva can cause infection unless mixed with blood from the infected person. At this stage the police don't know if the woman in this incident really is HIV positive or if she was merely attempting to alarm her assailant. We will bring you an update on this story at ten o' clock."*

"That must have happened just after we left," muses Tallulah, sitting in Jeff's living room with Barney begging for biscuit crumbs at her feet.

"Doesn't Nicole have a blue Avensis?" frowns Jeff. "You don't think it was her, do you?"

"No, they said this woman was in her thirties and, anyway, why would Nicole run away like that, leaving her car behind? It doesn't make sense. It sounds to me like the woman just got mad at the guy who accosted her and then panicked."

"You know I can't decide if crime really is worse these days or if, like our parents before us, we just *perceive* it as being worse because we're older and consider ourselves more civilized. It really does seem to me that things are worse now."

Tallulah nods in agreement and bends forward to slip Barney a small piece of her chocolate bourbon. "It's not just the cities any more; look at those two kids who broke in to my place. The lady PC at the station this morning was telling me how much trouble they have with drugs round here, especially in some of the larger villages. You know we never even *heard* about drugs and rape and murders when I was a kid but every time you turn on the news it's there. People don't let their kids play outside without supervision any more and if they *are* out on their own they're up to no good."

Jeff looks away from the TV and smiles. "Tally, you're sounding more like your gran every day!"

"Oh, don't say that! I'm just shocked that those kids were only sixteen and seventeen and they had the guts to break in to my house all for the sake of a few ounces of bloody marijuana. There I was, terrified every time I heard a noise at night and all the time it was just a couple of kids."

The seventeen year old boy had been caught late the previous night, skulking around behind some garages close to his parents' home in Hope. The bag of marijuana contained less than four ounces with a street value of about six hundred quid; hardly worth the attention of *serious* criminals. Both kids will probably get off with nothing more than a fine and a good ticking-off. It appears that they come from 'decent' homes and so it seems likely that this will be enough to teach them a lesson. The story didn't even make the news.

"You know, perhaps we should stop by Nicole's cottage on our way to the carol concert," suggests Tallulah. "I don't like to think of her being all on her own out there, especially when she's ill. She didn't look at all well this afternoon when we saw her."

"If you like," nods Jeff, "but it struck me that she wanted to be left alone. I'm not sure what's going on between her and Julian but Nicole strikes me as a bit of an opportunist. You should have seen the way her eyes lit up when I first took her over to Julian's place, she was all over him."

"She's just like most of the women we used to have as customers at Mr. B's. They're rich and spoilt and they always get their own way. They were born beautiful and it's a well-known fact that it's the beautiful ones who always get on in life. Even if you're thick as shit you can still get a great job because of the way you look. And Nicole strikes me as intelligent so she's got even *more* going for her. I still feel sorry for her, though. I don't know why but she always seems so sad even when she's laughing."

"There's more to her than meets the eye from what Ursula's told me. She's told so many fibs that nobody knows what is and what isn't the truth. I think she's a bit, you know..." and Jeff twirls his index finger against his forehead.

"Highly strung, I'd say. She just gets het-up about stuff that the rest of us would ignore. I've seen her get all twitchy and tense sometimes and it's like her whole body is on red alert. She's probably taking pills for it; that's something else that Americans are so keen on; swallowing pills for everything."

"So what about you, Tally? If you could choose any job you wanted; irrespective of qualifications or aptitude, what would you most love to do?"

"Oh I don't know," giggles Tallulah, "I've never really thought about it."

"Oh come on! Everybody's thought about it at some point in their lives. It's like dreaming about winning the lottery or wondering what it would feel like to be a film star or an athlete. My dream has always been to have a nice, respectable little antique shop selling only really good stuff; not the tat I sell now. Or maybe a Dutch-style coffee shop selling marijuana; with a lounge bar filled with floor cushions and hookahs so people could just lay around smoking their weed and chilling out."

Tallulah thinks for a moment before she admits that she wanted to be a bus driver when she was in infant school. Then she wanted to work in Woolworth's on the Pick 'n' Mix counter in the days when Chesterfield's branch of the store still had mahogany counters and potted palms. But instead of selling sweet in Woolies she went to *packaging* sweets at the Trebor factory and her dreams disappeared in a syrupy haze of pear drops and peppermint. "I think now, at my time of life, I'd like a job that isn't too physical but not an office job. I like working in shops; but small shops where they're run by a family is better. I'd hate to work somewhere like Wal-Mart. A book shop, perhaps? Or a little tea room like the one here in Castleton."

"So why did you stick it out for all those years slogging away at Trebor when you could have been doing something you would have enjoyed?"

"It never entered my head there was an alternative," admits Tallulah, sadly. "I was brought up to stick to a job and to accept the fact that work is the only way to make an honest living and is therefore a necessary evil. Nobody actually *enjoys* work! That was the basic idea behind it and I just accepted that. It was a hell of a lot more fun that being at school; at least in the beginning."

"So have you got any idea what you want to do now?" asks Jeff, turning off the television.

"Not really. My mind hasn't been on it recently and so I'm not going to think about it until after I've had my surgery. If they can't cure my cancer I might just want to go crazy; sell-up and travel the world. Who knows! I'm not in a great panic to find another job at the moment so I can wait until I find the right thing instead of taking the first thing that comes my way and I'm lucky that I don't have to worry about earning a huge wage."

Tallulah hasn't really thought much about finding a new job. Her mind has been pre-occupied with moving house, worrying about her health and coping with the drama of the break-in etc. With Christmas right on the doorstep she prefers to leave all those serious topics until the New Year but, for now, she would rather pretend that the next week will last forever.

A Whiff of Brimstone

The flight from Miami to London was hideous. First there was a two hour delay standing on the tarmac of Miami airport and then they experienced such violent turbulence for the entire journey that the seat belt signs were permanently illuminated. They couldn't even get up to go to the toilet unless accompanied by one of the cabin crew and the meal service was cut short which meant that Gideon didn't get his second bottle of champagne.

Arriving at Heathrow was a nightmare, especially for somebody who is experiencing severe Crystal Meth withdrawal. His teeth were clenched in an involuntary seizure and his body felt as though it was restrained and tightly-wound, desperate for release. Sweating and nauseous his pushed his way through the chaotic crowds at Arrivals, scanning the handwritten signs held aloft by the taxi drivers and chauffeurs. People blocked the exit, straining their necks to catch a first glimpse of relatives and friends, making it practically impossible to get through with luggage trolleys. Gideon had to restrain himself from screaming at the couple in front of him who suddenly abandoned their cart to hug their grandchildren. Girls wearing tinsel around their necks and people in Santa hats pushed and jostled while distorted announcements over the tannoy added to the general atmosphere of confusion and mayhem.

Finally Gideon spotted his driver and flagged him down. They went through to the car park garage and Gideon cowered by his suitcase in the frigid morning air while he waited for the driver to bring his car around. It was only just growing light and the sky was one solid sheet of dirty grey. Breath came from Gideon's chattering mouth in steamy clouds of vapour; he had forgotten what it was like to be really cold and his Florida clothes were totally insufficient.

As soon as he reached his hotel he called his friend Ian and a shifty-looking guy in a tracksuit brought him the gear within the hour. Gideon sat on the toilet and inhaled the smoke from the clean glass pipe he had been given and within minutes his head started to clear and the tension drifted away on a cloud of burnt chemicals. The nightmare of London immediately became a novelty to be savoured and he pushed open the bedroom window as far as it would go (a mere three inches to save desperate hotel guests from throwing themselves down to the pavement below) and gulped in great mouthfuls of damp English air. It is fifteen years since Gideon last experienced the foreign sights, sounds and smells of a European city and he was so high that the nostalgia brought tears to his eyes. What happened to those innocent days before they moved to Miami? Could it be possible that he was even the same person back then?

He couldn't face anything more than a couple of cups of lousy hotel coffee for breakfast but he took a shower, got changed in to warmer clothing and watched the TV with mild amusement. Everything seemed so quaint; from the size of the hotel bed to the electric kettle to the rinky-dink television programmes. His driver waited for him in the lobby and took him to the Hertz car rental place so that he could pick up his car and begin the journey out of London and up the M1 towards Derbyshire.

Getting out of the city was confusing and painfully slow but once he got on to the motorway he kept his foot down and enjoyed the exhilaration of driving at ninety miles an hour with the radio blasting out Christmas music. The car was equipped with a navigational system so all Gideon had to do was follow the instructions. He didn't even have to stop for gas. There was a narrowly missed accident when he decided to change lanes without indicating but apart from that his journey was uneventful and he reached Chesterfield by three o' clock.

He stopped at a motorway service station to get some more coffee and a Danish pastry and he refuelled on Crystal before stopping at a series of garages to pick up necessary supplies. The afternoon sky had cleared to an icy blue but there was a strong northern wind and Gideon bought himself a woollen hat and some gloves at one of the garage shops. He felt oddly conspicuous but it could have been paranoia caused by the drugs. Were people staring at him in a funny way?

It is dark now and bitterly cold but Castleton is festive with Christmas lights and Gideon feels as though he is driving through an old-fashioned Christmas card; the kind with painted horse-drawn carriages, gas lanterns and glitter sprinkled to look like frost on the trees. This illusion is completed by the brass band accompaniment of *Silent Night* on his car radio and he is almost tempted to pull in to the car park and seek warmth and refuge in one of the cosy-looking pubs. But Gideon isn't here for draught beer and horse-brasses; his drug-addled intention is to perform one simple act of vengeance and to hurry back to the safety of London. He can't pause to appreciate the bucolic conviviality of the pre-Christmas Derbyshire countryside, no, his intention is far less celebratory and he must drive past the coloured lights and the decorated trees in search of vindication from this gnawing sense of injustice that has plagued him now for days.

Brown Bread Cottage, when he finally reaches it, stands alone and vulnerable surrounded by a tumble-down wall and a garden of hardy evergreens and winter-dry perennials. It is a square building with windows like eyes; all of them dark but for the living room where the curtains stand open, revealing a cosy pink-hued interior with a low-beamed ceiling. Gideon reverses his car and pulls back down the lane, finding a convenient lay-by where he can park the car without drawing too much attention. He wonders if Veronica is at home. The light is on but there is no car outside the cottage and he presumes that she must have a vehicle of some kind; she's not the kind of woman who would actually *walk* anywhere.

He takes the three red plastic petrol containers from the back of his car and carries them back up the lane towards the cottage. Fortunately there are plenty of tall hedges behind which he can hide and he soon finds a suitable spot from where he can keep an eye on the cottage without being seen. The wind, when it blows, is cruelly cold and it blurs his vision as he squats in the grass, peering through the tangle of bramble and shrub. There is no movement inside the cottage but he keeps his eyes peeled on the lighted living room window and he waits.

He has his pipe with him and he decides to take another hit. It is difficult to keep the lighter flame steady in the buffeting wind but he turns his back to the gusts and cups his hand around the end of the pipe, inhaling urgently before the flame blows out again. He doesn't feel the cold so much when he closes his eyes. The familiar rush of energy propels him forward as though he is on a wild rollercoaster ride and he can't stop himself from smiling. She thinks she is so safe and protected in her little country cottage but Gideon waits and watches with a mounting sense of excitement. His plans are ill-conceived and unsophisticated but the consequences of his actions are of no concern right now; all he can think about is the rush of exhilaration when he finally shows Veronica what he's made of.

Half an hour passes uneventfully and Gideon is beginning to lose the sensation in his toes. His nose is dripping and even though he is wearing a fully lined coat the cold seems to reach under the cuffs and the collar like a creeping, malignant mould with frosty fingers. He anticipates and dreads each gust of wind and the desolate

sound it makes as it rustles through the barren branches
of the trees. He grows uncomfortable and impatient so
he decides to investigate behind the back of the cottage
to see if Veronica is visible from there.

The kitchen light is off but light from the living
room bleeds through and gleams dully against the glossy
painted cabinets. It doesn't look as though anyone is at
home. Fuck! How long will he have to wait here in the
dark before she comes back? He keeps to the shadows
but steps back to get a better view of the cottage. The
bedroom windows are vacant holes in the obdurate stone
of the cottage walls; they stare unblinkingly out across
the fields and Gideon looks up at them, straining his eyes
for signs of life.

And then he sees her. She is standing slightly
back from one of the window, partially obscured by a
curtain but she is definitely there. She must know he's
here because she keeps the lights out and her stillness
suggests that she is watching for something. Maybe she
heard his car earlier and has called the police? They
could be on their way right this minute and Ronnie is in
there trying to keep quiet until they arrive to save her.
Gideon will have to work quickly.

He runs around to the front of the cottage and
grabs two of the petrol containers from his hiding place
behind the hedge. Then he sidles back up to the cottage
and climbs over a part of the stone wall that has all but
fallen apart. Unscrewing the first container he starts
sloshing the petrol up against the cottage walls, following
the foundation line around the side of the house until the
first container is empty. He fetches the second and
continues his wild dance until the perimeter of Brown
Bread Cottage is completely fuelled with petrol. The
final gulp of petrol he tosses up against the little blue
front door and the sweet, intoxicating stench assails his

nostrils and he breathes deeply. It is a pleasant smell. It is the smell he used to love as a kid when fences were newly creosoted; the smell of garden sheds on hot summer afternoons. A whiff of brimstone perhaps?

And dipping some twigs in to the empty fuel container he ignites them with his lighter and throws the burning bundle up against the front door of the cottage. There is a sound like 'whump' as the petrol ignites in a satisfying billow of rich blue flames and then they chase around the base of the cottage, surrounding it like a saucepan sitting on the open burner of an Aga. Gideon steps away from the heat, admiring the way the flames leap up the sides of the cottage, catching on the dry remnants of the wisteria that twists and clings to the masonry around some of the windows.

He runs back to fetch the third container of petrol and unscrews the cap, watching for another appearance of Veronica in the upstairs windows. Soon she will come screaming to the surface; crying out for mercy and begging somebody to help her. Maybe she will pull open the front door only to be confronted by a wall of fire and maybe the vacuum she creates will drag the flames inside the cottage to ignite everything it touches? Gideon decides to throw more fuel around the front door and the lower windows just to make sure that Veronica doesn't somehow escape. He is laughing now and the sound is demented as he tears up the garden path with his slopping container of petrol. And just before he re-fuels the inferno he catches sight of her looking at him from the living room window. Through the blazing wall of violent flames the glass of the tiny mullioned window appears to be melting but Gideon can see her face quite clearly. She looks calm; impassive even and she stands quite still, her eyes dark and malevolent. She is wearing a black coat with a high collar and her hair is pinned up on top of her head; not at all her usual way of dressing. Probably all part of her disguise.

"BITCH!" screams Gideon above the roar of the flames, "FUCK YOU!" he shrieks in to the gusty, fume-laden wind and he tosses the contents of his red plastic container in to the greedy mouth of the fire.

Enemy Fire

Tallulah and Jeff pull up in Jeff's van as Gideon hurls the petrol in to the inferno that engulfs Brown Bread Cottage. An arc of flame appears to spring from the heart of the fire itself, eating the stream of clear liquid and igniting the plastic container still in Gideon's hand. He immediately drops the flaming container but in doing so the remaining petrol douses his trousers and sets them alight. Like a stunt man on a movie set Gideon stumbles backwards, towards the cottage gate, completely consumed by the fierce flames that streak up his body in a spontaneous flash of combustion. Instead of rolling on the ground to starve the flames of oxygen he keeps running, his arms waving frantically in the air like some kind of ghastly animated puppet and Jeff leaps out of the van.

"Jeff!" screams Tallulah, tumbling from the passenger side of the van but Jeff is running towards Gideon, removing his jacket as he runs, and as he knocks Gideon to the ground he smothers his head and shoulders with the jacket to try and extinguish some of the flames.

A bedroom window suddenly explodes, sending a shower of glass in to the cottage garden and the little house seems to inhale deeply, dragging the flames in to its lungs and then coughing them out in a shower of sparks. Tallulah can only watch from the side of the van; the heat of the fire is intense and her eyes blaze with the reflection as she watches Jeff and Gideon with mounting horror. Jeff appears to have put out the flames but the body on the ground is smouldering like a doused log and from this distance Tallulah can see nothing but charred clothing.

"My mobile's in the car, Tally! Call for an ambulance and the fire brigade!" Jeff is silhouetted against the flames that have now reached the roof of the cottage, licking their way under the eaves and gusting in the wind, setting fire to an adjacent tree. Tallulah dials 999 for the second time in two days and while she waits for the emergency operator to connect her there is a splintering sound as part of the cottage roof suddenly collapses and flames shoot skyward.

A police car appears in the lane even before Tallulah has spoken to anyone and it crunches to an abrupt stop just behind the van. There are two police officers; one of them jumps out of the car and runs over to Jeff while the second remains seated, talking in to a radio. There is somebody sitting in the back of the police car, pressed up against the window, staring out at the blazing cottage with horrified eyes. It is Nicole and she appears to be handcuffed to the seat in front of her. She doesn't acknowledge Tallulah, she merely stares at the cottage, her face a mask of astonishment, and the flames reflected in the car window appear to flicker around her as though she is staring out from the confines of a pizza oven.

A fall from Grace

L adybird, Ladybird
Fly away home,
Your house is on fire
Your children have flown

What a cruel, mindless little nursery rhyme that is and yet as Nicole watches Brown Bread Cottage go up in smoke from the back of the panda car she can't help but remember it from a far distant past of summer holidays and childhood pursuits. They used to capture the defenceless little insects in screw-top coffee jars; red and sometimes yellow and they would keep them imprisoned until they died. From an early age Nicole has been attempting to commandeer everything within her power, as though, in some small way, she needs the reassurance that ownership can bring. Ladybirds in jars, money in the bank, men wearing wedding rings; these are all signs of an insecure nature and despite Nicole's illustrious past she has never quite managed to shake off the shackles of her own deep-rooted lack of confidence.

Sometimes the most confident people are the ones who find it most difficult to live with themselves. They forge an impervious glossy shell of determination, intimidating people with their self-assured élan and efficiency as they stride through life barking orders at people who are too daunted to argue. But just beneath the highly-polished surface – like the crisp shell of a Smartie – there is a vulnerable chocolaty centre and it doesn't take more than a swift crunch to crack the candy overlay and to lay bare the delicate filling.

Nicole feels exposed and defenceless, handcuffed to the seat of the police car while Tallulah looks on with consternation and pity. How humiliating to be pitied by a woman who eats packet soup! How degrading to be gawped at as though she is some kind of circus freak when just a few months ago she was sitting in the toilet cubicle next to Paris Hilton! This is a fall from grace so squalid that it makes Nicole wish she had stayed in Miami and stuck things out with Gideon. An unfaithful husband and a sexually transmitted disease is nothing compared to this hideous mess; she has lost everything, including her dignity and now somebody has set fire to the cottage where, presumably, they thought she was hiding.

Was it Julian? Was it the ignorant little man at the petrol station? Or was it merely a random act of vandalism that happened to coincide with the unbelievable chain of events that have befallen Nicole in the last few days? She thinks of the voodoo dolls nailed to the churchyard tree and begins to wonder if all of this is a case of magic gone awry.

The wail of sirens heralds the arrival of the fire brigade and the ambulance and the wind blows thick smoke across the lane to envelop the police car, obscuring the view for a few seconds. She can taste the acrid fumes of petrol and scorched wood even though the doors and windows are firmly closed. The police officer continues to talk in to the radio, explaining that there is a body lying in the path; a body that appears to be lifeless and charred beyond recognition.

The police picked Nicole up just a few minutes after she attempted to flag down a car on the main road out of Macclesfield. She didn't have the strength or the willpower to take flight when she saw them slowing down and there seemed little point in denying that she was, in fact, the woman they were looking for. She didn't put up a fight when they asked her to get in to the car but she could tell that they were wary of her in the way one might be wary of a dog with a foaming muzzle. For her own amusement she could have growled or barked at them, baring her teeth, but she was cold and dizzy and merely grateful to sink down in to a comfortable seat. They asked her questions as they drove but she was too exhausted to answer. They said they were taking her to the station for questioning but first they wanted to go to the cottage to get some definitive identification; her passport, driving license etc.

The fire was clearly visible from a mile away and at first Nicole didn't realize the significance of that orange glow in the dark December sky. It wasn't until they pulled in to the lane that the sickening truth came to light and she gasped in disbelief. If there was such a thing as a thunderbolt from God she would have believed in it at that moment but Nicole has no religion to cling to and so she must accept the fact that bad things happen to bad people. The burning of Brown Bread Cottage is merely the culmination of a life so wicked and profane that it cannot be refuted. Just reward for a woman who deserves to burn in hell.

Life

I didn't stick around Derbyshire for Christmas; I decided I needed a change of scene and, remember, I have had *other* lives besides that of Robert Clegg; all of them equally important. I went to my old house in London where I died in 1952. The family that lives there now are remarkably wealthy considering that the neighbourhood was predominantly working-class back in the fifties.

The youngest daughter saw me on the landing one night when she got up to go to the loo and she virtually screamed the place down. I heard her describing me to her mother as an 'old man with white hair and glasses wearing a tie and an unbuttoned cardigan' and it was quite the dinner party conversation over the Christmas break, I can tell you.

My name was Cedric Johnson. I was a greengrocer until I retired in 1949 and my little shop is still there near the Angel tube station. It's a newsagents' now run by an Indian family and they've turned the upstairs stock rooms in to a little flat. Very cosy. My brother, Harold, was in the theatre business; an agent and very well thought of around those parts. He's a transsexual computer operator in the Czech Republic at the moment; goes by the name of Gizela but has absolutely no psychic abilities so I've not had much success contacting him.

It's seven months now since Robert Clegg died and, as always, the passage of time weakens my ability to connect with the life I have left behind. I can *observe* but direct communication is becoming increasingly difficult unless I go through a professional medium. Ursula sees me sometimes but she keeps it to herself and occasionally, just for the hell of it, I scare people on the Snake late at night; right at the curve where my car went over the edge. Not everybody sees me, of course, but every now and then I stand in the headlights of a car and see the terrified expression on the driver's face as they swerve to avoid hitting me.

I went down to the bottom of Ladybower dam to see the submerged village of Ashopton and found it not in ruins as I'd imagined but totally intact and bustling with life. Beneath the murky waters I watched people going about their daily routines as though totally unaware that they were drowned. Of course the village was evacuated before it was flooded to create the dam but the people who lived there haunt the streets and buildings as though captured on a piece of film that repeats itself over and over again. I stood outside the window of a bakery and watched them preparing dough on a long scrubbed-pine table. I rapped my knuckles against the glass and yelled at them but they didn't even look up. I wasn't quite sure who was the ghost; them or me.

I can feel a meditative period approaching. Like animals and reptiles during the cold winter months, spirits go in to hibernation from time to time. Sometimes we can lie dormant for centuries and sometimes just for a few weeks. It is a time to reflect on past lessons and to decide the course of the next incarnation.

When I decide to move on – when my spirit inhabits another earthbound body – I will remember nothing of Robert Clegg or the lives of those around him. When a child is in its mother's womb, or is a one-year-old, it is not in a fit state to remember anything long term - so whether we like it or not, it actually makes sense that most adults can't remember anything from before a very young age, let alone from before this life.

But I'm in no hurry.

Life on Earth – or any of the other inhabitable planets for that matter – isn't easy but it has its rewards. And like J. M. Barrie once said; 'Life is a long lesson in humility.'

Simon Temprell

Tallulah

How time flies when you're having fun; or so they say.

Today is the longest day of the year; the twenty-first day of June; the Summer Solstice; Midsummer's Day. Ursula is preparing to celebrate the season this evening with a garden party and an outdoor ritual so she has been busy setting things up with Petra and a couple of other friends all afternoon. Tallulah watches them from her kitchen window while she waits for the kettle to boil; the back door is open to let in some air and a fat bluebottle drones lazily as it bounces off the glass in a vain attempt to escape.

She takes her camomile tea through in to the living room where the temperature is a little cooler. The old deck chairs are still here from Christmas but Jeff has been helping Tallulah to strip the wallpaper so the walls are now unfinished plaster; streaky with water marks and patchy with Polyfiller. Since Tallulah started working at the nursery she has developed a passion for houseplants and the living room window is framed with a tangle of thriving greenery. Ferns and spider plants in hanging baskets and sprawling wine-stained Coleus compete for space with the vibrant pink and salmon flowers of the hectic Busy Lizzies grown from seed.

She doesn't actually work in the gardening section of the nursery complex; she supervises the running of the adjoining craft gallery where they sell paintings and pottery, hand-knits and glassware. It is an old converted barn with a working water wheel, a small courtyard and, opening on to the courtyard, a vegetarian café called Gardens. Petra now works weekends as a waitress at the café and Tallulah has acquired a taste for tofu and lentils. She cooks healthy vegetable casseroles and wholewheat scones and is learning to make her own wine.

The phone interrupts her brief reverie and she places her mug on the bare floorboards and goes back in to the kitchen. It is Gran calling to complain about the heat and to speculate on the possibility of a thunderstorm.

"It's that close, duck and although they haven't mentioned anything on the forecast I'm wittling that there's going to be some thunder this evening. I'm sitting here in my underskirt, I'm that hot!"

"I don't think there's going to be any thunder, Gran," assures Tallulah, peering out at Ursula who is balancing on a step-ladder stringing up lights between the trees.

"It's not natural, this heat. They reckon it's going to be almost ninety by Friday and we've not had a decent downpour for a fortnight. They'll be enforcing a hosepipe ban soon and then my lawn'll go to pot. I just had a call from Ted in Bournemouth, it sounds like he's having a good time even though the boarding house is noisy at night. I thought he might be feeling a bit depressed without June, after all it's only been six months since she passed, but he reckons the change of scenery is doing him good and he sounded happy enough. Jack Smith has been showing him where he used to live when he was bombed out of Southampton and has been taking him to see his friends. He was in the RAF when the war was on and spent a lot of time in Egypt and Africa. He didn't get married until he was fifty-six so there's hope for you yet, duck!"

"You never know," chuckles Tallulah, straightening the mugs on the mug-tree.

"Well he had two wives and they both ended up in wheelchairs. He cared for them on his own and our

Ted reckons he's a smashing cook. He's on to his third wife now, some woman called Florrie from Cheadle. He can look after himself and doesn't really need a wife but they were both lonely. Their flat looks over the sea and it's worth five hundred and twenty thousand so he's well endowed."

Tallulah resists making a joke out of that last statement, knowing that Gran doesn't like 'smut'.

"Molly and young Wayne from the crescent went to New York and hated it. They were on the go all the time and Molly was taken ill on the plane coming home. The doctor reckons she had a slight stroke and she's only fifty-three so it makes you wonder but Mrs. Reynolds says it's their lifestyle. Oh and she says she's sorry she forgot your birthday; she's sending you a card today. I wouldn't bother if I was her, still that's her affair. I think if they don't get to you on the day it's futile."

"Well it's nice of her to remember me, anyway," mollifies Tallulah, twisting the phone cord between her fingers and wondering if her tea's getting cold.

"I'm worried about our Beryl's lad going to live in London. I expect you've seen on the news the concerns about bombings on the tubes again. It's just as bad as the Blitz and I think it'll carry on as there doesn't seem to be any security. It's *that* frightening; violence seems to be everywhere. How's work, duck?"

"Oh, it's great. I've got the next two days off but we were run off our feet last weekend. I'm going down to London myself in a couple of weeks for a craft fair. Jeff's going down with me and we're going to make a weekend of it. His friend Julian's got a flat we can use – right next to Harrods!"

"Well you just be careful, my lass. You don't want to find yourself pregnant at your time of life."

"Gran!" exclaims Tallulah, "what do you take me for? I keep telling you that we're just friends."

"Eye, that's what Edward said about Mrs. Simpson and look what happened there! You two are joined at the hip and you're not telling me that he's not got designs on you so look sharp and think on. Not that I'm against it, mind you; he seems like a lovely chap and you could do with a man in your life. I'd like to see you settled before they carry me away in my box."

Tallulah refrains from comment. She is trying to keep her engagement secret from everyone but Ursula and Petra until the ring's ready. Jeff had it specially designed by a bloke who works with Julian and it's a one karat solitaire in white gold. And as for her sex life, well nothing has changed in that department; Jeff and Tallulah have decided to wait until after they're married, much to Petra's disgust.

Gran cuts her conversation short when she notices a couple of 'them buggers from number twelve trampling on my pansies' and Tallulah returns to her lukewarm tea.

The afternoon is peaceful and she thinks she might take a little nap before starting on the dinner. It's only a salad tonight but she wants to boil a few new potatoes and make a quiche from the recipe she got on Delia Smith's website. The doctors are very supportive of a healthy lifestyle and combined with her twice daily dose of White Powder Gold and the Jazzercise classes in Macclesfield once a week she feels better than she has ever felt in her life. She is a cancer survivor with both breasts intact and although nobody knows for sure why the tumour had shrunk by the time she had her surgery in January she is completely convinced that it was Rob's magic powdered gold that did the trick.

Simon Temprell

"Tally!" shouts Petra from the back door, "could you make us a cup of tea? We're parched and Ursula's fused her electric with all these bloody extensions."

"All right!" calls Tallulah, draining her mug and getting up from the creaking deckchair. "No rest for the wicked," she mumbles to herself as she pulls off a couple of brown leaves on her ficus plant and heads back to the kitchen to fill up the kettle.

Veronica

Oh dear, the judge consigned to poor Nicole's case is a close friend of Julian Smythe and he showed little sympathy when faced with the evidence before him. The televised video tape of Nicole attacking Kevin Thompson in the garage forecourt led to additional charges of vandalism from the manager of the NCP car park in Sheffield where, in a blaze of mindless fury, Nicole cracked the window of a parked car with a brick.

"In light of your obvious problems with self-control," said Judge Threadneedle, "and your disregard for community and private property, I am sentencing you to two hundred hours of community service and mandatory psychological evaluation. I have considered the various alternatives but feel strongly that Ms. Rustin should atone for her unacceptable behaviour by giving back to the HIV/AIDS community and so I am recommending that she work with one of the many charities involved with the cause."

So, for the first six weeks of the New Year Nicole was obliged to pass out condoms at youth clubs, to prepare meals for hospice patients and to work in the charity shop selling second-hand clothes and cheap brica-brac in an environment that was as far removed from that of Harvey Nichols as night is from day.

"What's this filth?" challenges Nobby Charmers, leaning forward to peer in to his teacup with distaste.

"It's tea, Dad," explains Veronica patiently, "what does it look like?"

"It looks like it's stewed, that's what it looks like. You've left it too long in the pot."

"Well let me put some more hot water in it then."

"Hot water? You think that's going to make any difference? Stewed is stewed and unless you're prepared to make a fresh pot, don't bother."

"I don't know why you want tea in this weather," sighs Veronica, flapping a listless hand in front of her face, "there's a nice jug of iced tea with lemon in the fridge, why don't you have some of that instead?"

"I've told you before, Veronica, I don't want none of that bloody cold tea. You're not in America now you know! Iced tea, iced coffee and even bloody iced *soup* if you're to believe what they tell you on the telly! I've never heard anything so bloody ridiculous."

"Please yourself," snaps Veronica, shifting sideways on the uncomfortable little chair by the open window. There's not a breath of wind and her father's flat faces a brick wall just a few feet away so there's no view either; just a green stain where the gutters are broken and some mustard-yellow moss that grows between the crumbling mortar. There is a distinct whiff of urine and Veronica turns back to her father, wrinkling her nose in disgust.

"Have you pissed yourself again?" Her father's chronic incontinence requires constant vigilance and she's already mopped twice today. She's got him sitting on a pile of old newspapers and a couple of bin bags but he still manages to wet the upholstery.

"I think my catheter's come out again. It's all this bloody tea you keep giving me. I was better off with the home help, at least he knew what he was doing; you're about as useful as a wet fart."

"Oh thanks very much!" retaliates Veronica, jumping up from her seat and snatching the cup from the arm of her father's invalid chair.

She goes through in to the tiny kitchen, slamming the door behind her. The remains of a Frey Bentos steak and kidney pie sits, congealed and forlorn, on the draining board and a fly crawls across the surface of the pastry. It's too hot to think straight in this cramped little flat but she's already been for a walk along the sea front and it's too depressing to contemplate another until it cools down a bit.

Her parole officer says that Veronica should be happy she's got a roof over her head. Having lived in America for fifteen years her social security payments are deficient and they're not going to shell-out for a place for her to live when her father's got a perfectly good spare room. She's not working because her medications make her feel exhausted most of the time and she's been having problems with her kidneys so she's surviving on disability payments; such as they are. Being HIV positive doesn't cut much ice with the government these days and unless you're totally incapacitated you're supposed to be out there earning money like everybody else.

There was a glimmer of hope when Veronica found out that Gideon had died of third degree burns and despite the fact she was prosecuted for 'malicious intent' following the petrol pump debacle she imagined that she could return to Miami and live off what was left of Gideon's fortune. Think again, Veronica! Gideon had already changed his will, leaving everything to his niece and nephew in Ohio with absolutely no provision for his estranged wife. A few personal possessions were forwarded to Veronica in a cardboard box when the condo was sold but, basically, she was left with nothing.

Initially she thought she would return to Miami but then there was the problem of health insurance. In America, without decent health insurance, there is not much hope for anyone with a chronic illness and unemployment benefits are far less lenient than in England. Her medications cost almost a thousand dollars a month, not to mention the regular doctor's visits, blood-tests etc and that's before she even thinks about finding a place to live and paying the regular monthly bills for food and utilities. America – the golden land of opportunity – is merely gold-plated and beneath the thin metallic glitter there is nothing more than poisonous lead. It is as superficial as the red carpet that leads to the Oscars; it is as shallow as the walls of Cinderella's Castle and Mickey Mouse's manic grin.

So Veronica had no choice but to remain in England and to suffer the indignity of moving in with her recalcitrant father; a man who sucks on his bitterness as though it were a boiled sweet. At first he refused to accept her as his lodger but the combined force of the health service and the benefits office proved more powerful than his paternal reluctance and he grudgingly accepted her in to his home.

"This is my daughter, Veronica. She's got AIDS."

"Dad, I don't have AIDS. I'm HIV positive."

"What difference does it make? You're diseased and nobody wants you near them."

And he has said this so many times now that Veronica has started to believe him. It's true; there are some people who prefer not to make her acquaintance when they hear of her affliction and others who surreptitiously sneak to the bathroom if they shake her hand or brush up against her in the hallway. It doesn't matter how much information they give out on the TV and in magazines people still think that they can catch it from a toilet seat so Veronica prefers to keep to herself.

Fortunately for Veronica neither the man she accosted nor Julian ever contracted the disease so at least she is spared the guilt and persecution of that possibility. But Gideon's death affected her more profoundly than she ever imagined it would and she holds herself personally responsible for the tragedy that befell both him and Daphne. Sometimes, at night, she wakes up in a cold sweat and she can feel the indelible grip of fear clutching at her throat like invisible fingers. She suffocates like Daphne, she burns like Gideon and in her dreams she is running, always running.

She throws the remains of the steak and kidney pie in to the flip-top bin and rinses out her father's teacup. It is that soulless hour between afternoon and evening; the time of the day that she hates more than any other. Neighbours watch the early evening news, eating their fried eggs and chips smothered with Daddies sauce. Holiday-makers return to their guest houses and hotels after a day on the beach with sand between their toes and sunscreen stinging their eyes. And Veronica contemplates another early night with a library book and the taste of regret, like a dirty penny, spoiling the flavour of the cheap white wine that she drinks from a champagne glass.

The End

Intents & Purposes